Arden swallowed, knowing that his real question had nothing to do with addresses or phone books.

Garrett was asking if his suspicions were accurate, and she couldn't bring herself to answer. There was a huge difference between not tracking down a man to deliver life-altering news he probably didn't want to hear and actually lying to his face.

He took a step closer. "You seemed so startled to see me the other day. Terrified, as a matter of fact."

Feeling cornered, she took deep breaths, trying to lower her elevated blood pressure.

"Maybe I'm completely off base," he continued, "but extenuating circumstances have made me more distrustful than I used to be. If I'm wrong, you can laugh at me or indignantly cuss me out. But tell me the truth, Arden. Are you carrying my child?"

HOME ON THE RANCH:
COLORADO SECRETS

——————— ✿ ———————

New York Times Bestselling Author

TANYA MICHAELS

PATRICIA THAYER

**Previously published as *Her Secret, His Baby* and
*A Colorado Family***

⬥ **HARLEQUIN** HOME ON THE RANCH

(H) HARLEQUIN® HOME ON THE RANCH

ISBN-13: 978-1-335-00868-8

Recycling programs
for this product may
not exist in your area.

Home on the Ranch: Colorado Secrets
Copyright © 2020 by Harlequin Books S.A.

Her Secret, His Baby
First published in 2013. This edition published in 2020.
Copyright © 2013 by Tanya Michna

A Colorado Family
First published in 2017. This edition published in 2020.
Copyright © 2017 by Patricia Wright

This edition published by arrangement with Harlequin Books S.A.

For questions and comments about the quality of this book,
please contact us at CustomerService@Harlequin.com.

Harlequin Enterprises ULC
22 Adelaide St. West, 40th Floor
Toronto, Ontario M5H 4E3, Canada
www.Harlequin.com

Printed in U.S.A.

CONTENTS

Tanya Michaels, a bestselling author and eight-time RITA® Award finalist, has written more than forty books full of love and laughter. Tanya is a popular event speaker, an unrepentant Netflix addict and a mother of two. She lives outside Atlanta with two teenagers who inherited her quirky sense of humor and a spoiled bichon frise who has no idea that she's a dog.

Books by Tanya Michaels

Harlequin Western Romance

Cupid's Bow, Texas

Falling for the Sheriff
Falling for the Rancher
The Christmas Triplets
The Cowboy Upstairs
The Cowboy's Texas Twins

Harlequin American Romance

Hill Country Heroes

Claimed by a Cowboy
Tamed by a Texan
Rescued by a Ranger

The Colorado Cades

Her Secret, His Baby
Second Chance Christmas
Her Cowboy Hero

Visit the Author Profile page at Harlequin.com for more titles.

HER SECRET, HIS BABY

TANYA MICHAELS

Dedicated with gratitude to Barbara Dunlop—
wonderful author, friend and dinner
companion.

Chapter 1

Never in her twenty-five years had Arden Cade done anything so rash. *What was I thinking?* Although she usually woke in gradual, disoriented stages, this morning she was instantly alert, hoping to discover the previous night had been a dream—a vivid, thoroughly sensual dream.

But there was no disputing the muscular arm across her midsection or the lingering satisfaction in her body.

Physically, she was more relaxed than she'd been in nearly a year, her loose limbs at odds with her racing thoughts. Her first impulse was to bolt from the bed, putting distance between herself and the still-sleeping cowboy. She hesitated, not wanting to wake Garrett before she'd had a chance to gather her composure. Besides, his body heat and the steady rumble of his breathing were soothing. Beckoning. It was so tempting to snuggle closer beneath the sheets and—

Don't you learn?

Cuddling into his heat was what had landed her in this situation. But she'd been cold for so long. She'd needed to feel something other than suffocating grief. If only yesterday hadn't been the ninth of March.... What the hell had made her think scheduling a photography job would keep her too busy to mourn?

Memories of the night before flooded her—the despair that had gaped like a chasm, the encounter with a charming stranger, the reckless bliss she'd found in his arms.

"If you don't mind my saying so, ma'am, people usually look happier at wedding receptions." The man's teasing tone was deep and rich, unexpectedly warming her.

She had to tilt her head to meet his clear gray eyes. Knowing her clients deserved better than a photographer who depressed the guests, she struggled for a light tone as she gestured toward the crowded dance floor. "I was feeling sorry for myself because I'm not out there," she lied. "I love to dance."

A slow grin stole over his face, making him even more attractive. As the younger sister of two ridiculously good-looking brothers, Arden didn't impress easily, but this man made her pulse quicken.

"I'd be happy to oblige," he offered. "I realize you're working, but I have some pull with the groom. Hugh was my best friend in high school."

His casual words pierced her. Arden had kept the same best friend from preschool into adulthood, rejoicing three and a half years ago when the sister of her heart married Arden's oldest brother and became her sister-in-law. This was the first March 9—Natalie's birthday—since the car accident that had killed Nata-lie and her toddler son, the first March 9 in over two decades Arden hadn't spent with her friend.

"Rain check," she'd managed to respond, abandon-ing the stranger to snap shots of the twirling flower girl.

After the reception ended, Arden should have gone home, but facing her dark, empty apartment seemed unbearable. She packed her equipment, then sat in the hotel bar while ice melted in her untouched whiskey. Time passed with excruciating slowness.

Then Garrett Frost walked in, his earlier suit re-placed with a casual button-down shirt and a pair of dark jeans that somehow made him even more devas-tatingly handsome.

"I'd offer to buy you a drink, but..." He raised one jet-black eyebrow at the liquor she was clearly ignoring.

"Guess I wasn't thirsty, after all."

Their gazes locked, and she wished she had a camera in hand to capture his mesmerizing eyes. He's beauti-ful. Sculpted cheekbones, full mouth—

"If you're gonna look at me like that," he'd drawled softly, "it's only fair you tell me your name."

"Arden. Arden Cade."

He extended his hand. "You still want that dance, Arden Cade?"

She'd accepted. Sometimes what a woman needed most in the world was to be held....

"Mornin'." Tinged with sleep, Garrett's voice now was every bit as compelling as it had been last night— when he'd breathed her name as he slid into her.

Arden! Focus! Last night's impulsiveness was one thing. She'd been emotionally raw, had needed to feel alive in some primal way. But she couldn't rationalize a repeat performance. She'd had only two sexual partners before, and they'd both been serious boyfriends.

She scrambled for the edge of the bed, trying to secure the sheet around her as she moved. "Yes, it is. Morning, I mean. Time for me to go."

"Don't hurry on my account." He lay back on his pillow, grinning at her in utter contentment. His appeal was more than physical good looks. She was drawn to his easy confidence, how comfortable he seemed in his own skin.

"Checkout's not 'til noon," he continued. "Thought I might order us an obscenely large breakfast from room service. I'm starvin'."

So was she, Arden realized. After months of being numb, of having no appetite whatsoever, the hunger felt both foreign and exhilarating. "I could eat," she blurted.

"Good. I'm gonna hop in the shower, then we can look at the menu. I'll only be a minute. Unless you want to join me?" He gave her another of those lazy smiles that left her dizzy. Garrett made love the way he smiled. Completely and thoroughly, in seemingly no rush.

"N-no." She ducked her head so that her long dark hair curtained her face. It was probably bad manners to look appalled at the thought of being naked with a man who had rocked your world mere hours ago. "I'll, uh, wait."

He sauntered across the room nude, and Arden resisted the urge to sneak a final glance. Not that her resistance held for long. He was male perfection.

And he'd been exactly what she'd needed last night. As unplanned and perhaps unwise as her actions had been, she had to admit she felt…lighter. She could almost hear Natalie's mischievous voice in her head. *Damn, girl, you really know how to celebrate a birthday.*

Arden squeezed her eyes shut. *I miss you, Nat.* That ache might never go away, but it was time Arden stopped letting it drag her down like a malevolent anchor. Natalie would have hated how listless she'd become.

The sound of the shower in the adjoining bathroom pulled Arden from her reverie. Garrett had claimed he'd be back in a minute. What was she going to say to him? All she really knew about him was that his family owned a cattle ranch several hours south of Cielo Peak and that he'd come to town for the Connors' wedding. She didn't know how to be glib about what they'd shared, and she didn't want to burden him with a heavy emotional explanation about the losses she and her brothers had endured. Wouldn't the simplest solution be to leave now, without an awkward goodbye?

She zipped her wrinkled dress, trying not to think about how she'd look to anyone she passed in the lobby. Cielo Peak attracted plenty of tourists, especially during the Colorado ski season, but there were fewer than fifteen hundred year-round citizens. The Cades were well known in the community; gossip about Arden hooking up with a guest at an event she covered would not enhance her professional reputation.

Her hand was already on the door when she stopped abruptly, recalling how Garrett had touched her the night before, his maddening tenderness. He'd made her nearly mindless with desire, and it had been the first time in months the pain had receded. Among her many conflicted feelings this morning was gratitude. He would never truly understand how much he'd given her, but she didn't want him to think she regretted being with him.

She grabbed the pen and notepad that bore the hotel logo and scribbled a quick note. It wasn't much, but it helped ease her conscience.

Garrett, thank you for last night. It was...

A barrage of words filled her mind, none of them adequate. Suddenly, the water stopped in the bathroom. Adrenaline coursed through her. She crossed out the last two words and wrote simply *I'll never forget you.*

Chapter 2

Six months later

Justin Cade shuddered at the brochures on the kitchen table. "I will paint nursery walls, I will assemble the crib, I might be wheeled into a few hours of babysitting once the peanut is born, but no way in hell am I attending birth classes with you." Then he flashed his trademark grin, a mischievous gleam in his blue-green eyes. "Unless you think there will be a lot of single women attending?"

Arden ignored the question. He'd already proven he wasn't comfortable dating a single mom. Justin, the middle Cade sibling, had raised casual dating to an art form and steered clear of women with complicated lives. The ski patrolman didn't like being stuck in a relationship any more than he liked being stuck indoors.

Thank God he's a more dependable brother than he is a boyfriend. "I didn't pull out the brochures to show you, dummy. I'm going to ask Layla to be my labor coach. She's coming over for dinner in a couple of hours."

Back in June, when the "first trimester" nausea Arden had thought would disappear actually intensified, she'd hired a temporary assistant to keep up with the administrative side of the studio. High school Spanish teacher Layla Green had been happy to make some extra money over the summer. The women's friendship continued to grow even though Layla had quit to prepare for the new school year.

"Layla, huh?" Justin crossed the small kitchen to pour another glass of iced tea. He frequently joked that the desert theme of her red-and-yellow kitchen made him extra thirsty. "She's good people. Cute, too."

"Hey! We've talked about this. You are not allowed to date my friends. Your one-hit-wonder approach to relationships would make things awkward for everyone. I was even a bit nervous when Natalie…" She trailed off, the memories bittersweet.

The sharp sting of missing her best friend had lessened over time. As Arden progressed through the trimesters, she found herself thinking of Natalie as a kind of guardian angel for her and the unborn baby. After losing so many loved ones in her life, it seemed cosmically fitting that Arden had conceived on Nat's birthday.

"You wondered if it would hurt your friendship when Natalie and Colin first started dating?" Justin asked. "To be honest, I thought the age difference would be a problem, that they wouldn't have enough in common for it to be long-lasting. But she made him damn happy."

While Arden was finally healing after the deaths of her sister-in-law and young nephew, Colin had withdrawn further. Not only had he taken a sabbatical from his job as a large-animal vet, but he'd also recently announced that he was putting his house up for sale.

She leaned an elbow on the table, propping her chin on her fist. "I'm really worried about him."

"Colin will be okay." But the way Justin avoided her gaze proved he was equally concerned. "He's always okay. He's the one who holds us together."

Their mother had died the winter Arden was in kindergarten, their father a few years later. Although a maiden aunt had come to live with them, it had been Colin who had essentially raised his younger brother and sister. He'd been so strong. But this most recent shattering loss—burying his wife and child? It seemed as if something inside him had broken beyond repair.

Justin dropped down next to Arden's chair, squeezing her shoulder. "He *will* be okay. Maybe selling the house will help him let go, give him a chance to move forward with his life."

Arden placed her hands over her distended abdomen. "Do you think this makes it harder, my having a baby? I'm sure it reminds him of Danny." Her voice caught on her nephew's name. He'd been a wide-eyed, soft-spoken toddler with an unexpectedly raucous belly laugh. His deep laugh had caused double takes in public, usually eliciting chuckles in response.

"If you're happy about Peanut, then we are happy for you," Justin said firmly. "But if you want to offer

Colin some kind of distraction, I'm sure he'd be eager to track down the jerk who knocked you—"

"Justin!"

"The jerk responsible for your being in a blessed family way."

"He wasn't a jerk. He was…" A gift. Even after six months, she vividly recalled Garrett's ability to make her temporarily forget everything else in the world, the power of his touch.

Justin recoiled with a grimace. "Seeing that look on my little sister's face is disturbing as hell. You sure you won't tell us who he is so we can punch his lights out?"

"He doesn't live anywhere near here." Thank God. Most of the locals hadn't been brazen enough to ask outright who the father was, but the mystery had caused whispers behind her back. Some of the teachers in the district had begged Layla for information, but Arden— who'd shared only the vaguest details—had sworn her to secrecy. The first time Arden had encountered Hugh Connor in town after her pregnancy began to show, she'd held her breath, wondering if Garrett had ever mentioned their night together to his friend. But Hugh had merely asked for a business card because he planned to recommend her to a business colleague looking for a good photographer.

Meanwhile, Garrett lived in a different region of the state, on a ranch he'd told her had been in his family for generations. He had deep roots there. Maybe even a girlfriend by now. Arden didn't plan to repay the kindness he'd done her by upending his existence. They'd used birth control during their night together, and the news that it had failed would most likely be an unwelcome shock.

It had taken her weeks to process the news that she was expecting, but she knew firsthand that life was precious. She chose to see conceiving this baby as a miracle. *Her* miracle.

Garrett Frost held his parents in the highest regard. An only child, he worked alongside his father running the Double F Ranch and was impressed with the man's drive and integrity. Garrett's mother, the one who'd spent many afternoons giving him advice in their kitchen while she baked, had always been wise and articulate. So why, today, had Caroline Frost lost the ability to string together a coherent sentence? Ever since the restaurant hostess had seated Garrett and Caroline at a small booth, she'd been spluttering disjointed, half-finished thoughts.

"Breathe, Momma." He took the breadbasket out of her hand. As jittery as she was, she was about to send the rolls flying to the floor. He gave her a cajoling smile. "You wanna tell me why you're as nervous as a kitten in a dog pound?"

Her gray eyes clouded with worry. "You've always hated surprises," she muttered. "Not that it's your fault if you take this badly! Anyone would…. I don't— Lord, I've messed this up before I even started. But I don't know how to make it better. Easier to hear."

Okay. Now *he* was nervous. Garrett waved away the approaching waitress. Something was very wrong. He doubted his mom wanted an audience for whatever she needed to explain. Although, if she had something personal and difficult to tell him, why had she suggested going to a restaurant?

They could have easily had a conversation in his parents' main house or in the luxurious cabin Garrett had built on the back forty. The most logical explanation for her dragging him this far from home was so they could speak freely without any risk of his father overhearing. Was something wrong with him? Long, arduous days of ranch work could take a toll, and Brandon wasn't getting any younger. But his father was direct to a fault. If there was bad news to be delivered, he would have told Garrett himself, not delegated the job to someone else.

"Momma, is everything all right with you?" he asked slowly. "Is there some irregular test result or something I should know about?"

"With me? I'm fit as a fiddle." But she'd gone completely pale.

"Oh, God. Then it *is* Dad?"

Caroline did something he hadn't witnessed since the day of his high school graduation. She burst into tears. "No. And y-yes. Your father's quite ill. B-but it's not wh-wh-what you think." Taking deep gulping breaths, she clutched the edge of the table in a visible effort to regain her composure. "I'm so sorry. Brandon isn't your father."

Garrett punched up the volume on the music in his truck, but it was pointless. Not even the loudest rock and roll could drown out his tumultuous thoughts. He pounded his fist on the steering wheel, rage rising in him like a dark tide. Tangible enough to drown him.

For the first day after his mother's avalanche of revelations, he'd been too numb to feel anything. Once emotion rushed in, he'd realized he had to get away from the ranch. Away from her. She'd had thirty years to tell the truth but had never said a word—not to him and not to the man he'd always believed was his father. Now she'd made Garrett an unwilling accomplice in keeping her adulterous secret. "I swear it was only the one time," she'd sobbed. "A lifetime ago. Confessing my sins to Brandon might ease my conscience, but why wound him like that?"

Her single indiscretion had been with a longtime family friend, recently hospitalized Will Harlow. Complications from Will's diabetes had irreparably damaged his kidneys. Though his condition was currently stable, renal failure was inevitable. Without a kidney transplant, his prognosis was grim. Caroline insisted they couldn't tell Brandon now. "If Will died with animosity between them, your father would never forgive himself!"

How had Brandon remained oblivious to the truth for all these years? He was an intuitive man. Certainly perceptive enough that he would notice the awful tension between his wife and son. So Garrett impulsively announced that he was spending Labor Day weekend with Hugh Connor.

"I don't know exactly when I'll be back," Garrett had warned his dad. "With calving season behind us and time before we need to make winter preparations, can you spare me?"

Brandon had readily agreed that he and their hired hands could cover everything, adding that Garrett didn't seem himself and maybe a week of R & R was just what the doctor ordered. Garrett's sole motivation had been escape; he hadn't consciously chosen Cielo Peak as his destination. Had he named the town because he knew it wouldn't sound suspicious, his visiting an old friend?

Or was he lured by the heated memories of a glorious night spent with Arden Cade?

Their encounter had left such an impression it was haunting. She appeared in his dreams at random intervals. He'd developed a fondness for brunettes and had caught himself unintentionally comparing a date to her. Over the summer, while packing for an annual weekend with some cousins, he'd discovered Arden's note stuck to the lining of his suitcase. *I'll never forget you.* Was that sentiment invitation enough to look her up while he was in town?

She was a beautiful woman, and over six months had passed. Even if she still resided in Cielo Peak, there was likely a man in her life. Unless, like Garrett, she was between relationships? Maybe he could casually broach the subject with Hugh.

When Garrett had phoned his friend, it had been to ask for suggestions of a not-too-touristy rental cabin that wouldn't already be booked for the holiday weekend. He hadn't actually planned to stay with Hugh and Darcy, who were practically newlyweds. Learning of his mom's infidelity had soured Garrett's opinion of wedded bliss, and he doubted he'd be great company. But Hugh was stubborn. Besides, Garrett secretly questioned whether too much time alone with his thoughts was healthy. After all, he was having trouble surviving just the drive, battered by emotional debris from Caroline's bombshell.

He fiddled with the radio dials again, trading his MP3 playlist for a radio station. A twangy singer with a guitar droned on about his misfortunes. *You think* you *have problems, pal?*

Garrett faced not only bitter disillusionment about the woman who raised him and unwilling participation in her long-term deception, but also a monumental medical decision.

Despite Caroline's emphatic vows that her fling with Will was an isolated event, that they didn't harbor any romantic feelings for each other, the man had never fallen in love with anyone else. He'd remained a bachelor with no children. Garrett was his best hope for a close match and voluntary organ donation, which would drastically shorten the wait.

"I know you need to think about this," his mother had told him. "No one wants you to rush a decision." But they both knew Will didn't have forever.

If Garrett agreed, would he feel as if he were betraying his father? If he said no, was it the same as sentencing a man to die?

He was mired in anger and pain and confusion. Little wonder, then, that his mind kept turning to that night he'd shared with Arden, the perfect satisfaction he'd experienced. Right now, it was difficult to imagine he'd ever feel that purely happy again.

Chapter 3

Arden sighed wistfully at the seafood counter. "I miss shrimp."

"Throw some in." Justin indicated the grocery cart he was pushing for her. "How about this? I'll pay if you'll cook." Even with the holiday sales price, it was a generous offer. Since ski season hadn't started, he was scraping by on a reduced off-season salary working for a local ambulance service.

After a moment of letting herself be tempted, she shook her head. "Nah, I've read warnings that pregnant women should avoid shellfish. Skipping them completely might be overreacting, but I really want to do this right, you know?"

She rarely missed her mom, having been so young when Rebecca Cade died, but she sure could use a woman who'd experienced the wonder and worry of impending motherhood. Her only living aunt who'd had children was well over sixty, her memories of pregnancy and childbirth hazy and outdated. Arden hesitated to take advice from a woman who'd chain-smoked and enjoyed cocktail hour through all three trimesters. Cousin Rick never had seemed quite right in the head.

Arden changed the subject, eyeing her brother curiously. "You know, you've been hanging around an awful lot lately. Does this sudden fascination with helping me have anything to do with missing Elisabeth?" Though Justin's relationships never lasted long, Arden thought she'd sensed genuine regret after his most recent breakup—and not only because he missed the job as hiking guide and first-aid administrator at the lodge Elisabeth's family owned.

"What? No. I barely think about her. *You're* the one who keeps bringing her up!"

I am? Arden wracked her brain, trying to recall the last time she'd mentioned Elisabeth Donnelly.

"I'm giving up my Sunday afternoon because you shouldn't be lifting things," he added virtuously. "What would you have done if I hadn't been here to grab the pallet of bottled water?"

"Um, asked any one of the numerous stock boys for assistance?"

He shoved a hand through his dark brown hair. "Humor me, okay? I have two siblings I care the world about, and one of them, I don't have a clue how to help."

So he was overcompensating by lending a hand with her menial errands? That she could believe.

"Besides," Justin drawled, "being such a good brother makes me look all sensitive and whatever to any single ladies we encounter. Major attraction points."

On behalf of women everywhere, she socked him in the shoulder. "You go to the freezer section and get us an enormous tub of vanilla ice cream. I'll grab caramel and chocolate syrup."

"And some straw—"

"Of course strawberry syrup for you," she added. There was no accounting for taste. "Then we'll need bananas. Meet me in produce, okay? I'll make chef salads for dinner and sundaes for dessert."

He turned to go, then hesitated. "Should we invite Colin to join us? Granted, he's not exactly Mr. Fun these days, but…"

"I'll call him," Arden promised. "But you know he'll probably decline. Again."

"If the situation were reversed, he wouldn't give up on either of us. Maybe it would help if you pick up some of those minimarshmallows for the sundaes. He's a sucker for those."

"Minimarshmallows?" she echoed skeptically. "That's our plan?"

Justin shrugged. "Hey, we all have our weaknesses."

Garrett wheeled the shopping cart into the produce section, absently navigating as he consulted Darcy's grocery list. He'd asked her to let him do the supermarket run as a way to pay the Connors back for room and board. It was more diplomatic than saying he needed a break from the doting couple.

Conversation between Garrett and Hugh had been uncharacteristically stilted. Garrett wanted to confide in his friend but hadn't quite worked up the courage. It felt disloyal to tell anyone what Caroline had done, and it rocked Garrett's sense of identity to admit Brandon wasn't his father. He'd never said the words aloud, and they were harder than he'd expected.

The other potential topic of discussion Garrett wrestled with was Arden Cade. He'd started to ask about her half a dozen times, but stopped himself. After their intimate night together, she'd left without saying goodbye. That seemed like a strong indicator that she wasn't expecting to see him again.

Blinking, Garrett whipped his head around in a double take. A dark-haired woman in his peripheral vision had triggered his notice. *You're pitiful.* Just because he'd been thinking of Arden, now random shoppers looked like her?

Or, maybe… Could it actually *be* Arden? The long fall of shiny brown hair was familiar. He could recall its silky texture between his fingers. Given the crappy week he was having, had fate decided it owed him a favor? He hadn't figured out a casual way to look her up, but he couldn't be blamed for a chance encounter.

Steering toward her, he asked hopefully, "Arden?"

"Yes?" She smiled over her shoulder but froze in recognition, his name on her lips so soft he saw it rather than heard it. "Garrett."

He couldn't believe she was here—and even more beautiful than he remembered. Her cheeks were rosy, her aquamarine eyes bright and lively. He couldn't recall noticing a woman's skin before, but Arden's creamy complexion beckoned him to touch her.

Garrett realized two things at once: he was staring, and she didn't look happy to see him. Then he came up alongside her, getting his first real look at her profile, and had a startling third revelation. Arden Cade was pregnant.

It wasn't immediately obvious until one saw her stomach. She seemed to be carrying the baby completely in front. From behind, other than the curve of her hips, there hadn't been— Good Lord. He was ogling a pregnant woman.

He swallowed. "So. How've you been?" He punctuated his question with a wry glance at her abdomen. He knew nothing about pregnancy. His understanding was that women didn't show for a few weeks, although Arden was slim enough that perhaps it was more obvious on her than it would have been on someone else. He had no real sense of whether she was four months along or eight.

That was a sobering thought. Was there a chance she'd already been carrying when they'd made love? The possibility upset him beyond any rational justification.

"I, uh…" Her eyes cut to the side, as if she were seeking help. Or scoping exit routes. "It's good to see you."

Wow, are you a bad liar, sweetheart. "You're obviously busy." He gestured to the bananas she'd been perusing. "I won't keep you. I'm staying in town with the Connors for a few days, and when I saw you there, I thought I'd say hi."

The tension in her shoulders eased fractionally. "Hi." She managed a smile, but it didn't reach her eyes.

"Arden? Is there a problem here?" A broad-shouldered man approached, his tone possessive as he practically rammed his cart between Arden and Garrett. He was a tall son of a gun, even had an inch or two of height on Garrett.

"No problem, Justin. Except that I'm…feeling sick." Her progressively ashen color backed up her claim. She dropped the produce bag she'd been holding into the cart. "Get me home. I can come back later for anything we missed."

"Don't be ridiculous. *I'll* come back." When he glanced at her, Justin's features softened. But the glare he aimed at Garrett was flinty with suspicion.

Garrett's stomach dropped. He'd known there was a good chance Arden would be involved with someone. So why was his disappointment at being right so keenly bitter?

Wait a minute. His eyes narrowed, and he met Justin's unblinking stare. Those blue-green eyes were a lot like Arden's. And the thick brown hair they both shared? Arden's was streaked with honey and gold, while the man's was more like coffee grounds, but the resemblance was unmistakable.

A broad grin stretched across Garrett's face. "Is this your brother?"

"Damn right." The man took a step forward. "And *you* are…?"

"Justin, please." Arden's voice trembled. "I have to get out of here."

"Right. Sorry. Let's go."

With a hasty, departing wave from Arden, they were gone. Garrett stood there, bemused.

Had she truly been unhappy to see him, or did her not feeling well explain her behavior and the grimace she'd tried to cover? At first, he'd thought her skittish demeanor was due to the awkwardness of running into a fling while her significant other was nearby, but that wasn't the case. Maybe he'd misread the situation entirely.

But as he began piling groceries into the buggy, he

conjured her face again. He could have sworn the emotion he'd seen in her eyes was…fear. Why on earth would Arden be scared of him?

"Great dinner," Garrett complimented his hostess. Personally, he'd been too preoccupied to taste a bite of the meal, but Hugh had wolfed down his roast beef with gusto, so Garrett felt reasonably sure of his statement.

Darcy Connor, Hugh's pretty blonde wife, beamed from across the kitchen table. Her gregarious nature seemed at odds with the cliché image of a part-time librarian. "Lavish praise, doing the shopping for me— when word gets out about you, my single girlfriends are going to be lining up at the front door."

"Since you cooked, we can do the dishes," Hugh volunteered.

"Another time." She shooed them out of the kitchen. "Garrett just got here yesterday. You still have lots of catching up to do."

"Isn't she terrific?" Hugh asked adoringly as they relocated to the living room. He grabbed a television remote from the side pocket in his recliner, flipping through channels until he found a college football game. "If you'd told me when I was a freckled, fifteen-year-old comic book collector that I could get a woman like that to marry me…"

Garrett snorted. "You were also six feet tall and the team quarterback." His auburn-haired friend might well have freckles and an interest in superheroes, but he hadn't spent his teenage years lonely. "As I recall, you went to senior proms at three separate high schools."

Hugh grinned. "Did I? Before Darcy, it's all a blur. What about you, man? You had a pretty active social life, too. I was surprised you didn't bring anyone to the wedding."

Boy, would that night have ended differently. A month prior to the wedding, he'd been dating a woman he'd planned to take to the ceremony, but they'd ended things when she got a job offer that took her to the east coast.

"Speaking of your wedding," Garrett said with studied nonchalance, "I never got to see how the photos turned out. Isn't there an album or something?"

"Darcy," he called to his wife, "you have a willing victim here. Garrett asked to see wedding pictures." Turning back to Garrett, he added, "Narrating our photos is one of her favorite hobbies, up there with bird-watching and snowboarding. I warn you, the collection is massive. There's the professional album our photographer put together, then the one Darcy crammed full of everything from wedding shower pics to the honeymoon."

"I remember the photographer," Garrett said. Understatement of the year—she was seared into his memory like a brand. "Arden, right?"

Hugh smirked. "Why, you looking for a photographer? Maybe planning to have some of those glamorized portraits done? You'd look pretty spiffy in a sequined cowboy hat."

"I think I ran into her at the grocery store earlier. The woman I saw was pregnant?"

"That's her, Arden Cade." Hugh clucked his tongue. "Poor kid. Being a single mom can't be easy under the best of circumstances, much less with gossips buzzing about the dad."

Garrett leaned forward on the couch. "Why? Who's the dad?"

"It's a big mystery. Far as anyone knew, she wasn't seeing anyone. Maybe it was a long-distance relationship with an out-of-town guy. People were shocked when she turned up pregnant and even more shocked those two brothers of hers didn't march the dude responsible into a shotgun wedding."

The fear he'd seen on Arden's face today flashed through his mind, and a completely insane thought struck him. *He* was an out-of-town guy. They'd used condoms, but those weren't effective one hundred percent of the time, were they? He'd heard stories.

"Out of..." His throat was so dry he had to try again. "Out of curiosity, do you know how far along she is?"

Hugh regarded him suspiciously but didn't challenge the bizarre question. "Hey, Darce? You have any idea how far along Arden is in her pregnancy?"

Darcy appeared in the doorway between rooms, drying her hands on a green-and-yellow-checkered towel. "Around six months, maybe? She said she's due the week of Thanksgiving."

Garrett's blood froze. *Six months.*

No, he was crazy to contemplate it. It was unfathomable that the woman who had been so open and expressive beneath him would keep a secret of this magnitude, cruelly excluding him. She knew he was friends with the Connors and could have found him easily. She could have called, emailed, sent a telegram—something! This was just his imagination running wild.

The unpleasant combination of newfound cynicism and sleepless nights had colored his judgment. The odds that Arden was pregnant by him… They'd used condoms, and they'd only been together one night.

Then again, Garrett himself was living proof that once was all it took.

"Layla, I am in trouble." Arden leaned back in the leather office chair, resenting the way it creaked. She hadn't gained *that* much weight. "Deep, deep trouble."

"Don't panic," her friend counseled over the phone. The words of wisdom were somewhat muffled around a bite of sandwich. In response to Arden's frantic text that morning, Layla was taking her lunch break in her car, away from the curious ears of students or fellow teachers.

"But he's here! Why is he here?"

"Um, didn't you say you met him because he was in town for a good friend's wedding? Makes sense that he'd occasionally visit said friend. The part I can't believe is that you saw him Sunday, yet waited until Tuesday to let me know."

"Because I spent yesterday in denial," Arden mumbled. She'd never been comfortable discussing her night with Garrett. It had felt so private, something meant only to be between them. Maybe if she'd known Layla back then, or if Natalie had still been alive… "Am I being punished for having a one-night stand? Am I a bad person?"

"Don't start pinning those scarlet *A*'s on your maternity clothes just yet. The fact that you'd only been with two men up until then is pretty solid evidence you're not a tramp."

"No, the fact that there had only been two previous lovers in my life is evidence that I have very large,

very overprotective brothers," Arden said without ran-
cor. Her brothers' local influence had probably helped
prevent some impulsive mistakes in her teens. She nervously twisted the cord on the phone. "I think Justin
suspects Garrett is the father. What if *Garrett* suspects
as much?" So many emotions had rampaged through
her when she'd seen him. She hadn't exactly maintained
a poker face.

"Did he give you any reason to think that?"

"Not really. He was making small talk. I was busy
freaking out."

"Then let's not borrow trouble," Layla advised. "Are
you going to—"

"Oops, work beckons," Arden interrupted as the
door to her studio swung open. "Maybe we can meet
for dinner?"

"I don't know. I've got a stack of practice tests I have
to grade so I can figure out how much my students forgot over the summer and plan accordingly. But give me
a few hours to talk myself into it, and I'll text you later."

Arden disconnected, calling out, "Be with you in
a second."

Over the summer, Layla had acted briefly as receptionist, but for the most part, Arden had always run a
one-woman shop. She didn't get many random drop-ins.
Customers usually called or emailed to schedule an appointment or, in the case of big events, to ask preliminary questions and do price comparisons.

Coming around the edge of her desk, she steadied
herself with her hand. She was constantly readjusting
to her ever-changing center of gravity.

"Hope I'm not interrupting your work." That smooth
deep voice was exactly the same as it had been the first

time he'd spoken to her, sending tremors through her body. Garrett Frost stood in the center of her reception area, cowboy hat in hand, an unreadable expression on his face.

Adrenaline surged, making her head swim. "Garrett." Her hands moved reflexively to cover the baby bump. That happened a lot lately when she was apprehensive.

He misinterpreted the protective gesture. "If you're trying to hide that you're expecting, it's a little late."

"I… I…" *Say something.* Preferably something intelligent. "Can I get you a cup of coffee?"

It wasn't until he shook his head that she realized she hadn't brewed any. She'd given it up during the pregnancy and hadn't been expecting clients for another few hours. Thank goodness he hadn't taken her up on the offer—her pride balked at the idea of making herself seem more ridiculous. She hadn't exactly been articulate at the grocery store.

"I'm sorry I was rude the other day," she said. "You took me by surprise. It was a shock, running in to you there."

"You weren't the only one stunned," he said pointedly. His gaze dropped before returning to her face.

"So, uh, how'd you find my office? Did your friend Hugh mention I was in this shopping center? I hope he and his wife are doing well." Her pulse was racing, and she heard her babbled words as though from a distance.

"Actually, I looked you up myself. Knowing your name and that you owned a photography studio was enough. It's not difficult to find someone, if you bother to look." His gray eyes were like thunderclouds. "If, for instance, a woman needed to locate a man, even one in a different town. I don't think there are many Garrett Frosts who are part owners of Colorado cattle ranches, but maybe I'm wrong. What do you think, Arden?"

She swallowed, knowing that his real question had nothing to do with addresses or phone books. He was asking if his suspicions were accurate, and she couldn't bring herself to answer. There was a huge difference between not tracking down a man to deliver life-altering news he probably didn't want to hear and actually lying to his face.

He took a step closer. "You seemed so startled to see me the other day. Terrified, as a matter of fact."

Feeling cornered, she took deep breaths, trying to lower her elevated blood pressure.

"Maybe I'm completely off base," he continued, "but extenuating circumstances have made me more distrustful than I used to be. If I'm wrong, you can laugh at me or indignantly cuss me out. But tell me the truth, Arden. Are you carrying my child?"

Chapter 4

Garrett had mentally rehearsed different ways this confrontation could play out—from her scoffing at his ludicrous accusation to her tearfully confessing all and begging his forgiveness. But he hadn't imagined her collapsing.

Her eyes rolled upward and she crumpled in on herself.

"Arden!"

He bolted toward her with just enough time to get his arms around her before she fell. What was he thinking, intimidating a pregnant woman? What if he'd caused harm to her or the baby? He lowered himself to the floor awkwardly, supporting her weight as he cradled her against his chest.

She blinked up at him, and it was such a relief to see those blue-green eyes open. At least she was conscious, although her chest rose and fell with alarmingly rapid exhalations. "G-Gar—"

"Shhh. Catch your breath first." He stroked her hair back from her pale face, feeling like an ogre. If he was right about the baby, then Arden owed him a major apology, but no matter how angry he was, he never would have deliberately hurt her.

She raised one shaky hand to press against her heart, her expression pained. "Water?"

He shrugged out of the lightweight denim jacket he'd been wearing, rolling it up as a makeshift pillow beneath her head. There was a water dispenser in the corner of the room, and he half filled a paper cup. "You have a history of fainting?" he asked. Maybe if this was something that happened routinely, he wouldn't feel like such a bastard.

"Only twice." She sipped her water, her words halting. "Overheated camping. Blacked out another time. When… I got bad news."

He wasn't sure whether this technically counted as fainting—had she lost consciousness completely? Was there a chance it would happen again when she was alone? "Should we get you to a doctor?"

She bit her lip, still struggling to breathe normally. "Probab— Probably overkill, but… The baby." Her eyes filled with tears, the palpable fear in her gaze knifing through him.

"Better safe than sorry." He helped her to her feet, noting her rocky balance.

"We have to lock up," she said. "Keys in my purse. Second desk drawer."

He got everything she asked for, then helped her out to the truck. She leaned against the seat, eyes closed.

There was a lot they needed to say to each other, but it was challenge enough for her to give him rudimentary directions to the hospital.

The emergency room was fairly empty on a Tuesday afternoon. A mother sat in the far corner trying to coax a little girl to stop crying, and a burly man watched a daytime talk show with one eye while holding some kind of compress over the other. The blonde nurse working the admissions counter gasped softly when she spotted Garrett and Arden.

"Arden! You okay, hon?"

"Probably. I feel silly being here, but I think I fainted. Heart beating too fast, got dizzy…"

"Then you did the right thing by coming in." The blonde eyed Garrett with blatant curiosity but didn't ask who he was. "You two have a seat and fill out the forms on this clipboard. Oh, and this one for Obstetrics." She passed over a pale green sheet of paper.

Garrett caught sight of a long list of questions. None seemed as crucial as the one looming in his mind. *Who the hell is the father?*

"Need any help with those?" he offered.

"No!" Arden clutched the paperwork to her chest, not meeting his eyes. "I got it."

They sat down and she fumbled through her purse, retrieving her license and insurance card. Her hands were shaky as she muttered, "Damn, I hate hospitals."

He'd never thought much about them one way or the other. It occurred to him that Will Harlow could be in a hospital bed at this very moment, praying that his biological son agreed to give up a kidney.

Fury filled him, resentment at the secrets that had been kept. He struggled to keep his voice soft, nonthreatening. "Arden, you owe me an answer." At least here, if she became overwrought by his questioning, there were medical professionals twenty feet away.

"I know." She turned to him, the tears shimmering in her apologetic gaze an unmistakable reply. Still, he couldn't quite force himself to accept the truth until she added out loud, "It's you. You're the baby's father."

Garrett hadn't thought he could ever be more shocked than when he'd learned about his mother and Will. He'd been wrong. *I'm a dad?* If he hadn't retreated to Cielo Peak to cope with the last bombshell a lying woman had dropped on him, he never would have known.

He clenched his fists against his thighs. "What were you planning to tell the kid? Children should know who their fathers are!"

The clipboard trembled in her grasp. "To be honest, I hadn't thought that far ahead. I was already a couple of months pregnant by the time I realized what had happened, and the discovery was mind-blowing. I needed time to adjust."

He knew the feeling. But he was too angry to sympathize.

"Garrett, I—"

"Someone from Obstetrics is on the way down with a wheelchair." The blonde admissions nurse walked toward them. "They'll get you in a real room instead of one of these E.R. cubicles, probably put you on a fetal monitor for an hour or so to make sure the baby's not in distress. Ask you some questions, maybe take some blood, check for anemia. You want me to contact either of your brothers, hon?"

"No! The last thing Colin needs is another phone call

from a hospital E.R.," Arden said adamantly. "And I figure calling Justin would be awkward for you."

"You mean because he dumped me?" the woman asked with a wry smile. She seemed more amused than heartbroken. "Don't worry, I knew what I was getting into with that one. It was fun while it lasted. Talking to him won't upset me, I promise. Would you like him to be here?"

"Not unless I'm going to need the ride." Arden slid a questioning glance in Garrett's direction. "Are you planning to stick around?"

He folded his arms over his chest, smiling for the nurse's benefit. "You couldn't get rid of me if you tried, sweetheart."

Arden studied the ceiling intently, as if the answers to her problems might magically be found in the speckled tiles overhead. She'd gained a momentary reprieve when Garrett stepped out of the room so she could change, but he'd be knocking on the door any second. She hadn't missed his smirk when she'd asked for the privacy—after all, he'd already seen her naked. That was how they'd landed in this mess.

"Not that I think you're making a mess of my life," she whispered guiltily, as if the baby had heard her tormented thoughts. Arden was plenty grateful for her child. She was just second-guessing her decision to raise the child alone, Garrett none the wiser. *But I am alone.* She and Garrett had no real history or future. How was she going to share the most precious thing in her life with a man she barely knew?

Instead of knocking, Garrett cracked the door open

a quarter of an inch, calling out before entering. "You decent in there?"

In a thin piece of fabric that tied behind her and left most of her back exposed? Hardly. "Close enough, I guess."

He strolled into the room, filling it with his size. Having grown up with brothers, she normally found the presence of a strong man comfortingly familiar. But now trepidation rippled through her. Her brothers had never been as furious with her as Garrett seemed.

She expected him to interrogate her about the baby, but he surprised her. "That nurse downstairs—" he began.

"Sonja."

"She asked about your brothers. Not your parents?"

Arden kneaded the hospital blanket that covered her lap. "They're both dead. My brothers are pretty much all I have."

"Two of them, right? Colin and Justin?" At her nod, he continued. "Is this why Justin looked like he wanted to put his fist through my face at the grocery store— because I got you pregnant?"

"I think..." She averted her gaze. "I'm not sure what he picked up on between us, but I think he suspects you're the dad. He couldn't know for sure, though. I never told anyone who the father was."

"No kidding." Despite his soft tone, the biting sarcasm in his voice made her flinch.

"Garrett, I'm sorry. I—"

"Don't!" This time, he wasn't soft-spoken at all. Even he looked taken aback by the vehement outburst. He cleared his throat. "I've heard that particular phrase far more than any man should in one week. Enough already."

She frowned. Someone besides her had reason to apologize to him? Whoever it was should feel grateful to Arden—it was doubtful anyone else's transgression topped hers.

Garrett paced the room. Although he might have regained verbal control, forcing himself to *sound* calm, he couldn't mask the tension radiating from his body. "So is there a specific reason you hate hospitals? You mentioned Colin and emergency rooms. Did—"

"Knock, knock!" The cheerful voice preceded a gray-haired doctor poking his head inside the room. "I'm Dr. Wallace. I hear we're having some dizziness and tachycardia today?"

Why did doctors speak in plural like that, Arden wondered, as if using the royal we? "Does *tachycardia* mean my heart tried to pound through my chest?" she asked wearily.

"It's when your heart beats abnormally fast, yes. There are several reasons it can happen during pregnancy." Dr. Wallace went over the possibilities while looking at the vitals the nurse had collected. Then he checked the baby's heartbeat. "Just a precaution, of course. We have no reason to think anything's wrong with the little guy. Or gal."

Arden had grown accustomed to the use of fetal dopplers in her OB appointments and the reassuring *whoosh-whoosh* sound, but she'd forgotten this was Garrett's first time. He went completely still, the restless anger that had been palpable a few minutes ago fading into wonderment. His eyes widened.

"That's the heartbeat?" he asked reverently. "It's fast."

"Well within the standard range," Dr. Wallace assured them. But as Nurse Sonja had predicted, the doctor wanted to monitor Arden and the baby for some readings before letting them leave the hospital. He pushed Arden's gown up farther, the preliminary gel a cool tickle against her skin.

Although the sheet on the hospital bed kept her lower half covered, embarrassment heated her face. The last time Garrett had seen her unclothed, she'd looked a lot different than she did now.

When she was younger, Arden had stayed in shape by trying to keep up with her two athletic brothers. She'd been trim most of her life, and grief after Natalie's and Danny's deaths had robbed her of her appetite. Since her pregnancy had begun to show, she'd often felt awkward, but never fat—a growing baby was a healthy one. At the moment, however, vanity reared its head. Would Garrett be repulsed by her swollen body?

Why should you care if he is? Their night together had been amazing, but it had also been a one-time occurrence. It wasn't as if she wanted him to find her attractive. Even if she did, she suspected not contacting him about the baby had forever tarnished her in Garrett's eyes.

Within moments, the doctor had the sensors in place. "You try to relax, young lady, and I'll be back to check on you later. Meanwhile, I'll have the nurse bring you some water. It's important to stay hydrated."

All too soon, he was gone, leaving her and Garrett alone once more.

"You want to have a seat?" she offered. It was a small

room, and the only chair would put him in uncomfortably close proximity to her. Yet almost anything seemed preferable to his earlier pacing. His taut strides made her think of caged predators.

He sat, but kept shifting position, obviously ill-at-ease. "Have you, um, had other problems during the pregnancy? Everything okay with you and the baby?"

"The doctors say everything's normal, even my being sick as a dog well into the second trimester." But she worried sometimes. It was frustrating to wake up with a sharp pain at three in the morning and have no one she could talk to about her fears. Early on, she'd posted a question to an online forum for soon-to-be-mothers. Despite a couple of helpful responses, the possibility of misinformation and the discovery that some people were far too willing to share horror stories had kept her from doing so again. "Apparently nausea can be a good sign that the baby's nice and strong. Plus, my being too sick to run the office alone led to hiring Layla, and she became a good friend. I...needed a friend."

Did Garrett hear the ache in her voice, the echo of solitude that had plagued her for so many months? What he'd said down in the emergency room was true. She *did* owe him answers. Starting with the night they'd met.

"My brother Colin married my best friend several years ago," she said haltingly. "Natalie and I had been best friends since kindergarten, the year my mom died. Colin's a great guy, but he's always had too much responsibility. He rarely laughed. Natalie changed that. She changed him. He doted on her and their baby boy. But then Nat and Danny were killed in a car accident."

Garrett watched her silently, obviously unsure what to do with this information but not interrupting.

"It destroyed Colin and devastated me. The day your friend Hugh got married? That was Natalie's birthday, the first one I didn't get to spend with her as far back as I could remember. I was in a lot of pain that day. Meeting you was about the best thing that could happen to me. You were…" She broke off, assailed by memories that seemed excruciatingly intimate with him sitting only inches from her side. He'd been by turns tender and passionate, driving her need to such a sharp peak that there'd been no room in her for any other emotion.

On sheer impulse, she reached over and squeezed his hand. "Thank you."

He looked taken aback. "Uh, my pleasure."

"Having a baby was the furthest thing from my mind," she added. "At first I was too shocked to be scared or happy. But I've been around death, too much of it, and the idea of bringing a new life into the world… This may sound insane to you, but it almost felt like a goodbye present from Natalie. Some sort of cosmic full circle."

"And there wasn't room in that circle for anyone else?" He abandoned his chair in favor of resumed pacing.

Six months ago, he'd helped heal her hurting. The last thing in the world she wanted was to wound him. Another apology hovered on the tip of her tongue, but she recalled his hostile reaction to her previous attempt.

"I hardly knew anything about you," she reminded him. "I tried to imagine how my brother Justin would react if he discovered, completely out of the blue, that a near stranger was carrying his child. It was daunting. By the time the nausea and confusion subsided, months had passed. You could have had a serious girlfriend, plans for the future I would be ruining! Telling you seemed like too big a risk. After a lot of sleepless nights, I decided it would be best for my child to have no father than one who might resent it."

He stopped his pacing and stared her down. "So you were protecting both me and the baby by keeping the news to yourself?" His chuckle was like broken glass. "I wonder if all mothers have this gift for rationalizing dishonesty."

All mothers?

The slight knock at the door made them both jump, and a nurse entered with a pitcher of ice water and some plastic-wrapped cups. She drew up short, her smile fading as she registered the tension in the room.

"I hope I'm not interrupting," she said hesitantly. "Dr. Wallace asked me to bring some water."

Garrett nodded his head at her, making a visible effort not to appear intimidating. "Much appreciated, ma'am."

The nurse smiled at him before asking Arden, "Is there anything else you need?"

Yeah, a do-over button. Or, barring that, the words that would make Garrett understand what she'd been feeling, her belief that she was making the right decision for all three of them. What were the odds that the hospital stocked second chances and forgiveness alongside the antibiotics and lime Jell-O?

After her release from the hospital, Arden had tried to talk Garrett into driving her back to her car. "You can follow me home if you're worried about me," she'd proposed. But he'd categorically refused. Now, as she struggled to keep her eyes open, she found herself grateful for his inflexibility. If anyone had asked her a few hours ago, she would have sworn the day's events had left her too shaken to sleep for a week. But one of the periodic side effects of pregnancy was a full-body fatigue so encompassing it bordered on paralysis.

By the time Garrett pulled his truck into her driveway, the September sun was dipping below the horizon.

"This is it." She smothered a yawn. "Home sweet home." In terms of square footage, the cozy two-bedroom house was actually smaller than her former apartment. But once she'd learned she was pregnant, she'd wanted to own something, a place that was all hers. *Mine and the baby's.*

Besides, while walking up three flights of stairs every day might have been one of the lifestyle choices that helped keep her in shape, it would be more difficult to navigate while carrying boxes of diapers and an infant car seat. She'd traded all those steps for a neatly fenced-in postage stamp of a yard. Did it look sad and despondent to a rancher who was used to the open range, hundreds of acres of pastureland where cattle grazed beneath the Colorado sky? Based on Garrett's grudgingly solicitous manner, from not leaving her side at the hospital to not letting her get behind the wheel, she wouldn't be surprised if he insisted on walking her inside. Would he judge the meager surroundings inadequate for his child?

"This is a really good school district," she blurted.

He quirked an eyebrow at the spontaneous announcement.

Her face warmed. "Just thinking ahead." By five years, plus or minus. Even though she might not be living here when it came time for the baby to go to kindergarten, she was doing her best to make all the right decisions.

She slanted a glance at Garrett's stony profile. Ironically, she may have already botched her biggest parenting decision thus far.

As he helped her down from the truck, she couldn't help noting that his hand was warm and calloused. How did a man with labor-roughened skin caress a woman with such silky gentleness? The way he'd touched her— *Whoa.* Where had that memory come from? She shook her head as if she could physically dislodge the mental image.

He frowned. "Everything okay? You look flushed."

"Pregnancy comes with a lot of weird side effects." Like hormones in hyperdrive. Mostly, those hormones had manifested themselves in very vivid, very detailed dreams that made her blush the next morning. One of the more anecdotal pregnancy books had mentioned the phenomenon, and the author advised women to enjoy the perk. But it was disquieting to experience that surge of lust in front of Garrett.

She yanked her hand out of his. When his expression grew even stormier, she tried to mitigate her action with a lame explanation. "I, ah, need to get my keys." As she unlocked the front door, her stomach emitted an embarrassing rumble. Hunger ran a close second to exhaustion.

"I'm starving," he commented. "Didn't get around to eating lunch today."

"Me neither."

"Let's get you situated and decide on a plan for food. Maybe I can whip up something for dinner."

"I don't know about that." She stepped inside, flashing a sheepish glance over her shoulder. "My grocery shopping got cut short the other day. The kitchen's not fully stocked."

Should she mention the nearby pizza place that delivered? Would she be able to sit through a meal in Garrett's presence, or would nerves keep her from eating? She appreciated how civil he was being, but the friction between them was as pointed as it had been when he strode into her office today. She was too drained to withstand much more.

Needing to get off her feet before she fell off them, she made a beeline for the ratty armchair she'd found at a rummage sale years ago. She'd had it steam-cleaned with the distant plan of someday reupholstering. Since she'd never gotten around to that part, the chair looked like blue-plaid hell, but it was inexplicably comfortable.

Garrett was slow to follow. After a moment, she realized he was examining the framed pictures on her wall.

"Did you take all of these?" he asked.

"Yes."

Portraits of Justin and Colin were scattered among a jumble of other subjects, from a black-and-white shot of a stone well to a close-up of a light purple dahlia bud in midbloom. There was a landscape photo taking up too much space; she'd squeezed it in to replace the family picture of Colin with his wife and son that had been exiled to temporary storage in her closet.

"You're very talented," Garrett said. "Darcy and Hugh showed me their wedding album. They were thrilled with your work."

She swallowed, briefly closing her eyes. "Do they know about the baby?" Had Garrett told them about how she'd jumped into bed with him, shared his suspicions that this baby was his? Lord, what they must think of her. "I mean, of course they know I'm pregnant, I've seen them in town. But do they know…?"

"That I'm a daddy? How the hell could I have told them when *I* didn't even know?" he exploded. He began pacing, not that there was much more space here than he'd had in the hospital room. In a slightly calmer voice, he asked, "Does the idea of anyone knowing we were together bother you so much? I've never felt like a woman's dirty secret before."

"It's not like that," she said miserably. "It has nothing to do with you." She recalled the pitying looks her teachers had given her after her father died, the local news stories after Natalie's crash. She hated for anyone to have reason to talk about her and her family. But Garrett shouldn't be penalized for her hang-ups.

He rubbed his temple absently. "It's not as if your neighbors are gonna buy that the stork brought the baby. So who cares if they know it was me?"

"I'm handling this badly." She sighed. "I've never… I'm pretty inexperienced."

"You mean because you're a first-time mom?"

"Inexperienced with men. And, um, sex in general." At his startled look, she added, "I'd had sex before— just, infrequently. And only with long-term boyfriends I knew really, really well. I'm *not* ashamed of what happened between us. I'm just at a loss for… If I say 'I'm sorry' again, are you going to yell?"

His sudden grin was so unexpected and striking that it made her knees weak. *Thank God I'm already sitting.*

"No yelling," he promised.

"Thank you. I am sorry. I don't know what I'm doing." There were manuals and chat rooms, even documentary-style television shows that revolved around pregnancy and birth. But none of them had outlined the protocol for how to weather whispered rumors, or break the news to appalled, overprotective brothers or how to cope with the gorgeous one-night stand you'd never expected to see again.

His smile faded. "If you'd told me the truth, maybe we could have figured it out together. For the record, since you broached the subject today, there's no girlfriend, serious or otherwise."

The declaration warmed her far more than it should have. *Not because I'm interested in him romantically, but because I'd hate to complicate a third person's life with all of this.*

"Based on what Hugh said, can I safely assume there's no guy in the picture?" he asked.

She almost laughed at the suggestion that she was dating anyone. How many men fantasized about meeting a gal who barfed for months on end, then began steadily swelling to the size of a beluga? The hint of vulnerability that flickered in Garrett's gaze sobered her. Did he worry that someone else was poised to play the role of father to his child?

"No guy," she said softly. *Except you.*

His tense shoulders lowered the merest fraction of an inch. There was relief and something less definable in his eyes. Possessiveness? Awareness sizzled through Arden, replacing her earlier lethargy with something more energetic. And far more complicated. Her voice caught in her throat.

Changing the subject, he clapped his palms together. "Point me in the direction of the kitchen. I'll check out the dinner options."

"I wasn't kidding about rations being low." She used the arms of the chair to hoist herself upward. "But I think we can manage salad and some grilled cheese sandwiches."

As someone who lived alone, she wasn't used to anyone else puttering around in her kitchen. Letting him wait on her would just be too weird. "Can I offer you something to drink? I don't have any sodas or beer, but there's lemonade or filtered water. I could brew some tea."

"Lemonade sounds great." He trailed her into the kitchen.

"I'll get glasses. Lemonade's in the fridge," she directed. "And there should be some fruit salad left."

He turned to the refrigerator but stopped when he caught sight of the sonogram photos secured with promotional magnets from the Donnelly ski lodge. The first picture was from so early in the pregnancy that the baby was a mere peanut-shaped blip; a circle the doctor had drawn in ink showed where the heart was. But the other pictures were from a recent appointment. It was easy to make out the baby's head and profile.

"So, um, that's the little guy. Figuratively speaking," she clarified. "I have no idea what the gender is. I've decided to be surprised." She'd had trouble explaining her decision to friends and family, but there had been enough ugly surprises in Arden's life. Why not revel in one that was wonderful? "I've been calling the baby Peanut since I'm not sure what pronoun to use."

Garrett traced his thumb lightly over the edge of a photo. "These are amazing. To have such a clear look at someone who's not even… I've looked at bovine sonograms, but this—"

"Did you just compare pictures of our unborn child to those of *cows?*" she interrupted with mock indignation. Reaching around him, she pulled butter and cheese from the refrigerator.

He shrugged. "Hey, it's the life I know. Sleep with a cowboy, you gotta expect the occasional livestock mention."

"Good to know. I'll keep that…" *In mind for next time.* The thoughtless words evaporated from her lips. Next time? With whom? Certainly not him.

For starters, her major lie of omission probably guaranteed there would never be anything tender between her and Garrett. That aside, romance of any kind had dropped completely off her list of priorities for the time being. She hoped that, eventually, she and Garrett could overcome the strain between them for their child's sake, and develop a smooth, cordial relationship. Romantic entanglement was a risk that didn't make sense. Long-distance dating was difficult under the best of circumstances, and if they braved a relationship, only to have it end badly… *I'll take 'Ways to Make an Awkward Situation Even Worse' for a thousand, Alex.*

No, definitely not worth the gamble.

Casting about for a neutral topic, she placed buttered bread in the skillet. Since he'd made the joke about livestock, she decided that maybe his ranch was the safest subject.

"When you first told me what you do for a living," she began, "you sounded like you really love it. Do you think you would have eventually found your way into ranching even if you hadn't grown up surrounded by cattle and horses?"

He leaned against the kitchen counter, considering

the question. "I honestly can't say. It's so much a part of who I am that I never gave any thought to another line of work. If I had to be cooped up inside an office like Hugh every day, I'd go stark raving mad. Running the Double F alongside my father... He's a hell of a man. I always wanted to be—" He broke off, his jaw clenched. Tension lined his rugged face.

Was there conflict between Garrett and his dad? Arden flipped the cheese sandwiches, backtracking quickly. "What about your mom?" Her voice was too shrill with forced cheer, and she struggled to sound natural. "Are the two of you close?"

"Not currently." He set the bowls of fruit salad on the table with a muted crash.

Strike two. "Any, uh, brothers? Sisters?"

"Only child."

She chuckled bleakly. "You with no siblings, me with no parents. It's like, between the two of us, we have enough puzzle pieces to make a whole family."

"A family." His expression darkened. "Maybe under different circumstances, we could have been. Maybe I would've known what it was like to teach my own son how to ride a horse, how to drive a tractor." He stared her down, so much pain in his steely gaze that it stopped her breath. "You know what? I'm not hungry, after all. Guess I'll head back into town."

Garrett, wait. At least eat something before you leave. She followed him, but her protests never made it any farther than her mind. She'd made a sufficiently disastrous mess of things for one night. Given his charged mood and her own emotional unpredictability, it was probably best to let him go.

He hesitated at the door, his look almost menacing.

"I'll be in touch soon. Like it or not, we have a lot to discuss. I won't be a stranger in my child's life, Arden." With that, he left.

Possibly to do online research on Colorado family law and paternity rights. He'd looked furious. Was he enraged enough to challenge her for custody?

She pushed the horrible thought away. Garrett was a good man. Yes, she'd screwed up by not telling him of her own volition that he would be a father, but the baby wouldn't be here for another few months. She prayed that was enough time to somehow make this right.

Chapter 5

Garrett pulled over at the end of Arden's street and texted Hugh, asking if his friend could meet him in town. Fifteen minutes later, both men were parking their vehicles outside Hugh's favorite bar. The place didn't look like much—the lot was gravel rather than pavement and a couple of the light poles had burned-out bulbs—but Garrett had been here before and knew that the food was good and the drinks were reasonably priced.

"Thanks for joining me," Garrett said, his words brusque but sincere. "Feels like I've been asking you for a lot of favors lately. Hope I didn't interrupt you and Darcy's dinner."

"Nah, she's got book club at a friend's and isn't even home. For tonight, it's just us guys." Hugh squinted at him in the dim lighting. "So this might be a good time to finally tell me what brings you to town. Besides my obvious awesomeness."

Garrett had no idea where to begin. The astonishment over his mother's confession was still fresh, but now there was the tangle of Arden's deception, too. He felt battered by lies and weighty decisions he needed to make. "What would you do if Darcy ever lied to you?"

"What, you mean like about how expensive a pair of boots were?" Hugh asked.

"No. About something major."

Shaking his head, Hugh reached for the door to the bar. "She wouldn't do that."

Isn't that what Garrett had told himself twenty-four hours ago? That Arden Cade wasn't the kind of person who would hide her pregnancy from the baby's father? Lord, had he been wrong. But maybe he shouldn't be surprised. Apparently the closeness he'd felt between them during their night together had been merely superficial. An illusion. What did he really know about her?

That she's a talented photographer and a young woman who's lost too many people in her life, that she's scared but already loves this baby fiercely. He didn't want to empathize with her, but he couldn't help admiring how she'd dealt with the deaths of her best friend, her nephew and her parents. Even though he was avoiding his own mother right now, the thought of either of his folks dying one day turned his stomach and made his flesh clammy.

The men stepped inside and waited for the hostess to find them an available booth.

Amid the bar's many neon lights, the concern on Hugh's face was unmistakable. "I don't want to push, but, buddy, you look like you're gonna snap if you don't talk to someone."

It was a fair assessment. "Okay, but this conversation will require some time. And definitely some beer."

"Cannot believe you're gonna be a daddy," Hugh slurred. It wasn't the first time he'd made the declaration. "I assumed it would be me before you. Since I'm, you know, actually married."

"Hey, I figured it would be you and Darcy first, too." Accepting reality was a cyclical process, one he'd been stuck repeating all day. It was like trying to unknot gnarled fishing line—each time he thought he was making progress, he'd have to start all over again.

"Have another glass," Hugh suggested sympathetically. He'd gone through more than half the pitcher while Garrett, now the designated driver, was busy spilling the story. Or at least an abbreviated version of it. He got through the upsetting news of his mom's affair, which had spawned this trip, to the secret of Arden's pregnancy. But he left aside the issue of Will needing a kidney transplant for now. It was too much for one night.

Garrett shook his head. "I don't think a second beer is really a long-term solution." Considering how Justin Cade had glowered at him the other day, maybe Arden's brothers would ultimately drop him off a steep cliff and eliminate the need for long-term plans. "Look, about Arden... I don't think she's really eager for people to know who the father is. The details—"

"Are her business. And yours," Hugh said firmly. "I won't keep secrets from my wife, but don't worry. Darcy and I won't spread any gossip."

"Y'all are the best," Garrett said, genuinely grateful. For the first time in days, he felt as if he could count on someone. Life had thrown him nothing but curveballs lately, and it was nice to be reminded that he had people in his corner. Hugh was as good a friend now as he'd always been in the past.

Garrett found himself nostalgic for the much simpler past. The present was full of perplexing psychological land mines. And he had no idea what to do about the future.

While Arden unlocked her studio early Wednesday morning, Justin impatiently shifted his weight behind her.

"Your secrecy is freaking me out," he complained. "First you were cagey about why you needed me to drive you to work this morning, now you won't tell me why you've called a family meeting."

The three siblings had long ago agreed that Cade family meetings were never to be called lightly and that attendance was mandatory.

Arden shot him a quelling look. "Of course I'll tell you—when the other part of the family gets here."

Justin went straight for the coffee supplies in the corner and began filling the pot with water. "You had a 'dizzy spell' yesterday and a friend drove you home," he commented. "Which friend? If it was Layla, you would've said so. I know there's something you're leaving out. You were a lousy liar as a kid, and you haven't improved with age."

She stood next to the coatrack, shrugging out of her jacket. "I got dizzy enough that I went to the hospital, okay? But I don't want Colin to know, so you'd better not mention it. He does *not* need any extra reason to worry that something will happen to me or the baby."

Justin was quick to agree. "My lips are sealed. Look, I'm as concerned about him going round the bend as you are. But you can tell *me* this stuff, okay? I'm too shallow to stay up nights obsessing over other people's safety."

The big faker. "No, you're not." The women he jilted might think of him as a heartless beast, but Arden knew there was more to him than that. Why was he so reluctant to let people see his caring side? "You've been a fantastic brother these past few months, and I don't know how I would have coped without you."

"Ah, is that what the family meeting's about?" he asked, spinning around a low-backed chair and straddling it. "Am I getting a medal for outstanding brothership? Is there a cash award involved? Because there's this new girl who works at the deli across from the ambulance station, and I would love to take her out for a night on the town."

Ignoring him, she booted up her computer for the day. Given Justin's flippant personality, he might be kidding about the girl at the deli. But if he was serious, she'd rather not know. His hit-and-run dating habits were too exasperating. She'd never seen him happier than he'd been with Elisabeth Donnelly. She understood that Elisabeth's life had changed drastically after being named guardian of a little girl, but she believed Justin had made a grave mistake walking away from the woman he loved. A gust of wind swept through the studio when the front door opened again, and her heart jumped to her throat. *Colin.* While she'd decided that this conversation with her brothers was necessary, she dreaded having to go through with it. Silly, really.

Wasn't the hardest part telling them she was pregnant in the first place? Relatively speaking, explaining who the father was should be a piece of cake.

She watched her brothers exchange greetings. Colin's hello was terse, his voice a low rasp. He had his motorcycle helmet tucked under one arm, and his rich brown hair had grown shaggy, falling across his forehead. It almost covered his turquoise eyes, which resembled hard stone in more than just color. All in all, not someone you'd want to encounter in a dark alley.

It tugged at her heart that he tried, for her benefit, to smile. Even if it was a dismal failure. "Morning, Colin."

"You…look good. Glowing and all that."

"Thank you." She hugged him, trying not to be offended by how he stiffened at her embrace. The man who'd once cuddled her after nightmares and skinned knees could no longer bear to be touched.

He patted her on the back, then stepped away. "You haven't called a family meeting since you told us you were expecting. What's wrong?"

She heaved a sigh. "Didn't I say in the message, like ten times, that everything was okay and not to worry? That I just needed to talk to you guys?"

"Maybe this is when she tells us she's having twins," Justin mused.

"No." She led them to the table where she normally showed clients their photo selections, and they all took a seat. "This is when I tell you about the baby's father."

"About damn time." The playfulness vanished from Justin's gaze. "Tell me you've talked to him and that he's taking responsibility for what he did."

"What *he* did?" She rolled her eyes. "Where do you think I was in all this?"

Colin held up a hand, looking pale. "No details!"

She interlocked her fingers, trying not to fidget while she searched for the right words. "I told you that you guys didn't know him—"

"Which I've always found suspect," Justin interjected. "We know pretty much everyone you know."

"Well, I didn't know him, either," she admitted. "He was an out-of-town guest at a wedding I shot. I'd only met him that night."

"You went to bed with a total stranger?" Colin roared. "And didn't have safe sex?"

Her face flamed, but she didn't get the chance to explain that they'd used protection.

"Do you have any idea how dangerous that was?" Justin demanded.

"Hey." She slammed her palms down on the table. "*No* yelling at the pregnant lady. It's not good for me or Peanut. We were careful. Or tried to be." She wagged her finger at Justin. "And you don't get to comment on my love life, you hypocrite. How many women have you slept with whose last names you didn't even know?"

He ground his teeth but didn't argue.

"I needed that night. It was Natalie's birthday, and I just—" She broke off, assessing her oldest brother. There was a time when his late wife's name made him flinch. Now he stared woodenly ahead. Difficult to tell whether that was progress.

She swallowed hard, picking up the thread of her story. "The next day, Garrett left town and went back to his regularly scheduled life. I was stunned to learn I was pregnant, but I saw it as a gift. Almost like… Natalie's gift to me. I didn't see him as part of the equation. Until he came to town for an unexpected visit."

"The guy from the grocery store!" Justin declared. "It's him, isn't it?"

She nodded. "He deduced that the baby is his, and he's justifiably *irritated*." The emphasis she put on the word kept it from being a laughable understatement.

Colin's scowl deepened. "What did he say? If he thinks he's going to upset *my* sister, I—"

"I do search and rescue," Justin said. "I know plenty of obscure places where no one would find his body."

"And you two boneheads don't understand why I wouldn't tell you who he was? Garrett isn't the one who messed up. He thought he was taking a few days in Cielo Peak for rest and relaxation, he wasn't expecting his life to get turned upside down. The thing is, I'm not sure how long he's staying and I need to…fix this. I don't want him hating me. Or suing me for custody. Or—"

"He threatened to take your baby?" Colin's voice was raw murder.

"No! That's an over-the-top, sleep-deprived worst-case scenario." The most recent of her 2:00 a.m. panic attacks, which ranged from concerns about genetic predispositions to wondering how difficult it would be to master the art of nursing. "Justin, if you're not on call tonight, I want to invite Garrett to dinner so you two can meet him."

"Absolutely," Justin said with relish. He and Colin exchanged bloodthirsty glances that detonated Arden's temper. A tsunami of conflicting emotions and pregnancy hormones crashed over her.

"Enough with the insane big-brother crap!" she thundered. "I don't need someone's knees broken. I need *support*. Mom's not here to hold my hand, to soothe my panic when I suddenly can't remember how long it's been since I felt the baby move. Nat was my best friend in the world, and she would've been supportive without judging me, but she's gone, too. After Thanksgiving, something between the size of a five-pound and ten-pound bag of potatoes is going to come *out of my body,* and then starts the *really* difficult stuff! I have to figure out how to raise a kid alone. Do I make enough money as a photographer? Even with Layla's generous offers of weekend and summer babysitting, how will I be able to take as many jobs? I've been terrified of screwing up, yet it seems like I already have. I kept Garrett in the dark, and I have no one but myself to blame if he detests me. One family dinner isn't going to make things right, but it's a start. You two are going to help me. You will come to my house for dinner, and *you will be nice!* Got it?"

Belatedly, Arden realized she was breathing hard. And standing. When had she shot out of her chair?

"Damn." Justin turned to Colin, lowering his voice to a stage whisper. "So much for *you* being the scariest Cade."

As someone who loved being outdoors, Garrett should be having more fun. The scenery was breathtaking, and the crisp bite to the early autumn air was a refreshing counterpoint to the bright sunshine. He knew Darcy had suggested this midmorning hike to keep him entertained while Hugh was at work, but Garrett spent a lot of hours with stoic ranch hands and equally nonverbal cows. He was unprepared for Darcy's nonstop, effervescent commentary.

"Don't you worry," Darcy had chirped on their drive

to the trail's entrance. "Hugh told me everything, and I won't pester you with questions about you-know-who. We're going to get your mind off your problems!"

Evidently, her treatment for a troubled mind included two steps: fresh air and more information on birds than any normal human being could process in a lifetime. The summer day he'd first met Darcy, he'd commented on the finch tattoo across her shoulder blade and learned she loved birds. But he'd never known until now how much ornithological detail she could pack into a discussion.

Although, weren't discussions multisided? This fell more into the category of an academic lecture. Somehow, she'd worked her way around to the topic of orioles and their intricate nests, which she called "engineering marvels."

"They're really quite spectacular," she continued happily.

Garrett hoped his eyes didn't glaze over, or he might end up aimlessly walking off the mountain. He made a nominal effort to listen, but he was busy imagining an oriole hatchling hit with the news that his father was some other bird. *Actually, son, you know that cardinal a couple of trees over? I was going to tell you when you were old enough....*

The shock of Arden's pregnancy had temporarily eclipsed the reason Garrett had escaped to Cielo Peak in the first place. But now thoughts of Will Harlow were bubbling to the surface. Earlier, after navigating a particularly steep part of the trail, Darcy had become winded and asked to pause for water and a chance to catch her breath. She'd remarked that ranch work obviously kept Garrett in tip-top shape.

Garrett was beginning to realize that he often took his health for granted. He could climb mountains, gallop across a pasture on horseback or go for a spur-of-the-moment jog. *Or have really athletic sex with a woman you met at your friend's wedding reception.* Meanwhile, there was a man potentially dying whom Garrett might be able to save.

The funny thing was, if his mother had simply told him their old friend Will needed a kidney, Garrett probably would have agreed to be tested for compatibility. His driver's license already had him listed as a willing organ donor. But the way she'd gone about it… What would Garrett tell his dad? How long would recovery from surgery prevent working on the ranch?

It would be easier for Garrett if his dad knew the truth, if Brandon could give his understanding and approval of the decision.

"Oh! Warbler." Darcy's voice was a delighted whisper. She abandoned what she'd been saying and made her way up the path, reaching for her binoculars as she went. Garrett stayed where he was, drinking in the silence.

A few minutes later, she returned, holding her cell phone out toward him. "You should see these shots I—" The phone began playing an obnoxiously catchy pop song Garrett dreaded having stuck in his head for the rest of the day.

"Hello?" Darcy answered. Her eyes widened. "Arden! This is a pleasant surprise. His number? I can do better than that. He's standing right here. Garrett, it's for you."

Knowing who it was ahead of time didn't stop him from experiencing an electric jolt at the sound of her voice.

"I'm so glad I caught you." Arden's tone was husky.

With nerves, or something else? "I didn't have your cell number, so I thought maybe your friends could help me track you down. I hope you don't mind?"

Aware that Darcy was watching with avid curiosity, he bit back the retort that the only thing he minded was Arden *not* tracking him down months ago.

"No, I'm glad you called. Has, um, something else happened?" She'd seemed completely stable when he'd left her house last night, but what did he know about pregnancy?

"With the baby, you mean? We're both fine," she assured him. "It's just… I was up all night thinking. About us."

His heart did an odd somersault in his chest. It was uncomfortable yet not entirely unpleasant.

"Like you said, we have to decide how this is going to work," she said, "how involved you'll be. For better or worse, we're a part of each other's futures. I think we owe it to ourselves to get to know each other."

His undisciplined thoughts strayed to how intimately he knew her. Clearing his throat, he turned away from Darcy. "Sounds reasonable."

"I'd like you to meet my brothers," she added shyly. "They're a big part of my life."

That half of the proposition sounded a lot less appealing than the first part. "If I have to."

He could hear the grin in her voice. "They're not that bad. Once you get used to them. I know it's short notice, but do you already have dinner plans?"

"Nothing concrete." The Connors would understand his absence—and could point the police in the right direction if the Cade menfolk helped him disappear.

"Then how about my house, seven o'clock?"

"I'll be there." He disconnected, thinking how bizarre it was that, without having been on a single date, he and Arden had progressed to the meeting-the-family phase. But then, he supposed that wasn't as unusual as getting a woman pregnant without ever having dated.

"That is not lasagna!" Arden slammed the oven door in frustration.

"It isn't?" Layla asked hesitantly.

"No, that is soup. I've made freaking lasagna soup." Arden covered her eyes with her hands and battled the urge to cry. Or swear. Or break plates. Any of the three might make her feel better, but none seemed like a productive use of her time with guests arriving in less than an hour.

"It smells wonderful," Layla assured her, coming closer to inspect the pan through the oven window.

"Thanks. But I screwed up. Normally I buy oven-ready lasagna noodles. You don't have to boil them first." Arden's words grew more rapid as she recounted her mistake. "You just add some water to the pan before baking, but the store was out of my preferred kind and I had to get regular noodles, only I was distracted so I added extra water even though I didn't need it, and it doesn't look as if the extra liquid is absorbing so now—"

"Breathe!" Layla gently squeezed Arden's shoulder. "In case you haven't heard, four out of five doctors are now saying oxygen is important."

Arden rolled her eyes, momentarily abandoning the pasta diatribe. "Oh, good. Make jokes."

The petite redhead grinned. "Well, it seemed like a better way to fix your hysteria than slapping you." She took a peek at the lasagna. "That's not too bad. Worst-case scenario, your sauce is slightly runnier than usual, but I bet it'll still taste great. You know your brothers will eat anything you serve them."

True. They'd been her test subjects in the early years, when she'd first been learning to cook. But Garrett...

"I wanted to impress him," she admitted. "At first, I looked up fancy recipes online, but that felt pretentious. I also considered a steak dinner, which I rejected because it seemed too on-the-nose for a cattle rancher." And those were only the food deliberations. She didn't want to admit how much thought she'd put into her appearance. After changing three times, she'd settled on a silky, oversize deep purple blouse with a pair of stretchy black leggings—her feminine pride had balked at pants with built-in maternity panels. Thankful that pregnancy was making her hair so full and shiny, she'd pulled it into a high ponytail.

"Honestly," Layla said, "I doubt Garrett will pay much attention to the food, not with everything else you've given him to think about. You yourself hardly ate for months, until the surprise wore off."

"You're confusing surprise with nausea. I couldn't hold down a damn thing." But she understood her friend's point. No matter what she served, one dinner would not magically solve the problems she and Garrett faced. "Did I remember to thank you for stopping by? You're a lifesaver."

Layla had brought a loaf of fresh bread from the bakery to go with the lasagna and salad. She'd also lent a hand with setting the table and chopping vegetables, doing her cheerful best to keep Arden calm. A tall order, since the two brothers who'd never fully approved of any man in her life were about to meet the stranger who'd fathered her baby.

"I don't suppose you want to stay for dinner?" Arden asked a bit desperately.

"Can't. I have a PTA thing, remember? But I will call and check on you tonight. Partly because I care and partly because your life is way more engrossing than mine." An only child, Layla was always fascinated by stories of Arden's brothers. Now that Garrett had been added to the mix, Layla said talking to Arden was better than watching television.

They both stiffened when the doorbell rang. Arden glanced at the digital clock over the stove. "It's not even close to time! None of them should be here yet."

"Relax," Layla advised. "For all you know, it's the mailman dropping off a package."

But when Arden followed her friend to the foyer, they saw Garrett through the wedges of decorative glass that framed the front door. He was striking in head-to-toe black that started with his cowboy hat and stopped with his boots.

"Whoa," Layla whispered, her hushed voice filled with awe. "Is that him?"

"Yep."

"A man that virile can probably get a girl pregnant just by smiling at her. You didn't stand a chance."

Arden opened the door, trying to look welcoming instead of exasperated by his untimely arrival. "H-hi."

"I'm early," he said without preamble. "I thought maybe I could help. And that if I arrived before your brothers, I'd be less likely to walk into some kind of ambush."

Layla laughed, and Arden shot her a look.

"This is my friend, Layla Green. She dropped by to assist, too. Great minds thinking alike and all that." She moved out of the way, allowing Garrett to step inside and shake Layla's hand.

"Nice to meet you, ma'am."

Ever since Arden had seen him at the supermarket, she'd been assailed by trepidation, viewing him through the eyes of a woman with reason to avoid him. But seeing him now, through Layla's openly appreciative gaze, she remembered how she'd felt that first night, how drawn she'd been to the handsome wedding guest with his slow, beckoning grin and silvery eyes that made all kinds of mysterious promises. In his hotel room with her that night, he'd fulfilled every one of those unspoken promises.

Heat suffused Arden. Her body had been so hypersensitive lately that the idea of him touching her skin now—

"Arden?" Garrett's voice was strangled.

"Y-yes?" She guiltily met his gaze, wondering if her thoughts had been clear on her face for everyone to see.

"I should be going," Layla said brightly. "You kids… have fun." Her car keys jingled as she pulled them from her cardigan pocket, and she scampered out of the house.

Come back, Arden wanted to call after her. *Save me from myself.*

Garrett reached over and pushed the front door shut without ever taking his eyes off her, then slowly advanced toward her. With the wall at her back, she had nowhere to go. Not that she had the willpower to make an escape, anyway. "You have to promise me something, Arden."

Anything.

"Do *not* look at me like that in front of your brothers. They'll have me run out of town before dessert."

"I, ah…" She wished she could feign confusion. It was so undignified to be caught mentally undressing him. "Sorry. Pregnancy hormones are— Words fail me."

Seeming intrigued by her explanation, he raised his hand, brushing the back of his knuckles over her jaw. "You think it's because of the pregnancy?"

"Yes." That and his return to Cielo Peak. "S-something to do with increased blood flow. The books say it's perfectly normal." Like swollen hands. Or heartburn. But she couldn't find her voice to mention those less charged symptoms.

"I haven't been able to get you out of my head all day," he said hoarsely. "Maybe that's the real reason I'm here early. After you called this morning, I started with platonic intentions, trying to think about what happens once the baby comes. But the longer my thoughts lingered on you, the more I couldn't help remembering…"

Her lips parted. Oh, God. Was he going to kiss her?

If he didn't, did she possess the self-discipline *not* to kiss him?

Somewhere in the furthest reaches of her desire-fogged brain, a small voice reminded her that her brothers would be here eventually. The last thing she wanted was for them to walk into her house and catch her seducing Garrett.

She held up both her hands, theoretically to ward him off, but when her palms met the hard wall of his chest, need spiraled through her. "We can't do this now."

"Now?" His eyebrows rose, and he grinned down at her.

"Er…it's probably not a great idea for later, either, but— Can I get you a drink? I could use some ice water. You heard what Dr. Wallace said about staying hydrated." She tried to duck away nonchalantly, putting a safe distance between them, but given the current proportions of her body, it was difficult to move casually. She waddled toward the kitchen, suddenly neurotic about what she looked like from behind.

"Whatever's cooking smells delicious," he said.

"Fingers crossed. I'm, uh, not sure the sauce is going to be the consistency I wanted. Guess we can always order take-out," she joked wanly.

"After you, the woman carrying my child, slaved over a home-cooked meal? No, ma'am. I don't care what comes out of that oven, we're eating it. My momma raised me better…" His expression, which had matched the protective warmth in his voice, grew shuttered as he trailed off.

She recalled when she'd asked him the other day if he and his mother were close. He'd said "not currently." Were they fighting? Estranged? A pang of melancholy stabbed her. She hoped he didn't let some argument or difference of opinion deprive him of a relationship with his mother. Life was short.

"Garrett, this may be out of line, but—*oomf.*" She pressed a hand to her midsection, where her unborn child had taken up soccer. Or was possibly audition-ing for the Rockettes.

"You okay?" Garrett was at her side in a heartbeat.

"Fine. The baby's just kicking."

How was it possible to look ecstatic and apprehen-sive at the same time? His gray eyes flickered with both emotions. "Can I... Would you mind if—"

Instead of waiting for him to finish floundering through the request, she took his hand and settled it over her tummy. Another dramatic jab occurred, and while the high-kick routine being performed among her internal organs wasn't exactly comfortable, she was glad the movements were forceful enough for Garrett to feel them.

He gazed at her with such reverence it was humbling. "We really did make a baby." He said it like a blessing rather than an accident, and she felt closer to him in that instant than she ever had to anyone else.

Her eyes welled. "We really did."

He grazed the side of her face with his thumb, wiping away a tear. Then he bent and kissed the spot.

"Garrett." It was a plea, and they both knew it. She was already stretching up to meet him, anticipation siz-zling through her veins. She inhaled his clean mascu-line scent, which triggered a cascade of sense memories from their night together. It had been six and a half months since this man had kissed her. If she had to wait another six and a half seconds, she'd spontane-ously combust. His lips brushed over hers, barely mak-ing contact, more tease than touch, and a small sound of need escaped her. Then he kissed her for real, taking possession of her mouth.

Sensation shot through her, igniting every nerve ending in her body. Her skin tingled, her breasts ached, her nipples tightened. She met his tongue with her own, gripping his shoulder with one hand and plunging the other through his hair. She was dimly aware of his hat hitting the floor. He tightened his hold on her hips, tugging her closer. While her shape made it difficult for them to be as perfectly aligned as she would have liked, he was near enough for her to feel his erection. She moaned, shifting restlessly in her attempts to nestle against him.

Abruptly, Garrett straightened, his breathing ragged. "I heard a car door."

No, no, no. *Not now!* She could barely form a coherent thought.

He leaned down and bit her bottom lip. "Rain check, sweetheart."

She was still leaning against the wall trying to catch her breath when the front door opened. Justin called out, "Hey, sis. I see we already have company?"

In addition to putting his hat back on, Garrett had grabbed a dishtowel and a bowl from the rack next to the sink, making it look as if he'd been helping in the kitchen rather than ravishing her. Holding the towel casually in front of him, he extended his free hand. "We didn't formally meet the other day. I'm Garrett Frost."

Her brother hesitated, and Arden cleared her throat to remind him of his promise to behave. "Justin Cade." He turned to her. "I wasn't expecting anyone else to be here yet. Thought I'd show up a few minutes early and see if you needed any help."

"Garrett and Layla both had the same idea—you just missed her," Arden added innocently, as if she and

Garrett had been chaperoned rather than making out in her kitchen.

"Well, I can take over where she left off. You don't need to be on your feet."

She knew from a lifetime of experience that arguing never stopped either of her brothers from fussing over her. "I'll sit, but get the lasagna out of the oven for me, okay? It's got enough problems without the edges burning."

"Problems?" Justin scoffed. "Your lasagna is kick-ass." He shot Garrett a suspicious glance, as if the cowboy were to blame for Arden's uncharacteristic lack of culinary confidence. Both men reached to pull a chair out for her at the same time, nearly colliding. Justin took a step back, his expression mulish. "Hell, Arden, you could drop it on the floor first, and I'd still eat it."

Was that supposed to be flattering?

Garrett squared his shoulders, rising to the challenge. "Same here. I already told her we'd be eating anything she served, no matter how bad it is."

Arden smacked her forehead with her palm. She'd expected some blatant displays of testosterone tonight, but she wished they'd leave her food out of it. Nonetheless, she knew how tough her brothers could be on other males in her life, so she offered Garrett an encouraging smile. He responded with a wicked grin that made her think he was mentally replaying their kiss. She blushed, earning a frown from her brother. Justin stepped between them to place salad dressing on the table, jostling Garrett in the process.

Why had she thought this dinner would be a good idea?

In an attempt to keep the men occupied with something other than sizing each other up, she almost asked for a volunteer to slice the bread. Then she decided she didn't want either alpha male holding a knife until they'd decided to play nice. When she heard Colin's motorcycle roar into the driveway, she barely stifled a groan. *Oh, goody. Because he excels at lightening the mood.*

This should go well.

Chapter 6

Garrett had immediately recognized that Justin Cade didn't like him. Yet, compared to Colin, Justin was a welcoming ray of sunshine. Colin didn't even smile when he greeted his sister. He squeezed her shoulder in what was probably meant as an affectionate gesture, his aquamarine eyes scanning her face intently as if convincing himself she was well.

Then he turned his head toward Garrett, his voice wintry. "You must be the father."

The wrong one of us is named Frost.

"We've heard about you," Colin added, his expression just shy of a sneer.

Garrett would have bristled at the cold animosity if Arden hadn't told him about her brother's tragic past. Was it difficult for Colin, who'd lost his own child, to be around a man who'd so casually, inadvertently, stumbled into fatherhood? "I'm Garrett. Arden's told me a lot about you, too."

She smiled, her expression a little desperate. "Now that we're all here, we should eat! Hope everyone's good and hungry. I know I am!"

From the way Justin raised his eyebrows, Garrett guessed Arden wasn't typically this high-strung. "My sister's nervous." Justin leveled the words at Garrett like an accusation, holding him responsible for Arden's increased stress. Considering that Garrett's conversation with her yesterday had landed her in the hospital, perhaps Justin had a point.

"Not at all," Arden denied. "I'm not nervous, I'm starving. You know, eating for two now."

"You have any sisters, Frost?" Justin asked.

Garrett shook his head. "Only child." This information was met with a curled lip, as if not having siblings was a personal failing or meant he didn't value family. "My parents and I are very close." Except, of course, that his dad wasn't actually his father but didn't know it. And Garrett wasn't technically speaking to his mom.

Other than that, they were a tightly knit unit.

Arden shepherded everyone to the table. Her brothers sat at the two ends, and Garrett found himself with the best view in the house—directly across from Arden. He couldn't recall ever seeing anyone who blushed as easily as she did. Was it that increased blood flow she'd mentioned? Whatever the reason, her rosy cheeks made her look as if she'd just come in from the cold. Which made him want to cuddle her in front of a fireplace. And exchange more searing kisses. The memory of how she'd tasted left him hard and wanting.

It was a damned inconvenient feeling, seated as he

was with her overprotective guardians on either side. And he still hadn't sorted out his emotional state. While part of him could understand why Arden hadn't come after him to tell him about the baby, he was still furious. A man had a right to know if he was a father. *Or if he wasn't.*

"Frost?" Justin's voice was sharp, and Garrett realized Arden's brother was trying to hand him the plate of bread slices.

"Thanks." He took a piece and passed the plate along to Colin.

Arden looked from Garrett to her eldest brother. "You two have a lot in common. Cows, sheep, horses. Colin is a large-animal veterinarian."

Garrett wondered if the aloof man was better with animals than people. "That so?" he asked, not sure where he was supposed to take conversation from here. He struggled to think whether any of the heifers in the Double F herd had demonstrated any symptoms he could ask about. In the Frost household, Caroline didn't stand for any discussion of parasites or erosive lesions at the dinner table, but desperate times called for desperate measures.

"Was," Colin said. "I was a large-animal vet, but I'm scaling back to more generalized services."

Arden froze with her fork halfway to her mouth. Her speared piece of lasagna fell to the plate with a gooey splat. "What do you mean, more generalized?"

"Traveling. Doing odd jobs on ranches. I've got plenty of contacts throughout the state." Colin shrugged, not meeting her eyes. "You knew I was making some changes."

"But I thought they'd be local changes—that you'd

find somewhere else to live in Cielo Peak, maybe re-sume your practice someday." Agitated, she swiveled her head toward Justin. Was she checking to see if he'd known about this, or imploring him to intervene?

Although Justin took a more subtle, playful approach in his response, he didn't seem any happier than his sister. "If you go on walkabout, who's gonna keep me and her out of trouble?"

Colin made a short, bleak noise that Garrett belatedly identified as a laugh. Or a mutated cousin of one, any-way. "It's been a long time since I was able to take care of anyone. I'll stay until the baby's born, but then…" He changed the subject, putting Garrett on the spot. "What about you? Will you be staying in Cielo Peak much lon-ger, or heading back to your own ranch?"

Good question. "I haven't decided. I came here plan-ning to stay a week, but I may have to extend that."

"Must not be very important on that ranch if they can spare you so easily," Justin said.

"Justin Alexander!" Arden sounded very much like a mom, making Garrett grin. "You will not be rude to my guest under my roof."

Instead of looking shamed, the man turned to Gar-rett. "Any chance I could persuade you to finish this conversation under my roof? A whole different set of rules apply there."

Garrett ignored him, focusing instead on Arden, who'd seemed so distraught over her brother's leaving. Over losing another person. "I can't stay in Cielo Peak indefinitely, but I'll figure out a way to be here for the birth," he said quietly. He could give a rat's ass what Justin or Colin thought of him, but he wanted Arden to know he wouldn't desert her.

She swallowed. "That could be hard to plan ahead. The doctors are estimating November thirtieth, but due dates are notoriously unreliable. Especially for first-time mothers."

Not to mention that having surgery to remove a kidney could seriously decrease Garrett's mobility. But those were details to be hashed out later, when he had more information. "I saw the brochures on your counter. Do you need a partner for those birth classes?"

She hesitated. "Technically, my friend Layla is signed up to go with me."

"And if she hadn't, I was going to," Justin said with a thin smile. "So we've got it covered."

"Oh, please!" Arden rounded on him. "Weren't your exact words last week *no way in hell?* I wouldn't let you come with me to scam on vulnerable women."

"I don't do anything of the sort," Justin protested. "I may not be looking for anything long-term, but *I* don't exploit women." He slanted Garrett a glance that made his fists curl.

Garrett hadn't exploited anyone. Hell, he was the wronged party here.

"I want to be involved," he told Arden stiffly. "This is my child, too." He wasn't sure yet how they would make the situation work from two different parts of the state, but being some faceless, distant entity in his own kid's life was not an option.

The brothers Cade exchanged significant looks. Apparently, neither of them appreciated his asserting paternal rights. Their hostility was beginning to goad Garrett past polite behavior.

Colin leaned forward, his body language aggressive. "I don't have much family left. Arden means the world to me. I hope you'll forgive my old-fashioned heavy-handedness when I say, you'd damn well better not hurt her."

How dare they act as if he was the bad guy? "I would never physically harm a woman, but you may have meant emotionally. Something along the lines of betraying her, maybe? Keeping secrets? Lying to her about the most important event of her life?" he snapped. "No, I wouldn't do *that* to anyone, either."

"Garrett." Arden's feather-soft voice was full of pain and remorse. All three men heard the tears quavering in her tone.

Justin was out of his chair in an instant. "You son of a—"

"No! He's right," Arden said. "I think Garrett and I should talk alone."

"Leave you alone with the jerk making you cry?" Justin demanded. "What kind of brother would do that?"

"The kind who is respecting his sister's wishes," Colin said wearily, getting to his feet. "We've met him, we know what he looks like. If we need to find him to kick his ass at some future date, we will."

This time Garrett held his tongue. He was too glad to see them go to take the bait. And he regretted his impulsive outburst. He hated to see Arden cry, and it wasn't in his nature to lash out at a pregnant woman. But the anger was a fresh wound. Had it only been yesterday that he learned the earth-shattering truth? His temper had been simmering, and Arden's brothers had provoked him past reason.

With the two men gone, silence permeated the room like a dense, chilly fog. *What now?* The night he'd met

Arden Cade, everything between them had happened so naturally. He'd never felt so instantly connected to anyone else. This ironic reversal of fortunes would have been laughable if it weren't so maddening.

"I should apologize for my brothers," she began tentatively.

Garrett expelled a heavy breath. "No. You aren't responsible for their actions, only yours."

She began shredding her paper napkin into tiny pieces. "And that's the problem, isn't it? My actions. Or inaction."

"Yes," he said bluntly. There were a lot of things to like about Arden, but none of them erased her selfish decision. He wasn't sure he'd be able to completely forgive her. If he hadn't happened to be in the grocery store at that exact moment, she could have kept her secret indefinitely.

There would have been a child in the world who was *his* and he never would have known.

He would have missed birthdays and recitals and graduations. Illnesses, homework struggles, dating advice. Garrett had been raised to believe there was nothing more important than family and, at a time when he needed that anchor more than ever before, Arden would have taken his own flesh and blood from him.

She said she wanted what was best for her child. Had she really believed that raising the kid with no father, with unanswered questions and secrets, was better than letting Garrett be a part of their lives? The sting of that was indescribable.

"You must hate me." Her words were thick with self-recrimination.

"No. Whatever I feel for you…it's a lot more complex than that." It wasn't an easy admission. Understanding his reaction to her was difficult enough in his own mind, much less out loud. He began clearing dishes from the table.

"You don't have to do that."

"This is what I've been trying to tell you—I *want* to help. I want to be a decent father." And he didn't want to harden into this angry, unrecognizable version of himself. He wasn't sure how to forgive Arden. Or his mother. Or Will. But the alternative… He turned on the hot water. "I realize your brothers despise me, but I'm glad I met them. Colin was something of a wake-up call. I found something out last week that destroyed my view of the world. I've been very…bitter ever since. Cut off from the people in my life. Even though you love your brother, and vice versa, he's isolated. I don't want to be like that."

"He's damaged," she agreed, fighting a sob. "And God, I wish I knew how to help him."

Garrett rinsed the dishes wordlessly. The pat answer was that she had to give her brother time, but how did he know that would work? He'd never faced losses of such magnitude. How much time was enough?

He felt Arden watching him, wondered what she was thinking. That he'd ruined her family dinner, perhaps?

"This thing you found out," she asked, "was it about your mother?"

"Yes." Was he ready to share something so personal? *She's having your baby, it doesn't get much more personal than that.* He scrubbed a plate with escalating force. "My mother had an affair thirty-one years ago. My dad—Brandon Frost, the man I know as my dad—isn't really my father."

"That must have been hard. But it doesn't change the relationship you have with him. Does it?"

"Not in theory, but she still hasn't told him the truth. I don't know how to be around him, lying to his face day in and day out. The only reason she finally told me is because my biological father is dying." It was the first time he'd said the words aloud, and the severity of the situation struck him anew.

"Oh, Garrett. Do you know him?"

"He's a family friend. He spent a couple of Christmases with us here and there, sent me a check for way too much money as a high school graduation gift." Which made a lot more sense in retrospect. "He has diabetes, and his condition has messed up his kidneys. He needs a transplant. My mother told me about him because she wants me to consider giving him one of mine."

Arden's gasp was audible.

He shot her a grim smile over his shoulder. "See? You're not the only one with family drama."

While Garrett finished with the dishes, Arden excused herself to the restroom. It was a lame attempt to get a few minutes by herself and collect her scattered composure. Was there a single emotion she hadn't experienced tonight? She sat on the edge of the bathtub, trying to find her balance. She'd been off-kilter since Garrett kissed her, unprepared for the enormity of her desire. The chemistry between them certainly hadn't dimmed over the months.

Once her brothers had arrived, she'd felt both gratitude for their concern and outrage at the way they'd treated Garrett. She'd gone through dismay and sympathy and shock. *And guilt.* The guilt was staggering.

In the past few days, she'd witnessed Garrett act with honor and periodic tenderness. Despite any hard feelings he harbored toward her, he was a gentleman, one willing to face up to his responsibilities. Embrace them, even. Maternal instinct told her he would make an excellent father. And she'd almost denied him that.

Her time with her own parents had been cut unforgivably short—what would she give for another day with her dad? Yet she would have sacrificed her child's time with Garrett.

"Arden?" There was a soft knock at the door. "I don't mean to intrude, but I was starting to worry."

Good hostesses didn't hide from their guests. "I'm fine." Physically. Mentally, she was a wreck. "Out in a minute."

Listening to his retreating footsteps, she closed her eyes and tried to relax by counting to ten and doing some meditative breathing. Deeming her efforts pointless, she gave up and joined Garrett in the living room.

"If I ever invite you to my house for a dinner party again, remind me that I suck at this, okay?"

"Oh, I've had worse evenings." He steepled his fingers beneath his chin. "There was a night I got salmonella poisoning at a county fair. And then there was that incident with a bull who'd been incorrectly tethered at an auction barn."

It was miraculous that, with all she'd put him through in the past twenty-four hours, *he* was trying to make *her* feel better. She sat next to him on the sofa, trying to ignore his now-familiar scent. "I wanted this to go differently. I wanted us to…" Her body tingled with the memory of his kiss. If only things between them could be as simple as finding sanctuary in each other's arms. "To be friends." She wanted to ask if that was possible but was afraid of his answer.

"I have an OB appointment Friday afternoon," she continued. "There's no sonogram or anything. The most interesting thing about the whole visit is that I have to drink a solution for the glucose screen beforehand but if you want to come…"

"I'd love to."

Feeling that she was offering too little, too late, she was driven by a need to include him in as many baby preparations as possible. "Would you be hopelessly bored going with me to shop for the nursery this weekend? For months, I didn't really buy any baby stuff because I was paranoid about something going wrong and too queasy to move. Then when I got my energy back, I was so focused on making up for lost time at work that I never got around to registering. I have portrait sessions at the studio all morning Saturday, and the high school hired me to take pictures at the homecoming ball Saturday night, but I'm free Sunday."

"Then it's a date. But after Sunday, I'll have to leave town. At least for a few days."

"To check on the ranch?"

"Yes." He looked away, the tension lining his face making her feel protective. She wanted to smooth his brow and soothe his troubles. "And to set up a couple of medical appointments of my own."

"Because of your fa— That man you told me about? You've decided to help him?"

"I don't even if know if I'm a good candidate," he

said noncommittally. "Finding that out is probably step one. I don't know what will happen next."

His words resonated with her. Never knowing what came next was the story of her life.

On Thursday, Arden met Layla for lunch at a barbecue place down the street from the school. Her friend had called the night before, as promised, but by the time Layla got home from her PTA event, Arden had been too drained to discuss her evening. But Layla had been off-campus for a meeting that morning and was free for lunch before her next class.

"So?" Layla pounced as soon as Arden walked into the restaurant. "I want to hear everything."

"Shouldn't we order our food first?" Arden asked. "You should eat before you get back to the school."

"This is my planning period." Layla rubbed her hands together. "I have almost an hour." But she waited patiently, allowing non-Garrett-related small talk while they walked to the register and placed their orders.

Arden struggled to hold up her end of the conversation. The second or third time she lost her train of thought, Layla frowned.

"Rough night, or is hunger sapping your mental energy? You don't seem yourself," her friend observed.

"It's been a…challenging morning." She'd love to vent about her earlier photo session from hell, but not with other townspeople in earshot. It was bad for business to publicly bash the clientele.

"You snag us a table," Layla directed. "I'll fill our cups."

Arden took the plastic tent marker with their number on it and sank into one of the only empty booths, right next to the window. The sunshine streaming through the glass made it seem like a much warmer day than it was. Unfortunately, the brightness only added to the discomfort in Arden's throbbing head. She massaged her temple with her thumb, hoping her afternoon clients weren't as difficult as this morning's.

She'd met with Mrs. Merriweather, a woman who wanted to surprise her husband with framed pictures of herself for his birthday. Normally, Arden tried several different backgrounds and cameras along with a variety of poses, so that the customer ultimately had plenty of options for purchase. But Mrs. Merriweather had argued about everything from the "unflattering" light to the way she was positioned. Early on in the process, she'd asked about Arden's own husband and when Arden answered that she was single, Mrs. Merriweather had glanced pointedly at Arden's stomach and sniffed in disdain.

By the time Arden left the studio for lunch, she was feeling a lot of pity for the unseen Mr. Merriweather.

"Here you go." Layla set a drink in front of her. "Food should be out soon. Sometimes getting a bite to eat helps when I have a headache."

"Thanks. I guess dealing with an opinionated client all morning was too much to take on top of not being able to sleep last night."

"Does it make you feel better to know you weren't alone?" Layla's smile was impish. "I couldn't sleep, either. The curiosity about how your dinner went was eating me alive!"

"Dinner was a fiasco. My brothers were complete asses." Annoyance flared again, but it was tempered with worry. "Colin's leaving town. I knew he was selling his place, but I thought he'd find something smaller, without so many memories. He's talking about looking for ranch work. It doesn't sound like he has a real plan, just some haphazard idea of jumping on his motorcycle and seeing where he ends up."

"Maybe that's what he needs," Layla said cautiously. "Grieving is a process everyone goes through differently."

"He told me he'll stick around 'til the baby's born. Garrett wants to be here for the birth, too. He's going with me to a doctor's appointment tomorrow."

"So you two are on friendly terms?"

Did wanting to tear his clothes off in her kitchen count as friendly? That had been the high point of the night, but there had been a lot of turmoil after that. "I've damaged his trust," she said somberly. "I don't know if it will be possible for us to ever be close. And the sexual awareness is confusing."

"Confusing? He's a hot cowboy. From where I sit, the sexual awareness makes total sense."

"That's not—" She paused when the waitress came over with a tray of food.

"Here you are, ladies. One pulled pork spud with a side salad, one sandwich plate. Enjoy!" Her smile dimmed suddenly, and Arden followed her gaze. Justin was walking toward their table.

After the waitress beat a speedy retreat, Arden rolled her eyes. "Don't tell me," she said to her approaching brother. "You dated her briefly."

He squirmed, not meeting her gaze. "It didn't end as amicably as I'd hoped. Hi, Layla. Mind if I take a seat?"

"Don't you dare!" Arden interrupted before her friend could reply. "I shouldn't even be speaking to you after that ridiculous, chest-beating macho display last night."

"I did not beat my chest," he countered. "The rest of it…may be accurate."

"Go find your own table. Better yet, find Garrett. And apologize."

"Returning to my classroom to conjugate verbs with sophomores is going to be really dull after this," Layla said to no one in particular.

"Sounds dull no matter when you do it." Justin hitched his thumbs in his front pockets, adopting a contrite expression. "Look, Arden, I'm not about to apologize to Frost. But if I did anything to upset you—"

"If?" she squeaked.

"I'll, uh, just let you two continue your lunch," he backtracked. "We'll talk later, sis."

As he shuffled off in search of a seat, Layla chortled. "It always cracks me up to see you put your brothers in their place. It's like watching a kitten scold a rottweiler."

"Kitten?" Arden echoed dubiously. "More like a hippo. I've never felt so ungainly." Part of the magic in Garrett's kiss last night was that, even while she hadn't been able to get as close as she'd wanted, with the baby wedged between them, he'd made her feel sexy as hell. She hadn't felt bulky or undesirable in the slightest.

"Penny for your thoughts."

"Nope." Arden doubted a penny was the going rate for adult pay-per-view, and that seemed to be the direction her mind was headed. Lusting after him was futile. She wasn't sure they could achieve friendship, much less anything more. But with her body chemistry all out of whack and the knowledge of just how good she and Garrett were together, it was difficult to keep her longing in check.

She rubbed her temple again, glad her afternoon was booked solid. It would keep her too busy to dwell on this unwise attraction or to worry about her oldest brother.

But, several hours later, as Arden's headache was evolving into a full-blown migraine, she felt less grateful for her afternoon lineup, especially Mrs. Tucker's twins. The three-year-old girls were…well, monsters. No other word was adequate.

When they were asleep, they were probably adorable.

Seeing them through the front window in their matching houndstooth dresses with brightly colored pockets, collars and belts, Arden had experienced a misguided instant when she thought they were cute. A fleeting notion. Before they were fully inside the studio, problems erupted. Odette, who didn't want to have her picture taken, had gone limp. Mrs. Tucker literally had to drag the child through the door. Meanwhile, the other twin, Georgette, was screaming that Odette had taken her purple crayon. The accusations were delivered at the highest possible decibel level and punctuated with flying fists. She pulsed with rage. Arden wondered if three-year-olds could have strokes.

"Could you watch her for just a moment?" the beleaguered Mrs. Tucker asked with a nod to Odette. "I'm going to take Georgie into the restroom to wipe her face and fix her hair before we get started." The little girl's red-and-yellow bow had been no match for her hurricane of temper.

As soon as Mrs. Tucker was out of sight, Odette lodged herself beneath a heavy train table Arden kept in the lobby for children. "No pick-sures!" the girl shrieked.

Arden's skull felt as if it were being squeezed in a vise. Her chest hurt, and the self-doubt that welled up within her was suffocating. What if her child was exactly like this? Would Arden know how to correct the situation lovingly, or would she overreact and set a bad example? Would she become like Mrs. Tucker, with her glazed eyes and resigned air of defeat?

By the time Mrs. Tucker wrestled both of her daughters in front of the backdrop, their dresses were askew, neither of them had hair bows anymore and Georgie's nose was running steadily.

"Um…" Arden peered through the camera and absently adjusted some settings, but nothing she did was going to make this a picture worth purchasing. "Would you rather do this on another day Mrs. Tucker? I'm flexible."

The woman gaped. "Are you *crazy?* Do you know what I had to go through just to get them here in the first place? I am not going through that again." She jabbed a finger at Arden's protruding abdomen, as implacable as the Ghost of Christmas Future pointing to the grave. "You'll understand soon enough."

Chapter 7

"You don't look so good." Garrett regretted the words even as they were leaving his mouth. Why would he say something so stupid? He blamed a late night of researching organ donation until his eyes had crossed. Giving Arden a sheepish smile, he jerked his thumb over his shoulder, toward the lobby. "How about I step out, then come back in and start over?"

Her chuckle was wan. "Not necessary. I don't kick people out of my office for telling the truth."

His offer to pick her up for the OB appointment had been twofold—he was serious about them getting to know each other better, and it seemed silly to take more than one vehicle. But it also seemed lucky that he was here since she looked too tired to drive herself. He wouldn't be surprised if she fell asleep on the way to the doctor's office.

"Are you okay?" he asked. "No more fainting spells?"

"Nothing like that," she assured him, rising from her desk chair. "I just had a rough day at work yesterday, followed by the headache that wouldn't die. My medicinal options are limited now that I'm pregnant, and I was too uncomfortable to sleep."

"I wish you'd called me," he said, not sure why he made the rash statement. What would have been accomplished by her calling? Chatting on the phone wouldn't have been fun for someone with a killer headache, and it wasn't as if he could have lullabied her to sleep. Garrett did not sing. The world was a better place for it.

Her expression mirrored his own incredulity. "You do?"

"Dumb, huh? I'd just like to feel useful. While I'm in town, feel free to phone day or night. If your heart starts racing too fast again or if you want someone to bring you pickles and ice cream." When she made a face at the silly cliché, he added, "Not literally. I meant, any craving you have that I could help satisfy."

Her eyes widened, and he reconsidered his words.

"Food cravings." Although, now that his mind had started down that path… Arden had confessed that one of her recent pregnancy symptoms was amplified desire. How would he respond if she called him in the middle of the night, her voice husky with need, and—

"W-we have to go." Her face was a brighter red than the scarlet mallow wildflowers that blossomed near the ranch every summer. "I already drank that sugar solution, and I need to reach the office at a certain time for the test to be valid."

"Right. After you." He almost felt guilty about his undisciplined lust, but he knew it was mutual. The way she'd kissed him a couple of days ago… *Dammit, Frost, pull yourself together.* This was a medical appointment, not a third date.

While they walked to his truck, he apologized for being distracted, hoping he could play it off as sleep deprivation rather than ill-timed sexual fantasizing. "As it happens, I didn't get much rest last night, either. I read living donor FAQs and articles about Colorado transplant centers into the wee hours." When he'd finally hit the pillow, terms like *laparoscopic* and *antigen match* had continued to swirl behind his eyelids.

"It must be daunting, the idea of going through such a physical ordeal."

He opened her door, shaking his head wryly. "Says the woman soon to have a baby?" A kidney was a lot smaller than an infant. And, *if* he went through with it, he'd get to be unconscious for the whole thing.

He was fastening his seat belt when he noticed Arden nibbling at her bottom lip, drawing his attention to her mouth. A man could get lost there.

"Something on your mind?" he prompted.

"Sort of. It's none of my business, though."

"We're becoming better acquainted, remember? I'm interested in your opinion."

"After I found out I was pregnant, I went on this information binge. I marked a bunch of sites on the internet, bought a stack of books, started DVRing this documentary-style show that follows expectant mothers. But none of those resources could give me what I really needed. Deep down, I wasn't looking for stats on fetal development and the most popular baby names, I was looking for peace of mind. Acceptance of the situation. It's commendable that you're doing your homework, preparing yourself with facts, but I don't think sites on renal transplants will give you the answers you're looking for."

He tightened his grip on the steering wheel. Could *anything* give him the peace of mind she mentioned? He knew he had to talk to his mother, but whenever he mentally rehearsed the conversation, it spiraled into disjointed recriminations. They'd only communicated through texts since he'd arrived in Cielo Peak.

"You want to know the horrible truth?" he asked quietly. "A big part of me hopes I'm not a good match, because then the decision's out of my hands. I don't want to deal with these mixed emotions about my dad or Mom or Will. Cowardly, isn't it?"

"Human," she amended, blessing him with unconditional compassion. "You've had so much dumped on you in the past, what, week and a half? It's mind-boggling. Don't beat yourself up over needing time to process it. I've watched people deal with bad shocks before, and it can involve anything from going catatonic to drinking too much and picking bar fights. The way you're handling everything is…amazing."

"Thank you. And thank you for listening. I tried to tell Hugh about some of this, but couldn't quite put it all into words." Despite Wednesday's awkward silences, maybe Garrett's initial impression of her had been right, after all. "You're very easy to talk to."

She sniffled, diverting his gaze from the road as he checked on her.

"Did I say something wrong?" he asked in alarm.

"No. You made me think of Natalie. Her willingness to listen was one of my favorite things about her. There was nothing you couldn't tell her, and I miss that so much. It was major praise, hearing that someone saw a bit of that same quality in me." She fluttered her fingers in front of her eyes, as if that might stop her from getting weepy. He wasn't sure he followed the logic behind the action. "This is ridiculous. I'm crying at everything lately. I sobbed over a banner ad on a recipe site the other day."

He laughed, hoping she wasn't offended. It wasn't mocking laughter. The truth was, he found her sentimentality kind of adorable.

"Turn left up here," she instructed.

"So is the crying strictly a pregnancy thing?" he asked. "I mean, are you someone who normally needs a box of tissues during a sad movie, or is this just a hormone-based anomaly?"

"I'd love to say I'm usually tough, but I'm not. Pregnancy is magnifying everything about me. I've been known to cry at soup commercials. At least those are thirty seconds of actual story, with endearing characters. Banner ads are a new low! The sad-movie question is moot, though. I try to avoid them. What the heck's wrong with happy endings? We could use more of those in film and in real life."

Her wistful tone pierced him, making him want to shield her from any more sadness. She'd said *he* was amazing for coping? Honestly, this was the first time in his life he'd been tested. He'd always been healthy, had lived in a home with loving parents and had done perfectly well in school. He'd never loved anyone enough to propose, but he'd never been lonely or suffered through a traumatic breakup, either. Arden, on the other hand… She was only twenty-five, and she'd had to survive enough upheaval for two lifetimes.

"You need to get in the right lane before the next light," she said.

"Got it." He flipped on his blinker. "So, no sad movies. Comedies, then?"

"Actually, I'm a sucker for action movies. Possibly because I grew up in a house full of guys. I'll take the original *Die Hard* over the majority of chick flicks. And I like the action stuff with a science-fiction angle."

Arden kept navigating, but between directions, they exchanged DVD recommendations and got into a spirited debate over which sequel in a futuristic spy franchise was the worst. By the time he parked in front of the medical building, she was in much higher spirits than when he'd first arrived at her office. Her eyes sparkled with humor as she facetiously tried to convince him the hilariously bad '90s flop *Vengeance Before Breakfast* was the best movie of all time. Did she know how beautiful she was when she smiled liked that?

She stopped abruptly in the middle of her animated grenade-scene reenactment. "You're staring. You know I was kidding about it being a great movie, right?"

"Didn't mean to stare. I'm just glad to see you're feeling better. No more pinched look around your eyes, and you got your color back." Leaning toward her, he traced his finger up the slope of her cheek. Her skin was silky beneath his touch. *What are you doing?* He dropped his hand. "We should get inside."

A long interior hallway led them to her doctor's practice. Garrett opened the door for her, then hesitated, feeling unexpectedly like an invader in a foreign land. Surely it was normal for fathers-to-be to attend some of these appointments, but today, he was the only guy. Women of all ages, shapes and sizes sat beneath huge framed black-and-white photos. Some of the poster-size shots focused on a pregnant belly, others were of mommies cuddling newborns. The carpet was pale pink, and the chairs were cushioned in an assortment of pastel colors.

He was overwhelmed with a clawing need to run out and buy power tools. Or work on his truck.

Instead, he followed Arden to the check-in window, where she let the woman behind the counter know the exact time she'd ingested her test solution. The receptionist said someone would take her back momentarily to draw her blood, but then she'd have to return to the waiting room until an exam room was available.

"We're pretty busy today," the woman added unnecessarily.

They weren't able to find two unoccupied chairs next to each other, but a woman in her mid-fifties scooted over to make room for Garrett. He gave her a grateful smile.

"Sorry about the wait," Arden told him. "But at least I got to drink that syrupy stuff before we came. When Natalie was pregnant with Danny, she had to drink at the doctor's office, then wait a whole other hour after her appointment. I would have felt awful for making you sit here that long."

In spite of his earlier discomfort, he heard himself say, "There are worse ways to spend time than an extra hour with you." It should have been light, teasing, but it came out wrong. His voice was too sincere. The fact that he couldn't tear his gaze away from hers wasn't helping.

Her face flushed a soft, becoming pink.

The sight knocked loose a piece of trivia in his mind, and he grunted in acknowledgement. "Huh. You blushed earlier, and it brought to mind a scarlet mallow. I just remembered the other name for that flower. Cowboy's delight." Disturbingly appropriate.

"Arden Cade?" A woman with a clipboard called Arden's name over the drone of conversations taking place.

"I'll be right back." Arden stood, slow to break eye contact. As if she didn't want to leave him. Not that it was much of a compliment that she'd rather stay with him than have a needle stuck in her arm.

The older woman who'd changed chairs for him struck up conversation. "First-time parents?"

He laughed. "Is it that obvious? She's read a bunch of books, but I don't have a clue what I'm doing."

"My husband was the same way. Don't think he'd ever held a baby until our first was born. He for darn sure had never changed a diaper. Parenting is all about on-the-job training. You'll do fine. Just love her and love the little one. Be patient with her for the rest of the pregnancy—it gets worse before it gets better. But the first time that infant's tiny fingers wrap around yours, you'll know it's all worth it."

He nodded weakly, even though he felt a little sick inside. On-the-job training? He might not have that opportunity. How were they going to handle custody? He would never challenge Arden's right to raise their child, but he didn't want his son or daughter to only see him on holidays and periodic weekends. Would she be willing to move? It would be a major life change—and she had her brothers to consider—but, in theory, she could take pictures anywhere. He couldn't very well bring one hundred head of cattle to an apartment in Cielo Peak.

He looked forward to teaching his son or daughter to ride horses, to show them around the ranch where he'd spent his entire life, the land that was in his blood. Loving his child would be easy. He was already half-smitten, and the birth was months away. But loving Arden? After what she'd done? The stranger meant well, but her counsel wasn't applicable in his situation.

To discourage further conversation, he grabbed a magazine off the nearby end table, opened to a random page and tried to look engrossed. His thoughts were racing, and he didn't even see the words printed in front of him. Nor did he notice Arden's return.

"Wow," she said, craning her head to see what he'd been reading. "I didn't know you were so interested in… the best remedies for hair-coloring disasters?"

"What?" He shut the magazine, and bold purple type on the cover caught his eye. "'Thirty-six ways to please him in bed?' Damn, are they overthinking that. You want to please a guy in bed, show up."

That startled a giggle out of her. She covered her hand with her mouth, as if embarrassed, and sat down. "Just show up? Sounds pretty passive."

"I don't remember you being the least bit passive, sweetheart."

She didn't blush or turn away. Those blue-green eyes locked on his as she tilted her body toward him and lowered her voice. "No, I wasn't, was I? As soon as you put your arms around me on that dance floor, I knew what I wanted and went for it."

Heat flooded him, shooting directly to his groin. Was kissing her in the middle of the reception area a bad idea?

Arden nibbled her bottom lip. "Can I ask you something?"

"Yes." *Whatever you want.* He'd give her the keys to his truck right now.

"Why me?" She spoke just above a whisper, and he had to get closer to catch every word. "That night... I'd never done anything like that before." She looked down, toying with a loose thread at the hem of her coat. "Is it normal for you? I have brothers. I know men have casual sex, I just..."

He was as charmed by her sudden shyness as he had been by her boldness a moment ago. "For the record, I don't think there was anything *casual* about what happened between us. I've never slept with anyone else that quickly."

"No?" she asked hopefully.

"My best friend had just gotten married. Happy as I am for him, it was odd to think he was settling down, buying a house, eventually having kids. Meanwhile, I'd broken up with a girlfriend a few weeks before and was feeling, not lonely, exactly, but restless? Then I saw you. And I forgot about everyone else. Even though it was Hugh's reception, I would have bailed in a heartbeat if you'd gone with me."

She peered at him through her lashes. "Professional photographers don't ditch the events they're working. Bad business. But it sure would've been tempting."

"Arden Cade?"

Her head jerked up guiltily, as if the nurse had caught them doing something illicit. "That's me." She turned to Garrett. "Okay, this is the part you can come back for. We'll probably get to hear the heartbeat again."

Plus, he got to remain in her company, which was far more enticing than it should have been.

* * *

Arden was familiar with the procedure by now. First, the nurse sent her to the restroom with a cup, then took her vitals—including weight. Face warm, Arden asked Garrett if he wouldn't mind waiting farther down the hall. He smirked but did as requested. Then the nurse showed them to room number three, sliding Arden's chart into the plastic file slot on the door.

Thankfully, for the visit she had today, Arden didn't need to disrobe, but she still felt oddly exposed atop the examination table.

Her doctor was Jason Mehta, an OB whose own wife happened to be expecting. Normally he was all smiles and full of anecdotes that put Arden at ease. But today, he entered the room looking troubled. He drew up short when he spotted Garrett; this was the first time she'd ever brought anyone with her.

"I am Dr. Mehta." He extended a hand. "Pleased to meet you."

"This is Garrett," Arden said. "He's the father. I thought he might like to listen to the baby's heartbeat, hear for himself that everything's going well?" Her nervousness made the last part come out as a question. Maybe Dr. Mehta was having a stressful day and his expression didn't have anything to do with her pregnancy.

His next words ruled out that optimistic thinking. "What did the nurse tell you about your blood pressure?"

"Nothing. She wrote it down on the paper but seemed in a hurry to get me processed. You guys have a really full lineup today."

"She must have wished me to discuss it with you, so I could allay your concerns."

Arden straightened. "There's reason for concern?"

Garrett moved from his post by the door to her side, taking her hand. His thumb brushed back and forth over her hand. She appreciated the soothing gesture, but it couldn't completely prevent her alarm.

"Let's not panic," Dr. Mehta said. "Your blood pressure's never been a problem prior to this, and it was not abnormally high going into the pregnancy. Is it possible you've been under stress lately?"

A strangled laugh escaped her. "You could say that. Plus, I've barely slept the last two nights. Didn't I read somewhere that there's a correlation between lack of sleep and elevated blood pressure?"

"So this is probably an isolated occurrence." The doctor eyed her sternly. "You, young lady, need your rest. The blood pressure spike may well prove to be nothing of consequence, but this is after your twentieth week. I would not be doing my job if I didn't ask some follow-up questions. Any nausea lately?"

"Not in weeks." On the contrary, she'd been feeling pretty good. Especially when Garrett touched her, causing a giddy buzz of sensation. She darted a sidelong glance in his direction. When he was this close, could he tell the effect he had on her?

"Any swelling?" When she glanced pointedly at her stomach, the doctor chuckled. "I meant in your extremities. What about headache?"

"She had a killer headache last night," Garrett blurted. "Why? Does that mean something?"

Dr. Mehta made a noncommittal noise, jotting notes on her chart. "Have you suffered blurred vision?"

"Well, yes, but I've had migraines in the past that

frequently mess up my vision. I didn't think it was related to the baby."

"Hmmm. The good news is, there's been no protein in urine—at least, not more than the normal trace amounts."

Arden wanted to cover her face with her hands. She was more attracted to Garrett than any man in memory, and even if nothing was going to come of that, she'd rather he not be subjected to discussions about her bodily fluids. She snuck a peek at Garrett, who looked hyperalert, like a soldier at attention. As if he were memorizing everything Dr. Mehta said and avidly awaited instruction.

The doctor put a hand on her shoulder. "You are a healthy young woman. It's likely everything is fine. But you need to come back next week so we can check your blood pressure again and rule out preeclampsia. Meanwhile, to err on the side of caution, try to stay off your feet. I won't prescribe complete bed rest if you swear to me you'll take it easy."

She craned her neck to look up at Garrett. "Better cancel our nursery shopping trip for Sunday. That might be too much after a full day of work Saturday."

"What exactly does this day of work entail?" the doctor interrupted.

"I have a number of portrait sessions scheduled and the big high school dance Saturday night. I'm the official photographer," she explained.

He scratched his chin. "And that would involve walking around and taking a bunch of candid shots in a noisy ballroom as well as being out late? Absolutely not. You should reschedule the other Saturday sessions, too. Unless you can promise me you'll be taking all the pictures from a chair without moving around much and that none of your clients are going to be demanding and in any way raise your blood pressure further."

She thought of Mrs. Merriweather and the Tucker twins. "Um…"

"That is what I thought."

"But…" Her eyes stung. "I'm a professional. I can't just flake out on everyone."

"Even professionals cancel when there is a medical necessity," Dr. Mehta said gently. "Arden, your baby needs you far more than the high school students do."

He was right. She knew he was right. But she'd already been worried about how the baby would affect her work *after* the birth. She was thrilled to become a mother, but babies weren't cheap. Photography was how she kept a roof over her head. She wasn't sure the high school administrators would be able to find anyone good on such short notice. If they did, would she be losing their future business to an unknown competitor?

She blinked rapidly, trying her damnedest not to cry in front of Garrett or the doctor. She was only able to half concentrate on the rest of what Dr. Mehta said during the visit. Thank goodness Garrett was there to help catch whatever she missed. Finally, the doctor left them, reminding her to make a follow-up appointment with the receptionist.

Garrett stepped to the edge of the table and pulled her against his chest for a comforting hug. It was exactly what she needed, but, unfortunately, she lost the battle with the tears she'd been struggling not to shed. The front of his shirt grew damp beneath her face.

"Y-you must think I'm s-so selfish, caring more about my j-job than—"

"Hush. I don't think that at all, sweetheart."

She sniffed. "I had to cut back while I was sick. Now that it's passed, I've been trying to take as many jobs as possible, to save up for—"

"Arden." He drew back so she could see his expression. "Don't worry about the money. I can help with that. What I can't do is keep this baby any safer. I know we haven't talked specifics yet—hell, this time last week, I didn't even know you were pregnant—but Peanut is my responsibility, too. No, not just responsibility. My *gift,* too."

She was dazed by his generous spirit. Not the financial generosity, but his emotional openness. Some men would be demanding a paternity test right about now to make sure the kid was even theirs before offering to pay a dime. She knew from his candor Wednesday night how angry Garrett was, yet he was at her side, hugging her. And when he talked about the baby, there was real caring in his voice.

Guilt seized her, raw and wrenching. This wasn't how parenthood should have begun for him. It should have been with someone he loved. She could easily imagine his joy at hearing the news for the first time. He probably would've brought flowers for the woman, a big floppy teddy bear for the baby. He should have been there from day one, and she could never give that back to him.

She swallowed hard. "I need to go pay and set up that appointment. Heaven knows they need the room back."

"If you need another minute, they can wait," he said gruffly.

"I'm good." It was a lie, but one designed to put him

at ease. She realized she was feeling as protective of him as he sounded about her.

They returned to the front of the building and arranged her next visit. She almost asked Garrett if he would come with her but bit her tongue. He'd mentioned that he would need to leave Cielo Peak. His entire life was elsewhere, and he had pressing concerns of his own. He couldn't drop everything to hold her hand.

Both of them were quiet on the ride back to her studio. Arden was dreading the phone calls she needed to make, rehearsing what she would say to the clients she was about to disappoint. "Rescheduling the individual sessions shouldn't be too bad," she mused aloud. "I can offer them a big discount for their inconvenience. It's losing the high school business that bothers me. All the future potential—yearbook photos, prom, graduation."

"I wish to God I knew the first thing about cameras. I'd go in your place," he vowed.

She smiled despite her sour mood. "You've already gone above and beyond the call of duty."

He snapped his fingers. "You mentioned yearbooks. Don't high schools usually have student staff, kids who take pictures for the yearbook and student newspaper? Maybe several of them could cover the event for, I don't know, extra credit or something. I realize they'd be amateur pictures, but if the school uses more than one person, there could be a decent assortment of photos to choose from."

Plus, she wouldn't be handing a competitor her job on a silver platter. Bonus. "It's worth at least mentioning to the principal," she agreed. "Or maybe I could broach the suggestion with the journalism teacher first. I kind of know her a little, since Jus—"

"Let me guess. Your brother dated her?"

"You catch on quick."

"What is he, pathological?"

Truthfully, she couldn't tell if Justin was afraid of being alone or afraid of being with someone. Or both. But it seemed traitorous to discuss her brother's flaws with Garrett. "Anyway, I'll call the teacher when I get back to the studio. If I can get her jazzed up about your suggestion, she might help me convince the principal. Thank you—it's a really good idea."

"Wanna see if I can go two for two?" Garrett gave her a winning smile. "I have another great idea. Promise you'll hear me out before you answer?"

"Sure." She owed him that much.

"Come to the Double F with me."

"What?" It was the last thing she'd expected, an invitation to meet his family and see the homestead. Was he serious?

"Assuming that it's okay with your doctor, I can take you there for a long weekend. Maybe bring you back Tuesday. You're going to be miserable, canceling all your jobs this weekend, and I hate to think about you cooped up in your house, worried about that next appointment. Aren't fresh air and open spaces healthy? You'll come back rejuvenated with a suitably lowered blood pressure."

She laughed at his coaxing. "You know that for a fact?"

"I know I'll be worried about you the whole weekend if I can't check on you for myself," he admitted. "You have to see the place sometime. However we decide to manage this, our child *is* going to spend time there, right?"

"Yes." The word nearly got lodged at the back of her throat. There was no question that Garrett deserved time with the baby, but the thought of being separated even briefly stabbed right through her. For six months, this baby had been entirely hers. She already loved it more than anything in the world.

"You're too good a mother to let your kid stay somewhere you'd haven't already assessed," he said matter-of-factly. "So come with me now, before the baby's born and your schedule gets even more hectic. Who knows? Maybe you'll fall in love with the place."

Her worst fear—falling in love with yet one more thing she couldn't hold on to. One more thing that would break her heart.

Neither of the Connors was home when Garrett returned from dropping Arden off at work. He'd told her to call him when she was on the way home this evening so he could meet her at the house. "I'll help pack," he'd insisted. "You can supervise. From a comfy spot with your feet propped up and a glass of water in your hand." His tone had brooked no argument.

She'd groused some choice phrases about "high-handed males" but she'd agreed. After all, they both had the same goal—protecting the little one.

Using the spare key Darcy had lent him, Garrett let himself inside, thinking that it was probably best his hosts couldn't see him now. In spite of everything, he was grinning like an idiot. Knowing that Arden would be on his ranch, the land he'd loved since he was a boy, filled him with a sense of triumph and more joy than was strictly logical. As soon as he'd first wondered if she might one day agree to move, he'd been steadily consumed with a need to show her the Double F.

She was emotional right now, and he could imagine how a conversation where he asked her to uproot her entire life would go. It would simplify matters if she'd already grown fond of the area surrounding his home. Relocating might give their unorthodox family their only legitimate chance at bonding. Maybe he was getting ahead of himself, but it was invigorating to nurture some small spark of optimism in the pit of confusion his life had become.

Unfortunately, there was one thing he had to do before he took Arden to the ranch. He had to call his mom. So far, he'd responded to her texts but had managed to put off actually speaking to her. In every message she sent, he could feel her anxiety like a sunburn abrading his skin.

If he called the house now, his father would probably be outside, still working for the day. Assuming Caroline was home, she should be at liberty to talk. Should he practice what to say? Bitterness swamped him. He'd been raised on the propaganda that he and his parents could talk to each other about anything, yet now he had to rehearse just to endure a ten-minute phone call with his own mother?

Best to get this over with, then. Sitting at the Connors' kitchen table, he pulled his phone out of his pocket. He was up and pacing before the first ring had finished.

"Garrett? Oh, thank God." Her voice was full of maternal reproach. It made him crazy that, in spite of the position she'd put him in, *she* could make *him* feel guilty. "I've been worried sick!"

"It wasn't my intent to worry you by not calling," he said stiffly. "I told you I needed space. But I'll be coming home tomorrow, at least temporarily. If you talk to Will—" damn, those words were hard to say "—tell him that I've made a preliminary appointment consultation. My understanding is that's followed by up to a week in the hospital with testing to find out if I'm a good candidate. That's not to say I've decided one hundred percent to go through with the procedure even if I am, but—"

"It's a start. We're both so sorry to have to put you through—"

"Don't!" He didn't want to think about his mom and Will as a unified "we." The idea of the two of them, his *parents,* discussing him behind Brandon's back... His free hand clenched into a fist. Knowing he couldn't hurt granite, he took a swing at Darcy's countertop. It stung like a bitch, but left him feeling calmer. "There's something else I need to tell you. I'm bringing someone with me to the ranch. A woman named Arden Cade."

"Oh?" Beneath the expected surprise was a note of what sounded like disapproval.

"Is that a problem?" he asked defensively. He was a grown man with his own house on the acreage. He'd had overnight guests and weekend visitors over the years.

"Garrett, you're in a very tough place right now. Not quite yourself, and I don't want you doing anything drastic that you might regret later. I know a lot about regrets," she murmured. "Knee-jerk reactions to stress and jumping into—"

"I do not want your advice on relationships." He also didn't want to argue with her or listen to more apologies. "I'll text you before we hit the road. See you tomorrow."

He hung up the phone, angry with his own rudeness

and her hypocrisy. He wasn't fourteen, looking for her wisdom on girls. How could she act as if their mother-son dynamic hadn't been irreparably altered?

If he hadn't gotten so ticked off, maybe he could have done a better job explaining his and Arden's situation. *Or not.* The righteous fury that had burned through him when he learned about his child was still there, boiling below the surface like lava, but other powerful feelings were developing, too. The instinct to shield her and the baby from all harm. The driving need to kiss her again. The appreciation for her inviting nature—when he wasn't actively angry with her, she was easier to talk to than almost anyone he knew.

The more time he spent with Arden Cade, the less he understood just what their situation was. Now they'd be together for three days in his one-bedroom home. Would he come out of this weekend with answers? Or just more questions?

Chapter 8

Arden stared out the truck window, suppressing the need to ask for another stop this soon after the last one. Garrett's parents were expecting them for lunch. *At the rate we're traveling, we might make it to the ranch in time for a midnight snack.*

He pointed at a green exit sign. "I'm gonna get off here. Help me look for a place to stop."

"Don't do that on my account," she managed to say, her tone brittle. As much as she appreciated that he'd come over to help with packing and dinner last night, it was a tad humiliating. On top of having to cancel paying jobs this weekend, she couldn't accomplish basic tasks? Not being able to ride for ten minutes without needing to scout out another restroom intensified her mounting frustration.

"Oh, this isn't for you, it's for me. Old junior rodeo

injury." He tapped his side. "My hip jams sometimes. Need to stretch my legs."

The corner of her mouth quirked. "You expect me to believe that load of horse manure?"

He grinned, unabashed. "Hey, I'm trying to salvage your pride here. The least you could do is play along." When he winked at her from beneath the brim of his black cowboy hat, she couldn't help but laugh.

They changed lanes to make their way toward the exit ramp, winding up behind a huge truck that said Lanagan Brothers across its back doors. "Speaking of brothers," Garrett said, "what did yours say about our little road trip?"

She bit her lip.

"You *did* tell them? We'll be gone three days, and I know you wouldn't want them to worry."

"I was planning to call them from the road," she said brightly. "At a safe distance. Like maybe your parents' driveway."

He smirked. "That explains why I didn't find Justin at your front door this morning. I half expected to see one of them waiting with a duffel bag and the announcement that he was tagging along."

"With time, I think you could all become friends." Her words came out with less conviction than she'd hoped.

"Don't sweat it. Everyone's families come with their own peculiar baggage. Mine especially."

She saw the way his fingers tightened on the steering wheel, and her heart ached for him. One of the reasons she'd agreed to this trip was because she knew he'd been avoiding his mother in Cielo Peak. Arden didn't want to provide an excuse for him to stay away from home, away from his problems. Still, the thought of his parents made her uneasy. She'd been astonished that Garrett was bringing her to meet the Frosts without first warning them that she was carrying their grandchild. She hoped this wasn't, on a subconscious level, petty retribution—him springing this shock on his mother after she'd dropped her own bombshell. *Bound to be the most awkward introductions in the history of Colorado.*

When she'd tried to suggest giving them a heads-up would allow his parents more time to adjust, he'd become prickly, so Arden had dropped the subject, aware that he already had ample reason to be irate with her. Other than that, he'd been the perfect travel companion, thoughtful and funny with decent taste in road-trip music.

"Aha!" Garrett indicated a billboard for a family-owned place that was both a diner and a country store.

They followed the directions and reached a building that looked like an adorable stone cottage on steroids. There were two separate entrances at either end. Garrett parked near the door leading into the shop.

He unbuckled his seat belt. "Want a souvenir for your collection?"

This had been his running gag for the day. The first time they'd stopped, she'd remarked that she hated to use an establishment's restroom without buying something. So he'd jokingly purchased her a shot glass while he waited. At the following two places, he'd presented her with a postcard and the gaudiest ink pen she'd ever seen in her life, closer to the size of a rolling pin. It was a feathered monstrosity that played bird calls when you pressed buttons on the barrel.

He'd looked inordinately proud. "I've outdone my-self. How am I going to top this?"

She'd pursed her lips to keep from giggling. "You are only allowed to buy me bottled water for the rest of this trip, you lunatic."

As they strolled up the sidewalk, she reminded him firmly, "Just water. Got it?"

He tipped his hat at her. "Yes, ma'am."

They stepped inside, and a blonde woman behind the cash register called out a friendly hello. Arden headed for the sign that said restroom, smiling inwardly when she heard Garrett ask the blonde to point him in the direction of the bottled water. A few minutes later, Arden reemerged and discovered that the blonde had come around the counter, abandoning her post to stand much closer to Garrett. She was practically draped across him as she laughed at something he said.

To be fair, Arden assumed the woman needed his proximity for body heat. After all, the tiny little thing was wearing a cropped sweater with low-slung skinny jeans. Exposing so much midriff, she must be chilly. Beneath the fluorescent lights, a dark orange jewel winked in her navel. A pierced belly button and a flat stomach. Arden sighed, recalling her own reflection in the ladies' room mirror. She felt like a bloated, overripe tomato in the bulky coat she wore—its bright red color had been so appealing in the store, but now…

Garrett suddenly turned, as if sensing her presence. "There you are. I got the water. Anything else you need?"

Only to get out of here. She shook her head. "Ready when you are."

The blonde pursed her lips in a pout, laying her hand

on Garrett's arm. "Leaving so soon? You should stay and have some lunch at the diner. The bison burger is my favorite, but we also have a wonderful Denver omelet and green chili."

"Actually, we already have lunch plans," Arden said, sidling closer to Garrett. Since she'd made a beeline for the restroom when they walked in, it was probable the blonde hadn't gotten a good look at her yet. Once the cashier realized Arden was pregnant, would she assume Arden and Garrett were a couple?

Whether the woman noticed her or not, she didn't put any space between her and Garrett. She managed to reach for the business card holder on the counter without ever taking her eyes on him. "Next time you come through this way, give me a call. Maybe we can have that lunch together."

He didn't take the card. "Appreciate the offer, ma'am, but I'm not in these parts often."

His refusal should have mollified Arden, but her temper was still smoldering when they got back into the truck. Not that she had any claim on Garrett, or cared who he found attractive. But wasn't there a code between females, an inherent rule that you didn't flirt with another woman's guy right in front of her? Garrett wasn't hers, of course, but the blonde hadn't known that. The rational conclusion, after seeing them together, was—

"I got you something to go with the water." Garrett rustled the brown paper bag in his hand, and she wondered what he would pull out of it. Snow globe? A decorative plate featuring the Sangre de Cristo Mountains?

A squeak of excitement escaped her when she saw the familiar gold wrapping. "Are those what I think they are?" Manners temporarily forgotten, she lunged for the package. "They're my favorite! How did you know?" These particular caramel-filled, individually wrapped chocolate medallions weren't always easy to find. She never would have thought to look in a kitschy little market on the side of a low-trafficked road.

He grinned, clearly pleased with himself. "There were some in the candy dish on the coffee table at your house. I recognized the logo when I saw it again in the store."

"Oh, these are the *best!* I could kiss y—" She broke off abruptly, then wished she hadn't. It was just a stupid expression. By stopping midsentence, she gave the words more weight than she should have had. "Thank you."

"You're welcome." But he didn't start the truck. He was watching her, and she could feel the heat in his gaze.

A shiver of awareness ran through her. For the first time, Arden wondered if she'd gotten in over her head when she'd agreed to this trip.

In spite of the circumstances under which he'd left, driving through the wrought-iron archway of the Double F filled Garrett with the same sense of joyous homecoming it always had. He loved his home, these sprawling ranges of short-grass and sand-sage prairie where generations of Frosts had made their living. His grandparents now resided in an assisted-living home in the nearby town, but Brandon brought them here at least one weekend a month for Sunday supper. During some visits they all fished at the spring-fed lake, other times they simply played cards on the wraparound porch that circled the two-story brick house.

Garrett lived farther back in a modest one-story. He experienced a wave of excitement mixed with nerves as he imagined showing Arden his place. When he'd left, he certainly hadn't been expecting to bring someone back with him. Would she like his house? Would she be cataloguing all the potential dangers to a baby? The good news was he didn't have stairs. But when he considered all the other possible hazards, it made his head spin.

"I'll buy outlet covers the next time I go to town," he announced. "That's a standard part of baby-proofing, right? I'm completely open to making whatever changes necessary. Just let me know what needs to be done."

She was quiet, the silence heavy around them. Was she thinking about all she still needed to do to prepare? He knew she'd hoped to take care of the baby registry this weekend and that she was worried about how fast time was flying. Or was her pensiveness caused by the idea of the baby being here with him and, by default, not with her?

His parents' house was directly in front of them. "Do you want to stop here, or would you rather come back after we've had a chance to drop off our bags at my place and freshen up?"

"We've already made them wait long enough. Let's get out here." But her tone was bleakly unenthusiastic as she shrugged back into her coat.

Garrett had a sudden paralyzing moment of doubt over his decision to bring her. Was it too stressful, meeting his parents like this? What kind of selfish idiot subjected a pregnant woman with dangerously high blood pressure to a nerve-wracking situation? "We don't have to do this, sweetheart. We could turn around and—"

But Brandon and Caroline were already hollering their greetings as they hustled down the porch steps. Obviously, someone had been keeping watch for his truck.

Arden's smile was sad, her tone wistful. "They sure are eager to see you."

She was unmistakably missing her own parents. His reservations about this trip evaporated. Even though he and Arden weren't dating, they were still linked by the baby. Given time, his parents, the only grandparents her child would have, could become like Arden's honorary extended family.

They climbed out of the truck just as his parents reached them.

"'Bout time you got your butt back here," Brandon chided with gruff affection. "I'm too old a man to be running this place by myself."

Garrett blew out his breath in a rude noise. "Good thing we have half a dozen employees, then, huh?" He threw his arm around his dad's broad shoulders and hugged him. Looking at him now, with a fresh perspective, Garrett wondered why he'd never noticed there was no resemblance between them. Brandon had brown eyes and sandy-blond hair, though it was liberally streaked with silver under his ubiquitous Stetson. His build was more compact than Garrett's, his features blunter.

If Garrett hadn't inherited his mother's coloring and facial characteristics, would the truth have come out sooner?

He nodded to Caroline, using introductions as a way

to put off embracing her. "Dad, Mom, I want you to meet someone very special. This is Arden Cade."

As she lifted her hand in a timid wave, her coat slid, giving them a much clearer look at her figure.

"Oh, sweet mercy," Caroline breathed, her hand flying to her mouth. She impaled Garrett with a gaze full of impatient questions. "N-nice to meet you. I'm Caroline Frost."

Arden shook the woman's hand. "I've heard a lot about you."

Garrett was impressed at Arden's warmth. There'd been no irony in her tone despite all she knew about his mother.

"And you," Arden said, turning to his dad with a broad smile, "must be Brandon Frost. Your son really looks up to you."

Brandon cleared his throat twice, then hugged Arden with almost comic gentleness, as if he were worried she might break. "So, um, how long have you and my son known each other?"

"We met at Hugh's wedding," Garrett said. "About six and a half months ago."

Pink swept across Arden's cheeks, and she shot him a reproving glare. Was she annoyed that he'd told the truth? He glared back. His father was being lied to enough without Garrett further prevaricating.

Brandon glanced between the two of them, then dropped his arm around Arden's shoulders in a protective manner. "It's cold out here today. Let's get you inside, young lady." He steered her toward the house, their heads close together as if they'd known each other for years.

Caroline whistled under her breath. "Wow. He's a

good man, but I'm not sure I've ever seen him take to someone *that* fast."

Garrett had no intention of lagging behind and being forced into conversation with his mom. She'd no doubt have questions and opinions regarding his pregnant guest. It was only on the top step of the porch that he temporarily slowed, his gaze straight ahead, his voice low.

"Do you know if Will…has his condition changed?"

"No," Caroline said from behind him. "Dialysis and prayers are still the status quo."

He acknowledged her words with a curt nod and stepped inside the house, trying not to feel as though the life he'd known there had been an illusion.

Arden had expected a polite interrogation, but Brandon wasn't asking her any questions. Was he waiting until they were seated at the lunch table, or until he'd had a chance to discuss the facts with his son first? At some point, Brandon or Caroline would ask Arden how far along she was or when she was due and they'd be able to piece together that Arden had jumped into bed with him immediately after meeting him. Would they mentally brand her a shameless hussy? Would they assume it was typical behavior of hers, sleeping with men she didn't know? Might they even worry she was some kind of gold digger who'd schemed to entrap a cattle baron?

Oblivious to her inner monologue, Brandon Frost seemed content to squire her through the long hallway leading to the dining room. The walls were covered with pictures of Garrett through the years. The Frosts obviously doted on their son.

Her mood brightened when she spotted an eight-by-ten of Garrett in elementary school, grinning at the camera with that mischievous smile Arden knew. In the photo, the smile revealed that his two top front teeth were missing. "That is so cute! He's adorable." Since she had no idea whether she was carrying a boy or girl, she rarely imagined what her child might look like. But suddenly she had a visual. Oh, how she'd love to have a miniature version of this face glowing up at her as he told her about his day.

"Adorable?" Garrett echoed from down the hall. "Hale, hearty cowboys such as myself are not *adorable*."

She tapped the frame. "This picture says otherwise. I may have to start calling you cutie-pie."

"You may also have to walk back to Cielo Peak," he responded.

Brandon clucked his tongue. "No talk of leaving yet! You two just got here." He gave Arden a knowing smile. "When he took off last week, with very little explanation, I wondered what was so important in Cielo Peak. Guess now we know. Reckon you've been meeting him on those periodic weekend trips he takes?"

"Actually, no," Garrett said. "There's nothing romantic between me and Arden."

Her face flamed. She'd entertained the far-fetched notion that springing her on his parents like this was minor revenge for his mother's affair. It was slowly dawning on Arden that she might have had the right idea but the wrong target. At the moment, it seemed an awful lot like a vindictive response to her hiding the pregnancy.

She wasn't the only person who'd gone red in the

face. Brandon's expression had also grown ruddier. "Oh. But I thought…" His gaze, full of confusion, fell to her stomach.

"It's your son's baby," she confirmed, raising her chin imperiously. Irritation with Garrett bolstered her confidence. "Perhaps the more accurate statement would have been there's nothing romantic between us now." Or ever again. She blasted Garrett with a fulminating glare, then—proud of how serene she sounded—told Caroline, "Something smells wonderful."

"She made Garrett's favorite," Brandon said.

Seeming eager to move on and dispel the tension, he led them into the dining room. A dark cherry oval table had been set with plates and silverware. Goblets of ice waited to be filled with beverages, and the sweet buttery aroma of cornbread wafted from the woven basket at the center of the table.

"I'll get the sweet tea while Caro checks on the casserole," Brandon said pointedly. He might as well have held up a sign declaring that he was giving Garrett and Arden a moment alone.

She wasted no time. Maybe some women employed the silent treatment, but she'd been raised by two brothers who'd taught her how to stand up for herself and, when the occasion called for it, swear like a sailor. "You ass," she hissed. "Is this why you didn't want to tell them ahead of time that I'm pregnant? Because you thought it would be more fun to make everyone uncomfortable and paint me as some kind of skank with loose morals?"

"Fun?" he echoed in an incredulous whisper. "Explaining a baby I knew nothing about until this week to a mother I can barely look in the eye and a father who's no relation to me? Yeah. Good times, Arden. Fine, maybe I could have used a smoother approach—"

She snorted.

"—but I will not lie to them about us. They deserve better. And so do you," he said unexpectedly. "I could mislead them about our relationship, but, trust me, you don't want that. Feeling like someone's secret, waiting for the other shoe to drop…"

Her anger slipped a notch. Garrett had been wonderful at the doctor's yesterday and for most of today. She'd known this homecoming would be challenging for him. Maybe it shouldn't have caught her off-guard that his terse explanations had been so graceless.

"And nobody who spent as much as thirty seconds with you could think you're a skank," he said earnestly. "I meant what I said to my parents. You're special. My dad never takes to people that quickly."

Bemused, she took her seat at the table while Brandon filled everyone's glass with tea. Sometimes there was such tenderness in Garrett's tone, yet other times, contempt flashed in his eyes. She recalled what he'd told her after the dinner with her brothers, that he didn't want to be a bitter, angry man. She could see him wrestling with the ways he'd been wronged. She hated that she'd contributed to that inner struggle.

Caroline returned with some kind of cheesy chicken casserole that made Arden's mouth water. The two women sat across from each other, while Garrett and his father sat on either end. Both men had removed their hats for the meal and set them on a side table.

Settling her napkin in her lap, Caroline looked at Arden. "I probably should have thought to ask before now—you don't have any food allergies, do you? Or foods you can't tolerate during pregnancy?"

"I'm avoiding shellfish and a few other items for the time being, but mostly, I can eat everything. And this looks delicious."

"Thank you." Caroline ladled a portion of the casserole onto her husband's plate and passed it back to him. "There are so many people in our church now with dairy or nut or gluten allergies. I never know what to bring to potluck anymore."

"I feel terrible for the Sunday school teacher, Bess Wilder," Brandon said. "Poor woman's allergic to chocolate. She's never once been able to eat Caro's award-winning brownies. Our friend Will has it worse. Diabetic." His expression grew shadowed. "'Course, now he has more to worry about than just missing out on dessert."

Arden noticed that Garrett had gone stock-still, his entire body rigid. And Caroline's gaze darted between her husband and son—she looked like a trapped animal that didn't know where to run. Garrett had said his biological father was diabetic and a family friend. Her heart squeezed in sympathy. It couldn't be easy to bite back the truth whenever Will's name was mentioned.

She wished she was sitting closer to Garrett so she could hold his hand or rub his shoulder. A silly impulse, perhaps, since patting his shoulder would do nothing to improve his circumstances, but she wanted to lend him strength. The way he had at her doctor's appointment yesterday.

Arden couldn't help stealing glances at Garrett throughout the meal. He'd barely eaten a bite, even though the recipe was supposedly one of his childhood favorites. Brandon ate almost absently, spending most of his time studying his wife, a concerned frown creasing his brow.

It seemed up to the women to make conversation, and Arden wasn't surprised when the first question came.

Caroline set her fork down. "So, the two of you met at Hugh's wedding? Are you a friend of—what's his wife's name?" She glanced toward Garrett, who acted as if he hadn't heard the question.

"Darcy," Arden related.

Brandon chuckled. "Freckled Hugh Connor, the kid who used to squeal in terror if his folks tried to make him ride a pony at the fair. Can't quite picture him as a married man."

"Well, he's grown now." Ostensibly, Caroline's reply was for her husband, but her gaze was locked rather desperately on Garrett. "His pony phobia was *years* ago. The past isn't always relevant to the present. I'm sure he's a much different person." Her every sentence and gesture seemed an attempt to reach out to her wounded son, who continued to silently stonewall her. It was painful to watch.

Arden wondered what the future held for her and her own unborn child. Would she ever do anything her son or daughter couldn't pardon? That would cut a mother to the quick. "I wasn't actually there as a guest," she told Caroline. "I was the photographer."

"Photographer, huh?" Brandon asked. "That an interesting line of work?"

"Some days, it's more interesting than I'd like. I learned early on that any portrait sessions including children or animals tend to be unpredictable."

"And do you like working with children?" Caroline

asked. Her voice was tinged with sadness. Because of the current strain between herself and her now-grown child?

Arden squirmed in her chair, trying not to dwell on her tortuous afternoon with the Tucker twins. "I love it." *Mostly.*

"If you don't mind my asking, will this be your first child?"

"Yes, ma'am."

"*Our* first child," Garrett said unexpectedly. "I should have figured out sooner a better way to tell you that I'm going to be a father. To be honest, I'm…still adjusting to the idea myself."

"Well, becoming a father is momentous. And becoming a grandpappy?" Brandon looked delighted at the prospect. "Hell, Caro, we're getting old."

"Speak for yourself." She sent him a mock scowl, and he grinned back at her. Despite today's undercurrents of tension, it was evident the two of them were crazy about each other.

"How about your folks?" Brandon asked Arden. "Are they excited to have a baby on the way? Do they have grandchildren already?"

Her eyes burned with emotion. "My mother died when I was five, and my father followed her into heaven a few years later."

"Oh, you poor dear." Caroline's tone was distraught. "You're all alone, then?"

"Not completely. I have two older brothers. I'm sure they'll be good uncles." Assuming Colin was around. His growing restlessness scared her. What if he jumped on that damn motorcycle and disappeared, convinced his siblings were better off without his gloom and damaged psyche?

"We'll love the baby enough for two sets of grandparents!" Caroline vowed.

"We plan to register for baby stuff soon," Garrett said, "so you'll have opportunities to start spoiling your grandchild even before he—or she—gets here."

"You don't know the gender?" Caroline asked. "How soon can they tell that?"

"I wanted to wait until the baby's born to find out," Arden said. "I don't care if it's a girl or boy, as long as the little peanut's healthy."

Brandon nodded. "I'm proud to have a son to carry on the ranch and the family name, but I would have loved a daughter, too." He gave Arden a smile so welcoming that her throat constricted. For a split second, she felt a wave of utter belonging.

She was confident these two people would love her child, and she wanted that for the baby. The chance for grandparents was a gift she wouldn't have been able to offer as a single mom. But it hurt, the Frosts' acceptance of her. It was a cruel tease, showing her something she hadn't had in a long time but couldn't keep.

Or was she, as Layla would say, borrowing trouble? Life was short. Perhaps she should try to appreciate the blessing of this day and take the future as it came.

"Caroline, can I help you with the dishes?" she offered, wanting to repay their hospitality.

"Absolutely not!" Garrett objected. "There were multiple reasons I brought Arden home with me this weekend, but a major one was to keep an eye on her and make sure she doesn't overexert herself. Dr. Mehta says her blood pressure is too high. He didn't go so far as putting her on strict bed rest, but she's supposed to stay off her feet."

Brandon studied her, seeming to sense her frustration. "Don't you fret. Maybe I can't give you the standard walking tour of the ranch, but we can take the Gator."

She stared at him blankly.

"All-terrain vehicle," Garrett clarified. "We've got several kinds of transportation on the ranch, from tractor to snowmobile, but my favorite mode has always been horseback. I'm getting up early tomorrow to ride the perimeter and check fencing. See if there are any repairs we need to make before the serious winter weather rolls in."

"I've never been riding," she said. "I think I sat on a horse to get my picture taken at a birthday party when I was little, but that's about it." Justin and Colin had loved skiing and snowboarding. They'd been more eager to get her on the slopes than in a saddle.

"After the baby comes, maybe we—" Garrett stopped, catching himself. Whatever the future held, Arden doubted his girlfriends down the road would be thrilled about him spending recreational time with his former one-night stand. Even if—especially if—she was the mother of his child.

He recovered admirably, making it look as if he'd interrupted himself to say something else. "Hey, Dad gave me an idea. You wanted to register for baby gifts, but the doc said to stay off your feet. Don't most big stores have those motorized carts now? You can drive from one end of the store to the other."

She knew he meant well, but the suggestion highlighted the grating powerlessness she'd felt ever since the doctor said she had to cancel her jobs this weekend. It was mortifying to feel helpless, prohibited from simple tasks like dishes and shopping. Plus, though she was reluctant to admit to such pettiness, motoring around on one of those carts would chafe her ego. She was a young, comparatively athletic woman in the prime of her life! It had been bad enough standing next to Garrett while that crop-topped blonde with the bejeweled belly button flirted with him. She could just imagine following him around like some giant parade float while lissome salesgirls fawned over him and offered their assistance.

"Another option," Caroline said, "is to register online. We like not living in a city, clogged with traffic and malls, but I have to admit, being able to use the internet for shopping makes it a lot easier."

"Oh, yeah," Brandon grumbled good-naturedly. "She can whip out a credit card and buy anything her heart desires at any hour of the day. Hurray."

"So I suppose you want me to cancel those gifts I ordered for your birthday in November?" Caroline teased. She swung back to Arden. "Speaking of November, do you have plans for Thanksgiving, dear?"

"Only if you count having a baby," Arden said, trying not to gulp. She couldn't wait to meet her child, but thinking about the birth process was still daunting. She kept trying to skip over that part in her mind and look forward to Christmas. Last year had been the first holiday season since Natalie's and Danny's deaths; Arden hadn't even dredged up the energy to put up a tree. She and Justin had exchanged gifts and toasted each other with heavily spiked eggnog. Colin had insisted on being alone. This year, she planned to celebrate the biggest gift of her life.

"I've read all the recommended books," Arden said, "and I'm signed up for classes through the hospital, but I'm a nervous wreck."

"I understand completely," Caroline admitted. "The whole time I was carrying Garrett, I was convinced something would go wrong again."

"Again?" Arden asked.

"Oh! I…is that what I said?" Visibly shaken, Caroline bolted from her chair and carried her plate to the kitchen.

Brandon excused himself, gathering up more dishes and leaving to check on his wife.

Arden glanced at Garrett, who seemed confused. Had Caroline been pregnant before she had him? "Do you know what that was about?" she asked softly.

He shrugged. "Not a clue."

"Maybe we should give them some space," she suggested.

When Caroline returned a few minutes later to ask if anyone had room for dessert, Arden shook her head. "Actually, I'm more tired than hungry. I was just asking Garrett if we could take our stuff to his house. I may stretch out and take a nap."

"Of course. You two just come back when you're ready this evening. We'll have dinner and maybe play some card games." Her smile lacked its previous luster, but she was obviously trying to project cheer. "Have you ever played pinochle, dear? Brandon and I are formidable. Regional champs."

"Never tried it, but good to know I'll be learning from the best," Arden said.

"Thank you for lunch, Mom." But Garrett didn't so

much address Caroline as the pale blue wall over her left shoulder.

As they left, Arden snuck one last glimpse at Mrs. Frost, who stood alone in the center of the dining room, shoulders slumped in dejection. She was staring down, so Arden didn't get a look at her expression, but her body language was clear. She was a woman with a broken heart.

"My house isn't very big." Garrett pulled their bags from the truck, feeling foolish for having stated the obvious. His house had always been more than adequate, focused on the exact luxuries he wanted and none of the unnecessary extras his mother had given up suggesting—like vases or "curio cabinets." What the hell was a curio? "It's kind of like yours, actually. So the peanut should feel right at home."

In his peripheral vision, he saw Arden flinch.

"Does it bother you, when I talk about having the baby with me? I'm not trying to separate you from Peanut, you know. I just want to be a father." His throat tightened. "Do you know how many milestones I'll miss? It's unlikely I'll be there for the first step or the first word. At best, they'll probably be blurry videos I get to see weeks later on your phone." If she'd had her way, he wouldn't have even experienced those.

"Garrett…"

There wasn't a damn thing she could say to change the circumstances or take back what she'd done. Shaking his head, he strode toward the house.

He unlocked the door and held it open for her, letting her step into the living room first.

The look she gave him over her shoulder was wry. "So this place is like mine, huh?"

Granted, she didn't own a big-screen television or a leather sectional sofa, but the analogy wasn't completely off-base. "Maybe without some of the homier details," he admitted.

On the mantel he had a framed picture of himself with his parents and grandparents and a much smaller photo of his favorite horse. They were the only photographs displayed anywhere in his home. He suddenly felt self-conscious about that, given Arden's profession. But mountains and spectacular sunsets and countless stars winking down at his porch were part of his daily existence. Why miniaturize them for capture in insignificant pewter frames when he could experience them firsthand?

"The good news is, I have plenty of room for baby paraphernalia," he joked.

The furniture was sparse, but that helped keep the modest-size house uncluttered. His philosophy was that he didn't need much, so for the belongings he *did* purchase, why not buy the best? He'd spent most of his budget on the high-end sectional sofa but skipped over a kitchen table. Between bar stools at the counter, folding TV trays and meals at the main house, he figured he was covered. Did Arden see an indulgent bachelor pad? He had to admit, his style of living wasn't necessarily compatible with having an infant or toddler in the house.

He scratched his jaw. "Guess I need to change more than just the outlet covers, huh?"

She hesitated as if there were something she wanted to say but thought better of it.

"Arden?"

"I actually am tired. Is there a place I can lay down for a while?"

"Right this way." He took her to the master suite. Something potent jolted through him. He'd always been sexually drawn to Arden, but having her here by his bed made the desire more primal. More possessive.

She took in her surroundings. "This isn't a guest room."

"Don't have one anymore. This house was over seventy years old. I did a complete remodel, including knocking out the wall between two small bedrooms. Figured less was more. Literally. You'll sleep in here, I've got the living room. The middle section of the sofa pulls out into a surprisingly comfortable double bed. Bathroom's right this way."

"Whoa." She gaped at the spacious tub. Its hot-water jets were perfect for easing sore muscles after days of sunup to sundown labor. "That's big enough for two people, easily."

The mental image was vivid and instantaneous. He tried not to groan at the thought of slicking soap over her dewy skin. The morning they'd woken up together in that Cielo Peak hotel, he'd hoped she'd join him in the shower. Instead, she'd stolen away without a backward glance.

He cleared his throat. "Unless you need anything else, I'm headed to the barn to help my dad." Putting much-needed space between himself and his alluring houseguest. "I've got my cell phone with me."

Although Garrett truly loved the ranch, he didn't think he'd ever been this eager to tackle menial chores.

There was a specific calm that came with the familiar tasks—cowboy Zen his dad had called it once.

He found Brandon starting the tractor.

"About to haul hay," the older man called. "Wanna lend a hand?"

"Sure." Garrett stepped up onto the platform step and held on. The tractor chugged toward the round bales they would use to stock feeders. Sometimes the two men rode in companionable silence. Garrett knew today would not be one of those days.

Brandon came out swinging, raising his voice to be heard over the engine. "You gonna do the right thing and marry that purty gal?"

"Dad, I told you, it's not like that between us. We aren't dating." Relationships required trust. These days, Garrett was feeling pretty cynical about the institution of marriage in general. But that wasn't something he could discuss.

"I don't know what you mean by *dating,* but whatever you did was enough to get her pregnant." Brandon made a derisive noise. "You were brought up in a good home, with parents who loved each other. Didn't think you were one of those men with dumb-ass priorities, the ones too afraid to grow up and settle down."

"That's not it at all," Garrett said, defending himself. "And you're making an awfully big assumption that even if I asked her, she'd say yes. Arden…has been through a lot. She told you she lost her parents. About a year ago, she also lost her best friend and young nephew in a car crash. She's…in a delicate place emotionally, picking up the pieces."

A wholly unexpected stab of guilt twisted Garrett's insides. Whether he'd known it or not, Arden *had* been emotionally vulnerable the night he'd slept with her. He hadn't meant to take advantage of her loss. All he'd known was that the beautiful stranger made his blood boil with need. Hell, she still did.

Arden had said she wanted them to be friends. Did she have any feelings for him beyond that? She'd kissed him at her house but had been quick to blame pregnancy hormones. Had she been trying to tell them that her body might want him, but, aside from the ungoverned chemical reaction, she wasn't interested?

"Caught your momma and me off-guard," Brandon chided, "springing Arden on us like that. Don't get me wrong. We're happy to meet her. She seems like good people. But your momma… Long before we had you, there were miscarriages. Caro's tough enough to hold her own against a coyote or a snake, but she wasn't emotionally prepared to spend the afternoon with a pregnant woman."

Garrett didn't know what to say. "How come neither of you mentioned any of this before?"

His dad shrugged. "Never saw the need. Why dredge up old pain when it's in the past?"

They reached the bales and began the process of lifting them for transportation to the feeders. For now, conversation was over. But his dad's words kept replaying through Garrett's mind. Did Brandon truly believe it was better for the past to lay undisturbed? Caroline Frost insisted that telling her husband about her long-ago indiscretion would cause him pointless grief, that it was a fleeting mistake with no consequence on the present.

Except that wasn't true. Garrett was the consequence. Brandon always talked about the Double F as if it were the family legacy. But right now it felt as if their legacy was comprised of unintentional pregnancies and women who kept secrets.

Striving to push aside the doubt and questions—at least for one afternoon—Garrett threw himself into the familiar rhythm of feeding the cows. He envied the herd their simple existence. As far as his own life was concerned, it felt as if no decision would ever be simple again.

Chapter 9

Arden suppressed a yawn, staring out the window at hundreds of twinkling stars. "I may have to spend the night in the truck. I'm too stuffed to move. Not that I'm complaining."

"I have to say, my mother went all out. She must really like you."

Was he really that blind? *Arden* wasn't the one Caroline was trying so hard to win over. "I would've said it was more a case of slaughtering the fatted calf to welcome home the prodigal son. In this case, literally." The Frosts' freezer was full of prime beef they themselves had raised. Had it been strange for him as a boy, eating a steak that might have had a name only a few months ago?

"I'm not that *prodigal*. I was only gone for a week."

"Nonetheless, she's happy to have you home. Happy and scared. She's afraid you won't forgive her."

"You think I *want* to be angry with her? I didn't ask for any of this. Waffling between all these emotions sucks. It's confusing. And exhausting." As they walked toward the house, a motion-sensor light flooded the yard.

She took the opportunity to steal a better look at his expression. Did he classify her in the "any of this" he hadn't asked for, one of the factors currently screwing up his life? She would never, ever wish away the baby, but for the first time, it occurred to her to wonder what would have happened if she hadn't been pregnant when she'd encountered Garrett in the grocery store. Would they have met for a drink, maybe? Reexplored their physical connection? Would there have been a chance for them to develop something more?

"I know what you mean about the emotional exhaustion," she said. "When Natalie and Danny died, I was livid. But maintaining that level of outrage over the unfairness of it all left me depleted. Listless. It was a long, slow climb up out of that pit." Her night with Garrett had been a major catalyst in that process. She only wished there was more she could do to help him with his own personal crisis.

Inside, he asked, "Ready to turn in?"

"No. I slept too long this afternoon," she said ruefully. His bed was impossibly comfortable. "But if you're tired, I can read or something."

He didn't answer at first, and she wondered what he was thinking. Would he prefer the solitude of his own company? Or was he as reluctant to say good-night as she was? "How about we look into that online registry idea?" he suggested finally. "My computer's in the bedroom."

Fifteen minutes later, as Arden wiggled her bare toes and sipped from a steaming mug of generously honeyed chamomile tea, she decided that Caroline Frost was a genius for having thought of this. Arden had changed into a pair of pajamas, and Garrett was stretched out next to her in a pair of plaid flannel pants and a well-worn charcoal T-shirt, his muscles delineated beneath the thin cotton. This was *so* much better than rolling alongside him at a retail warehouse like his fat cyborg friend.

They hadn't gotten to any of the fun stuff yet—the actual scrolling through products and clicking on anything and everything that looked useful. Garrett was still inputting their basic information, listing her as the main contact and her address for shipping. She thought about what he'd said earlier, that his wanting to spend time with the baby was nonmalicious and that she was welcome to spend time here, too. After tonight, she could almost imagine doing so. Caroline and Brandon had entertained her with stories of Garrett's childhood and ranch life; they'd coaxed her to talk about herself and said her brothers sounded like absolute princes— which had earned a sarcastic guffaw from Garrett.

She nudged his ankle with her foot. "You have a strange surname."

"Frost? That's not weird."

"It is for a family this warm. Thank you for bringing me here. Your parents are wonderful people. *You're* wonderful." When the time came that her child was spending weekends and holidays and summers here without her, she would always know that the kid was in good hands.

But now was not the time for such bittersweet

thoughts. She wanted to distract herself with cute one-sies and colorful board books, not dwell on the challenges to come. "Maybe I should've typed," she mocked him. "Even with swollen hands, I could go faster than you."

"Not my fault," he grumbled, moving his fingers in an inefficient, hunt-and-peck fashion. "Your pajamas are distracting me."

She blinked. "My pajamas?"

"They're sexy."

The sky-blue drawstring shorts printed with bright yellow rubber duckies and the voluminous matching top? "Are you on crack?" A walking lingerie ad, she was not.

"Rubber ducks are for the bathtub," he said, as though this made something resembling sense. "Ever since what you said earlier... I might have pictured you in the tub once or twice."

A sweet, piercing heat flooded her. "Oh." He'd pictured her there? She was surprised by the intensity in his tone, how much he wanted her. True, they'd had incredible sex together, but that had been months ago. Before she'd damaged his trust. Before her body had morphed to its current shape. "Did you, um, picture yourself in the tub with me?"

He jerked his head up, looking startled by the question. Then he set the laptop on the comforter and leaned very close. "Yes." His breath fanned over her skin. "Would you like to hear the details?"

"I... No, I..." Frankly, she'd rather have a demonstration. But no matter how loudly the reckless words echoed in her head, she couldn't bring herself to voice them.

"I understand." He picked up the laptop again as if nothing had happened. She tried not to hate him for that. Her breathing was shallow, her palms were clammy, her nipples were hard points. He resumed the uneven staccato of his typing.

Arden gulped her tea as if it were a miracle cure for lust, and immediately cursed.

"Whoa. Some language." Garrett looked impressed at her imaginative vulgarity.

"I was raised by older brothers," she said by way of explanation. But since she'd burned her tongue, it came out as *I wath raithed by older brotherth*. Very sexy. No wonder a gorgeous cowboy who could probably have his pick of any woman in the state spent time fantasizing about her. *Sheesh*.

"Okay, all done filling out the online form," Garrett declared. "Do you have a checklist of everything we need?"

"At home. I didn't pack it this weekend. But we can get started and always add items in later." She scooted closer so she could see the screen better and directed him to consumer reviews and safety reports on the car seats that interested her the most. It took them over forty minutes of research and debate to decide on a seat, a crib and a high chair.

He hesitated, his hand hovering over the mouse. "Should we register for two cribs?"

It was a fair question, and she tried not to balk. "How about this? We register for a playpen. It's basically a portable crib that you can fold up and throw in the back of the truck. Not only would it work well here at your place, you could easily schlep it over to your parents' for a few hours in case you wanted to visit with them or they offered to babysit."

After a number of big items had been selected, they began surfing the site just for fun. "Why are there no baby cowboy hats?" Garrett demanded. "That's a travesty!"

She had a sudden mental image of a little boy with Garrett's shimmering gray eyes, a too-big cowboy hat dipping comically low over his forehead.

"Oh, dear Lord." His befuddled tone snapped her out of her reverie. "Now I've seen everything."

"What is it?"

"Baby Booty Balm. Then there's another brand called Butt Spackle. Can't these people just call it diaper rash ointment? Leave the poor kids some dignity."

A succession of memories drifted through her mind—mental snapshots of Danny dressed like a bunny at Easter when he'd only been four months old, him covered in mud after he'd discovered a puddle in the yard, and streaking bare-assed through a dinner party once when he'd emphatically decided his father was *not* going to change his diaper.

"Hate to burst your bubble," she said, "but I'm not sure infancy and toddlerhood come with a lot of *dignity*."

"You never know," he quipped. "Our kid could be special."

Of that, she had no doubt. They made a few more selections, and she realized that the soothing chamomile had done its job. A peaceful lassitude was seeping through her bones. With Garrett next to her, making jokes about their son or daughter, she felt more tranquil and lighthearted than she had in weeks. Not wanting the moment to end, she tried to smother her yawn, but he noticed.

"Why don't we shut this off for now?" He clicked on an icon to bookmark the page, and she noticed some of the other sites in the "favorites" library. Most of them were about kidney transplants and living donors.

"Interesting reading," she remarked. She didn't want to pry, but she hoped that by giving him an opening, he'd know she was available to listen.

"Kidneys are among the most common organ transplants," he said. "And, if I read this one article right, doctors don't actually remove the bad kidney to replace it. They leave it in there and do some kind of... I don't know, arterial rerouting? Like when someone used to hack their neighbor's cable. So whenever Will gets a new kidney, he'll be walking around with three of them inside." Garrett frowned. "Three's an awkward number."

"How do you mean?"

"What was your impression of my parents together?" he asked. "As a couple?"

The question surprised her, but it meant a lot to her that he valued her opinion. "From my perspective as an outsider, it looks as if they're crazy about each other. I can't imagine why your mother was ever with someone else, but if she says it ended years ago, I'd believe her."

Garrett jammed a hand through his hair. "You may be right. I mean, I certainly never saw anything when I was younger to make me suspicious. I always thought my parents were devoted to each other, a shining example. I wanted, someday, to find what they had."

Was he angry not just that Caroline had betrayed her husband but that she'd betrayed Garrett's long-held ideal? Parents were human beings, too. Yes, his mom was flawed, but he was still lucky to have her.

"I think the affair bothers me more because Will Harlow never married," he said. "He'd bring an occasional date to dinner, but I've been racking my brain and can't remember his ever having a serious girlfriend. It makes me wonder if his feelings for my mother were as platonic as she'd like to claim. Did he ever really move on? And does it matter? Even if he's been pining for my mother her entire marriage, is that a reason to deny him a kidney?"

She gave in to the impulse she'd had earlier today to comfort him. Now that they weren't separated by his parents' dining-room table, she put her arm around his midsection and hugged him tightly, resting her head on his chest. He went very still at first, but gradually relaxed, dropping one arm over her shoulders and stroking her hair with his other hand. It was very quiet in the room, only the whir of his laptop providing background noise.

Finally, he broke the silence. "You know I have a consultation scheduled for Monday? That's the first step, followed by several days, up to a week in the hospital. There are physicals, blood tests, psych evaluation…" He sounded overwhelmed.

"I could go with you on Monday," she ventured. "You know, for moral support."

"I'd rather you stay here."

She sat upright. "Are you sure? I know hale-and-hearty cowboys don't admit weakness, but it might be easier for you with someone there."

"Just the opposite. My dad really likes you."

What did that have to do with the price of skis in Denver?

"I already despise that I can't tell him where I'm going," Garrett said hollowly. "Bringing you with me would be like a double betrayal, making you an accessory to the crime."

"Garrett, you may end up saving a man's life—a man your father cares about deeply, by the way. That's hardly a crime." She decided to lighten the mood. "If you end up spending a week in the hospital, can I at least come visit you? Feels like it should be *my* turn to see *you* in one of the embarrassing paper gowns that covers essentially nothing."

He arched an eyebrow. "Here I thought you were being compassionate and supportive, but really you were angling for a look at my ass?"

"Is there a law that a woman can't be nurturing and ogle at the same time?"

He laughed at that, and his smile made her feel as if she'd won the lottery. Their gazes held a fraction of an instant too long. If he asked again whether she wanted to hear the details of his scandalous bathtub daydreams, she'd say yes this time. But he did the sensible thing and held his hand out for her mug.

"I'll wash these out. You can go ahead and brush your teeth, then I'll take my turn."

He gave her plenty of time. She was already in bed with the covers pulled up to her chin when he disappeared into the bathroom. Listening to him gargle mouthwash, she giggled in the dark. She'd lived alone for years and was unaccustomed to sharing the mundane, yet somehow poignant, intimacy of these daily routines.

The bathroom door opened, and Garrett shut off the light. Her eyes needed a moment to readjust—she could hear him but not see him very well. The man had a fantastic voice, rich and addictive like caramel.

"I'm not going to wake you before I saddle up in the morning," he reminded her. "No reason for us both to be up at the crack of dawn. Dad bought me some pastries when he went to town this morning. They'll be out on the counter. There's also a bowl of fruit and plenty of milk and juice. Mom used her spare key to stock the fridge when she heard I was bringing a guest. If you want anything more substantial for breakfast or need company, give Mom a call at the house. Dad bought her a used golf cart a few years ago so she can zip between all the buildings on the property as long as there's no snow on the ground.

"On the other hand," he continued, "if you feel like taking advantage of the opportunity to sleep in, no one would blame you."

"Feels a bit antisocial," she said. "To come all this way to meet your family, then waste half the day in bed." Plus, Brandon still owed her that tour he'd promised. He said the spring-fed lake was particularly beautiful. And he wanted to show her the spot on this very ranch where, thirty-six years ago, he'd proposed to Caroline.

The mattress dipped as Garrett sat next to her. "I think your obstetrician would see it as 'resting,' not 'wasting.' And you're nearly seven months pregnant. Being a little antisocial is your prerogative, okay?"

"Yes, sir." She gave him a jaunty salute.

He sighed. "Why are you mocking me?"

"Force of habit. I grew up with two well-meaning

but domineering brothers, so irreverence tends to be my default mode whenever a man tells me something that's for my own good. Not that you were domineering. You're being considerate."

"I try. It hasn't been the easiest thing this week, but I do try. The considerate thing now is to leave you alone so you can sleep."

For a bare second, she thought he might kiss her good-night. Instead, he brushed his thumb over her bottom lip, tracing the sensitive outer edge and doubling back to curve across her top lip. Unable to help herself, she caught the pad of his thumb between her teeth, biting gently. He sucked in his breath, the gasp unnaturally loud in the stillness.

"Arden." That warm caramel voice spilled over her, making her toes curl beneath the sheets. "Even if I wanted to act on the attraction to us, I'm not sure it would be safe for you."

He had a point. In the unlikely event that her blood pressure didn't go back down and Dr. Mehta diagnosed her with preeclampsia, she needed to exercise caution for the duration of her pregnancy. The last thing she wanted to do was risk Peanut's safety.

She felt ashamed. "I'm sorry."

"Don't be." There was so much banked heat in his eyes, she imagined she could see them glowing.

When he headed for the doorway, she succumbed to a moment of weakness and called him back. "Garrett? I know we shouldn't…do anything stimulating. But do you really have to sleep on the couch? We've shared a bed before." She'd slept in his arms over six months ago and hadn't had that kind of closeness with anyone since. Once the baby came, she would have her hands full. It could be a *very* long time before she was serious enough about another man to spend the night with him.

The thought gave her a pang, as if imagining a hypothetical man in Garrett's presence was disloyal. What if...what if she'd already found the man she wanted? *Then you probably shouldn't have elected to cheat him out of the news that he was a father, especially not at the same time he was grappling with the most important woman in his life being a liar and adulteress.* With his scars and trust issues, she almost felt sorry for the next person to date him.

"You want me to stay?" he asked.

"I do." She held her breath.

"Then scoot over, and don't hog the covers."

"Can I put my icy cold feet on you?" she asked sweetly.

"Not unless you want to hear a grown man shriek like a little girl," he said as he slid beneath the sheets.

She rolled to the other side, fluffing her pillow and smiling at his nearness. Then she chuckled. "Figures. He does this every night—it's half the reason I never get decent sleep anymore." She reached for Garrett's hand and placed his palm over her abdomen. "Peanut seems to be gearing up for the 2028 Olympic gymnastics team."

"You called the baby *he*," Garrett noted. "So you're thinking men's gymnastics, then? Maybe we should have registered for an itty-bitty set of parallel bars."

"It was just a slip of the tongue, not true maternal instinct." The power of suggestion—she'd been visualizing their child as a boy ever since seeing all of Garrett's baby pictures. By the time they'd returned to the main house for dinner tonight, Caroline had pulled out even more albums for Arden to peruse. "We should register for equipment used in both women's and men's gymnastics. Think that site we were on has anything in a miniature vault?"

"They'd better. If they've neglected to stock cowboy hats for newborns *and* essential gym equipment, we may have to take our business elsewhere."

She laughed and, as though responding to the sound, the baby rolled beneath Garrett's hand. "Peanut seems happy," she said. In fact, she herself felt dangerously content.

Snuggled against Garrett now, it was difficult to remember that he was the same person who'd baldly announced to his family earlier today that there was "nothing romantic" between him and Arden. He'd admitted that he was trying extra-hard to be considerate, and he knew from her visit to Dr. Mehta that she shouldn't be exposed to extra stress or conflict. Garrett was humoring the pregnant lady. Just because he'd agreed to her request to stay with her tonight didn't mean anything had changed long-term, that he'd forgiven her.

Still, despite what her logical mind knew to be true, her last absent thought as beckoning oblivion enveloped her was *my family*.

Caroline Frost must have been standing at her back door, keys in hand, just waiting for Arden's call. Scarcely three minutes after Arden phoned to say she was awake and showered on Sunday morning, Caroline appeared on the porch.

Garrett's front porch wasn't nearly as elaborate as his parents' wraparound veranda, but it was wide enough to accommodate a white swing and two padded chairs. In the spring, it was probably a beautiful place to enjoy the breezy sunshine and watch birds and small animals flit across the pasture.

"Come on inside," Arden welcomed Caroline. "Although, I feel a little foolish issuing the invitation, me being a temporary guest and this house having belonged to your family for generations."

They walked into the living room, where Arden had set out a pot of decaf coffee and pastries on the table.

"I hope you won't think of yourself as a mere guest for long." Caroline settled onto the couch, her expression earnest. "I'll admit, when Garrett told me he was bringing you home this weekend, I had mixed feelings. Nothing personal, dear. I only questioned the timing. But now I'm delighted you're here. I saw the way he looked at you last night. You may be exactly what he needs."

Suddenly Arden wished she'd taken Garrett's guidance about sleeping in this morning. This was the most carefree she'd seen his mother since they arrived, and Arden was about to rob her of her optimistic happiness. "Mrs. Frost—"

The woman harrumphed an unsubtle reminder.

"Sorry. Caroline. I appreciate the compliment, but you know your son and I aren't dating."

"Maybe not at the moment," she said knowingly.

"Maybe not ever. I lied to him. About the baby."

Caroline looked startled. "How do you mean?"

"I never called to tell him he was going to be a father. I'd planned to be a single mom with him none the wiser. And, frankly, I'm not sure he'll ever forgive me. That's not to say he's nurturing a grudge or being unpleasant to me," she was quick to add. "He's been…wonderful, very conscientious about my health and not upsetting me unduly. But there's a barrier between us. I don't know that it will ever completely go away."

"I see." Caroline's hand trembled slightly as she poured two mugs of coffee. "My son's certainly been through a lot. I wish I could promise you that forgiveness will come, but I'm the last person who can say that. Did he tell you that we had…not quite an argument, but a difficult conversation before he left?"

"He told me. About you and Will."

Caroline covered her face with her hands. "What you must think of me!"

"If there's one thing I've learned, we all act rashly at one time or another," Arden said wryly.

"I wanted to explain the whole story to him, my frame of mind at the time—not that it excuses what I did. But he was too damn mad. When he left the ranch, I had no idea how long he'd be gone or what he'd say to Brandon when he returned. I love my husband, Arden. With my heart and soul! I hate myself for what I did to him…but how do I regret having Garrett? My other pregnancies— Oh, but this isn't an appropriate story for a young woman expecting her first child. I don't want to frighten you."

Arden appreciated her thoughtfulness, but Caroline Frost seemed as if she desperately needed a friendly ear. "I can probably take it. I grew up with the acute awareness that bad things happen. Often without rhyme or reason. One person could live a charmed life and the neighbors next door could lose their grandmother and their dog and have their house burn down all in the same week. I'll try not to let your misfortunes make me paranoid." *Try* being the operative word.

"You're sure?" Caroline licked her lips nervously. "Oh, if you weren't in a family way, I'd pour a healthy dollop of whiskey into both our coffees. Brandon loves this ranch almost as much as he loves me. He grew up here and planned to run it with his two brothers. But one was killed in Vietnam. The other overdosed."

Arden sometimes forgot that tragedy could be just as prevalent in other families as it had been in hers.

"When we got married, he talked all the time about having children. I think he hoped our kids could recreate the dream he lost when his brothers died. I wanted a big family, too," Caroline added with a sad smile. "We hadn't been married a whole year the first time I got pregnant. We were beside ourselves with joy. I lost the baby in the first trimester."

"I'm so sorry." Miscarriages in early pregnancy weren't uncommon, but Arden could see in Caroline's gray eyes—so like her son's—that the memory still haunted her.

"I was devastated, but the doctor assured me it wasn't a sign we'd done anything wrong or couldn't have children. After some time passed, we found out I was expecting again. This time, we didn't tell anyone. I wanted to safely pass that three-month mark first. We never made it that far."

Arden wanted to weep for her. It was easy to imagine the excited young bride and her groom with their dreams of children filling the brick house, playing hide-and-seek in the stables, gallivanting through the pastures, chasing after bunnies and chipmunks.

"Brandon and I never fought while we were dating,"

Caroline continued, "and we've rarely fought during our marriage. But that was a terrible time for us. Tension was so high. We didn't know—should we try again? Every time we came together as husband and wife, I was torn between half hoping we had conceived and praying we didn't. Then it happened. I was pregnant. I made it all the way to five months." She stopped, hiccupped, tried to catch her breath and stave off the gathering tears.

"You don't have to tell me the rest." Arden felt like hell for encouraging her in the first place. "Really. It's none of my—"

"No, it's okay," Caroline said bravely. "I should have talked this all out with someone a long time ago. You're doing me a favor. That last miscarriage was the worst. The doctors weren't even sure I could have a baby after that. Brandon was enraged, having lost his brothers and repeatedly losing the babies. I was despondent. We barely spoke, neither of us knowing what to say or how to make it better. The only time either of us laughed was when his friend Will joined us for dinner or to play cards. When the doctor told me it was okay to have relations again, Brandon wouldn't touch me.

"Looking back, I think it was fear. He was afraid to cause me more physical or emotional damage. At the time, it felt like rejection, like I was defective. A piece of livestock he'd sell off because of inherent flaws. We had a horrible argument one night, and he took off."

Arden was so caught up in the tale she forgot to breathe. Even though she'd seen firsthand that the Frosts had overcome their tribulations, it was easy to imagine how scared and alone the woman had felt so many years ago, wondering where her husband had disappeared to and if he would be all right.

"Turns out, he'd holed up in a friend's hunting cabin to think. That's one thing about Frost boys, sometimes they have to go out on their own before they can figure out how to be with the ones they love. This was before the days of cell phones, and I was inconsolable. Bad storms swept into the area the next day, and Will came to look after me. Tornadoes in the area knocked out the power. Will and I lit some candles and made up pallets in the basement, planning to spend the night down there. We talked about Brandon and I cried, afraid he didn't want me anymore. Afraid no man would want me because there was something wrong with me. I…" She broke off on a wail.

When she'd regained a measure of composure, she finished. "It just happened. I know that sounds awful, like I'm not taking any responsibility, but I know I betrayed the man I love." She sounded lost.

Arden handed her one of the napkins from the table, taking another to dab her own eyes.

"The storm was the impetus Brandon needed to come home. As soon as the roads were cleared, he raced back to check on me. Will begged me not to tell Brandon what we'd done. He said that with everything Bran and I had already suffered through, he could never forgive himself if *he* was the straw that broke our marriage. For years, he wouldn't even come to dinner unless he had a date with him—a buffer, I guess. After Brandon and I made up, it took time to coax him back into our bed. He's a man. He doesn't pay attention to details like gestational calendars, unless it's calving season, but the timing didn't line up."

"You knew he wasn't the father," Arden observed.

Caroline nodded. "After the delivery, my doctor did a procedure to keep me from having more kids. He'd formed a theory that Bran and I were...incompatible, medically speaking. We're so blessed to have Garrett. He's ours in every way that counts. I never would have told him otherwise if it weren't a matter of life or death." Her voice was a naked plea, an entreaty for forgiveness that wasn't Arden's to bestow.

Tears were streaming down both their faces, and Arden hugged her tightly. They sat like that for a while, two mothers both understanding the compulsion to do right for your child amid a minefield of possible wrong choices.

Caroline straightened. "I've wondered, at times, if Will had an inkling of the truth, but we didn't speak of it through my entire pregnancy. As an infant, Garrett once had to go to the E.R. because his fever was too high. I realized there may come a day when there was a medical necessity for Will to intervene. Maybe donating blood or answering questions about patient history, whatever. For the sake of my son, I had to talk to Will, to make sure we were on the same page in case there was ever a future crisis. I never imagined it would be the other way around, that *he* would be the one needing assistance. Garrett may be too angry to see it right now, to remember it, but Will Harlow is a good man."

"I don't think I can convince Garrett to help Will," Arden said apologetically. "That's a deeply personal decision. But I will seize any opportunity to persuade him to forgive you. For his sake and yours. The time we get to spend with our loved ones can be too brief."

If anything happened to Caroline without Garrett first absolving his mother, he would never find peace again.

"Thank you. I'm probably the last person in the world who should give another woman advice, but I'll do it, anyway. As you may discover, Frost men are not always easy to love. But loving them is worth any trials along the way."

Long after Caroline left, her words remained.

Arden could picture them hovering over her like cartoon thought bubbles. *Love Garrett?* That would be total folly.

Feeling suddenly claustrophobic in the house, she wrapped herself in a thick blanket and went out to the porch. Arden had thought herself in love once or twice in the past, but those men were dim memories now. She couldn't imagine a time when Garrett would be a "dim" anything. The larger-than-life cowboy had made more of an impression on her in one week than a past boyfriend had made in a year. The pregnancy muddied the issue. Her feelings for Garrett were tangled up in the love she had for their baby.

If they'd met and dated without this automatic bond between them, would she even be having this mental debate? Was she falling in love, or was she simply overcome with gratitude? Not only had he given her Peanut, but this weekend he'd also given her a sense of home and family she hadn't experienced in a long time.

Much as she adored her brothers, their family was undeniably fractured. She was increasingly frustrated by Justin's glib refusal to let people get close to him, and it felt as though Colin were growing more detached every day.

Motion caught her eye, and she lifted her head, focusing. In the distance, a black horse galloped past, its rider clad in a dark brown duster and a familiar cowboy hat. Even at this distance, her body quivered with yearning, making a mockery of her deliberations.

Whatever she felt for Garrett Frost, it was a hell of a lot more than gratitude.

Chapter 10

If Arden had thought she was discomfited on the trip to the Double F, with the ordeal of meeting Garrett's parents looming large in her mind, it was nothing compared to the drive back to Cielo Peak on Tuesday morning.

Garrett had returned from his donor consultation the day before more withdrawn than she'd ever seen him. He'd told his father he wasn't feeling well and asked Brandon to fetch Arden to the main house for dinner. At bedtime, he'd gone straight to the fold-out sofa and she hadn't bothered to issue another request that he join her. He obviously craved space, and she refused to be that needy.

What had Caroline said on Sunday? That Frost men had to work through things alone?

Men were fools. Colin was also a believer in solitude

over catharsis, but she couldn't see that it was working out for him. Arden would have lost her mind years ago without Natalie and, more recently, Layla. Even Caroline, who'd only just met her, had said her talk with Arden left her feeling more unburdened than she had in a long time.

"I had a long chat with your mom." Breaking the silence in the truck was far more jarring than she'd intended. Like a loud crash at midnight in a perfectly still house. Grimly determined, she plodded on. "It was very enlightening. I think if you heard what she had to say—"

"I'd what?" His head swiveled toward her, his tone lethal. "Stop caring that she betrayed her husband and her vows? Stop caring that I'm another man's bastard?"

"Well, no." She gulped, clinging to her resolve. "Arden, I don't want to talk about this."

"Maybe not, but you should, anyway. You can't just let it eat at you."

"Actually, I *can*. I don't answer to you."

Perhaps his scornful tone would have deterred another woman, but she'd had a lifetime of practice with stubborn males. She continued as if he hadn't spoken. "You know she messed up. What you don't know are the extenuating circumstances, what she was going through at the time."

"Yeah, you're an expert at justifying deception and questionable decisions. No surprise you're siding with her."

Anger boiled up in her. She'd been sincerely trying to help, and he'd thrown it back in her face, not even bothering to see the big picture. "Do you even know how freaking lucky you are to have a mother who loves you? Who's knocking herself out to win your forgiveness? Maybe I am siding with her—I'm *glad* she had the affair. Otherwise, you wouldn't be here. And I care about you, you jackass."

That stunned him into silence. The admission had come as a bit of a surprise to her, too.

After a moment, he snickered. "'I care about you, jackass'? You steal that from a greeting card?"

She tapped her head against the window. "I guess it's safe to conclude our child is gonna have something of a temper."

"A fair bet." A few minutes later, he added, "I shouldn't have taken your head off. The donor consultation yesterday left me in a foul mood. That's not your fault, and neither is what my mother did."

He didn't address the other part—when he'd accused her of deception and bad decisions. No matter how well they might get along at times, she was fooling herself if she allowed herself to believe for a second that what she'd done was behind them.

"I have to figure out what I'm going to tell my father if I check into the hospital for days on end. I *hate* having to lie to him. That's the part I can't forgive, you know. If she'd made an isolated mistake thirty-odd years ago, I'd like to think I'm a big enough person to let it go. But this isn't an obsolete aberration, it's ongoing. It's my life. We're lying to him every damn day. You think I'm a jerk because I haven't forgiven her yet? Well, I'm having trouble forgiving myself, too."

She squeezed his hand. "Garrett, you haven't done anything wrong."

"Really?" He flashed his teeth in a humorless smile. "Because it sure doesn't feel like I'm doing anything right. What would Dr. Mehta say about my arguing with you when we're supposed to be decreasing your blood pressure?"

"I promise not to rat you out," she said solemnly.

"You'll call me after the appointment Thursday, won't you?" Garrett asked. "Put me out of my misery? Otherwise, I'll worry. Arden, I...care about you, too."

She wished he sounded happier about it, but, for now, she'd take what she could get.

Arden almost threw her arms around Dr. Mehta in an enthusiastic hug. Was that outside the bounds of an acceptable doctor-patient relationship? "So the baby and I are fine?"

Being a medical professional, he was hesitant to give a clear yes or no. They probably had to attend lawsuit avoidance seminars that trained them how to be so evasive. "Your blood pressure's still elevated above what I would like," he said, "but it's gone down since last week. We'll keep monitoring, but given the significant improvement, this probably isn't a serious condition. Get plenty of sleep and hydration, and watch your salt intake. Don't overexert yourself, and try to minimize stress."

They talked about her being scheduled to work a bar mitzvah Saturday afternoon, and he cleared her to proceed as scheduled, as long as she tried to take it easy for the first half of the day. Garrett's prediction that all she needed was a restorative weekend at the ranch may have been right on the money.

Once she reached her car in the parking lot, she scrolled through her contact list to find Garrett's name, grinning in anticipation of sharing the news.

"Hello?" He yelled the salutation over the considerable background noise of some kind of motor. "Arden, is that you?"

She pulled the phone away from her ear, raising her voice so he could hear her. "Yep. Calling with important news. Guess whose blood pressure is down? This girl's!"

Even with the background motor noise, she clearly heard his sigh of relief. "We definitely have to celebrate when I come to town next week."

They'd decided that it made sense for Layla to remain her official labor coach since she lived locally and due dates were difficult to pinpoint. However, Garrett wanted to be part of the process and was planning to visit Cielo Peak to attend a couple of the birth classes. Arden couldn't believe how badly she was looking forward to seeing him. How was it possible to miss him so much after only a couple of days?

Even sleeping alone was more difficult after the two nights she'd spent cradled in his arms. He'd rubbed her back when she couldn't sleep, spoke to her in a low, drowsy murmur that seemed to even soothe the baby, taming some of Peanut's wilder, 3:00 a.m. somersaults. Would it be a mistake to tell Garrett he could stay with her instead of the Connors? Hugh and Darcy had generously offered their guest room on an as-needed basis for the duration of Arden's pregnancy.

"Thanks for taking the time to let me know," he told her.

"Hey, we're in this together." And not just the pregnancy. On Friday, she sent him several non-baby-related texts after a hilariously chaotic photo session with a family of seven. Then around eleven on Sunday night,

Garrett texted her to find out if she was awake because he couldn't sleep. Upon discovering she was up, too, he called.

Arden lit a few candles in her otherwise dark bedroom and curled up in bed with some caramel-flavored hot chocolate and the phone.

"Is it too late to take you up on the offer to listen if I needed to talk about that kidney thing?" he asked.

Only a guy would call the generous act of giving part of yourself to save another human being's life *that kidney thing.* "The offer stands," she assured him.

"I've scheduled my check-in date for testing the week of Halloween. It's going to require time away from the ranch. Would I be a terrible person if I let Dad believe I was coming to see you?"

Understanding how much the dishonesty bothered him, she knew it had probably cost him something to ask. "I'm happy to be your alibi if you need one."

"Thanks. There's only so much lying I'm willing to do, though. I've made a decision, and I need a second opinion. If, after they finish the blood work and paperwork and mental evaluations, they conclude I'm not a good candidate, then I'll keep Mom's secret. Why hurt Dad with the truth? But if I go through with this organ donation, she's got to tell him. I could be looking at up to six weeks of not being able to do my usual activities around the ranch, and Dad's gonna need a reason. Kidney and cornea transplants are pretty commonplace, there's minimal risk to me."

For her own peace of mind, she'd needed to hear him reiterate that. If anything were to happen to *Garrett*...

"The possibilities of rejection and dangerous infection are on Will's end, but still, this is a major procedure. I can't lie to my father about it."

"I understand that. I imagine Caroline will, too. She knows more than anyone the kind of man she raised."

"It doesn't sound like extortion? You can have my kidney, but only if you bow to my wishes?"

"No. Just…try to be gentle with her. No one can go back in the past and undo their actions."

There was a long pause, and she squirmed inwardly, trying to picture his expression. Was he wistful? Bitter?

"If you *could* go back," he said, "would you have done things differently? Found me, told me about the baby?"

She bit the inside of her cheek. The easy answer was yes. Now that she knew what kind of man he was—and how lucky her child would be to have him for a father—of course she'd say yes. But she hadn't known then. "I can't change what happened, Garrett. I can only hope you forgive me."

He was silent, not the response she'd hoped for deep down, but an honest one.

Changing the subject, he asked if Peanut had settled for the night or was awake and active. "Would it be weird to hold the phone to your stomach and let me say good-night?"

"Yes. I'd feel like a fool."

He talked her into doing it, anyway, and she was smiling when they disconnected their call, mentally counting down the days until she'd see him again.

Arden's first birth class was on a Wednesday evening, and she was touched that Garrett was making the trip even though he'd have to immediately turn around and go back. He and his father were driving to another ranch the next day to look at their herd and discuss trading some cattle. Garrett called her from the road to say he was running a few minutes behind and would meet her at the hospital.

True to his word, he pulled into the parking garage a few car lengths behind her. Her pulse stuttered in anticipation, and she smacked her palm to her forehead. She hadn't even seen him yet—was she really so far gone that she was reacting to the front bumper of his truck?

He came to her side while she was pulling out a duffel bag of supplies and a large pillow from home.

"How long's this session?" he teased, taking the duffel bag from her. "You look like you're planning to spend the night here."

"There are floor exercises. It said in the brochure to bring a blanket and pillow." They fell into step with each other and headed for the maternity wing. "Look, Garrett, I really appreciate your coming with me. I just hope you don't find these classes...silly. They're supposed to cover multiple types of birthing methods and new-age relaxation techniques. Some of it might get pretty touchy-feely."

He shot her a wicked grin. "Some of my favorite pastimes are of the touchy-feely variety."

She laughed, appreciating his easy, cheerful manner. He seemed far more himself now than when he'd brought her home last week. "Have you had a chance to talk to Caroline yet about your proposed compromise?" Maybe he was feeling lighter because they'd reached an agreement.

"Nope. Dad and I have actually been really busy, and since I won't have test results until November, there's not much to say to her on the subject." He reached forward to open the door for her.

"Things on the ranch must be going well. You seem pretty chipper," she observed.

His gaze met hers. "Maybe my good mood is just because I get to spend the evening with you."

And ten other couples, all of whom would be lying on the industrial-carpeted classroom floor, practicing pelvic positions and breathing. She grinned. If that was enough to put a spring in his step, then maybe she wasn't the only one falling hard.

The classroom was plastered with informational posters and smelled faintly of bleach. About half the pairs were already present and the instructor encouraged students to mingle and get to know one another. "No one can fully comprehend what new parents are going through quite like other new parents," she reminded them. "Make friends, compare notes."

Garrett and Arden were the only couple in this particular session who weren't husband and wife. Arden explained that Garrett was the baby's father and would be present for some of the weekly classes, but that her friend and labor coach Layla would attend the others. As they began the first set of exercises, Arden realized that it was going to be a little awkward with her friend here.

They did a take on "passive massage," where the men were supposed to lay their hands on their partners and visualize healing, supportive energy leaving their bodies and filling the mother's. Accompanied by the somewhat cliché recording of soft jazz interspersed with the sound of rolling waves and seagull cries, it could have been comical. But Garrett's touch made it an altogether different experience. She'd begun to crave his nearness the way some pregnant women ravenously craved peanut butter.

The exercise where she was supposed to mentally link with her cervix, however, was far less sensual. Finally, it was time to watch the evening's birth video. There would be one at every class, including footage of a water birth.

"Be warned, this may be pretty graphic," she whispered to Garrett as the instructor dimmed the lights.

"Not to compare you to livestock, but I have witnessed plenty of births. I know what to expect."

Yet ten minutes later, he was ashen. "It's different with cows," he mumbled when the class was dismissed. "I've never really thought about that happening to *you* before."

He seemed to be taking this hard—but this was nothing compared to what she imagined Layla's reaction would be to the explicit videos. *I'd better bring smelling salts with me next week.* She poked him in the shoulder. "Aren't I the one who's supposed to be a basket case?" she asked.

He looked chagrined. "Guess I wasn't really student of the week. Give me another chance?"

As many as it takes. "Of course. Besides, you did way better than that guy in the back who hyperventilated. Thanks again for coming with me. I owe you."

"Funny you should say that. I was actually planning to ask you a favor. Darcy's been requesting, rather insistently, that we consider a double date with them Sunday night."

Arden lost her footing for a second and grabbed his arm to steady herself. She stopped on the sidewalk, turning to face him. "Now, when you say *date*..." There were so many butterflies in her stomach that there was hardly room left for the baby.

"I know we're coming at this a little backward, but what if we actually tried dating? It seems like the sensible thing to do for our kid, and we do like each other." His grin was lopsided as he tucked a strand of hair behind her ear. "That's how we found ourselves in this position, right?"

She'd admitted to herself that she was developing romantic feelings for him. Were those feelings mutual?

Maybe not yet. He'd said he *liked* her and that dating would be *sensible,* but that was a foundation, wasn't it? Could they try building a relationship and see where it led?

And if it doesn't work out? They would be linked together for their child's entire life. The stakes were considerably higher than when her brother had broken up with a waitress and made it temporarily uncomfortable to have lunch at his favorite barbecue house.

"C'mon, sweetheart," Garrett coaxed. "Is the idea of going out with me that repellent?"

Not repellent. Beguiling.

She nibbled at the inside of her lip. Was this wise? She tried to imagine what guidance she'd give to Layla, or Justin or, years from now, her own child. Strategic retreat, or embrace the possibilities?

"All right, you're on," she decided. "It's a date."

Chapter 11

"I think it's so romantic that you're dating now!" Layla winced when a string of hot glue adhered to her finger. "Of course, most women don't wait until they're seven months pregnant to enter a relationship with the baby's father, but you're a unique individual."

"Thanks, I think." Arden was watching her friend in morbid fascination. So far, Layla had burned herself twice and cut herself with a pair of extra-sharp craft fingers. "It might be premature to say we're *dating* since our first date isn't until tomorrow night."

"But you've talked every night this week."

True. She'd already been mentally filing funny observations from her morning with Layla to entertain him with during their conversation tonight. "Why again are you the one who has to make these—what do you call 'em?"

"*Calavera* masks. For the multicultural performance the drama students are doing. I can't tell you how thrilled I would be if the theater teacher got transferred to another district," she huffed. "Just because she had some minor parts in a couple of movies out in California, the principal and PTA indulge her every whim. Don't get me wrong, I'm all for the performance, but everyone else ends up rushing to do the work whenever she has one of these last-minute 'brainstorms.'"

Arden laughed at her friend's sequined air-quotes. Sparkly beads and bits of feathers clung to Layla's glue-scarred hands.

The two women sat at Layla's kitchen table, and a dozen skull masks covering the painted wood surface. Of the four that were already adorned, Arden had finished three of them.

"You really saved my butt, agreeing to do this," Layla said. "I asked two of my honors students, Melissa and Phillip, to help. They've been dating since freshman year. They're so inseparable, they have one of those unified monikers—you know, where people mash their names together? Philissa."

Arden carefully brushed glitter onto the swirling pattern she'd created with glue. "So where are they?"

"Officially, Melissa remembered an SAT prep class she had to attend this morning and he woke up with a fever. Unofficially? I overheard some arguing in the hall at school. She accused him of hitting on a JV cheerleader. Note to self, don't rely on hormonal teenage couples." Layla stopped abruptly. "Hey! If you and Garrett make it work, your name will be Garden."

"*This* is the thanks I get for spending my Saturday making arts-and-crafts skulls?" Arden asked dryly.

"What you have against gardens? Seems fitting to me." Layla chortled. "You guys are obviously fertile."

"You know what I just remembered? *I'm* supposed to be at that SAT prep class, too."

"If you stay," Layla declared, "you get to taste-test the batch of Mexican wedding cookies I'm baking for after the performance."

"Done." Arden knew from experience that her friend's cookies were small, sugar-coated bites of heaven.

"Good, because there's something else we have to—damn it."

Laughing, Arden got out of her chair and reached for the hot glue gun. "Give that to me before we have to call 9-1-1."

"I have many impressive skills," Layla grumbled. "This just doesn't happen to be one of them. Okay, so about this other thing I wanted to discuss? Now that you two crazy kids have registered, I want to throw you a baby shower!"

"You do?" Arden was touched.

"Duh. That's what friends do for each other. That and make Day of the Dead masks, even though Day of the Dead isn't technically until November first. It sounds like Garrett enjoys being involved in planning for the baby, so I thought he'd like to come. But I don't think it should be specifically a couples' shower, since that would count me out. And both your brothers."

"You want my brothers to attend?" Arden asked skeptically. Colin would be visibly uncomfortable, a pall on the festivities, whereas Justin would be like a kid in a candy store, unabashedly flirting with any female guests. Too bad she couldn't invite his ex-girlfriend Elisabeth. She and Arden had been close until the breakup.

"Your brothers are your family. I know how critical family is to you."

That was indisputable. "Okay, so they go on the invite list. Who else are we thinking? Vivian Pike, for sure." Viv managed the personalized print store next door to Arden's studio. She specialized in customized stationery and cute business cards. "And Hugh and Darcy Connor." Not only had they been the reason Arden and Garrett met in the first place, but it would also be nice for Garrett to have some friends there.

Thinking of Garrett made her question the timing. In late October, he would be in the hospital. If he decided to through with the donation, she had no idea what the potential timetable for the transplant was. If they were going to have this shower, sooner might be better than later.

"Layla, I know it doesn't give people much notice, but if we keep it on the casual side, is this the type of thing that could be put together in a couple of weeks?"

"Are you kidding?" Her friend swept a hand majestically over the table. "Last-minute rush jobs are my specialty. As long as I don't have to hot-glue anything for your party, we're golden."

Garrett couldn't remember the last time he'd been nervous picking a woman up for a date. After all the time he'd spent with Arden, it was insane to feel nervous now. *No more insane than taking the mother of your child on a first date.* Maybe "sane" wasn't really their thing.

He parked his truck in her driveway, thinking that

his dad was partly to blame for his anxious tension. Before Garrett had left the Double F, his father had resumed hounding him about marrying Arden, urging Garrett to hurry.

"I don't get why you're dragging your feet," Brandon had scolded. "She's a great gal, and you know it. Do you want your kid to be illegitimate?"

Why not? Garrett had thought sourly. *I was.*

Garrett had always assumed he'd get married someday. He just wanted to find the right person, the way his parents had. It was sobering to think that, as many years as they'd been together, as much as they loved each other, Caroline had been unfaithful. How could a relationship between two people with such a solid foundation go so wrong? He was glad he and Arden were going to give a relationship a try, but that didn't mean he was naive. He knew there were bound to be mistakes and regrets lying in wait for them.

Which was hardly the right attitude to begin their date.

He pasted a polite smile on his face that became a real one as soon as she opened the door. God, she was lovelier every time he saw her. He suddenly wanted to kick himself for not bringing flowers.

Her gaze swept from his head to his feet, and she beamed at him. "Wow. You clean up well. Not that you aren't equally attractive in a coat and cowboy hat, but... wow. Am I underdressed?"

"No. You're perfect. And my clothes aren't *that* dressy." Okay, he'd swapped his usual jeans for black slacks and got a haircut yesterday, but it wasn't like he'd shown up in a tie.

She wore an ankle-length maternity dress in deep

green. The color made her eyes damn near mesmerizing.

"You look gorgeous," he told her as he stepped inside. The words weren't very suave or creative, but there
was enough ragged appreciation in his voice that she
couldn't doubt his sincerity.

"Well, I'm glad we were both in the same ballpark.
When I told you to surprise me with our destination,
I didn't realize I was making my wardrobe choice so
difficult."

"You could have called to ask for hints, like whether
we were going to be outside or whether the venue was
formal."

"That felt like cheating somehow." She tilted her
head. "So where *are* we going?"

"You'll see. Hugh and Darcy are meeting us there."
Part of him worried that adding another couple made
the evening less romantic, as if he wasn't trying hard
enough, but he wanted Arden to get to know the Connors better. He liked the idea that they could look in
on her if Garrett were unable to come to town for long
stretches.

"Don't let me forget to tell them about our shower!
Official invitations will go out later."

He frowned. "Shower?"

"Ah, I jumped ahead—sorry. Guess I temporarily
forgot to invite you to the baby shower. It's on my list
of things to talk about tonight."

He laughed. "You have a list?"

"Um…" She stared at the floor. "I'd like to say that
was a figure of speech, but if someone were to check
the memo section on my phone, they might find actual
bullet points. You don't understand what pregnancy

brain is like! I had to fill out a form the other day, and I blanked on my own address. So, yeah, I may have jotted down a few reminders of things that happened this week I thought you'd get a kick out of. It made me feel calmer, like I had some backup ammo in case we hit any awkward silences. Does this make me sound like a lunatic who doesn't know how to be spontaneous?"

"It makes you sound well-prepared and thoughtful." Qualities that were going to make her a great mom. Scratch that—qualities that made her a great person. They'd been so fixated on the pregnancy lately, their excitement for the baby, that he had to remind himself to stop and just enjoy *her*. Starting with tonight.

He stepped behind her to help her into her coat and resisted the urge to pull her body back against his. Her soft curves were tempting, but this was their first date and he wanted to be on time for meeting the Connors. "Ready to have a wonderful time?"

Arden was so busy absorbing her surroundings that she didn't hear the hostess the first time she offered to take their coats. "Oh! Yes, please." She shrugged out of the red wool jacket.

She and Garrett had arrived first. They were spending their evening at a dinner theater called the Twirling Mustache Tavern. Arden had been here once, years ago, to see a musical with Natalie. But the Tavern was actually known for its uproariously over-the-top melodramas. Audience participation was strongly encouraged.

Theatergoers were expected to cheer loudly for the hero, yell catchphrases along with the actors and greet any romantic moments with a synchronized "aww." But according to the playbill she'd been handed, the villains got the lion's share of the attention. Patrons could not only boo and hiss when a mustache-twirling bad guy tied a heroine to the train tracks or evicted a little old lady from her farm, but each table was also given a huge bucket of popcorn they were supposed to throw at the stage during evil deeds. House rules asked that customers *only* throw the popcorn, and not the actual bucket. It all sounded like a blast and, despite her emergency list of topics in case of awkward silence, she doubted silence of any kind would be a problem.

They explained to the hostess that friends would be joining them shortly and were escorted to a table for four very close to the stage.

"I don't know how well you got to know them when they hired you for the wedding, but I think you'll really like Hugh and Darcy. Although, word of warning?" Garrett said. "Darcy is a dedicated—one might even say, zealous—bird-watcher. If the subject happens to come up, we may be hearing about it for a while. Like, until November."

Arden chuckled. "So no mentioning birds, even in passing."

"To be extra safe, we probably shouldn't order the duck or chicken. But other than that one tiny quirk, the Connors are great."

"It would be pretty hypocritical of us to judge anyone for being quirky." She gave him a rueful smile. "We're not exactly the poster children for normal. How many men take a woman home to meet his parents before he's even been on a date with her?"

He brandished a piece of popcorn at her. "Are you saying I'm abnormal?"

"Psst!" Hugh Connor stopped at their table, his voice

a faux whisper. "I know you said you were out of practice at this, buddy, but generally speaking, it's not chivalrous to throw things at your date."

Behind him, Darcy was nodding in agreement. "I suppose you could make a possible exception for rose petals, but even then she might find it odd." She craned her head around her husband and waggled her fingers in hello. "A pleasure to see you again, Arden."

It turned out that Darcy and Hugh were regulars at the Tavern, and they recommended some of their favorite entrees. The food was delicious, but Garrett's smiles throughout the dinner were far more tantalizing than anything on the menu. Arden had enjoyed her time at the Double F with Garrett and his family, but there was no denying that being around his parents had caused him stress. Here in the presence of an old friend, no secrets to be kept or emotional baggage to overcome, Garrett was relaxed and witty.

What am I going to do? The more she saw of Garrett, the more she discovered to love about him. Her heart went out to the taciturn cowboy who was struggling with his sense of loyalty to each parent. But her heart absolutely melted for the charming date who knew all the right things to say and never failed to signal the waitress if Arden's glass of water was even close to getting empty. He was gallant and funny and caring. She couldn't think of any qualities she might want in a man that Garrett Frost didn't have in abundance.

Except maybe forgiveness? Against her will, she recalled how icy he'd been when Arden had tried to broker peace between him and his mother. While he seemed to be making gradual progress, it was slow. How long would it take his anger to fully dissipate? And what about Arden herself? He'd asked the other night if she'd do things differently, and he hadn't seemed pleased with her answer.

But those were needless worries. For now, they were having a fantastic evening together, and there was no reason to dwell on negative issues he might be well on his way to resolving.

During a particularly "dastardly" scene in the play, Garrett heckled the villain louder than anyone else in the audience, mercilessly pelting him with pieces of popcorn since he was at such close range. Without ever breaking in dialogue, the actor stepped down from the stage and upended the bucket of popcorn on Garrett's head. Arden and Darcy both burst into laughter, and Hugh choked on his beer.

Garrett laughed as hard as any of them, and the amusement in his silvery eyes gave her hope. He didn't look like a man consumed with anger.

Once the play ended, Darcy asked if they wanted to join her and Hugh at a coffeehouse that was open late and featured independent musicians. Arden thanked her for the invitation but admitted she was tired, then told the Connors she looked forward to seeing them at the baby shower.

The ride home nearly lulled her to sleep, but when Garrett walked her to her door, she was instantly, eagerly, awake. Her heart thundered. Surely he'd kiss her good-night? They'd kissed each other even when they *weren't* dating.

"Did you, um, want to come in for a drink?" she asked breathlessly.

He shook his head. "No drink necessary, but the gentlemanly thing would be to see you safely inside."

The wolfish grin he gave her beneath the front porch light made her think *gentlemanly* wasn't what he had in mind.

Once they made it to the foyer, he tugged her into his arms, his lips greedily claiming hers as if he'd been waiting to do this all night. She certainly had. Exquisite sensation blossomed inside her, hot and liquid. He speared his tongue into her mouth, making her lightheaded with pleasure. When he pulled back, she almost whimpered in protest.

"I promised myself I would kiss you good-night and leave," he confided.

"Already?"

"If we keep this up, sweetheart…" With a groan of surrender, he took her mouth again. Her jacket hit the floor, and his hand slid down from the curve of her shoulder to cup her breast. She sucked his lower lip in fervent approval.

And the baby picked that moment to kick—although it felt more like a cannon blast than a foot motion.

Arden could feel her cheeks reddening as she stepped back. *Way to kill the mood, Junior.*

Garrett's eyes glowed with humor. "Is that kind of like the kid walking into the room and catching his parents making out?"

"Pretty talented, considering ours can't even walk." She managed to laugh in spite of her frustrated libido.

He palmed her cheek. "I should go."

"You don't *have* to. We spent the night together at the ranch," she reminded him.

"Not after kissing like that, we didn't. I stay, you might not get much sleep."

Sounds good to me. She knew her need for him was

clear on her face—not to mention pulsing through other parts of her body.

He swore under his breath. "I'm not made of steel. We agreed to date, and I want to do this right. You pointed out the steps we've skipped, how we've done everything out of order up until now, and I think it's too important to be rushed. I want to send you roses tomorrow to thank you for a great time, start planning where I can take you next, call you during the week to let you know I'm thinking about you. I want to court you. You deserve that."

She let out a dreamy sigh. "That is the most romantic rejection I have ever heard in my life."

True to his word, Garrett did call her all during the next week—often right around bedtime. It quickly became her favorite part of the day. Hearing from him always gave her that little rush of exhilaration, but it was different at night, more intimate, less hurried. She curled up in the dark, closed her eyes and lost herself in his voice, pretending he was there with her.

He wasn't able to come to Cielo Peak the following weekend because he was managing the ranch while his parents were in Denver. Caroline was shopping in the city while Brandon attended a conference on winter grazing. Who knew there were such things? Arden had always pictured ranchers giving each other sage advice over fence lines, not holed up in the conference room of a Denver hotel, reviewing PowerPoint presentations about sod, rye and clover.

"But next weekend, when I come to town for the shower, I'll make it up to you by staying several nights," Garrett promised.

The Friday night before the shower, he called to tell her he couldn't wait to see her the next day. "I miss you."

"Want to prove it? When you stay in town this weekend, stay with me," she pleaded. "I don't want to be alone after the shower. I'll be all weepy over cute little outfits, and there will be nursery equipment I'll be impatient to assemble. I know you don't want me attempting to build furniture on my own."

He chuckled. "That's blackmail."

"Mmm, actually I think it's coercion," she said unrepentantly. Then, more seriously, she asked, "Will you at least think about it? Spending the night here could be your shower present to me."

"What makes you think I don't already have a present?"

"Really?" She spent a few minutes trying to wheedle clues out of him while he taunted her in classic juvenile I-know-something-you-don't-know fashion.

"So tell me again who's on the guest list for this shower?" he asked. "It feels surreal that I'll be celebrating the arrival of our baby with some people I've never even met."

"But you'll know the Connors and Layla, plus my brothers will be there." She got momentarily sidetracked. "I *wanted* to invite Elisabeth Donnelly. She's Justin's ex-girlfriend. They were great together, but she was the godmother for her college roommate's daughter. When her former roommate passed away, Elisabeth got custody of the little girl. The situation was too intense for my brother. I adore Justin, but he needs to grow up. If he had any sense at all, he'd get her back. I asked him if I could invite Elisabeth but he refused. I should have just asked her to come and not told him."

"You would've blindsided him? In the middle of our shower?"

"For his own good. You don't understand. He makes jokes all the time, but his happiness is superficial. Deep down, in his own way, I think he's nearly as miserable as Colin. He could benefit from someone scheming on his behalf."

"But not telling him she was coming would be the same as lying to him." Garrett's tone had taken on an edge. "You can't deceive someone just because you think you know what's best!"

She inhaled sharply, stung by his anger.

"If we're going to be in a relationship, Arden, I have to know you aren't going to rationalize away my right to the truth whenever it suits you."

"And *I* have to know that you can get past this!" She could only apologize so many times. "You had every right to be upset that I kept the pregnancy a secret, but I can't change that. And we weren't even discussing us, we were talking about my brother. I know my family a lot better than you do."

"Oh, really? Because you keep trying to pin Colin down and make him stay put. You don't seem as interested in what he needs as you do in keeping him close because it's what you need."

The implication that she was selfish sent her reeling. She adored her brothers and wanted the very best for them. Especially Colin! How many eighteen-year-old boys put their lives on hold to raise an annoying kid sister?

"You don't understand what it's like to have brothers or sisters," she shot back. "And you sure as hell don't seem to understand *me*."

With a muttered "Guess not," he told her he'd see her at the shower and ended the call.

"Oh, how I wish the punch was spiked," Arden lamented.

"If it was," Layla reminded her, "you couldn't have any."

"Maybe we could use it to sedate Garrett. Assuming he's even coming."

Layla paused in the middle of removing a plastic baby bottle from its packaging. "He'll be here. You guys had a fight—it happens. You're pregnant, with a hormonal probability of turning cranky, and it was late at night. He could've been tired and overreacted. Honestly, it was one argument. That's nothing compared to the kinds of things the two of you have endured. Together and separately."

"Lord, I hope you're right." Arden had lain awake for hours last night, rotating between crying jags, righteous fury and the almost visceral need to call him back.

"Of course I'm right! Now help me open the rest of these bottles."

"Why are there so many?" Arden asked. "Don't tell me these are what the guests will be drinking out of."

"Ha! No, these are for baby bottle bowling. Because yours truly is a genius, I planned all games where the equipment needed is actually extra baby supplies for you guys. Once I've got these all opened, where can I set up my lanes?"

They'd discussed having the shower at Layla's house, since she was the hostess and didn't want to create any extra work or cleaning for the mommy-to-be. But they'd decided it was silly to have everyone bring presents to her house when Arden and Garrett would simply have to load them back up for transport home. So Layla had come over bright and early to help Arden tidy up— and to listen to her vent about last night's catastrophic phone call.

"It started off so well," Arden said in disbelief. "He was as happy to be talking with me as I was with him. How did we make such a mess of it?"

"Sometimes phone conversations are more difficult than face-to-face. Long distance is hard, but you guys will get the hang of it."

How? After the baby was born, she'd be exhausted from middle-of-the-night feedings and barely be able to stay awake for their nocturnal chats—and that was assuming that a crying infant didn't make it impossible to hear. She'd adored her nephew, Danny, but when he'd been an infant, some of his ear-splitting crying spells had gone on for thirty minutes straight. Even if she and Garrett eventually mastered long-distance dating... to what end? What was their ultimate goal here? That she'd live in Cielo Peak, he'd work the ranch all week and they'd only be a family on weekends? Her memories of her own parents were faded with time, but she remembered two people very much in love.

Family was the most important thing in the world. Didn't her child deserve more than parents who were in a part-time relationship?

"Hey!" Layla snapped her fingers. "I know that look. Guests will be here within the hour. This is not a good time to fall apart. Besides, you know that if Justin and Colin get here and find you red-eyed over Garrett, they'll use it as an excuse to pick a fight with him."

"Good point." Telling herself that Layla had gone to a

lot of trouble to make today special, Arden got busy slicing up cucumbers for the cucumber-and-cream-cheese appetizers. The *whack whack whack* of the knife against the cutting board was cathartic, and by the time the doorbell rang, she no longer wanted to cry. Much.

She found Garrett at her front door, holding an armful of gold bags—her favorite chocolate and caramel medallions.

"I bought out three different stores," he told her. "Can you forgive me? I know you love your brothers, and you were only speaking hypothetically."

"Only if you'll forgive me, too. I should've been more tolerant of your point of view." She threw her arms around him, although he was holding too much candy to return the hug. "I'm so glad you're here. I was afraid you'd change your mind."

"And miss today? This is our first real family event. Wild horses couldn't have kept me away. Now, would you like to relieve me of some of this chocolate? Because I still have to unload all the real gifts from the truck."

As he brought in prettily wrapped pastel packages and gift bags, Layla mouthed a gloating *told you so* in Arden's direction. Arden merely laughed. She'd never been so elated to be wrong.

Shortly thereafter, Justin arrived, asking if there was anything he could do to help. He made jokes with Layla and Arden and was even passably friendly to Garrett. But when he and Arden were alone in the kitchen, his good-humored mask fell away, revealing sorrow.

"Don't shoot the messenger," he said. "But I bring tidings from our brother."

"He isn't coming?" She was as unsurprised as she was disappointed.

"I tried for over an hour to talk him into it, telling him it's what our parents would have wanted—for him to be here since they can't—but nothing worked."

"Thanks for making the effort. Maybe…maybe it is better for him not to be here." She didn't want to flaunt her burgeoning new happiness in front of Colin, and the baby shower she had once thrown for him and Natalie would probably have been etched in his mind all day. Replaying Garrett's words from the night before, she tried to focus on what her brother needed for his mental well-being. Maybe some men were like wounded animals, needing to skulk off on their own before they could heal. She resolved to stop smothering him with her worry.

The Connors' arrival was a welcome distraction. As it turned out, Darcy was nearly as besotted with babies as she was with birds. She cooed over the decorations, the planned games, the adorable gift tags on the presents that were piling up in front of the fireplace. And she kept reminding Arden and Garrett that after the baby was born, they had a ready and waiting babysitter.

"And that is officially the last time I say the *B*-word," Darcy vowed as she handed a diaper pin over to Layla. One of the ongoing shower games was that everyone fastened a diaper pin to their clothes, and if they were heard saying the word *baby,* another guest could claim the pin. Whoever had collected the most by the end of the party won a mystery door prize.

The final guests showed up, including Vivian Pike and Nurse Sonja from the hospital. As with all parties since the beginning of time, everyone ended up gathered around the snack table.

Justin grinned at the nurse he'd briefly dated. "Good to know that if this shindig gets too wild, we have a medical professional on the premises in case of emergency."

When Sonja asked Arden if she was sticking to her guns about not learning the gender ahead of time, Darcy followed up by saying, "Are you making lists of potential girls' names *and* potential boys' names?"

"I can help with that," Justin volunteered. "The name Justin, for example, is majestic and traditional. Teachers won't misspell it, kids won't pick on it. Also good are Justine and Justina for girls."

Garrett made a show of leaning toward Arden and whispering much too loudly, "Remind me why we invited him."

"Because we feel sorry for him." She smirked. "He's alienated all the women in a hundred-mile radius and thus has no social life."

"That is patently untrue," Justin argued. He turned to Vivian, who fell into the rare category of both being single and having never dated him. "For instance, have I alienated you yet? Justin Cade, nice to meet you."

They followed bottle bowling with an entertainingly ridiculous scavenger hunt and a baby-changing relay race where team members had to strip one outfit off of a baby doll and get a completely different one all snapped into place as quickly as possible.

"And Arden gets to keep all these clothes," Layla added. "I went with gender-neutral colors like yellow, which is just as easily masculine as feminine."

"The hell it is," Garrett whispered for Arden's ears

only. He obviously didn't think buttercup-yellow would be suitable attire for a son.

From across the room, Justin gave them a thumbs-up, as if he knew what Garrett had said and agreed whole-heartedly. It was the first sign of real bonding Arden had witnessed between the men, and it was heartening to think they might not kill each other, after all.

Layla sliced up the decadent cake she'd ordered from Arden's favorite local bakery, and the guests found spots in the cramped living room to enjoy dessert while watching her open gifts.

The Connors had purchased an adorable play mat labeled a "baby gym," and Arden laughed. "Did Garrett tell you our child is already an Olympian in training?" Garrett's parents went overboard with their gifts, which included both the stroller and the playpen from the registry. Arden rolled her eyes at Justin's present, infant shirts with slogans like Cuteness Runs in the Family. You Should Meet My Uncle.

"You are *not* using my kid to scam women," she said.

He laughed, then handed her a card with Colin's handwriting on it. "He asked me to deliver this." He lowered his voice. "I know he hates himself for not being here. He just couldn't."

Oh, what she wouldn't give to wave a magic wand and erase Colin's pain. If Colin needed to go somewhere else in order to eventually find his way back to them, she would support that. As she read the card he'd signed, sentimental tears welled in her eyes, then she gasped when she saw the amount of the gift card he'd placed in the envelope.

Garrett was equally startled. "Whoa. Is this to help

pay for newborn provisions, or is he single-handedly trying to put the kid through college?"

After everyone else's presents had been unwrapped, Garrett handed her a gift bag that he said was from him. "Nothing off the registry," he said. "Just a little something all kids should have."

She reached inside and pulled out a baby-size supersoft, red cowboy hat that inexplicably made her cry. It would be adorable on either a little boy or girl. There was also a chocolate-brown floppy plush cow.

"These are the sweetest things I've ever seen." She sniffled. She hugged the plush stuffed animal to her chest.

"Took me a while to find one that wasn't black-and-white. They shouldn't all be Holsteins!" Garrett complained. The man was serious about his cows.

She thanked him with a hug, but had other ideas about how she wanted to thank him once they were alone. It was Darcy Connor who seemed to guess Arden's feelings and subtly began directing guests to leave. Justin left with Vivian, and Arden didn't know whether to be amused or irritated. Finally, only Layla was left.

As the two of them straightened the kitchen, Arden told her, "You outdid yourself with the food. No one who was here will need to cook dinner tonight."

In between his trips carrying all the gifts to the eventual nursery, Garrett thanked Layla with a hug and a kiss on the cheek, flustering her.

"Sorry," Layla whispered to Arden. "I know he's yours, but damn, he's hot."

Finally, *finally,* it was just Arden and Garrett. Alone at last after she hadn't seen him for two weeks. Taking his hand, she led him to the couch but didn't sit with him.

"You never actually gave me a straight answer when I asked you on the phone. Are you staying tonight?" she asked shyly.

He nodded, his gray eyes intense. "The entire drive to Cielo Peak, I worried that I'd lost my chance to build something with you. I need to hold you, feel you with me."

Leaning forward, she kissed him tenderly. "Then we're definitely on the same page. Wait here?" she murmured near his ear.

Battling the impulse to race to her closet in an undignified sprint, she sauntered out of the room, giving him a sassy wink over her shoulder.

As often as she thought about him during the days and nights when he wasn't in town, she'd had ample time to play this out in her mind. While she didn't think of herself as specifically vain, any woman seducing a man wanted to look her best. No way in hell was she letting him peel industrial-strength maternity undergarments off of her. At least, not for their first time.

And, in a way, this would be their first time.

What seemed like a lifetime ago, she'd had sex with a good-looking and very kind cowboy who'd changed her life forever. But now, she was about to make love to Garrett, the man she'd come to know over the past month, the man who worked hard and knew how to make her laugh, the man who cherished family as much as she did, the man who acted as if he'd do battle to defend her honor but looked completely at home holding a snuggly stuffed cow.

She'd purchased a very simple nightgown. The silky

material was midnight-blue and fell from spaghetti straps to hit right above her knees. It wasn't ornate or lacy or sheer, but it made her feel sexier than she had in months.

Wearing nothing but the nightgown, she returned to the living room. Her senses were so heightened that the mere brush of satiny fabric against bare skin was arousing.

Garrett sat bolt upright, shock and pure masculine hunger playing across his face. "This may have been a strategic mistake on your part," he cautioned. "If this is what I get after we argue...well, I may be picking a lot of fights."

She smiled but didn't say anything as she continued her unhurried approach.

He leaned toward her, catching her waist in his hands and tipping her almost off balance as he pulled her forward. She thudded against him, soft and curved in all the places he was hard, and his heat went straight through the thin material.

He threaded one hand through her hair, angling her head to deepen their kiss until it felt as if they were fused together. Sensation built in the very core of her. Dazed, she realized that she'd begun rocking against his lap. He bit her earlobe, not hard enough to hurt, but just enough to penetrate the sweet hazy fog of desire enveloping her.

"Are you sure about this, sweetheart?" He took her chin in his hand, meeting her eyes and seeking assurance.

"Completely. All the stuff we unwrapped earlier is wonderful, but this is the only gift I really wanted today."

Needing no further urging, he reached down to tug off his belt while she fumbled with the buttons on his shirt. When he was stripped down to dark boxer-briefs, he repositioned her on his lap, kissing her like a man in a frenzy, leaving her mouth only to skim kisses across her sensitive collarbone. Meanwhile, his fingers traced maddening circles over her breast, not yet touching the sensitive peak. Without warning, he replaced his hand with his mouth, suckling her through the silky nightgown.

She cried out, her inner muscles clenching, tension already spiraling through her, pooling low where she was wet and wanting. Under his skillful attention, it wouldn't take long for her to detonate in his arms. *"Garrett."* She clutched the back of the sofa with one hand, crushing the upholstery in her fingers as she ground against him. He was hard as stone beneath her.

"Right there with you, sweetheart." As he shifted the hem of her nightgown to position himself, the straps slid down her shoulders. He tugged them farther, exposing her breasts to the cool air as he flexed his hips upward to enter her. He went slowly at first, not penetrating completely, savoring the moment and giving her time to adjust. But then he gripped her hips and thrust, wrenching another ecstatic scream from her. Her nerve endings were on fire with need. Using the back of the couch for leverage, she moved with abandon until the mounting tension began to ripple and spasm and finally exploded outward with such force it nearly blinded her for a second.

With a shout, he plunged into her one last time, then cuddled her against his chest.

Eventually, she realized she was practically panting and cursed herself for not having the forethought to place a glass of water nearby. "That…" She couldn't quite catch her breath enough to finish her sentence. But that was okay. There were no words adequate enough to capture what they'd just shared.

Chapter 12

Pale October sunshine stole through the window, and Arden experienced a childish urge to hide underneath her sheets. She resented that it was morning already and expressed her opinion with a rude noise along the lines of a raspberry.

Next to her, Garrett propped himself on one elbow. "You don't have to get up yet, you know. I realize some insensitive SOB kept you up half the night."

More than half, but that wasn't why she was feeling peevish. "I'm not tired. I just don't want… You're like a living, breathing sci-fi anomaly."

His eyebrows drew together. "Is that some sort of compliment on my performance? If so, I'll take it. But I don't get it."

"I think you disrupt the flow of time somehow. Whenever you're around, time flies so quickly it's unnatural. Then when you're gone…it feels like whole civilizations rise and crumble in the days when I don't see you."

He sifted his fingers through her hair. "I miss you, too."

When he climbed out of bed to take a shower, he invited her to join him, but she was feeling too blue to thoroughly appreciate the experience. He paused in the bathroom doorway. "You *are* going to be here when I get out, right? No running off and leaving me a note?"

That succeeded in drawing a smile. "One of the benefits of having sex with a woman in her own home is that she's unlikely to flee afterward. Of course, one of the drawbacks is that there's no room service."

"Don't be so sure," he told her. "I saw eggs in your fridge last night. You stay put, and think about what you want in your omelet. I owe you a breakfast in bed."

Thirty minutes later, he made good on his promise. He sat against her headboard, shirtless and barefoot, while she snuggled next to him in her favorite robe. She only had one breakfast tray, so both of their plates were balanced on it, giving them an excuse for extra closeness.

She moaned her appreciation at the fluffy, perfectly seasoned eggs. "This is terrific. How am I going to let you leave?"

"Maybe you don't have to. I did a lot of thinking while I was cooking. Dad always said I was stubborn, but I guess his lectures are finally sinking in."

She wasn't exactly following his train of thought, but as soon as he'd said maybe he didn't have to go, her heart had thumped happily. "You don't need to return back to the ranch soon?"

"No, I do. It's my job, and my life. I explained it wrong. When I leave, what if you came with me? My dad's been telling me since the day he met you that if I had the brains God gave a turnip, I'd take you off the market once and for all."

She gave him an incredulous look. "Off the market?"

"Marry you. And he's right."

"You can't be serious." Her brain whirled. What had happened to "let's not rush this" and "you deserve to be courted"? Okay, yes, they'd taken a big step forward last night, but she hadn't realized it was tantamount to getting engaged.

"Of course I am. I wouldn't joke about this." He swung his feet over the side of the bed, and she knew he'd be pacing within minutes. "Our baby received so many presents yesterday. Wouldn't the best gift be a stable home, a mother and father under one roof? We both know how important family is. Don't you want to provide that for the little one?"

She resented that line of reasoning. It sounded too much like he was trying to guilt her into the biggest decision of her life.

"It's the smart thing to do," he pronounced, irritating her even more.

"So if I don't say yes, I'm dumb *and* a bad mother?"

"What? How the hell did you make that leap?" He narrowed his eyes. "Wait, why wouldn't you say yes? We've both wondered how we're going to make this work long distance. You're alone here. At the Double F there's someone who can share the middle-of-the-night changings, built-in babysitting so you can keep working. Or you could stop working. I'll take care of you."

Now she shot out of the bed, too. It was a reminder

of everything intimate they'd shared during the night—
back *before* she'd wanted to throttle him—and she
didn't want to acknowledge those memories right now.
"I'm not alone here! I have Justin and Layla and my
studio. And, yes, I plan to keep working. I love being a
photographer, and I spent a lot of time building a professional reputation and cultivating word-of-mouth mar-
keting. You would expect me to drop all of that without
a second thought?"

Apparently, he would. He *had*.

He ran a hand through his hair, making it stand on
end. It looked as stressed out as she was feeling. "Is this
really so out of the blue, so unthinkable? In less than
two months, you're having my baby. In a perfect world,
we'd have more time to plan and discuss, but we didn't
go about any of this perfectly."

Irrational tears burned her eyes. Last night had
seemed pretty damned perfect. For that matter, she'd
accumulated a number of "perfect moment" memories
in Garrett's presence, even when it had been something
as small as laughing until her face hurt over the world's
ugliest souvenir pen. But to hear him tell it, he'd merely
been making the best of a bad situation.

Suddenly devoid of energy, she sank back down to
the mattress. "You said your father's been goading you
to get married since the day he met me? We weren't
even dating then."

"True, but he knew we were about to be parents. If
we get married before Thanksgiving, our child will—"

"*Before* Thanksgiving?" Was he delusional? They'd
never even discussed this before now, and he wanted to
throw together a wedding in five or six weeks? Tears
burned her eyes. He'd gone from telling his family there

was "nothing romantic" between them to insisting she become his wife. Obviously marriage meant very different things to each of them. "Garrett, why do you want to marry me?"

"I told you. The baby des—"

"My answer is no."

Garrett had left Cielo Peak in a raging bad mood that did not improve on his drive to the ranch. Arden had been unreasonable. She'd admitted she was miserable without him, but she refused to take the logical step so that they could be together. Even though it would make them both happy. Even though it was best for the baby.

Despite knowing his parents would want to hear about the shower and ask how she'd liked their gifts, he drove straight past their house. He needed to be alone. But fate had something different in mind. He'd barely removed his boots when his doorbell rang. He held his breath, debating how to proceed. He couldn't really ignore his own parents the way one might a door-to-door salesman.

"Son?" Brandon called. "We need to talk to you. It's important."

It had better not be about Arden. He'd had enough of his father's unsolicited advice on that front. *I tried, Dad.* She'd trampled his proposal with all the violence of a stampeding herd.

Years of ingrained obedience won out, and he opened the door for his father. Garrett did a double take, noting that his mom had been crying and that even his father's eyes were puffy. He experienced a moment of emotional vertigo— Oh, God. Had Will Harlow lost his battle with renal failure? "C-come in." Garrett cast his hand out to the side blindly, looking for something that would steady him.

They filed into the living room, no one speaking, until finally, Caroline said, in a voice so small it was almost inaudible, "Your father suggested that we invite Will for Thanksgiving next month. He has no family, and he's been so ill. It would be the charitable thing to do. And I just…couldn't. I couldn't go on not telling him anymore."

This wasn't about a downturn in the man's health? This was about Thanksgiving? Garrett's gaze dropped, zeroing in on his parents' joined hands. They were here as a unified front? Brandon hadn't driven into the mountains to process news of his wife's duplicity?

"You're not mad?" Garrett asked without thinking. "You don't care?"

"Of course I care, son. Especially for you. Your momma tells me you've been going through hell this last month, and I've never been prouder of you. You want to help a man who's critically ill, despite your anger. You tried to protect your momma by keeping her secret, but through it all, you've felt a strong pull of loyalty to me? We raised you good. And you had reason to be hurt. But only the two people *in* a relationship can truly understand what's happening between them."

Sometimes even fewer than two. Garrett, for one, had no idea why Arden had thrown away what could have been an amazing future.

"You don't know what that time was like for Caro, what I was like. I have a son, and Will may be dying. In light of those facts, holding a grudge seems pretty pointless. We just wanted you to know you don't have to hide it anymore. And we both fully support whatever you decide about the kidney donation. Suffice to say, Will Harlow won't be joining us for Thanksgiving. Not that I suppose it makes much difference to you. We figure you'll be in Cielo Peak."

With Arden, they meant. It was going to be difficult to feel thankful after her rejection.

Despite his relief over Brandon finally knowing the truth and his admiration that his parents had managed to weather such a significant betrayal, Garrett felt hollow. How could he be this bereft? When he'd first learned about Pea—about the baby, he'd assumed he and Arden would parent separately and platonically. It was only very recently that he'd begun to believe they could have more. They'd been on *one* date. How could he mourn the loss of something he'd never truly had?

His gaze went involuntarily to his parents' still-linked hands. Just because he'd never had something didn't mean he couldn't recognize the value of it.

Three teenagers posed against a pumpkin-patch backdrop in Halloween costumes ranging from zombie cheerleader to a two-headed mummy. But the scariest thing in the studio was Arden's unshakable gloom. What was the point in a soon-to-be mom taking a principled stand on her right to keep working if she chased off all her clients with her morose attitude?

"Great shots, girls." She put the camera away, trying not to think about when she and Natalie had been that age, the silly moments like these—funny BFF photos, staging "chance" run-ins with boys they liked, never having any idea the twists and turns their lives would take.

After the giggling teens had chipped in their money and selected the photo they wanted for their joint package, Arden was alone—free to put her head on her desk and cry her guts out. Except she couldn't. The woman who'd cried at greeting cards, soup commercials, random puppies she passed in the park and internet banner ads was completely empty. She'd been dry-eyed since Garrett stomped out of her house last week, unable to wash away the memory with cleansing tears.

Although she hadn't spoken directly to Garrett, Darcy Connor had suddenly discovered numerous reasons to call. The woman was obviously checking on Arden and the baby and making covert reports.

"Knock, knock." Layla stood in the doorway. As the teenage girls had happily announced, today had been an early release day for local schools. "This is an intervention."

"What?"

"Today, we close the studio early, go to your place and eat chocolate-covered caramels while we watch action movies with lots of car chases and explosions. Then, tomorrow, you start shaking this off, or I think your brothers are taking a road trip to the Double F and doing some damage. You remember your brothers, right? Big strapping guys who love you and are worried sick?"

"I'm not trying to worry any of you," Arden said apologetically. "I just…hurt."

"Oh, sweetie." Layla came around the desk to give her a hug. Then she pulled a caramel-filled chocolate medallion out of her pocket. "Here, want to get a jump start on the gorging?"

"No." Arden swatted the candy away. It made her think of Garrett. *Big surprise.* Everything made her think of Garrett.

"If you miss him so much, you could call him."

"And say what? Layla, the guy expected me to marry him without ever mentioning his feelings for me. He thinks it's rational to get married for the baby's sake, and, you know what? He may be right. There are probably people who do that and make it work. But I'm holding out for more than *rational*. He made it sound like a good mother would want her child to have a loving home with both parents, and I *do*. Enough that I'm willing to wait for the right situation, for a man who actually does love me. A man who gives his future with me the due consideration it deserves. I can't just pack up and leave Cielo Peak!"

Layla narrowed her eyes at her, lips pursed.

"What?"

"Don't scream at me...but are you *sure* you can't?"

"Hey! You're one of the reasons I'm staying. Do you want to get rid of me?"

"What I want is to see you happy. I know we couldn't go out for spur-of-the-moment pizzas if you left, but even living in the same town, we spend half our time on the phone. You'd be moving to a ranch, not the far side of the moon."

"I have a business I started from scratch. And the thought of leaving my brothers..."

"Maybe you'd be setting a good example for them," Layla suggested quietly. "Colin can't seem to find his way back to happiness, and Justin is too afraid of being happy to give it a fair shot. If you seized happiness with Garrett, it could give them hope, a blueprint to follow. I agree the man's proposal sucked, but let's look past that for the moment. Do you think he could make you happy?"

Arden stared into space, recounting all the small and

not-so-small ways he'd done just that, the unexpected joy he'd given her.

"C'mon, you can think it over on the ride to your house." Layla had already picked up Arden's purse and was bringing the red wool coat to her. "You said Garrett goes in for testing next week? Maybe you can call him Sunday night, after you've both had a chance to calm down and reflect. Wish him luck on the medical stuff and see how you feel talking to him."

Conjuring a ghost of a smile, Arden stood. "You're a very wise woman."

"That's what I tell my students. Let's go. Bad action movies await."

"I don't think so." Arden gasped, gripping the edge of her desk. "My water just broke!"

All the other ranch hands had called it a day. Garrett should, too. It was cold and dark. But where else would he go? His house was too quiet, too lonely. And up at his parents' house, Caroline's admission seemed to have brought her and Brandon even closer. With the weight of her secret lifted, Caroline was practically giddy. She danced around the kitchen to her old records while baking, a constant smile on her face. The house was full of the cinnamon-spiced aroma of pumpkin pie and happiness.

He'd rather be out shivering in the barn.

The cell phone in his pocket rang, and he had to remove one glove to answer it. He almost ignored the call since he didn't recognize the number. "Garrett Frost," he announced himself.

"Frost? This is Justin Cade."

Garrett groaned. Was the man planning to kick

Garrett's ass because he'd displeased Arden? "Look, if you're calling to bust my chops, you should know I *tried* to do the honorable thing."

"I'm calling because she's in the hospital." The swaggering man had never sounded so fragile. "How soon can you get here?"

By the time he reached the hospital, it was all over. Garrett was ravaged with self-blame. Why hadn't he been here with her? Had this happened because they'd had sex? Between all the machines in the hospital interfering with cell phone reception and Garrett driving through several "dead spots," he hadn't been able to stay in constant contact with Justin. Those moments of not knowing what was happening had been sheer hell.

What he did know was that Arden's membranes had ruptured a month too early. The doctors had given her antibiotics and had considered a drug to discourage labor as well as steroids to help speed development of the baby's premature lungs. But ultimately they'd decided the safest thing for both mother and child was an emergency C-section.

When he'd last spoken to Justin, that was all the man had known. Garrett burst into the maternity waiting room, frantic. Layla rose from a chair and ran to hug him.

"Tell me she's okay," he implored.

She nodded. "With the type of C-section they did, they had to knock her out. She's still asleep, but she should be fine. The baby was having a little bit of trouble breathing on her own, but she's on a ventilator in the NICU and—"

"She?" Garrett grabbed Layla's shoulders. The errant tears he'd fought since he'd jumped into his truck spilled over unchecked. "I have a daughter?"

Layla nodded emphatically. "Four pounds even. Name yet to be determined. Come on, her uncles are already upstairs watching her through windows."

Four pounds? Lord, she was smaller than a bowling ball but already had so many people in her life who already loved her. He followed Layla to the elevator bank. Now that the adrenaline in his body was starting to ebb, his legs felt too rubbery to take the stairs. The doors parted, and he was about to step inside the elevator when a nurse behind them called, "Family and friends of Arden Cade?"

He spun around. "Is she awake? Is she all right? Can I see her?"

The woman lowered her clipboard and gave him a patient smile. "Slow down there, sir. She's awake, but groggy. She'll experience some discomfort over her recovery period, but right now she's on some pretty strong painkillers. And, yes, you can see her. Only one at a time in the room until she's had a bit more rest."

"I'll go tell the guys." Layla squeezed his arm. "You tell Arden we all love her."

We all love her. God, he'd been an idiot. Why hadn't he dropped to one knee the last time he'd been with her, told her he'd never felt this way about another woman and begged her to marry him? He'd been cynical lately about matrimony and fidelity and honesty, but was that the kind of world he wanted to raise his daughter in? A place where people saw the worst in each other and didn't take risks with their hearts?

The nurse led him to a dimly lit maternity suite with a couple of guest chairs and a hospital bed angled so that Arden was reclining but not flat on her back. She was connected by IV to several different apparatuses and monitors. Wearing an unflattering hospital gown, tubes sticking out of her arms, plastic bracelets encircling her wrists, her damp hair sticking to a face bloated with the fluids they'd given her, she was easily the most beautiful woman he'd ever seen.

She blinked in confusion, as if trying to decide whether she was dreaming. "Garrett?" Her voice was slurred. "That you?"

"It's me." He came to her side, wondering if she'd let him hold her hand. Unable to stop himself, he leaned down to kiss her forehead. "Congratulations, I understand you have a beautiful daughter. But no way is she as beautiful as her momma."

"I need to hold her!" Splotches of color rose in her cheeks. "They put me under, I only glimpsed the hospital blanket and a blur and—"

"The nurse who brought me in here said they'll wheel you upstairs soon. They need to check some vitals first."

That seemed to calm her. She swallowed audibly, the sound dry and cracked, and he looked around for a pitcher of water.

"How'd you get here so fast?" she asked.

Fast? Under other circumstances, he would have laughed at the irony. "Sweetheart, those were the slowest, most agonizing hours of my entire life. I felt like I was stuck in another dimension and couldn't reach you. It was a living nightmare."

Her eyes slid closed once again. "You're here now."

After a night that passed in a fragmented series of narcotic impressions, Arden woke the next morning with a sense of awe. *I have a baby girl.* It seemed almost a dream, except for the pain in her midsection and the still-vivid memory of the fear she'd felt when the doctor had said they needed to do an emergency Caesarean.

Trying to remember how much of what she recalled was real, she turned her head to identify the source of snoring. She half expected to see Justin or Colin, but it was Garrett, his jaw covered in stubble, his legs hanging off a chair that transitioned into a twin bed about a foot too small for him.

"Garrett?"

He came awake immediately, his expression as chagrined as if he'd fallen asleep while he was supposed to be keeping watch. "I only closed my eyes for a minute."

She started to chuckle, but it hurt, tugging her insides in opposite directions. "You're allowed to sleep. How is she?"

"Healthy. She's upstairs in an incubator, but they say she's doing incredibly well for a preemie. She may have to stay in the hospital for a few weeks, but she should be home by Thanksgiving. My parents called about an hour ago. Would you mind if they come see you?"

"No, they should be here. Family's the most important thing in the world."

"Then you must be my family." He stood, coming to her side. "Because all I could think when I hauled ass to the hospital yesterday was that you're the most important thing in the world to me. You are my world. I'm sorry I didn't articulate that clearly enough until now."

She didn't know what to say. Could she trust what she was hearing, or were the drugs in the hospital very, *very* good?

"I can't wait to celebrate our first Thanksgiving as

a family," he said. "And Christmas! I'll put so many lights on the outside of the house the baby thinks she lives in Times Square."

"You...sound like you plan to spend a lot of time at my house. Don't they need you at the ranch?"

"I don't want to be here just for your recovery— or hers, no matter how much I love her. I want you, Arden. If I have to, I'll ask Dad to give the foreman extra responsibilities, hire some extra help. I'll stay in Cielo Peak as long as you want. If you'll have me," he said brokenly.

"But the Double F—"

"What's one ranch compared to the entire world?"

"Arden, is this bum bothering you?" Justin's teasing voice came from the door, and Arden was glad to see his familiar face—although it looked as if it had gained several new worry lines in the past twenty-four hours.

"I'm not sure," Arden began, "but he *might* have been proposing."

"In a hospital room with no ring?" Justin snorted. "Frost, my sister deserves a string quartet and a five-star meal."

"As soon as she's all better and you volunteer to babysit your niece, I'll take her out for those things. Right now, I'm improvising." He turned to Arden. "You asked me before why I wanted to marry you?"

She held her breath, almost afraid to hope.

He took her hand, his heart in his eyes. "Because I love you and always will."

"I love you, too." Joy filled her, and for a second she felt no pain at all. "And I'd like nothing more than to marry you."

Epilogue

Arden stood by her daughter's hospital crib, watching her sleep. "I hate that I'm going home without you, but I'll visit every day. And going home just means I can supervise Daddy while he gets your room set up perfectly," she whispered. "I'll tell you a secret, you've already got Daddy completely wrapped around your finger. Be careful with him. He may be a big, strong cowboy, but he's got a tender heart."

She couldn't believe he'd really been willing to move to Cielo Peak for them. She'd informed him that under no circumstances would she allow such a sacrifice. But they *would* have to remain for at least a few months, as their daughter got stronger. They'd relocate to the ranch sometime after New Year's and were hoping to get married around Valentine's Day.

Her husband-to-be was waiting for her in the hall,

having already said his temporary goodbye to their daughter. As soon as the drugs had begun to wear off and Arden started having longer stretches of lucidity, Garrett had asked if she'd decided on a name for a baby. During her pregnancy, she'd toyed with the notion of perhaps naming a daughter for Natalie. Or after her own mother. But those both felt off the mark now. There was nothing wrong with honoring the past, but Arden wanted to focus on the bright, bright future ahead of them. They'd christened their daughter Hope.

"Everyone's waiting downstairs," he told her, putting his arm around her shoulders. "If you want to change your mind, I can tell Mom that—"

"No, we agreed. Caro's going to stay with me while you finally get that testing done. You already had to postpone because of me. I don't want this hanging over your head, Garrett. The nurses are giving Hope the best care possible, and you know your mom will look after me and call you with daily—possibly hourly—updates."

"I just hate to leave you."

"I know, but we have a whole lifetime ahead of us. We can spare a week of that to find out whether you can help Will."

During the days she'd been in the hospital, Garrett had told her all about how Brandon had forgiven his wife's transgression. And Arden had thought about the many rich blessings she and Garrett shared. If they could bless someone else with a second chance…

Even though she was able to walk by herself, hospital policy dictated that she be taken to the exit in a wheelchair. Apparently, there was a waiting list for the chairs, because the nurse who said she'd be right back had yet to reappear. The elevator doors parted, but it wasn't the nurse who stepped off the conveyance. Both her brothers were loaded down with her belongings, ready to take them to Garrett's truck, and they were accompanied by Layla and the Frosts.

"We just wanted one last peek at Hope through the window before we go," Layla said sheepishly. "I can't wait until you can bring her home, and I get to hold her as much as I want."

"Sorry, honey," Caroline said. "I've got grandmother's prerogative. You'll have to wait in line."

"Her parents get first dibs," Garrett said firmly.

Affection and gratitude filled Arden. How was it possible she had ever felt alone? She looked from the group assembled in the hall back to her beautiful daughter, then up into the eyes of the man who loved her. *My family.* Hope didn't know it yet, but they were the luckiest two ladies in all of Colorado.

* * * * *

Patricia Thayer was born and raised in Muncie, Indiana. She attended Ball State University before heading west, where she has called Southern California home for many years.

When not working on a story, she might be found traveling the United States and Europe, taking in the scenery and doing story research while enjoying time with her husband, Steve. Together, they have three grown sons and four grandsons and one granddaughter, whom Patricia calls her own true-life heroes.

Books by Patricia Thayer

Harlequin Western Romance

Count on a Cowboy
Second Chance Rancher
Her Colorado Sheriff

Harlequin Romance

Tall, Dark, Texas Ranger
Once a Cowboy...
The Cowboy Comes Home
Single Dad's Holiday Wedding
Her Rocky Mountain Protector
The Cowboy She Couldn't Forget
Proposal at the Lazy S Ranch

Visit the Author Profile page at Harlequin.com for more titles.

A COLORADO FAMILY

PATRICIA THAYER

Chapter 1

Erin Carlton blinked several times, trying to stay awake as she drove along the Colorado highway. Last night's graveyard shift at the Mountain View Convalescent Center had been a rough one. During her rounds there had been two emergencies. Luckily, nothing too serious. Yet with Alzheimer's patients, you had to expect the unexpected, even if it was only to give them reassurance.

She leaned back in the cargo van's seat and began to relax her tense muscles as she focused on the majestic Rocky Mountains. A fresh start here in Hidden Springs had been a good idea. She'd made friends, been able to save money, but still she didn't have enough...yet. That was the reason she was going to this interview.

She glanced down at the written directions given to her for her appointment, not exactly sure of the location of the ranch.

If she got this part-time job, the money would be strictly for her special account. If she weren't so close to reaching her goal amount, she'd be home in bed, sleeping away the cool autumn day. But the money offered for this position was too good to turn down, even if she'd been warned ahead of time about the hard-to-deal-with client. Not that hard work ever stopped her before.

Erin turned off the main road and saw the sign to the Circle R Ranch, then another sign for Georgia's Therapy Riding Center. She smiled at the thought of her friends Brooke and Trent Landry, who were involved in the program for special-needs kids. If she knew how to ride a horse, she might help out, too. But this city gal didn't have any desire to take on a horse.

She drove through the ranch's main gate and followed the long row of white-slatted fence. There were several horses grazing in the green pasture. She passed the large red barn and several outbuildings that had recently been painted a glossy white.

She parked in the driveway of the large two-story gray-and-white house where two men were standing on the wraparound porch. She recognized Trent right away, and next to him was his stepbrother, Hidden Springs' new sheriff, Cullen Brannigan. She'd met him a few times when he'd been called out to the center. His new wife, Shelby, had brought the residents some desserts from her new bakery.

Erin parked next to the house and climbed out of the van. Trent came down to greet her. "Good morning, Erin." He hugged her.

"Morning to you, too. Sorry I'm late. My shift ran over."

Trent was a good-looking man, ex-military, and still

kept in shape. A few years ago, he took over his father's ranch and began raising cattle. And he found Erin's friend Brooke and had the good sense to marry her.

"You're not late," Trent said. "I told you if nothing else, this job would be flexible. You can work around your hours." He glanced at the man with him. "Sorry, Erin. Have you met Cullen Brannigan?"

"Yes. Nice to see you, Sheriff."

He smiled. "Same here, Erin."

Coming from Las Vegas, she'd met her share of phonies. From what she heard around town, these two men were as real as they came.

"Well, I appreciate you coming out and talking with us." Cullen blew out a breath. "Although I have to warn you, this patient isn't the most congenial person right now. And he needs to keep his rehab a secret. No one is to know he's here."

She tried not to show her concern. Who was this guy, an undercover cop? "I wouldn't tell anyone. Who is this person?"

Cullen exchanged a glance with Trent. "He's my twin brother, Austin. He's a champion bull rider who was badly injured about three months ago. His leg was damaged pretty badly, and he's had to have several surgeries. He's finally out of the hospital and is ready to rehab."

They didn't want her for a nursing job? "Do you need me to recommend a therapist?"

"No, Erin. We hope between your nursing and your experience with physical therapy, you might be able to help Austin. Brooke told me how you worked with your husband through his intense rehab."

Erin felt the familiar tightness in her chest. The pain

of losing Jared had faded some in the past eighteen months, but she'd always regret not being able to do more to help him. But her husband had to deal with more than a physical disability.

She glanced away, then said, "If his doctor is okay with me working with him, then I'm willing. When would you want me to start?"

Trent and Cullen exchanged a glance. What weren't they telling her?

"The doctor isn't the problem, but the patient might be," Trent said. "Austin hasn't been the easiest person to get along with. He's run off three other caregivers. So I'll understand if you want to leave right now."

"Bad attitude is understandable. Therapy is a lot of hard work, and most times painful. But if he wants to regain the use of his leg, he'll need therapy. Which rehab center is he in?"

Another look went between the brothers, and then Trent spoke up. "He's not in a rehab center. He's staying here at the ranch."

Cullen raised a hand. "He had all the equipment he needs delivered here. If you decide not to take this case, the fewer people who know the better."

"Of course. I never discuss my patients."

"You can't even mention that you know he's here in town. If the media get wind of his location, they'll be camped out all over the place."

She sighed. At the very least, she was fascinated just to meet this person. "When do I get to meet this man?"

"How about now?" Trent escorted her to a golf cart. "Austin has moved into the old foreman's house." She sat in the front seat, Cullen drove, and Trent climbed in the back.

The cart bounced along the gravel road that led to a smaller gray-and-white house. Cullen got out and escorted her up to the small porch. "Just remember my brother isn't at his best. So don't take anything he says personally."

She straightened. "Lead me to the tyrant."

"Don't say we didn't warn you." Trent opened the door, then called out, "Hey, brother. Someone is here to see you."

She followed the two men inside to the living room, where a dark leather sofa and a chair were grouped around a fireplace. Over the mantel hung a large flat-screen television. A dark brown rug covered hardwood floors.

"What a cozy room."

"Thanks. We've been working on the place ever since we knew Austin needed a place to recuperate." He started down the hall and called out again. "Austin…"

A string of curse words came from the back of the house, along with a crashing sound. All three of them ran down the hall.

Trent swung open the bedroom door, Erin close behind. She saw a man with scraggly, sandy-brown hair lying on the large bed, but his water pitcher was on the floor. The man caused her to do a double take.

Austin Brannigan was gorgeous. Rugged good looks, with a two-day growth of beard shadowing his strong jaw. His chest was bare, with a sprinkling of dark hair covering his well-defined muscles. Her gaze moved to a sheet that barely covered his waist and anything south of that. His left foot and calf were enclosed by a long removable cast, but still she got a glimpse of an angry scar peeking out the top.

"Like what you see, darlin'?"

Her attention darted back to his face, and those gray eyes zeroed in on her. She fought her reaction and lost. "Yeah, I do." She walked closer to the bed, channeling her years of nursing training. *Show him who's in charge.* "All except the attitude. So if you ditch that we might be able to work together."

Austin Brannigan tensed, but caught his brothers' smiles. He wasn't in the mood to be amused. His leg ached like the devil, and he hadn't been able to do the simplest tasks. "I take it you're the new recruit."

Her eyes narrowed. "I'll wait and see how the interview goes."

He stiffened. "I guess you're forgetting who's hiring you."

The pretty redhead strolled around the room as if she had a right to. Then she flashed those big emerald green eyes at him, and he felt a jolt of awareness deep in his gut. Damn.

She moved closer to the bed. "And I guess you forgot how bad you need me."

He might like this. He'd been without a woman far too long. "Oh, darlin', you have no idea." He caught the frown from Trent and Cullen, but ignored it.

The new nurse put her fists on her hips as her gaze moved over his body, stopping at the sheet. "Oh, I think I do." Quickly, her gaze returned to his face. "Okay, Mr. Brannigan. We can do this a few different ways, easy or hard. We work together as a unit and I'll help with your recovery, or we fight, which I guarantee will make it more difficult, or you can just tell me to leave. What will it be?"

He was used to being in charge. People did what he

wanted, not the other way around. But he had a feeling this woman knew what she was doing. He glanced again at his brothers in the doorway. "Do you mind leaving us alone?"

Trent looked at the woman. "Erin, it's up to you."

"I'm fine." She looked back at Austin. "I have a black belt in karate."

That brought a smile to Cullen's and Trent's faces. "Good luck… Austin." The door closed, shutting them in silence.

The woman spoke first. "My name is Erin Carlton, Mr. Brannigan. I'm a registered nurse and I've had some training in physical therapy, but I'm not certified. I know your sister-in-law, Brooke, from a time when we both lived in Las Vegas. I understand you're someone famous and you don't want anyone to know you're here during your rehab. Just so you know, I'd never reveal a patient's confidentiality."

He began to relax. "It's Austin."

She nodded. "Would you mind telling me what happened?"

Yeah, he did, but he began the story anyway. "My brothers might have told you some already. I was competing in the short round at the Frontier Days Rodeo last July and leading in points." Damn, he'd played the accident over and over in his head and never could understand how everything went so wrong. "I was thrown and got caught up in my rigging on my way down, and a two-thousand-pound bull named Sidewinder had his way with me."

He rubbed his thigh absently, trying not to relive the nightmare. "The doctor put my leg back together with the aid of a titanium rod. Now all I want to do is rebuild the strength in my leg and get back on the circuit."

Erin didn't react to his announcement. "Have you had any therapy?"

"Some, but I just got here this week." He nodded to the door. "There's a boatload of equipment in the bedroom across the hall. Dr. Michael Kentrell did the surgery. You should talk to him."

She nodded. "I plan to, if I take your case."

He frowned. "And I haven't decided you're the person for this job, either. What's your experience?"

"I told you, I'm a nurse and I presently work with Alzheimer's patients." Her gaze met his. "I do some therapy with my patients at the Mountain View Convalescent Center, but my most intense sessions were with my husband. He was wounded during his deployment in Afghanistan. I worked nearly a year on his therapy."

She was married. He glanced down at his ringless finger. "What were his injuries?"

She straightened. "Jared caught shrapnel in his calf and thigh, tore his muscles to shreds. He also had head trauma."

"Was he able to walk again?"

She shrugged. "Some, but he never gained total strength in his leg."

Austin wasn't sure what to say next, seeing the pain in Erin Carlton's eyes. Those pretty green eyes.

Did he want this distracting woman around all the time? Having her close, touching him, causing him to react? So far she was also the only person who'd dared to stand up to him. He doubted she'd be easy on him.

"If you work for me, how soon could you start?"

She blinked at the question, then recovered and said, "That all depends. I need to talk with your physician."

He nodded toward the dresser. "There's my medical file and instructions for my therapy."

She picked it up and began to read it.

"I was hoping that you could work every day. My goal is to get well enough to get back on the circuit. So I'll need someone who's dedicated to work with me. I've lost my top ranking for this year, but I plan to be back on the circuit as soon as possible." Most importantly, before he lost any product endorsements.

She looked up from her reading. "Firstly, I'll be working *with* you. And secondly, I have a full-time job at the center."

"That isn't going to work for me. I need you full-time with me."

She straightened. "There are only so many hours in a day, Mr. Brannigan."

"It's Austin."

"Austin. Like I said, I can't be in both places, and I can't function on no sleep."

"Then work *with* me exclusively." He tossed out an amount of money that was crazy even to him.

She couldn't hide her shock. "I won't give up my job at the center. Let's see what I can come up with. But if I agree to work with you, I'll have a few rules. Unless you're an invalid, which you're not, I won't clean up after you." She looked at the mess on the floor.

"That was an accident."

She didn't look convinced and held up the file. "May I take this with me to study your case?"

"If you're taking me on."

She nodded. "If we can work out a schedule."

He was suddenly excited she was working with him. He stared at the pretty redhead with those big green eyes. Her complexion wasn't pale or pasty; she had more of an olive skin tone.

Stop! he chided himself. He couldn't think of her as a woman. Besides, she was married to a soldier. *That makes her off-limits.* Not that he was in any shape to do anything.

Erin started for the door. "I'll get back to you tomorrow as soon as I make arrangements with my supervisor." She studied him. "Are you sure you want to pay the amount? It's twice the going rate."

He nodded. "It is if you're dedicated to helping me get back on my feet."

She smiled. "You're the only one who can accomplish what you need. All I do is help rebuild the strength in your leg. I'll help you walk, Austin, but you'll have to get yourself on a bull."

"Guaranteed, I'll do it."

"Good. I'll be back tomorrow afternoon." She walked out, and he found he wanted to call her back.

Damn, he had to get himself together if he was going to make this work. He had to forget that Erin Carlton was a woman. If he needed some stress relief, he had plenty of phone numbers of plenty of women. No. He shook his head. He needed to concentrate on regaining his status as top bull rider.

There was a knock on the door, and then Cullen stuck his head inside. "So you managed to find someone to help you with your crazy scheme."

"It's not crazy, bro. It's my profession, and I'm good at it."

Austin had grown up with the fact that Cullen was the good twin. The best student, a college graduate, and he even became a cop like their dad. Now he was the town sheriff with a smoking-hot wife, Shelby, and an adopted son, Ryan.

"I heard what the doctor told you when you came to from your concussion. Your leg is pieced together with metal rods. It might never be as strong as before. You've already gotten to the top in ranking, won every championship possible and made a fortune on endorsements. Why can't you retire now?"

"How would you like to retire from police work?"

"I would in a second. I've learned what's important, A." His brother tossed out the nickname as if they were still kids. "Find a nice woman and settle down. You own half this ranch—the possibilities are endless."

"I haven't found anything or any woman who I'd give up my lifestyle for."

"Okay, I'll get off my soapbox, for now." Cullen checked his watch. "I need to get to the station. Shelby will bring you some lunch. Do you need anything before I go?"

He sat up and slowly swung his legs over the side. "No, I can get around okay. Sorry I've been such a pain."

Cullen grinned. "Why should anything change? You've always been a pain in the butt, little brother." He walked to the door.

"Hey, you're only five minutes older than me." He sobered. "Hey, about Erin Carlton. Her husband... I take it he was in the military?"

"Yeah, Jared was a decorated marine. On his third deployment his Humvee was hit by an IED. There were complications to his injures." His brother held his gaze. "Sergeant First Class Jared Carlton died eighteen months ago." His brother started for the door, then stopped. "Just a little warning. This isn't your rodeo, so if you hurt Erin, you're going to have to deal with me."

"Hey, I'm the one with the bad leg."

Cullen didn't say a word as he walked out.

There was no need. Austin knew what his brother was talking about. He didn't have the best reputation when it came to women. Being in the rodeo made it easy to take his pick without having to think about the consequences. That was both a blessing and a curse.

Chapter 2

A few hours later, nature called and Austin finally got out of bed. He strapped on his booted cast, grabbed his walker, then made his way into the bathroom. After months flat on his back, being upright was a luxury he didn't take for granted anymore. Since he'd gotten out of the private hospital outside Denver, he'd decided he had to work hard to get back to the man he once was. That was why he was going to do everything possible to move on to rehab.

His thoughts turned to Mrs. Carlton. She was pretty enough, but a little short with a fuller figure than he preferred. So it was definitely a good thing he wasn't attracted to redheads. Besides, she had an attitude.

"Stop it, Brannigan. Even if you did find her appealing, you're in no shape to be sidetracked."

He needed to be focused only on his goal. Question

was, would Erin Carlton push him hard enough? He wasn't sure if she could, but he was intrigued when she hadn't backed down from him.

He washed up and looked in the bathroom mirror. After running a brush through his hair, he brushed his teeth. He'd forgo a shave until his brother came by later to help him shower. He knew his limits.

After he managed to get on a fresh pair of workout shorts and a T-shirt, he made his way down the hall. His leg throbbed like the blazes, but going back to the bed was too depressing. Besides, the doctor said there would be pain. It could take a good year before it went away, and that when the weather changed his leg might alert him to that fact, too.

Hell, he knew about pain. He was a bull rider.

The twenty feet he walked from the bathroom was agony, but he didn't stop. Finally he got to the sofa and sat down. Sweat broke out on his face as he pushed his walker to the side and gently lifted his leg to the coffee table. He eyed the long scar that peered out of the top of his cast.

Every day from now on, he'd be reminded how bad things were for him, and how lucky he was to be alive, even if he might have a slight limp for the rest of his days.

Exhausted, he collapsed back on the sofa and recalled how he'd begged the renowned surgeon to save his mangled leg. It had been touch and go for that first week, but the miracle surgery worked. Now the rest was up to him.

"Damn. I'm gonna fix this."

He closed his eyes to rest a minute and the next thing he heard was a knock on the door. He jumped and opened his eyes to see his sister-in-law pop her head in the door.

Shelby smiled. "You decent?"

"Never," he teased.

"Good." The pretty blonde walked in carrying a foil-wrapped dish. Quickly a delicious aroma filled the room.

Following behind Shelby was his nephew, Ryan. The cute kid was five years old and had a head full of golden curls that seemed to run wild. He was dressed in a henley shirt, a pair of jeans and roper boots. A miniature cowboy. The boy was still a little shy around his uncle Austin.

"Hey, Ryan. How's that horse of yours? What's his name?"

The boy grinned. "Cloud. He's great. I can ride all by myself."

"High five."

The boy smacked Austin's hand and giggled.

"Pretty soon Uncle Trent will have you chasing down calves."

The boy looked at his aunt. After the boy's mother died, Shelby took over the role of his mom. Once Cullen married Shelby last summer, he took over as the boy's father. "Can I go do that, Mom?"

"I think you need to ride around the corral a little longer before we let you go on a trail ride."

The boy smiled. "Okay."

Shelby looked back at Austin. "I'm glad to see you out of bed."

"It took a while, but I managed to get down the hall."

"Any progress is good," she agreed. "Are you hungry? I brought you some meat loaf and cheesy potatoes."

He groaned. "Sounds delicious. A person can only eat so much delivery pizza."

"Well, from now on, you'll be eating much better. I'll be bringing you some meals." She walked to the ancient kitchen that was open to the living space, with only a counter separating the rooms.

"You don't need to take care of me, Shelby."

She gave a bright smile. "I know, but I cook for Ryan and Cullen and there's always plenty. In case you didn't remember, I'm a chef. It's what I do."

His brother did good, finding this sweet lady with the twinge of a Southern accent in her voice. Originally from Kentucky, Shelby was to come here with her sister, Georgia, and nephew Ryan for a job. Before they left their small Southern town, Georgia's cop boyfriend killed her. Despite the tragedy, Shelby still brought Ryan here, where Cullen found her in the ranch house.

Why couldn't he also enjoy some of his brother's good fortune? "Well, if you insist."

Shelby went to the cupboard, got a plate and transferred the food onto it. "Should I bring the food out there, or do you think you can eat at the table?"

He needed to keep moving. "The table." He lowered his leg to the floor.

"I'll help you, Uncle Austin." Ryan moved his walker within reach.

"Thanks, Ryan." Austin managed to stand, then began his journey, the boy right beside him.

Shelby set down a place mat with flatware and a tall glass of milk. "Looks like you have a helper."

Austin managed a smile. "Yep, sure do." His strength was a little shaky, but he kept taking each step. Breathing labored, he reached the scarred maple table and sat down.

Looking worried, Shelby sat down across from him. "Are you sure you're not doing too much?"

He shook his head. "After the six weeks on my back, then another two weeks of restricted rehab at the hospital, the doctor deemed me fit enough to discharge me. It's about time I get on my feet."

"Sorry, I'm just worried about you, being out here all alone."

He dug into his food and savored the spicy taste of the meat. "I doubt with all of you around, I'll be alone much." He winked at Ryan. "I plan to be watching Ryan ride his horse soon."

The boy smiled at him. "Do you have a horse, Uncle Austin?"

Austin swallowed his food. "No, Ryan, I don't. I've been riding bulls for a long time. Now that I have a place to keep one, a horse or two might be a good idea."

His stepmother, Leslie Landry Brannigan, had died last year and left her ranch to her biological son, Trent, and her stepsons, Cullen and Austin. She'd loved all her boys unconditionally. Unlike his father, whom he hadn't been able to get along with since he'd been a kid.

"Pops can find you a horse. He brings lots of horses here."

Austin tensed. He hadn't had a chance to see his dad since he'd moved in here. Right now, he didn't want to deal with the old man.

Shelby's voice broke into his thoughts. "Those are for the riding center, honey." She turned to him. "Seems people have a lot of horses that need a home."

"That's good they have a place to go."

"Kinda like us," Ryan said. "We didn't have a place to go, but the sheriff let us stay here and he married us. Now you're here, too."

Shelby grinned. "And we're lucky to have you home. I want to keep you here, so I'll send some food that you can heat up easily. Maybe I can bring muffins and bagels by, too, when I bring Ryan home from school."

"Thanks—I'd appreciate it."

"You're very welcome. You need to put on some weight. To build muscle, you'll need extra calories." She watched him eat, then asked, "So Erin's going to be working with you?"

He arched an eyebrow. Had the woman broken her word already? "She told you?"

"Oh, no. Cullen called me after Erin left here earlier. And I haven't said anything, either. I know you don't want anyone to know you're staying here, but haven't the media had your accident on the news?"

He cringed, remembering how the tape had become an internet sensation. "Yeah, you can't do much these days without being recorded. I just don't want everyone knowing the extent of the injury."

"I'm sure your fans are worried about you."

"My fans aren't the problem. It's the sponsors who pay me to be on the circuit and advertise their products. They don't want to pay me if I'm not out there winning events."

She smiled. "Maybe you can advertise for me and my bakery. A Sweet Heaven banner would look good across your back."

Austin laughed, despite the pain in his leg. He

glanced at the bottle of pain pills on the counter. Damn, he didn't want to take them anymore.

"So you're willing to take on a washed-up, over-the-hill bull rider?"

"Austin, you're only thirty-two years old. Of course you're not washed up."

"I'm pretty old for a bull rider. It's a young man's sport. The life expectancy is usually about thirty. That's why I have to stay on top, so no one questions it. Well, they do, but if you're not making news, then you're not doing anything." He thought about what he'd just said and for the first time wondered why it mattered anymore. He glanced at Shelby and Ryan. He might have gotten a lot of money, but it seemed his brother was still richer.

The next afternoon, Erin glanced at her watch as she walked out of the doctor's office. She was still on a high after seeing the fertility specialist, Dr. Gail Evans, excited that she'd physically checked out for the IVF procedure.

At thirty-six, along with her previous failed attempts to get pregnant, she didn't have the luxury to wait much longer.

Now all she needed was the money. Enough for not only the procedure, but to support her and her baby for a six-month leave from work. Now that she had the Brannigan job, she could possibly afford to do both.

She desperately wanted to start the series of hormone shots soon, but she wanted the money in hand before she began anything. So many things could go wrong. She still wasn't sure about Austin Brannigan, or that working with him was a good idea. A bull rider? Correction—an arrogant bull rider. No doubt he was used to having his share of women on the circuit.

She climbed into her van, started it up and headed out of the parking lot. Maybe it was time to trade in the too-large vehicle. It had once been convenient for taking Jared around, and when she'd moved here to Hidden Springs, she'd packed nearly everything she owned in the back. For now, the cost of a new vehicle made her cringe. So she had decided to hang on to her van for a while longer.

She turned onto the highway, excited about her future for the first time in a long time. Her dream was finally going to become a reality. Someone with her DNA. Someone to claim her. A family.

She couldn't let anything go wrong. She'd already talked to her supervisor, Shirley, about conflicts with the schedule. Shirley assured her there wasn't a problem as long as she covered her shifts. Then she talked to the orthopedic surgeon, Dr. Kentrell, about Austin's case.

So she was headed to the Circle R Ranch to see Austin Brannigan. She had some questions about the man, but she was going to try to work with him. This money was too good to turn down. All she needed now was to have her new client sign a contract, and they would be good to go to start tomorrow.

In another twenty minutes she'd arrived at the ranch and driven by the main house and onto the gravel driveway that led to Austin's place. Coming around the grove of trees, she spotted something new parked beside the foreman's house.

A large crew-cab Dooley truck, and behind it was a fifth-wheel trailer. What caught her attention was the array of colors. The base of the vehicle was silver detailed with gold and black, and then on the trailer the writing announced World Champion Bull Rider, Austin "The Ace" Brannigan, along with a head shot of the man's face; along the bottom was a list of sponsors.

"There sure is no problem with your ego, Mr. B." Erin climbed out of her van and walked up to the porch. What had she gotten herself into?

In one of the other bedrooms that had been converted into a workout space, Austin sat on the weight bench, lifting the ten-pound weights as he looked at his manager, Jay Bridges.

"I thought you'd be further along," his manager said.

"Hey, the doctor only gave me the okay to start therapy last week," Austin told him.

Austin glared at the fifty-five-year-old man in his standard uniform of a dark suit and cowboy boots, worn even at the rodeo grounds. "So stop pushing me."

The gray-haired manager raised his hands as if he were innocent of any urging. "Whoa, you're the one who wants to get back on the circuit."

There was no denying Jay wanted his moneymaker back to making money. He'd built a reputation of being a go-getter. Austin had to admit he liked that about him.

Jay looked around the new equipment room. "I have to say, Austin, I'm impressed by all this equipment."

"I told you I was going to get back into the arena. I hired a therapist/trainer yesterday."

"I hope it's someone you can trust not to sell your story to the tabloids."

Before he could tell him any more, there was a knock on the door.

Jay frowned. "You expecting anyone?"

"Probably one of my brothers." He continued to lift the weights.

Austin got to his feet, but by the time he got his walker, Jay was already headed to the door.

Erin smiled as a stranger appeared in the doorway. "Hello. I'm here to see Austin Brannigan."

The older man held the door partly closed so she couldn't see inside. "I'm sorry—you must be mistaken. There is a Cullen Brannigan at the main house."

"I'm not here to see Cullen. I'm here to see Austin." She cocked her thumb toward the truck. "You know, the guy whose face is on the trailer. That's who I want to see."

The older man cursed. "Well, that's not going to happen. This is private property, and you need to leave before I have security remove you."

She folded her arms. "Since Cullen Brannigan is the one who hired me, I don't have a problem if you call the sheriff."

"Jay, who's at the door?"

Erin arched an eyebrow. "It's me, Austin, your therapist?"

"Oh, Erin," Austin called to her. "Please come in. Jay, let her in."

Still the man held the door, then reluctantly stepped aside and allowed Erin past.

She stopped and turned to the man named Jay. "If you want to keep Austin's location a secret, I suggest you hide that neon sign outside."

She walked toward Austin as he made his way to the living area.

"Jay, this is my new therapist, Erin Carlton. Erin, this is my manager, Jay Bridges. He drove my rig here."

Erin smiled at Austin. "I can see that. And I think the entire world will see it, too. Tomorrow, there's going to be riding lessons in the corral with several parents bringing their kids. I suggest you move it, at least the trailer."

Austin nodded. "I didn't think about that. Good idea. Let me call Cullen and see if there's room in the garage." He sat down on the sofa and reached for his phone on the table. He punched in the number and began to talk.

Jay walked over to Erin. "What are your credentials for this job?"

"I'm a registered nurse, and I have two years of therapy training. And I worked with my disabled husband."

"Enough to help Austin?"

"I think so," she said. "Better yet, Austin thinks so. Since he only hired me yesterday, we haven't even started yet. But I will work strictly with his doctor's guidelines."

Jay started to speak, but Austin cut him off. "Leave Erin alone, Jay. She's been checked out by my family and by me. Besides, you aren't going to win sparring with her anyway."

Okay, maybe she was beginning to like this man. Her gaze moved over his shorts and tank top. Whoa. He was just as impressive today as yesterday. Sadness took over when she recalled how Jared once looked all trim and muscular.

"Now, go park the trailer in the garage behind the main house," Austin said. "Cullen's there and he'll help you get it inside."

Jay nodded. "Okay, but I'll be back."

Austin got to his feet. "No, Jay. I don't want you here to distract me. I need to concentrate on my therapy. Cullen said he'll give you a ride into town so you can rent a car and get to the airport." He slapped the man on the shoulder. "Call me next week and I'm hoping to have something to tell you."

Jay started to argue, but closed his mouth. "You better call me, or I'll be on your doorstep." He turned to Erin. "Take care of him."

"I'll do my best."

Jay walked out, leaving them alone.

Austin turned to her. "I apologize for Jay. He's a little possessive with me. I can handle it, because he believed in me. And all my endorsements are because of his hard work."

What about the man on the back of the bull? Erin wondered. "So he's the brains behind your talent?"

Austin laughed. "You can say that. The man has even helped me plan for retirement."

"Well, since you don't want to do that yet, maybe we should get down to business." She reached inside her oversize purse, took out his medical folder and a piece of paper.

"I've talked with Dr. Kentrell. We went over your therapy schedule and exercises." She handed him the piece of paper. "So I drew up a contract for my service. It's pretty basic, but I need to protect myself."

Austin sank back onto the sofa and began to read. Erin wrote down the one-hour therapy sessions, twice a day for five days a week, and the dollar amount. The double price he'd offered her yesterday.

He held out a hand. "Do you have a pen?"

She reached back inside her bag, pulled one out and handed it to him. He signed with a flourish and gave paper and pen back to her with a smile.

She felt the reaction clean down to her toes. She had to stop this. "Okay, let's get to work."

Chapter 3

It had been the week from hell.

Austin felt pain and soreness in every muscle in his body. Erin had worked him hard during every session. She didn't believe in going easy, but that was what he liked about her. She'd shown up in the morning after her shift at the convalescent home ready to do her job.

At eight o'clock that morning, he made his way down the hall to the kitchen. He realized he was starting to move a little easier and able to put more weight on his injured leg. That made him hopeful.

He went to the refrigerator and took out some blueberries, then peeled a banana. After he tossed the ingredients into a blender, he added milk and powdered protein, then began to mix the concoction. As much as he wanted a cup of coffee, he needed the energy for his upcoming rehab session. The next hour would be grueling when Erin put him through the series of exercises. He smiled as he poured the smoothie into a glass. He was looking forward to it.

He had just finished his drink when he heard the key in the lock, and then Erin walked in. She was dressed in a pair of black tights and an oversize shirt. Her face was washed clean of any makeup, and her sloppy ponytail bounced as she walked toward him.

She smiled at him. Damn, she was too appealing. "Good morning, cowboy. Good to see you're up."

He shifted his stance. Oh, he was definitely up. "Yeah, well, I can't afford any more demerits."

"Good. I like your go-get-'em attitude."

"Do I get extra points for that?"

"First, you have to show me some hard work today." She walked up to the counter, took down a glass and poured some of the drink from the blender. "I'm gonna need something extra this morning."

He frowned, seeing the fatigue in her eyes. "Rough night?"

"One of my patients, Hattie, was frightened and kept crying for her son to take her home."

Austin's gut tightened watching the tears in Erin's eyes as she told the story.

"We had to restrain her."

"Why didn't her son come to be with her?"

She sighed. "He had been there most of the day, but Hattie only got more agitated with him in the room. That's the awful part about Alzheimer's patients—you don't always know what's best to do for them, and it can change every day. Patients get frightened because they can't remember anything or anyone. It's like they're trapped with strangers."

He could see Erin's intense compassion and got a glimpse of the personal side of this woman. She must be one hell of a nurse.

As if she realized she was exposing a side of herself she didn't want him to see, she turned away. "Sorry, I didn't mean to dump on you." She quickly offered him a smile. "Ready to get to work?"

He nodded and followed Erin into the bedroom. He sat down on the bench and removed his cast. He had a long knit sock to protect his calf and ankle and hide the ugly scar. She knelt in front of him and wrapped a small Velcro weight around his ankle. She looked up at him with those big green eyes. "Is that comfortable?"

He nodded, hating that she could get a reaction from him with just a look. "Yeah, it's fine."

With a nod, she began instructing him on how to do his reps. Moving up and down wasn't easy, especially not when she had him pause and hold it. It didn't take him too long to realize how weak he was, but he refused to cry uncle.

Over the next hour, Austin worked the weights, then the stretches as he labored to get through the series of exercises. He'd done some upper body strength training during his hospital stay, but nearly three months on his back had taken its toll. He'd always prided himself on his strength and agility. He didn't have much of that right now. He felt weak as a kitten.

"Okay, you're done for now." Erin handed him a towel and a bottle of water as he sat up on the bench.

"You sure?" He wiped the sweat from his face. "I mean, you forgot to use the torture device."

"I'll bring that out next week." She arched an eyebrow. "Come on, Austin. You knew this wasn't going to be easy. You're lucky to be standing on two legs. So don't rush it."

Okay, maybe she was right.

He took a drink and Erin did the same. She tipped her head back and took a long swallow of water from the bottle. A trickle of liquid found its way from her mouth to her chin, then down the long arch of her smooth neck.

He gulped the cool liquid, but it wasn't enough to chill his thoughts. Damn. He'd been without female company for too long, recalling the times when he could rodeo all weekend and have some left over for cele-brating. And he meant all night with the women. He brushed aside the memories as he looked down at his scar. He groaned.

The sound got Erin's attention. "Something wrong?"

"Just frustrated. I want to be able to do more, and not have it be so difficult to get there."

"Then use that frustration to drive you to do more, to go an extra step." She grinned. "You'll need it when I turn your sixty-minute sessions into ninety. And I'm not even going to charge you for the extra pain."

He straightened at her comment. Hell, she was right. He had to stop letting his pride get to him, or he'd never get strong enough to ride a bull. "Okay, you're on. I can deal with whatever you dish out."

"Good attitude." Her smile quickly turned into a yawn. "I hate to end this party, but I need to go home and get a few hours' sleep before I'm due back here."

Suddenly he didn't want her to leave. "Sure." He glanced at the clock on the wall. "Hey, you're not going to get much time." He got a crazy thought. "Why not just stay here and sleep?"

Erin looked at him and tried not to be shocked at his suggestion. "Oh, I can't."

"Why not? There's a bed in the other bedroom. It's only a twin, but I think you'll fit." He raised a hand. "Before you argue, by the time you drive to your apartment, sleep, then drive back again for the later session, you lose nearly two hours."

Erin couldn't deny she'd like the extra time. She hadn't been sleeping well lately. Maybe she was taking on too much. She'd rather it be that than this man distracting her.

"Okay, I'll just lie down for a while."

"No, you'll sleep until our next session. That's nearly six hours."

That sounded heavenly. "Okay, I'm too tired to argue. I'll stay. This one time."

With a nod, he reached for his brace and put it on. He stood with his walker and started out the door. "I'm not sure if there are any sheets that would fit it, but you can make do with a flat sheet."

Erin followed him out into the hall, and he opened a linen closet. There were stacks of towels and two sets of sheets for his king-size bed.

She took the linens from him, and their hands brushed in the awkward exchange. She jumped back and he frowned.

"I can make this work." Was she crazy? The man was her client. Yet she found that the simplest touch from this man sensitized her nerve endings. Why had her dormant sex drive suddenly been reawakened?

She glanced at Austin. Or was her condition just the result of this sexy cowboy? It was pretty bad that a man with a walker turned her on. Either way, she needed to keep a safe distance from him. And if she weren't so exhausted, she'd walk out the door. Instead, she was going to sleep in his house.

"I should go make up the bed." She turned and walked into the small bedroom. There was a pillow and a comforter covering the mattress. She quickly went to work adding the sheets. By the time she was finished, there was a knock on the door.

She answered it. Austin smiled as he reached out his hand, holding a T-shirt and a new toothbrush. "I thought you might like something to sleep in."

"What are you doing back here?"

Later that afternoon, Austin stood in the doorway, blocking the entrance to keep his business manager from coming in. Erin was still asleep, and the last person he wanted around here was Jay. He already made too much of her being his therapist.

"What do you mean, what am I doing here? You're not just my client, but also my friend, Austin." With briefcase in hand, Jay stepped over the threshold and into the house. "And I wanted to make sure you're doing okay."

Austin wasn't buying it. "I have two brothers and my father around." Not that the old man cared about him. "My two sisters-in-law keep me fed. So enjoy your off-duty time. Go on a vacation."

Jay frowned. "I wouldn't do that, not when you're still recovering. Besides, I need to keep all the fires going so people won't forget you. We're going to need to plan some big promotion for your comeback."

Damn, why did that make him feel so old? Hell, he

was old. He made his way to the sofa and sat down. "Let me get through this rehab, Jay. Then we'll talk."

The older man frowned. "Why? What's wrong? I knew it—that therapist you hired isn't working out. I can fire her for you. I know of this private rehab center outside Denver."

"No, Jay. I told you, I want to stay here while I recuperate. This is my home, my ranch." He realized he liked having his own place and his brothers around. "Besides, wouldn't the media find me easier in a rehab center?"

His manager shrugged. "You're probably right." He lifted his briefcase onto the table. "The other reason I'm here is I have some papers that need your signature."

Austin leaned back on the sofa. His leg had been throbbing since his last session, but he refused to take any meds. So he wasn't in the mood to go over any contracts, especially something new until he was sure of his future. "Just leave them and I'll go over them later."

Jay frowned. "They can't wait, Austin. They're tax papers. Look, just put your signature on the bottom where I made the *X* and I'll do the rest."

There were things about Jay he loved, like the fact that he'd taken him on as a client when he was a no-name bull rider. They both had made a lot of money on his talent and Jay's business cunning. Austin trusted him, but he wasn't foolish enough to sign anything blind, either. "Are you in town for a while?"

Jay shrugged. "I need to be in Dallas in a few days."

He stood and started for the door, hoping he could get Jay out of the house before he woke Erin. "Okay, I'll get them back to you before then. What hotel are you at?"

"Hotel? I thought you might offer me your guest room."

Austin turned quickly to tell Jay he needed his space

when he caught the end of the coffee table with his walker and it tipped him off balance. He did the wind-mill stroke with his arms, but he only managed to knock over a lamp, and they both crashed to the floor. Pain shot through his butt as he hit the hardwood.

Jay started over to help him when Erin came rushing out from down the hall, all that rich auburn hair flying around her sleep-ridden face. What got his attention was her state of undress. She was wearing his T-shirt that hung to midthigh. Oh, boy, those legs.

"Austin, don't move," she called and was kneeling down at his side. Her hands went to work examining his legs and arms. "Do you hurt anywhere?"

He brushed aside her concern and sat up. "Yeah, my bony butt."

She frowned. "Not your leg?"

A shadow appeared over them. He glanced up at Jay.

"Well, I can understand why you didn't need me here. Seems your therapist has everything under control."

Two hours later, the sun was setting over the moun-tains as Austin sat at the kitchen table enjoying the quiet peacefulness. In the dimming light, he could also see his brother Cullen's horses grazing in the pasture. Thanks to the heavy rainfall over the past few months, the grass was high and green. Soon, the snow would come to the area. Great for the ski resorts around Hid-den Springs, but hard on the cattle rancher. He didn't have to worry since he hoped to be gone by winter. He glanced down at his injured leg. Already he'd gained more physical strength.

His attention strayed when he heard the rattle of the old water pipes from the bathroom. He'd convinced

Erin to take a shower here so she could go straight to the center for her night shift.

Bad idea. His imagination was going wild. All he could picture was her naked body covered in soap, the spray massaging away her troubles and tense muscles.

Suddenly a knock sounded and Austin jumped as the door swung open and his twin brother walked in, carrying a large container of food. "Delivery for Austin Brannigan."

Well, that sure threw cold water on his erotic thoughts. Austin started to get up. "Hey, good to see you."

Cullen motioned for him to stay seated. "Let me come to you, A." He put the food on the stove, then came and sat down with him. "You're in for a treat tonight—Shelby's lasagna. There's also a green salad and garlic bread." Cullen hit the switch and turned on the kitchen light, showing off the room's flaws. Old knotty-pine cabinets and tiled counters, though the appliances were in much better condition.

"Are you sitting in the dark for a reason?"

"No, just watching the sun go down over the mountains. It's an incredible view."

Cullen straddled the chair across from him and gazed out the window. "It does look good. I like the repairs I put in, a lot of painting and new fencing. All in all, the place looks good."

"And I want to pay you for my share," Austin insisted.

"Let's get you in better shape first, and I'll have you work it off. The kids that come here to ride would get a kick out of meeting you." Cullen held up his hand. "I know—we'll wait until you're better."

Austin had to admit he was glad to be in his new home. "Not a bad place to recuperate."

"I guess if you get lonely, I can bring that trailer back here. I can see how you'd miss all that sparkle. The kids were all curious about that 'sparkly' house."

They both laughed, and then Cullen turned to face his twin. "Did I tell you I'm glad you're home?"

Austin could feel the emotions surfacing. "Yeah, you did. You know I'm not going to be here forever?"

"Yeah. Yeah. You're going back to bull riding. But I'd be happy if you'd use the ranch as your home base, and come back and visit your family, brothers and nephews." A grin appeared on his face. "And I'm hoping in the not-too-far-off future, a niece or another nephew."

Austin studied his brother. "A baby. You and Shelby are pregnant?"

Cullen shook his head. "No. We're both busy with everything else right now, especially Shelby's catering business and bakery. And my security business."

In the bedroom, Erin slipped on a fresh shirt she'd found in her bag, then straightened the room and started down the hall. She had a clean uniform at the center and time enough to grab some food on the way before her shift. She stopped, hearing men's voices. *Please, don't let it be Jay Bridges.*

She put her bag next to the sofa, then turned the corner to the kitchen as she called Austin's name.

"Hey, Austin. I just wanted to let you know that I'm leaving." She stopped, seeing the two brothers together. They might not be identical, but pretty close. "Oh, hi, Cullen."

"Hi, Erin." He stood and hugged her. "Hey, how's this guy treating you?"

"Not bad. I just have to listen to a lot of complaining."

"I can't help that. He was born that way." Cullen started out of the room. "Well, I need to get back home to the family. Enjoy the lasagna." He looked at her. "There's plenty for two, Erin. Stay and eat." He waved goodbye and left them.

She turned back to Austin. "I should really go, too."

"No, please, Erin, stay," he pleaded. "I hate to eat alone. Besides, I need to talk to you."

She was weak and relented. "Okay, only because it smells so good. I don't have much time, so you sit there, and I'll get the food." She moved around the kitchen, gathering plates and flatware. Once at the table she sat down across from him and cut a section of the casserole for each of them. She couldn't hold back a groan as she took a bite.

Austin stuck his fork into his mouth, but he couldn't taste anything. Damn if Erin wasn't distracting him again.

"What did you want to talk to me about?" she asked.

"Well, I was thinking about all the time it takes you running back and forth from here, then home and to work. All that trouble has to exhaust you, especially since your apartment is on the other side of town."

With her nod, he went on to say, "The ranch isn't that far from the convalescent center..."

With fork in hand, Erin paused. "What are you trying to say?"

"Well, it only makes sense, since you're running back and forth so much... I don't see why you can't just move in here."

Chapter 4

Later that night, Erin walked down the hall at the convalescent center. Everyone was sleeping soundly in her ward, or so she thought until she peeked into Hattie's room. She heard the quiet sobs and went to see if she was in distress.

The private room was dimly lit, and even with the patient's personal items and pictures, it still looked like a hospital. But sweet Hattie's Alzheimer's disease made it impossible for her to live on her own. With her husband deceased and her three children unable to care for her any longer, she needed to stay here. It was sad to see someone who once had been so vital and active be confined to a room unless medicated, or have an attendant assist her, including to the bathroom.

She walked to the side of the bed, the railing up to keep the slight woman from wandering off. She was crying. Erin immediately spoke her name, then placed a gentle hand on her back.

"Hattie… What's the matter?"

The older woman raised her head to show the tears that filled her blue eyes. Her bony veined hand reached out and gripped Erin's. "I want my Johnny. His last letter said he was coming home. He said the war was over, so we can get married now."

"Sshh…it's okay, Hattie." Erin knew that Hattie's husband had been gone for over five years, but in her heart and world, he was still very much alive. "He will be here soon. You know all that red tape in the army. Johnny wouldn't miss your wedding."

A sweet smile appeared on her lined face. Her eyes were bright with tears. "I can't wait to be his wife." She sighed. "And he looks so handsome in his uniform."

"I can't wait to meet him," Erin told her. "Do you want me to read his letter to you again?"

"Yes, please. I would like that." Hattie shifted against the pillows. "Johnny writes me the most wonderful letters."

Erin reached into the bedside table and took out a letter that Hattie's children had given her. How wonderful that in this woman's now-confused world, she remembered the love of her life.

Erin couldn't help but wonder if she would ever experience that kind of love. Once she thought she'd met the man of her dreams. She found that her husband's love hadn't been nearly as strong as she'd hoped. Over a year after his death, and she was still turned off men. Suddenly a picture of Austin Brannigan flashed in her head. Okay, maybe not all men.

She pushed the thought aside as she opened the yellowed paper and was transformed back over sixty years as she began to read, "'My dearest Hattie...'"

The next morning at nearly nine o'clock, Austin began to pace back and forth, and occasionally he looked out the window. Where was Erin? The session was to begin an hour ago. Had she decided not to come anymore since he'd suggested she move in here?

He leaned against the counter in front of the kitchen window, his leg aching like the devil. He reached for his walker. He still hated using the damn thing. He hoped that with Erin's help, soon he'd be walking on his own.

"But she needs to be here."

So where was his therapist? He was about to call her cell again when he heard her van coming up the gravel road. Seconds later she came rushing in the door. She was dressed in her familiar tights, oversize shirt and tennis shoes, with that silly large bag tossed over her shoulder.

"I'm sorry," she said. "I left work without my cell phone, and I was on my way back to get it when I got a flat tire. So I couldn't even call you."

He felt relieved. "Did you get roadside service to change it for you?"

She frowned at him. "Yeah, I'm roadside service. I'm just glad my spare had air in it."

Damn. He pictured her in all that traffic and didn't like her taking those kinds of risks. "I'm glad you're okay. I guess we don't realize how great cell phones are until we really need them."

"No kidding." She sighed. "I know we're running late, but would you mind if I had a cup of tea before we start?"

"Of course not. I think I'll join you."

She nodded. "Good idea. You sit down and I'll put on the water."

She moved around the kitchen efficiently, filling the kettle, then turned on the burner to heat the water.

She reached into the cupboard where there were several bottles of his pills. She found the one she wanted, then set it on the table. "Have you taken any pain meds this morning?"

He shook his head at her not-so-subtle hint. "You know I don't like how they make me feel."

"I've heard that argument a lot of times," she acknowledged. "But because you are in pain, you don't work to your full potential while doing the therapy. So just take it for the session."

She walked back to the table, causing her ponytail to swing from side to side. She looked so young and carefree, but the full curves said she was all woman.

His attention switched to her small hands as she dropped the tea bags into the cups. He recalled the feeling of those strong fingers against his sore muscles.

Her voice drew him back as she continued. "The pill is only effective for four hours. Weigh that against better results during therapy."

"What are you, a spokesman for the pharmaceutical company?"

"Just your therapist. You hired me for my guidance and abilities, so use them."

"How do you know I wasn't working hard?"

"Because I can see you tense and grimace during your workouts."

"Dang, woman, you're not going to let this go, are you?"

"Not as long as you're being so stubborn." She

opened the bottle, shook out one pill and placed it in front of him.

The kettle whistled and she filled both their mugs, then sat down across from him again. She sent him a challenging look that caused a reaction he hadn't felt in a long time. He glanced away, then tossed the pill into his mouth. He reached for the bottle of water and took a drink.

She smiled. "Good. I like my men cooperative." She brought the cup to her mouth and took a tentative sip.

"It's good that I'm still in that classification."

She arched an eyebrow. "Are we feeling a little emasculated?"

He looked away. "More like helpless."

"Considering the severity of your accident, you are a very lucky man. Not all are so fortunate, so don't go feeling sorry for yourself, cowboy, or I'm walking out the door. And that's another thing. One day, you will walk again. You might have a limp, but you'll be able to stand on your own two legs. So stop with the pitiful act."

Her words stung. "We signed a contract."

"You forgot to read the fine print, Mr. Brannigan. I only work with patients who give one hundred percent." Tears welled in her eyes. "You need to count your blessings. Not everyone gets a second chance. Excuse me." She got up and left the room before he could speak.

He heard the bathroom door close. Oh, boy. He needed to learn when to keep his mouth shut, or he was going to lose this woman. He just realized he'd be losing more than a therapist.

Erin looked at herself in the bathroom mirror. What was wrong with her, acting like a fool with Austin? She couldn't even blame it on last night with Hattie or the flat tire this morning. The problem was she needed to do a better job of handling her reaction to the man. That meant to think of him only as her client, a client who was paying her very well so she could have her dream.

She splashed cold water on her face, washing away any makeup left, but she wasn't going to take the time to reapply it. Good—a billion freckles should scare him off.

There was a soft knock on the door. "Erin…is everything okay?"

She released a long breath and opened the door to find Austin standing there with his walker.

"First, I need to apologize," she said. "I acted very unprofessional. I could say I had a rough night and morning, but that's still no excuse." She stole a glance at the too-sexy cowboy. "Truth is, Austin, I won't coddle my clients. If you want a babysitter, then I'm not the person for the job. I'm the person who's going to work you hard in every session. It's what your doctor ordered for your recovery. You knew it wasn't going to be easy when you started. So if we're not on the same page, I'll tear up our contract and leave."

"Damn, woman. You're tough." He grinned. "I like that, but that doesn't mean I won't complain. Hell, I'm paying you enough I should be able to bellyache now and then. So unless you need to yell at me some more, let's get started."

She felt relieved. "No, I don't want to yell right this minute, but I'll let you know. Come on—time to get to work." She walked out into the hall, then into the therapy room and waited until Austin got to the weight bench. She set the walker aside, then knelt down to remove the cast. She pulled down the protective sock and examined the wide, puckered scar.

"The incision has healed nicely."

"Still off-putting, especially to women."

Was he thinking about the women he wanted sex with? Of course, he was young and healthy, and had been without a woman for a while. She didn't doubt that was a long time for the handsome bull rider. That made her think about her own sorry sex life. It had been non-existent for years. Now all she needed to think about was a baby. Her baby.

She looked at Austin. "Some people might be, but if they care about you it shouldn't matter." She shrugged. "As a woman…it wouldn't bother me, that is…if I cared about the man." She glanced away when his gaze got too intense. "I mean, my husband had taken shrapnel in his leg, and it tore both the calf and thigh muscles." She quickly changed the subject back to him. "You've lost some muscle, so it will look a little different than your other leg. And since you live in boots and jeans, I don't see the problem."

That was enough questions. She stood, tied her shirt-tails into a knot at her waist. "We should get started while your meds are working."

The next hour passed quickly as she had him work with leg weights, then moved on to resistance training. He grunted and groaned as he did the up-and-down motions she instructed him to do.

Finally, she called a halt to the exercise and handed him an ice pack to put on his leg. "Since you worked so hard, I have a treat for you." She raised her hand. "Take off your shirt. I'll be right back."

Austin did as she'd instructed. What kind of torture was she about to think up now?

He didn't have to wait long. She returned carrying a folded table with a handle. She set it down on the floor, then pulled open the legs and sat it up. "This should help release some tension in your neck and shoulders."

She left, then returned with a sheet and towels. "How do you feel about a massage?" She spread a sheet on the table.

"I think I can be convinced." He got up on his good leg, and with two hops he was on the table, lying face-down. He laid his head on his folded arms.

She arranged the ice pack under his injured calf, and then she began to work her magic. First he felt the oil dribble on his back, then her hands. Oh, God. Her hands. He groaned as she moved those incredible fingers over his tight muscles. He tried to will himself to relax, but his body wouldn't cooperate.

"Okay, I'm begging you, never stop what you're doing."

"I'm glad you like it. Just part of the service when you work hard." He could hear the humor in her voice. "And you gave me a lot of effort today."

He felt her fingers move across his shoulders, down his back, then his spine. He shivered as those fingers dug into his waist. Whoa, what kind of magic was she working?

"How does that feel?"

"Heavenly."

Her hands continued their journey over his gym shorts to his thighs. Okay, his relaxation just turned to stimulation as her fingers dug into his muscles at the tops of his thighs, then slowly worked their way down to his knees. It was pure agony and getting even more uncomfortable, possibly embarrassing.

All at once, she stopped, then placed a warm blanket over him. "Rest. I'll be back in ten minutes." She left the room, leaving him aroused and aching. He turned his thoughts to all the different ways he could return the favor.

Later that day Austin wandered around the quiet house. He'd managed to convince Erin to stay and nap in the back bedroom. He knew she'd had a rough shift the night before, and he wanted her to get as much sleep as possible.

He sat down on the sofa and began surfing the channels on the flat-screen television. He needed to forget about the woman tucked into bed at the end of the hall. This time she hadn't borrowed one of his T-shirts. Did that mean she wasn't wearing anything?

He groaned and began punching the remote once again, needing to forget the auburn-haired therapist. Just hours ago, that same woman used her magical hands to drive him crazy. His body stirred with the memory.

Finally he gave up and tossed the remote on the coffee table. He made his way to the kitchen table and began going through the papers Jay left the other day. His manager was right. They were boring tax papers, along with his 401(k) reinvestment release.

At the bottom of the stack, he found a recent bank statement with a note attached from his accountant, wanting him to okay payment of some sort of hospital bill.

Austin usually went through the financials every month, but since the accident he hadn't had the chance.

Even though he trusted everyone who worked for him, he still needed to be alert about where his money was going. Most of his endorsement funds were put in savings and stocks. He wasn't foolish enough to leave everything in his one account. His attention was drawn to the bank's monthly electronic transfers, his utilities and upkeep on his condo in Denver.

Someday he'd hoped for a few acres with a house and barn so he could have a couple of horses. And now since his stepmother's passing, he owned part of this large ranch. He found he liked it here. Like Cullen had suggested, maybe this place could be a home base while he was on the circuit.

He frowned upon seeing an unfamiliar monthly transfer to one DJ Lynch. The name sounded somewhat familiar. He looked at the sum and decided he definitely needed to contact Jay before he signed anything. He also found a form to continue temporary power of attorney for his manager. Jay had had that control while he'd been in the hospital and under the influence of drugs, but now that Austin was back, he wanted to handle his own finances.

His silence was interrupted by a knock on the door. He checked his watch and wondered who would be coming by in the middle of the day. He stood, gripped hold of his walker and went to answer it.

He opened the door and found a tall, slender gray-haired man standing on the stoop. A strange feeling came over him, and he wasn't sure he could handle it as he stared at the man he hadn't seen in years.

"Hello, son. It's been a long time."

Cullen had told him that Neal Brannigan had retired from the police force, sold the family ranch outside Denver and moved here. Austin managed to find his voice. "Yeah, I'll say so, about ten years. What brings you by?"

He saw his father flinch, but he couldn't feel sorry for him. *You get what you give.*

"I was hoping we might be able to talk," his father said.

"So you can tell me how I've been wasting my life? No, thanks."

"I deserve that, but no, son, I only wanted to see how you've been doing."

"As you can see, I'm standing."

He smiled. "I'm happy about that."

Austin moved aside and allowed his father to come in.

His father glanced around the sparsely finished room. "The place looks good. A lot better since it's been cleaned and painted."

"Yeah, Cullen and Trent made it livable."

Neal Brannigan nodded. "It's good to have you here. I mean, I hate that you were hurt, but I'm glad you get to come here to be with your brothers."

"I'm not staying long," he warned. "As soon as I get the okay from my doctor, I'm back on the circuit. Nothing you say will change that."

His father raised a calming hand. "I'm not going to try to stop you. You're an adult and can make your own decisions."

Who was this man? Not the tough-as-nails police captain who'd been a no-show father. He never stood up for his sons and hated that one of them became a bull rider. Okay, so most parents wouldn't like that, either. "That's not what you told me the last time we were together."

"I hope I've learned from my mistakes."

This admission had Austin a little off center. "You're saying you want to see me ride?"

Neal nodded. "I've already had the pleasure a few years back in Lubbock, Texas." He smiled. "I believe you won that day."

Austin frowned, recalling that had been the last time he saw his stepmother, Leslie. "I remember Mom being there, but where were you?"

"I thought it might be better if you spent time with her." He saw the flash of sadness. "Leslie had just learned about her cancer. Even I didn't know the extent until much later."

Austin's leg began to ache, and he went to sit down at the table. He offered his father the other chair. "I wish I had known. I could have spent more time with her."

Neal sat down. "You know your mother. She didn't want you boys to make a fuss or disrupt your lives." His gaze went to Austin. "It's the way she wanted it, son."

Austin stiffened at the word *son* again. He was troubled that his father had suddenly remembered him as his child. "I'm sorry I didn't get back to the funeral last year. I was in Australia competing. By the time I heard the news, it was too late to come back in time."

His father raised his hand. "It's okay, son. Your mother knew you loved her. She was proud of you."

"I know Leslie was my stepmother, but I always thought of her as the real thing."

"She felt the same way about you boys, too."

Austin felt the old bitterness surface. "Yeah, she didn't question our choices like you did."

The old man cringed. "I know. I had to be right about everything, and look where it got me. I pushed you boys so hard I ended up driving you away. If there was a way I could change those years, I would. I'm most sorry for letting my job be my top priority." Those blue eyes met his. "I had sons and a wife who needed me at home. I apologize to you, Austin. You deserved a father to be there for you. I know I can't ask you to forget, but I was hoping while you're here you'd let me come by occasionally."

Austin felt a sudden weight on his chest. He didn't want to feel anything. He'd left home all those years ago to not deal with this man. So why now did he want the man's approval so badly? "I guess I wouldn't mind that."

Chapter 5

Two days later, after forty-eight hours off from the center and from Austin, Erin was ready to go back to work.

Or was she?

She'd planned to catch up on all the sleep she'd lost, grocery shop and clean her apartment. Sleep had eluded her, but her one-bedroom apartment looked pretty good. Her cupboards were stocked with food, but she had no appetite. As a nurse, she knew better than to let herself get run-down, especially holding down two jobs.

In a few weeks, if everything went as planned, she'd be beginning her hormone shots. She needed to be at her best, and not spend her time thinking about a man who'd be gone from her life as soon as he could stand on both legs. And seeing how hard Austin Brannigan worked during his therapy, it would be soon.

She drove her van along the highway, then took the

exit to the Circle R Ranch. How had he done without her? Even though he had a fill-in therapist, she still worried about him.

Better question, why was she letting this bull rider get to her? Never before had she allowed anything personal to happen between her and a client. Even during all the months Jared had been overseas, she'd never thought about another man.

Now she'd been spending her time looking up the rodeo cowboy on the internet. He was the face of the pro circuit with all his ads. Anything from cowboy boots to tight fitted jeans. And there was no doubt the man photographed well. That didn't mean he wasn't arrogant and a womanizer. She needed to stay away from him, outside of her job, of course. She had her future all planned out, and it didn't include another male. No, thanks. She'd been there.

She smiled as she drove up to the house and shut off the engine. Unless, of course, her baby was a boy.

The front door opened and she saw Austin. She climbed out and started to greet him when he stopped her.

"Where have you been? You're late."

She glanced at her watch. Maybe by a few minutes. "So dock my pay." Even in his fitted T-shirt and gym shorts, he wasn't so appealing at the moment. "Since when are you so anxious to start therapy?"

He shook his head. "I'm not. I just need something to distract me. And that therapist you sent me was a joke."

"Jason? You know he trains pro athletes? He volunteers at the center and was doing me a favor. What did you say to him?"

Austin stepped aside and let her into the house. He

hated that he took his frustration out on her. "Nothing. Okay, maybe he wasn't so bad."

"Not so bad? He should be the one who's handling your therapy."

He didn't want anyone else but Erin. "No. You're the one I hired. We have a contract."

"I know we have a contract, but if you keep yelling at me, you aren't going to like where I shove it."

Austin had to fight to keep from smiling. Damn, he'd missed her these last few days. Her freshly scrubbed face, sassy ponytail and sexy body in those tights. He quickly pushed aside his wandering thoughts. "Okay, okay, I'm sorry. It's just that it's been so boring around here."

She set her bag down. "What about your family? Haven't they been over to see you?"

He groaned. "All the time. It's great, but I feel like I'm about to crawl out of my skin."

She smiled. "Okay, how about this? We play hooky this morning, but only for about an hour."

He liked the sound of that. Miss Innocent Erin was stepping over the line. Okay, he was ready. "What do you have in mind?"

"Let me make a call first." She dug out her phone and punched in some numbers as she walked out of ear-shot. What was she up to? He didn't have to wait long, because she came back to him in a minute.

"Go put on a pair of sweatpants and a jacket."

"Why?"

She frowned. "You're on a need-to-know basis." She motioned for him to go. "Just do it."

Austin wasn't used to taking orders, not for a long time, but he was willing now if it got him out of the house. Using the walker, he made his way down the hall and dug through his limited supply of clothes. Maybe he could get Cullen to do a little shopping for him. He finally found a pair of sweatpants, and with a pair of scissors, he cut open the left leg to fit over his cast. Excited to get out of the house, he grabbed a hooded jacket, zipped it up, then headed out to the living room.

Erin had put on an oversize sweatshirt. "Ready?"

"You bet," he said and followed her to the door, grabbed a straw cowboy hat off the hook, then continued on.

Outside he was met by the bright sunlight. He tipped his hat lower and saw the golf cart headed their way.

"Hey, bro," Cullen called as he parked and got out. "I hear you're being a real stinker."

He couldn't deny he was disappointed to see Cullen. "Not any more than any other day. Are you our chauffeur?"

His brother pointed to his sheriff's badge on his uniform shirt. "Not today. I need to protect the good citizens of Hidden Springs, but I have no doubt Erin can handle the job." He looked at her. "Just leave him out in the pasture if he gives you any back talk." He nodded toward the mountains. "Just stay on the dirt roads and you should be okay. And Shelby sent along a care basket for your outing."

"We aren't going far," Erin said. "Just to get a little fresh air."

With that, his brother began to walk back to the main house. "I'll drive," Austin announced. Leaving his walker, he balanced on his good leg and took two careful hops and made his way to the cart.

"Not hardly," Erin answered.

"Why not? I won't be using my injured leg."

"That's right, because you'll be in the passenger seat, riding." She arched an eyebrow. "You do remember how to ride, don't you? Or do I need to draw horns on the front of the cart so you can pretend you're on a bull?"

He gripped the metal bar. The woman had a mouth on her. One day she was going to push him too far. "Okay, you win this one." He climbed in the passenger side.

Erin placed her bag on the backseat next to a wicker basket, then took the spot behind the wheel.

"Do you know how to drive one of these carts?" he asked.

She nodded. "I sometimes have to drive around the center when I go from building to building."

They hit a bump and she slowed down. "Of course, that was on a paved road."

Austin looked out at the horses grazing in the pasture. He knew most of the equines on the ranch were past their prime and were used at the therapy riding center. "Those must be some of Cullen's rescues. Could we stop?"

"Sure." She managed to get the cart pretty close to the fence.

He gripped the side of the cart and pulled himself up and out.

"Hey, wait," she called, but he was already out and had hopped two steps before she caught up with him at the fence. "Listen, Austin, you can't take these chances."

"Lighten up, Erin. I'm okay." He truly felt he was. In the past few weeks, he'd gained a lot of strength back.

"I wasn't going to stop you, just help you."

He looked down at those startling green eyes and

her hair blowing in the breeze. Damn, she was pretty. "I promise, the next time I'll wait for you."

"You better, or there'll be hell to pay."

Before he could think up some enjoyable torture for her, he turned toward the pasture. He stuck his fingers in his mouth and gave a sharp whistle. Soon two of the horses came to the railing. One was a gray gelding.

"Hey, guy. You must be Cloud. Ryan's buddy." Austin rubbed the horse's head and muzzle and inhaled his scent. He'd missed those familiar smells.

Erin watched a gentler side of Austin Brannigan. Mr. Tough Guy was a softy when it came to horses. "Seems you made a friend," she said.

"Yeah, I miss this." He gently stroked the animal. "It's been a while since I owned a horse. I have a chance to buy some property outside Denver. There are a couple of horses on the ranch that I wouldn't mind having, either. There was also a good-looking chestnut stallion named Wildfire and a sweet filly called Peanut."

So he'd thought about settling down. "Peanut? What kind of name is that for a horse?"

He laughed, and her heart took a little tumble. "Her registered name is a mile long. She's tiny, only about fourteen hands high. If you let her, she'll follow you around like a puppy."

Erin wasn't sure about horses. They were big and intimidating. Suddenly the other horse took notice of her, and before she could get out of the way, he nudged her. She jumped back with a gasp.

Austin frowned. "What? Don't tell me you're afraid of horses?"

"I'm not afraid. I'm just not used to being around them."

"So you're a city girl?"

"I grew up in Las Vegas, in town."

"Did you ever get to NFR there?"

"National Finals Rodeo?" She shook her head. "No, but I heard you did."

He gave her that cocky grin she'd come to expect, but also enjoyed. "I've been there a few times. And I walked away a winner, too."

"Good for you." She studied him for a moment. "Winning is important to you."

Even under the shade of his hat, she saw his expression change. "You get noticed when you're number one."

"You also get noticed if you do good things."

His shaggy blond hair brushed his collar as a sexy smile appeared on his handsome face. "And bad things, too." He winked.

"I have no doubt you're good at being bad."

He made his way closer to her. "Oh, yeah. That's all the fun."

She swallowed hard.

He turned his attention back to the horses. "Here are some things you need to know about horses. They're easily spooked, so talk in a soft, soothing voice. If you feed them anything like an apple or carrot, you flatten your hand out." He took hold of her hand to show her, and warmth spread through her. "They can't decipher food from fingers. They love being touched and stroked." He took her hand again and ran it along Cloud's forehead.

She couldn't help but smile. "He's soft." She looked at Austin and realized how close they were. So close she could see green flecks in his gray eyes. She glanced away. "I know this is fun, but you should get off your leg. So say goodbye to your friends."

She waited, then helped Austin back to the cart. "You ready to go back to the house?"

"No. Come on, Erin. You can't say you don't want to hang outside a little longer. Look around at this scenery. Inhale the clean air. Soon winter will be here and we'll be stuck inside."

"Okay, but you better stay in the seat, or I'll tie you to it."

He raised his hands in surrender. "I promise, I'll be good."

She saw that ornery grin. She didn't doubt Austin Brannigan was good at many things, but following rules wasn't one of them. "Now you're just outright lying." She didn't wait for an answer and pressed on the pedal and drove off.

Ten minutes later, she stopped under a grove of trees that overlooked the open pastures. "It's hard to believe a person is lucky enough to own all this land. You and Cullen are very fortunate."

He nodded. "Yeah, my stepmother was a generous woman. When Leslie divorced Trent's father, she moved to Denver. That's where she met my father, and took on not only raising her son, but ten-year-old twin boys."

Erin knew the sad story about the death of Trent's young brother, Christopher. The nine-year-old boy fell off his horse and died. The family never recovered from the tragedy.

"Leslie loved us. But I wasn't much of a son when I never came back home for visits. I'll always regret that."

"I met her once when I came to town when Trent and Brooke had baby Christopher. She seemed so sweet, and she beamed over her grandchild." She turned toward Austin. "You are lucky to have had her."

"Believe me, I know how fortunate I was, but I realized too late. My father kept reminding me of that all my life."

"That's a parent's job." Erin reached into the backseat and opened the small basket. She took out two travel mugs of coffee, labeled with their names, and handed Austin his. Next, she handed him the wrapped sweet roll. They sat there and ate their treats as the sun began to warm the day.

"Does your family live in Las Vegas?"

She wadded up the paper and used a napkin to clean the frosting from her fingers. "No, they passed away a long time ago. They were older by the time I came along. My mother died when I was in college. My father couldn't seem to manage without her and was gone the next year."

Austin turned to her, his intense gaze telling her he wasn't going to drop the subject. "That's tough."

She nodded. "Yeah, school was harder, but my parents left me enough money to get my nursing degree."

"Is school where you met your husband?"

She hated bringing up old memories. "Aren't we full of questions this morning?"

He shrugged. "Hey, my life has been an open book. Just getting to know you, too."

"Okay, here it is. I met Jared when he brought his friend into the emergency room where I worked. He was dressed in his Marine Corps uniform and he charmed the socks off me, and a lot more. I was barely twenty-three when we got married. He was a career soldier and was shipped overseas right after our honeymoon. Over the years, he went back several more times."

She felt the tears filling her eyes, and emotions clogged her throat. "On his last tour, he returned home as a disabled vet, and died eighteen months ago. I closed my business, Carlton Care Facility, sold our home and moved here to start over. End of story."

He flashed a concerned look. "I'm sorry, Erin. I didn't mean to bring up memories."

"It's okay." She turned the key. "We need to get back for your therapy." She was angry with herself because she knew it was never a good idea to get personal with a client. She had to keep focused on the one objective, having her new life, her baby. That was why she was doing this.

She glanced at the man across from her. Austin Brannigan wasn't in any part of her future.

After his therapy session later that day, Austin moved around the house quietly so as not to disturb Erin sleeping in the bedroom. He was surprised when she agreed to stay through his second workout, especially after he'd overstepped and asked about her marriage.

He sat down at the table and drank some water, wondering about the man she loved so deeply. What did that kind of love feel like? With his traveling from town to town, he'd never stayed anywhere long enough to get to know a woman. And that was how he liked it. No strings attached. He had more to do, more to achieve on the circuit.

He couldn't see himself settling down and having a family. Even after all these years, he could still hear his father's voice in his head, telling him what a disappointment he'd been to him.

Austin felt his chest tighten. What boy didn't want his father's approval? Yet nothing he did was good enough for Neal Brannigan. Even when the old man sat here the other day and said how sorry he was for being a bad dad, Austin still had trouble believing him.

Only sheer determination had him leaving home at eighteen and getting involved in riding bulls for a living. He looked down at his injured leg. If he couldn't get back into the sport, then he'd be a failure, just as his father predicted.

He chuckled. Not that much of a failure. Thanks to his talent for investing, he had enough money to do anything. Whatever the hell that was.

He heard a sudden cry. He stood, grabbed his walker and made his way down the hall, hearing Erin's distressed voice. He went to the closed door. When she cried out again, he went inside the dimly lit room. In the bed, she was thrashing around and crying out, "No! No! You can't leave me."

Austin went to her immediately and sat down on the mattress. He shook her arm. "Erin, wake up. It's me, Austin."

Her eyes shot open, and she gasped his name. "Austin. Oh, God." She launched herself into his arms, clinging to him like a lifeline.

"It's okay. I got you." His hand cupped the back of her head, trying to soothe her trembling. "Nothing's going to hurt you." He meant it. She was safe with him.

He held her for what seemed like an eternity, before she raised her head. She wiped at the tears in her eyes, but kept her head down. "I'm sorry. I didn't mean to break down like this."

"Hey, there's nothing to be ashamed of. You had a nightmare. Do you want to talk about it?"

She moved away from him. He immediately missed the feel of her body against his, the scent of her hair.

She wrapped her arms around her raised legs. "I don't know what happened. I haven't had that dream for so long."

"Do you remember what it was about?"

She nodded, and a tear slid down her cheek. "Yes. It was the night my husband died." Her watery gaze met his. "The night he took his life."

Chapter 6

The shock of Erin's words hit Austin hard. He wasn't sure what to do or say. "How can I help?"

She shrugged her shoulders. "What can anyone do? Jared decided that life wasn't worth the effort, so he overdosed on pills and ended it."

"I'm sorry" was all he could manage to say.

"No, I'm the one who should be sorry." Erin swung her legs around and got off the bed. "I don't usually dump personal business on my clients. It's not professional."

He watched her move around the room, the dimming afternoon light leaving shadows against the walls. She grabbed a pair of sweatpants off the chair and slipped them on under her oversize T-shirt. He got a quick glimpse of her legs, and a sudden charge zinged through his body.

"Well, we've been practically living together for the past two weeks," he continued, trying to refocus. "You've had your hands all over me. If that isn't personal, I don't know what is."

She glared at him. "Does everything have to be sexual to you?"

He couldn't help but grin, but mainly to relieve the tension between them. "Well, darlin', what do you think? I've got to live up to my reputation." He patted his bad leg. "Right now, it's all I got."

She raised a hand. "Just stop with the pity talk. There's more to life than losing a few women fawning over you. I'm sure when you're back on both legs, there'll be plenty of females who want to see your... scar." She stormed out of the room.

That stung. He followed, but she was already in the kitchen before he caught up to her. "That's not fair. My career takes me all over the country. And as you know, I'm not ready to give that up. And yes, I meet women."

She balked at his words. "That's just it. Women get to make all the concessions, and men get to do whatever they want. You breeze into town and make your conquests. Then you're gone."

It sounded worse when she said it. "Hold it right there. I don't bed every woman I meet. Believe me, if I partied as much as you claim I do, or the media, I could have never held on to my world ranking. I spend a lot of time working out to stay in condition. I don't drink much, and I try to get enough sleep, because I'm hauling a trailer across the country. If I did any celebrating, it was after the events."

Austin raked a hand through his hair. Why did he care about her opinion, anyway? "Yes, there have been women, and yes, I enjoyed their company, but also their friendships. The one thing I never did was make promises that I couldn't keep."

The room was silent as she put on the kettle for tea. She refused to look at him.

"Is that what your husband did? Make you promises he didn't keep?"

She shot him an intense glare. "It doesn't seem to matter anymore. Jared is gone, and I'm making a new life."

Austin saw her sadness and her anger. "What did he promise you, Erin?"

She shook her head. "I don't want to talk about it."

"I thought we were friends."

She arched an eyebrow. "You're my client."

"And friend. Because if you weren't, I'd never let you boss me around."

That brought a trace of a smile to her face.

"Well, you are bossy," he told her.

"Of course I am. It's the only way I can get you to work."

"You might try being sweet and see what it gets you."

Erin couldn't handle being congenial with the man. Austin was quickly tearing down her defenses, and she had no safeguard for that. The kettle whistled, and she turned off the flame. She reached for two mugs, inserted the tea bags and poured the water in.

They sat down and drank in silence until Austin spoke up. "I'm truly sorry about your husband, Erin. I can't imagine going through something like that."

She nodded. "I had good friends. Brooke has helped me a lot. Her mother, Coralee, was one of my live-in boarders at Carlton Care Facility. After Brooke found her sister, Laurel, then married Trent, she convinced me to move here, too."

"I, for one, am glad she did. I can't imagine going through this without your help."

"That's because I put up with your shenanigans."

He tossed his head back and laughed. Her heart raced seeing the handsome and carefree man. She understood why women were so drawn to him.

He squeezed her hand. "You're priceless, Erin."

"That's only because you insisted on paying me twice the money."

He sobered, his gaze locked on her. "And you're worth every penny. I've made so much of an improvement since you've taken over my therapy. I believe I'm on the road back." He grinned. "Those drill-sergeant tactics of yours are working."

His praise meant a lot to her. Darn, this man was coming to mean a lot to her. She glanced at the clock. "We better start our evening session. Are you ready for your workout?"

They both stood and headed for the bedroom. "Oh, I forgot to tell you. Next week you have an appointment with your surgeon in Denver. Do you have someone to take you?"

He looked at her. "Could I convince you to drive me?"

Say no. "I'm not sure about my schedule. Let me get back to you."

"I'd appreciate it. Thank you."

They had about made it to the room when there was a knock on the door. Erin looked at Austin. "Do you want me to get it?"

"Sure. You're faster."

She went and opened the door to find an older man of about fifty.

He touched the brim of his cowboy hat. "Evening, ma'am. I'm looking for Austin Brannigan. Is he here?"

"May I say who's calling?"

"I'm Dan Lynch. He knows me from the pro rodeo circuit."

Erin turned to see that Austin was on his way toward her. He looked past her, saw the man and smiled.

"Hey, Dan. What in the world are you doing here?"

Since Austin seemed okay with the stranger, Erin stepped aside and allowed him in the house.

Dan looked Austin over. "I'm glad to see you're doing so well. You were in pretty bad shape."

"Don't remind me, but thanks to a great surgeon, I'm back on my feet. Almost." Austin came up next to Erin. "Dan Lynch, this is Erin Carlton. She's my therapist and helping me get my leg strength back."

"Nice to meet you, Erin."

"You, too, Dan." She sensed the two had some business to talk about. She looked at Austin. "I'll go and get things ready in the equipment room. Don't be too long."

Austin watched Erin leave the room, then turned back to Dan. He wasn't sure why the man was here, but he was going to find out. "How did you know how to find me?"

"I contacted Jay Bridges. I told him I'd waited long enough and needed to see you in person."

Why wouldn't Jay tell him about Dan? "Okay, sit down and talk to me. How is Megan? She's about ready to graduate from college, right? I tried to call her a few times, but she never returned them." He thought that

was just as well. He didn't want to have a serious relationship.

Dan lowered his head. "She was diagnosed with leukemia last spring."

He'd cared about Megan. A lot. "Oh, God." Dan was
a single father, and he'd been bringing his daughter to
the rodeos since she was a little kid. She'd grown into
a beautiful twenty-four-year-old woman. " Do you need
my help? I have money for a specialist."

Dan shook his head as he blinked several times. "No,
it's too late. Meg lost the battle last month."

Austin swallowed. "She died?"

Dan nodded. "I would have gotten ahold of you
sooner, but you had the accident. Your manager wasn't
very cooperative, either." He blew out a breath. "And I
had so much to deal with."

He was in shock. "Damn. I'm so sorry, Dan." His
chest tightened, and suddenly he realized how much
he'd cared about her. "Megan was such a sweet person.
She didn't deserve this."

The older man studied him, then finally said, "I
didn't know you and Megan were…together. When I
found out, I can't say I was happy about it. And I also
knew that she's loved you since she was a kid." He
sighed. "And you always treated her special. I appreciate that."

Austin was ashamed. He had taken advantage of the
situation. "I hope you believe me. I cared about her, too.
But I knew that I could never be the man she needed."
He shook his head, trying to hold back his emotions, not
believing that she was gone. "What can I do?"

"I honestly didn't want to come here, but Megan
made me promise, so I didn't have a choice." He stood.

"She left something very precious for you. I'll be right back."

Austin laid his head back on the sofa and closed his eyes. Oh, God, not sweet Megan. How could she be gone? She'd probably been the best thing that ever happened in his life. They'd spent so much time talking and sharing things. She understood so much, and she'd cared about him. He hoped she'd known that he cared about her, too. Hearing the door open, he wiped away the tears that had found his cheeks. He sat up and saw Dan holding a baby carrier. He set it down on the coffee table.

Austin's heart began to drum in his chest.

Dan nodded. "This is your daughter, Lillian Katherine Brannigan."

Shell-shocked, Austin stared at the infant. She was cute, her cheeks were rosy, and her eyes were closed, so he couldn't tell anything about her, except she couldn't be his child, could she?

"Dan?"

"I'm only passing on what Megan told me. You're the father of her baby."

"Hell, Dan," he said, but the fight left him. He knew he couldn't deny it. Not after that weekend they spent together during her spring break. "Why didn't she contact me?"

The older man pulled an envelope from his pocket. "This is a letter from Megan. She said it will explain everything." He went outside and brought in two more bags. "There's food and diapers and clothes."

Panic surged through him. "You're leaving her here?"

Dan's eyes filled. "Hell, you think I want to? She's

my granddaughter, my wife's namesake. All I have left of my Megan. But I have rodeo contracts to fill over the next few months, and I need the money." Dan pulled a handkerchief out of his pocket and wiped his eyes. "If you'll allow me, I want to be in Lilly's life."

Still dazed, he answered immediately. "Oh, God, of course you can."

The older man's gaze narrowed. "Unless you don't want her, because I'll take her back home with me in a heartbeat and come up with a way to pay someone to care for her."

Austin looked at the baby. His baby. A protective feeling came over him. "Of course I want my child."

Dan straightened. "Megan said you'd step up and not turn your back on your child. She said it was because you knew what that was like to lose a parent."

Austin's heart squeezed as he looked down at the tiny bundle. "Of course I wouldn't turn my back on her. She's my daughter." The words sounded strange, as doubt crept into his thoughts. Could he care for this child? Give her what she needed and deserved? Damn, he was going to need help. "She's a Brannigan, and she's staying here with me."

Erin waited as long as she could. She checked her watch. She needed to be at work in about two hours. It was time to break up the party. She grabbed her bag and walked out to find the place quiet. Dan Lynch must have left. As she approached the sofa she found Austin holding something in his arms.

She gasped, seeing the tiny baby tucked against his chest, and her own heart began to pound. "A baby?"

Austin raised his head and nodded. "This is my daughter, Lilly Brannigan."

Erin's chest tightened painfully seeing her dream come to life, not for her, but for the playboy bull rider. "So her mother just dropped her off for you?" She couldn't keep the bitterness out of her voice. Quickly, she raised her hand before he could speak. "Not my business." She had to get out of there before her heart broke totally. She gripped her bag. "Since it looks like you won't be doing therapy tonight, I'll head out."

She headed for the door, and he called her back. "Please, Erin. You can't leave me. I can't walk, let alone care for a baby. I don't even have a place for her to sleep."

Erin wasn't sure what to do. On the verge of tears, she wanted to rip that cute little bundle out of Austin's arms and do some serious loving on her. "Where is the mother?"

"Megan died a month ago."

Her heart sank for the child's loss. "What do you want from me, Austin?" she argued. "I have to go to work in a couple hours."

"Just help me figure out what to do for tonight."

Erin hated that she wanted to stay, more than her next breath. She pulled out her phone and made a call. When it was answered, she said, "Brooke, I need a favor."

"Sure. What is it?"

"Do you have a portable crib or playpen Austin can borrow?"

There was a long hesitation, and then she said, "I do. Can't wait to know why he needs it."

"Please, just bring it over ASAP." She hung up and

called the main house, talked to Cullen and Shelby, and asked them to come immediately, too.

Erin then walked to the back bedroom, packed up her things and carried them out. She stopped and said to Austin, "Since you won't be needing me for therapy tonight, I'll be leaving."

"Wait. I need help until my family gets here."

She was tempted to stay, but once again, she couldn't let a man control her destiny. What did he want, for her to be the child's stand-in mother? At that moment, she wasn't sure what she should do. "They'll be here in ten minutes. I've got to go, Austin."

"Please tell me you're coming back." He looked at her, his face pale. "We have a contract."

She stole a glance at the precious bundle in his arms, already aching to hold her. "A baby wasn't included in the agreement."

"Then we'll renegotiate. You name the price."

She gripped the doorknob, fighting tears. "It's not always about the money, Austin." She paused, her resolve weakening. "I have to think about it." She walked out, the soft sounds of the baby starting to fuss tugging on her heart.

Austin looked down at his daughter. She blinked at him, then opened her startling blue eyes. Her chubby cheeks were rosy. Her hair was a hue of gold and soft as down. Suddenly her tiny rosebud mouth formed a pucker as if she were going to say something, but only bubbles came out.

A tightness spread in his chest, making it hard to breathe. In an instant, he'd fallen in love with Lilly Katherine.

Tears filled his eyes. "Hey, baby girl."

This time she made a cooing sound, and she gripped his heart even tighter. "I'm your daddy." The words were foreign to him. Wow. He wasn't this frightened when he had to face a twenty-thousand-pound bull. This precious ten-pound bundle scared the living daylights out of him.

What was he going to do? He didn't know anything about babies. He closed his eyes a moment and threw up a prayer. "Please, Erin, you have to come back to us."

A knock sounded at the door, and little Lilly jumped and looked frightened.

Cullen peered inside and began to complain. "You better have a good reason why you dragged us here so late…" Spotting the baby in his brother's arms, his eyes widened. "What the hell?"

Little Lilly didn't like the angry words and scrunched up her face, then began to cry.

Shelby rushed in behind her husband, and Ryan quickly followed behind. "Oh, my, a baby." She went to her brother-in-law and took the now-screaming infant. She began to rock her as she walked around. "It's okay, sweetheart." She looked at Austin. "Whose baby?"

Just then Trent and Brooke with their eighteen-month-old, Christopher, came through the door. "She's my daughter," Austin called out.

Shelby smiled as Brooke came closer and looked the baby over. "Well, she's definitely a Brannigan."

Over the next five minutes Austin's living room was chaotic while Lilly continued to scream at the top of her lungs. Shelby was rocking his infant daughter while Brooke heated a bottle. Ryan just covered his ears. Toddler Christopher was interested in the baby's toys. Once

Brooke returned from the kitchen with a warmed bottle and put it into Lilly's mouth, the room was silent again.

"Wow, she makes a lot of noise," Ryan said.

"Yes, she does," Cullen began. "Now, we need to know why there's a hungry baby in Uncle Austin's house."

"I told you. She's my daughter, Lilly."

Cullen sat down across from his twin. "I'm sure there's more to this story, like where is the mother?"

Austin had trouble with this part. "Lilly's mother is, or was, Megan Lynch." He went on to explain about his long relationship with Megan over the years, and how she lost her battle with leukemia.

Shelby put the baby against her shoulder and began to pat her back. "I'm so sorry, Austin. Oh, this poor baby."

Cullen said to his brother, "Are you sure she's yours?"

Shelby sent her husband an unbelieving look. "Are you kidding me?" She studied the baby in her arms. "She's got Brannigan stamped all over her. You and your brother's eyes and that dimple in her chin." Shelby got a dreamy look. "Oh, Cullen, she's adorable." Her gaze met her husband's. "Maybe we should rethink our decision to wait."

Cullen raised his hand. "One thing at a time. Austin will need help with Lilly." He nodded to his brother's bad leg. "How can you take care of a baby when you can barely take care of yourself?"

"I'll get my new cast from the doctor next week. So I can ditch the walker." Austin wasn't sure if he wanted to tell his plans. "And I'm hoping Erin can help me out."

He only wished that she were here so he could explain everything to her, too. He prayed that he would get the chance tomorrow. Problem was, he wasn't sure she would be back, and he couldn't blame her.

Erin's night only got worse. As if the patients at the center knew of her troubles, they added to them. Everyone seemed to need her attention, which normally she enjoyed. She was good with people and most of the time could handle about anything that came up. She'd sat with Hattie, but nothing she did calmed her. Finally they had to medicate the eighty-eight-year-old so the woman could sleep.

Erin went into the break room and got a sandwich out of her locker. She tried to eat, but couldn't block the sight of Austin holding his baby out of her head.

She couldn't deny she was jealous. She'd do anything to have a child in her life, and he had one just dropped on his doorstep. And he wanted her to help to care for his daughter. Could she do it? Could she fall in love with someone else's child, then get pushed out of her life when she wasn't needed any longer?

She shook her head. Why did Austin need her, anyway? He had a family, brothers and sisters-in-law who would be willing to help out until he got on his feet.

His therapy. That was her one and only job. She was paid to go back and help him. And now that could include having a baby in the house. How could she just ignore a child? She couldn't.

Shirley walked into the room. "Hey, Erin. I hear you've had a pretty rough night."

"Yeah, but it's quieted down."

Her supervisor sat down across from her. "I'm glad."

"Shirley, is there any chance I could cut two of my shifts from the schedule?"

The older woman frowned. "I thought you wanted all the hours you could get?"

"I do, or I did. My therapist job is taking on more hours, and I kind of want to see it through until the end."

Shirley nodded. "Well, Linda might be willing to take on more hours. I'll check the schedule, but I could probably cut you back to three days a week, ten-hour shifts."

Erin nodded. "Hold off until I talk with my client to make sure he still needs me."

Was she crazy to do this? To get more involved with Austin than she already was? All she knew was that sweet innocent baby needed her, and she couldn't walk away. So much for not getting personal with a client. Austin had stolen her heart; add in an adorable baby, and she didn't have a chance.

Chapter 7

Early the next morning, Austin stirred from his spot on the sofa when he heard the key in the lock. Erin. *Please, let it be Erin.*

The door opened and the petite redhead walked in. She turned and gasped at seeing him on the sofa and the small crib next to him. He put his finger to his lips to keep her from speaking. He tossed back the blanket and managed to get up. At the end of the sofa, he grabbed his walker, checked his sleeping daughter and followed Erin into the kitchen.

She leaned against the counter. "I see you managed to survive the night."

"Yeah, Brooke and Shelby helped organize things. There are bottles and enough formula for all day. I also found a list of instructions about Lilly's care from... Megan. She wanted me to know about my daughter."

Erin's gaze met his. "I shouldn't have run out on you last night. I apologize for that."

He shrugged, keeping his voice low so as to not wake the baby. "Everything you ever thought about me came true, huh?"

She couldn't even look at him, and that hurt.

"Shocked is more like it," she admitted. "You have a child now."

"Hey, I don't blame you for thinking the worst of me. I already think it of myself." He raised a defensive hand. "You didn't sign up for this. Whether you did or didn't, how do we move forward, or do we?"

She stared at him as if he came from another planet.

"I have a daughter now." The words were still strange to him. "Now that Lilly is here, I wouldn't trade her for anything."

"Of course not."

"Good. Now that we see eye to eye on that, I want you to know that I knew Lilly's mother for years. Megan Lynch wasn't just a random hookup. She worked with her father supplying the stock for the rodeos. She was sweet and caring."

Erin raised her hand. "You don't need to explain."

"Hell, I know I don't, but I want to," he said, hoping she'd see a better side of him. "Yes, Megan was younger, but she was a lot older than her years. I could talk to her about anything. I swear, we only had a friendship over those years, until last fall. It changed everything for me, but she never returned my calls, so I figured it was for the best. She was back in college, and I was headed for NFR. Now I have to live with the fact that because of me Megan died." His gaze met hers. "She had leukemia, but because she was pregnant, she refused any treatment until after Lilly was born."

"Look, Austin. I'm a nurse. I see tragedy on a daily basis. What Megan did was what a lot of mothers would do for their child. You can't blame yourself, because you weren't there."

His eyes filled with tears.

"Megan wants you to take over as Lilly's parent."

With his nod, Erin glanced away. She wanted to believe Austin could step up. Believe that he wasn't so shallow that he couldn't care about someone else besides himself. Now that he had a daughter, and with the mother gone, he didn't have any options. But she did and found she wanted to stay, at least to follow through with his therapy. She only had to figure a way to do it and not fall for both the dad and the baby.

She hesitated, then asked, "So now what are you going to do?"

"I'm going to raise her," he told her. "She's my child, Erin. But I'll need help, and I can't disrupt my family's busy lives. I can hire a stranger, but I trust you. I know this isn't in your job description, but I'll pay you well. Any hours you want to give me, at least until next week when I get the cast switched so I can walk on my own." He rubbed his hand over his whiskered jaw, looking tired. "I'm a fast learner."

"Just because your cast comes off doesn't mean you don't have to keep up with your therapy," she reminded him.

"I know, and that's even more important now because of Lilly."

Was he still thinking about returning to the circuit? "What about your dream of going back to the rodeo?"

"That's on hold. Right now, I'm only thinking about getting back on my feet for my child. I'll revisit that later. I still want you to keep working me hard. I need to be able to walk now more than ever."

"That'll be my pleasure." She leaned against the counter. "I talked to my supervisor this morning. She said she'd cut me back to three shifts a week, so I'll be able to stay here on my days off. I also have some vacation time, so until your doctor gets the other cast on, after tonight's shift, I can stay here for the rest of this week," she said, all the time thinking she was crazy for doing this.

His eyes brightened. "Oh, dear Lord, I could kiss you."

Her heart suddenly skipped a beat, but quickly recovered. "No need to get crazy, cowboy."

He raised a hand. "Sorry—I meant, I didn't know how I was going to pull this off."

She hesitated, then said, "Before you agree, there's something else I want you to know. It might cause you to change your mind."

He didn't even hesitate. "Just name it, and if I can help, I'll do my part."

She was taking a big chance, but she was tired of putting off her own dream. "I want to have a baby."

Austin sank into the chair at the table. This wasn't what he'd expected to hear. "Say again."

Erin held his gaze with those big emerald eyes that had him thinking about giving her what she wanted.

"I'm thirty-six, and time is running out for me to have a child."

"Thirty-six isn't old," he argued, thinking she looked

ten years younger. "You could find someone and get married again."

She shook her head. "No. No marriage. I only want a child. It was mostly my problem that my husband and I couldn't conceive. I'd planned to go through IVF treatment when Jared came home, but then he got wounded..." She paused and blinked several times. "I had to concentrate on his recovery..." She drew a shaky breath. "Then when he died, I couldn't move ahead."

Now he understood her reaction to the baby yesterday. "I'm sorry, Erin. Seeing me holding Lilly must have hurt."

"Not in the way you think, Austin. I'm happy for you. But I've dreamed of a family for so long. Unlike you, I have no other blood relatives. My parents are both gone, and there aren't any siblings." She managed a half smile. "I took your case because you paid so well, and that would help me afford the procedure and be able to take extra time off after my child's birth. That is, if I'm blessed with a child."

Austin felt his chest constrict. If anyone deserved a baby, it was Erin. His thoughts turned to the baby's father. Who would he be, some random sperm donor? He knew it wasn't his business, but there was no denying he cared about Erin.

He started to tell her that when a sound came from the other room. A discussion would have to be tabled until later.

Another soft cry filled the silence. "You ready to meet the newest member of the Brannigan family?"

Erin nodded. "Do you want me to go and get her?" she asked, looking hopeful.

"I haven't mastered carrying her and using a walker. So, yes, please go get her."

Erin hurried out of the kitchen, and he leaned back in his chair. What had he gotten himself into? Twenty-four hours ago, he had one focus: getting back on his feet. Now he was a father. Suddenly he had a lifetime commitment to another person. That scared the hell out of him.

Erin walked into the kitchen carrying the bundled baby in her arms. She had a loving smile on her face as she talked to Lilly. Austin found himself mesmerized by the sight of the two of them together. There was a slight tug on his heart.

"I wouldn't try denying this one, cowboy. She looks just like you." She handed the baby to him and he saw the sudden brightness in her eyes.

"My sister-in-law said the same thing. I don't see it."

"Here, keep her entertained until I heat a bottle."

Austin cuddled his daughter in his arms as Erin went to the sink and washed her hands, then went to the refrigerator and took out one of the bottles Brooke had prepared the previous night. She seemed so natural at falling into the routine.

"Oh, yeah, she does," she told him as she heated a pan of water on the stove. "I hope you know how lucky you are."

"I do. At the same time, I'm scared to death. She's so little, so fragile. What if I'm too rough with her?" Lilly grasped his finger and tried to stick it into her mouth. "And look, she wants to eat my finger. That can't be healthy."

"That's what babies do. They put everything in their mouths." Erin smiled. "Don't panic. They need to build up their immune system. Just keep all dangerous things out of reach, especially toxic cleaners and sharp objects. But you have a few months before she starts crawling around."

After a couple of minutes, Erin took the bottle out of the hot water and shook out a few drips on the inside of her wrist. "That should be about right."

She handed him the bottle. "Have you fed her yet?"

"Yes—last night." He slipped the nipple into Lilly's eager mouth. She latched on and began to suck.

Erin sat down next to him. "Lilly's mother, Megan? Do you know if she breast-fed her daughter at all?"

Austin thought back to the letter he'd read and reread several times through the night. How Megan refused any lifesaving drugs during her pregnancy because she didn't want to harm her baby. How she got to spend those precious few weeks with her child. Although he was still angry that she didn't contact him.

"Her letter stated she did the first few days, but then since she'd refused chemo during her pregnancy, they wanted her to begin treatment immediately. But it was already too late." His watery gaze met hers. "She made so many sacrifices for our daughter. And I wasn't even there to help her."

Erin reached over and touched his arm. "If the dates are correct, I believe you were in the hospital at the same time, too. Besides, you're here now, Dad." She brushed her hand over Lilly's head. "And this little one needs you."

"And I'm going to try to be here for her," he told her. "And I mean that, Erin. I'm not asking you to raise my daughter. I'm asking you to help me until I'm standing firmly on both feet."

She nodded, looking down at the baby. "Let's do this

week to week. Starting first with the doctor's visit in four days, then see where to go to from there."

Austin studied her, suddenly remembering what she'd been talking about. "It seems Lilly interrupted us earlier. Do you mind telling me about this IVF treatment?"

She glanced away, but he saw the sadness in her green eyes. "I shouldn't have mentioned it."

"I'm glad you did. Will this procedure help you have a baby?"

She shrugged. "There's no guarantees, but for those who have trouble conceiving, it's hope. The biggest problem is, it's expensive."

He raised his daughter to his shoulder and began to pat her back. "How expensive?"

She shook her head.

"I can look it up on the internet."

She finally gave him an amount, and he tried not to react.

"I take it you've already looked into it."

"Yes, I have a fertility specialist. As soon as I finished with your therapy I was going to begin treatment."

"Why wait? Make your appointment and start them now."

The morning flew by in a whirlwind of activity. Austin had to watch from the sidelines as Erin took over. After feeding and bathing precious little Lilly, she had put her down for a nap. Then she kept going with his scheduled hour of therapy. He had a new determination to drive him to do his best workout.

By the time he finished, Lilly had woken up again. After the second feeding, he'd played with his daughter, hoping to tire her out. Erin had fixed lunch for them both and they ate at the coffee table while entertaining the baby. Finally Lilly crashed and Erin put her in the bed. Then he convinced Erin to go lie down, too.

"Come get me when the baby wakes up," she whispered as she stood.

He waved her off. "Just go to sleep."

As she walked off down the hall, he couldn't help think about how blessed he'd been to find this woman. She had every right to walk out with the added burden, but she agreed to stay and help with Lilly. He was also starting to feel more for her than a working relationship. He truly liked Erin, and he needed to keep it there, too. He'd be foolish to even think about starting anything with her. They both had their futures planned out, and nowhere did they come close to being the same, except for having children.

He leaned his head back on the sofa. A little less than twenty-four hours ago all he had to worry about was himself and his leg healing. Now he was a father. His entire life had changed with Lilly. He needed to make sure his child was taken care of. A call to his lawyer was important to add her in his will.

He also needed to buy some baby things. His daughter had to have a bedroom, too. There were only three in the house, and with one being the workout room, he was short a baby nursery.

He thought about Erin asleep in the last bedroom. He couldn't put Lilly in there. That wasn't fair to her. She needed a good night's sleep. A sudden picture of Erin's sexy little body asleep in his king-size bed flashed through his head. All that red hair spread across the pillow, those green eyes dark with desire. He blinked and opened his eyes. He gasped and sat up straighter, and began to concentrate on anything that would cool off his body.

Damn. He didn't need to think about her that way. She was his therapist and now the baby's nurse. He couldn't give in to thinking about satisfying his own need. He was a dad now.

There was a soft knock on the front door, and then it opened. His father peered inside. Oh, no. Austin didn't need to have a lecture about being irresponsible. Instead, Neal Brannigan smiled and walked in. "I hear I have a granddaughter," he whispered.

Austin put his finger against his lips and nodded. He reached for his walker and got to his feet as his father looked into the crib at the sleeping infant.

After taking a quick glance at the child, Neal followed his son into the kitchen.

His father spoke first. "Sorry. When I heard the news, I couldn't wait for an invitation to come and see her."

Austin sat down in the chair. "Lilly only arrived yesterday. I hadn't planned a party."

His father raised a calming hand. "I know, son. I only stopped by to take a peek at her and see if you need anything from the store."

Okay, he was surprised by his father's offer. "What? No lectures on my behavior, or how I should have been more careful?"

Neal shook his head. "You're an adult, Austin. And besides, look at that darling angel you have. You're a lucky man. Your mother, Mary, always wanted a little girl. It just never happened for us." His smile brightened again. "Now I have a granddaughter to love on."

Maybe this wasn't so bad. "How are you at baby-sitting?"

"Well, it's been a while, but I'm pretty sure I can recall a few things. Remember, your mom and I raised two babies at once." His eyes glassed over. "Those were the days. You two boys had us coming and going. You were the worst. If you were awake, you'd wake up Cullen. Even back then you were getting him into trouble."

"I did?"

"Who do you think taught him how to climb out of the crib? It's no wonder you ride bulls. Anything for a challenge."

Austin felt a tightening in his chest. His father remembered all this? "Yeah, I guess I always liked living on the edge."

There was silence for a few seconds, and then his father said, "Have you decided what you're going to do?"

He shook his head. "Just that I'm going to raise my daughter."

Neal nodded. "I know that. What I meant was, what are you going to do immediately? Are you staying here to raise Lilly? Do you need some help?"

"Honestly, I haven't thought past finding her a room in this house. Erin has agreed to help out for a while, but as soon as I'm on my feet, I'm on my own."

"You're not, son. You have family around."

Warmth spread through his chest. "I appreciate that, but I have to go back to work eventually and make a living."

Neal frowned. "What about all the money you made in endorsements?"

"It's invested, but I'd planned to use it for my retirement, not to live on for the next forty to fifty years."

He shook his head. "Do I have to think about all this right now?"

His father raised an eyebrow. "So are you still thinking about going back to bull riding?"

Austin tensed. He didn't want this argument. "I'm not saying that, but it has been a very lucrative career for me." He raised a hand. "Maybe we shouldn't discuss this." He'd always known how his father felt about his choice of career, how disappointed he'd been in his second son for following the rodeo. "We're never going to agree." Austin couldn't understand at thirty-two why it still mattered so much.

Worse. He had a feeling it always would bother him that his father couldn't be proud of him. No matter what, he swore his daughter would never feel that way about him.

Chapter 8

The next morning, Erin was dragging as she pulled up in front of Austin's house. She'd gotten off from the center a little early, so the sun wasn't even up yet. Maybe she could manage a few hours' sleep before the baby woke up.

She put the key into the lock and opened the door. In the dim light, she stopped to see the shirtless Austin stretched out and asleep on the sofa. Her heart swelled when she saw the tiny infant curled up on his well-developed chest, her little bottom tucked up in the air.

Oh, my. She wasn't going to survive these two. Austin Brannigan was difficult enough to ignore, but add this adorable little girl and Erin was a goner. The most sensible thing to do would be to turn around and walk out the door. Instead, she took off her sweater coat and knelt down beside the lovable twosome but didn't know what to do. Should she disturb them? Of course, safety won out. But before she could wake him, his eyes opened and locked on hers.

"Erin?" he breathed in a low, husky voice that had her thinking about hot, passion-filled nights with this man. *Whoa, stop that.*

"Yeah, it's me," she whispered. "What are you doing with Lilly?"

"She wouldn't go to sleep. Every time I put her down she started to cry. It broke my heart." He rubbed his stubble-covered chin. "We need a rocking chair."

"I think she's got your number, cowboy. She also needs to be in her own room."

"I know. That's why I decided to move you into my bedroom."

"Excuse me," Erin whispered, but not soft enough, and the baby stirred.

Austin rubbed the infant's back until she settled down. "Just hear me out. You move into my room. I take your twin bed and move it into the therapy room. Then Lilly can have your old bedroom."

She was touched. "You're too big for a twin bed. No, since I'm not staying long, I'll move into the therapy room." She stood and carefully lifted Lilly off Austin's chest, then bundled her into a blanket to keep her warm before placing her in the crib.

Once the baby settled down, she turned to see Austin reaching for his walker. Then he followed her into the kitchen.

She tried to ignore his bare chest, but gave up. Okay, she'd seen him half-naked before, but so early in the morning, and him half-asleep… She glanced away. "Look, you can't give up your room to me. My stay here is only temporary at best. But you're right—Lilly will sleep better if she has her own room. Then we don't have to walk around whispering."

Austin was still trying to wake up. When he saw Erin so close he had to fight to keep from reaching for her. "Well, we better come up with something, because don't you move in today?"

She nodded. "I brought some things over in the van. I'm officially on vacation for the next week."

He couldn't help but smile. "I wouldn't exactly call taking care of us a vacation."

"Speak for yourself, Brannigan. I'm going to enjoy this week. So don't give me a hard time and spoil it."

He raised a hand. "Not me. If you get turned on by spit-up and dirty diapers, who am I to change your mind?"

She nodded. "Okay, after I feed Lilly her breakfast, would you mind if I took a few hours to sleep?"

"Sure. Go now. I can handle the bottle, and I've figured out how to change a diaper. We can play for a while, and when you get up you can give her a bath and dress her."

Erin nodded. "Then we need to go shopping for some baby things. Unless you want to order everything online."

He shook his head. "I'm really tired of being cooped up. A road trip sounds good. Do we have a safety seat for Lilly?"

"Yes—her carrier snaps into a base that fits in the car."

"Okay, then. Now, you go lie down and get some sleep. Then we'll hit the road."

She eyed him cautiously. "We're only going into town to Baby World."

Who would have thought he'd get so excited about shopping? Most of his clothes had come from companies that wanted him to advertise their brand, so everything had been shipped to him. Now he was shopping for baby clothes.

"I feel like I've been held prisoner for the last four months. It doesn't matter where I go. I'm hoping we can stop for lunch, too."

"Well, while you think about that, I'm headed off to dreamland for a few hours." She walked out of the kitchen, and he had to fight to keep from following her. He wouldn't mind a little dreaming with this woman. He quickly shook off the thoughts. He wanted Erin Carlton to stay, and if she knew what he was thinking, she'd surely run far away.

Three hours later in the shopping center parking lot, Austin managed to get out of Erin's van on his own. On the drive into town, he'd decided she needed a safer vehicle, especially if she was going to be driving them around. He didn't want to think about the trip to Denver in a few days.

With Erin holding the sleeping Lilly in the carrier, and him aided by his walker, they made their way into the store. She grabbed a shopping cart and attached the carrier, and they headed back to the baby crib section. There were so many choices that he was dizzy.

Erin stepped closer. "Remember, this is furniture Lilly will use through her first few years, and you can even add a youth bed for when she's a toddler."

"Pick whatever you think is the best."

He had refused to bring a wheelchair. So he sat down

in one of the rocking chairs, which was surprisingly comfortable, and big enough for him.

A blonde salesclerk came up to them. She smiled. "Hello, I'm Michelle. How can I help you?"

"Well, Michelle, we need a baby bed and dresser," he told her. "And many other things, too."

If the thirtysomething woman recognized him, she didn't say anything. He was happy about that. He looked at Erin. "I'm going to leave this up to you, but add this chair to the list."

"Good choice," Michelle said. "My husband had that model and he clocked a lot of hours in it with our boys. Do you like the caramel color, or it also comes in dark chocolate or ivory."

"I think I like this color."

Michelle nodded and turned her attention to Erin, who made a suggestion of a crib and dresser that were maple and a contemporary style that he liked, too. He gladly entertained Lilly while Erin and Michelle moved on to the clothing section to get some basics for an infant. The salesclerk suggested several stretchy little suits in pink and yellow and green. A couple of dresses that the women were making over were tossed in the pile.

Over the next hour they filled the cart with bottles, diapers, clothes, sheets, blankets and a mobile for the crib, and a few other toys to stimulate a baby. Right now, the baby in question, Lilly, had decided to take a needed nap.

At the checkout, his MasterCard consumed the total that would scare most people, but his daughter deserved that much from her father.

Michelle handed him the receipt. "Thank you so

much, Mr. Brannigan. My husband isn't going to believe me when I tell him you were in today. We're happy to see you're recovering from the accident."

"Thank you, Michelle. You have a piece of paper?" She nodded and handed one to him. "What's your husband's name?"

"Jake."

He wrote a short note and gave it back to her.

Michelle beamed. "Thank you. You and your wife come back anytime."

"We will, and I'll ask for you." He waved, trying not to react to the comment or correct the mistake. "No doubt you'll see us again."

After the promise of a late-afternoon delivery of the furniture, the stock boy loaded up the van with the other baby items. Then they climbed in for their next stop. Lunch.

Erin climbed in the driver's seat and looked at him. "Are you sure you're feeling okay?"

"Yes, I'm fine. What about Lilly?"

"She's sleeping." Erin stopped at the light. "Of course, that doesn't mean she won't wake up and demand to eat. Do you want to stop at the B & B Café, or we can go next door to Sweet Heaven and see your sister-in-law Shelby."

"Let's go there," Austin said. "There's less chance of running into a large crowd of people."

Ten minutes later, Erin found a place to park in the small lot next to the storefronts on Main Street. Austin got out, retrieved his walker and waited for Erin to get Lilly. They walked into the small bakery and catering business. The bell rang overhead, causing Lilly to jump and wake up, and she immediately began to fuss. They moved across the room to the corner and sat at a soda-shop-style table just as Shelby came out of the back.

"Well, I'll be." She smiled. "So they finally let you out of the house."

Austin grinned. "Just for a few hours, but we had to buy some supplies for the kid. Believe me, she needed a lot of stuff."

"And they outgrow it all so fast." Shelby glanced at Erin before she went to the baby. "So he roped you into being the chauffeur today, huh?"

"I volunteered for a few weeks." They set the carrier on the table and quickly Lilly wasn't putting up with being ignored any longer.

Shelby stepped in. "May I hold her?"

"Sure. Would you mind if I heated her a bottle?"

Cradling the baby in her arms, Shelby nodded toward the kitchen. "You'll find a pan in the bottom cupboard next to the refrigerator." After Erin left, Shelby turned to Austin. "So she's playing mom to the little one here."

He didn't like that term, but basically she was. "Erin is helping me out. I can't move around easily just yet."

Standing, Shelby swayed back and forth as the baby sucked eagerly on the pacifier. "You're taking on a lot for a guy who enjoyed the single life."

"I won't turn my back on my child." A strong protective feeling came over him. "Besides, I'm already in love with the little munchkin."

"She's adorable. She gets my mama juices all revved up." His sister-in-law got all dreamy-eyed. "I'd love to have Cullen's baby, but right now, we're both trying to start up two businesses and raise Ryan."

"That's understandable." He thought of Erin and her wanting a baby. After seeing her with Lilly, he knew she'd make a great mother. He'd done some research online last night to check out the IVF procedure. Since she didn't have a husband, who was going to be her sperm donor? Could she just pick a random father for her child?

"Austin."

He glanced up to see that Erin had returned with the bottle. "What?"

"Do you want to feed her?"

"Sure," he said and took the fussy baby from Shelby. Once situated in his arms, he gave her the bottle, and silence filled the air.

Shelby smiled. "That girl knows what she wants and nothing else will do. Excuse me—I have customers." She went back to the counter to take their order.

Erin sat down across from him. "How do you feel? Did we overtire you?"

He was taken aback by her comment. "I'm fine. Okay, my leg might ache a little, but not like it used to."

"That's because you've been moving around a lot more today." She looked concerned. "You're gaining strength back, but I still don't want you to overdo it."

He looked down at the baby sucking on the bottle. She was already half finished. He took the nipple from her rosebud mouth, then raised the baby to his shoulder and began to pat her back like he'd been instructed to do. After a few minutes there was a husky burp. "Good girl." He cradled her in his arms again and fed her the rest of the formula.

Lilly had barely finished her meal before she was asleep again. After one more burp, he placed her back into the carrier and tucked a blanket over her. Erin set the baby seat on the floor between their chairs.

About that time, Shelby walked over carrying two plates with oversize turkey sandwiches on crusty rolls and a side of warm potato salad. She went back and brought them two frosty glasses of iced tea. "This is my newest sandwich on the menu. I hope you don't mind sampling it for me."

"Not at all," Austin said. "I'm so hungry." He took a big bite of his sandwich, and the sweet cranberry sauce surprised his taste buds. "This is good." He took another.

Erin joined in. "I like the cranberry sauce. Nice combination."

Shelby beamed. "Good. I'm glad." Another customer came in and she took off again. "Excuse me."

Erin watched Austin to see if he was having any discomfort with his leg. He did look tired, but that was because of the new baby. She glanced down at the sleeping infant. She was so precious that she needed to come with a warning sign. Too late; Erin had already lost her heart.

"She's perfect, isn't she?"

Erin looked at Austin. "Yes, she is. And of course she's sleeping right now."

"Is this normal?"

Erin nodded. "Pediatrics isn't my specialty, but yes. She's only three and a half months old. That reminds me—you should make her an appointment for a checkup."

He nodded. "I have Lilly's medical records. Can you recommend a good doctor?"

"You might want to talk to Brooke and Trent about where they take Christopher."

"I will. I want to make sure I'm doing everything right."

"We can't always, but as a parent, just trying and loving your child is the most important. So enjoy these naps while you can, because once Lilly is up more, she'll want to be stimulated. That means you get to entertain her. That's why I got the mobile for her crib and the hanging toys for her carrier. She'll need something to focus on. Soon, you'll be reading her stories."

She paused, seeing the panic on Austin's face. "It's okay. You're going to do fine."

"How do you know all this stuff? What if I mess up?"

"Oh, you'll do that for sure."

He glared at her. "Thanks for the vote of confidence."

She smiled at his panicked look. "Hey, you're not perfect—no parent is. But you learn from your mistakes, and just let your child know how much you love them." She couldn't help but think about her own baby. Would it happen? Would she have the chance to be a parent?

She tried to concentrate on her sandwich, but soon gave up trying to finish the other half. "I'll take this home and finish it later."

Austin winked as he dropped a couple of twenties on the table. "Keep a close eye on it, because it might disappear."

They stood up and Erin got Austin his walker. Then she got Lilly, and Shelby handed over a basket of food as she walked them out. "Here, this is for later. I'm so glad you're getting around better, Austin." She hugged him, then Erin. "If you two aren't doing anything this weekend, come by for supper on Saturday night. Cullen is going to barbecue."

"Sounds good," Austin said as he got a nod from Erin. "Thanks for lunch."

Erin strapped the baby in the backseat, then took Austin's walker and followed it up. "Okay, let's go home."

"I have one more stop," Austin told her. "There's a car dealership at the edge of town."

Erin frowned. "Why? You have a truck."

"I need a more practical vehicle now that I have a child. A dependable car that you can drive, too."

She went around and climbed into the driver's seat. "My van is dependable." Even she didn't sound convincing to herself. She thought about all the times she'd used it to drive patients to the doctor, and her husband to therapy.

She put the key in the ignition and turned it. The engine cranked but didn't start up. After several attempts, the engine finally turned over. "Okay, it might need a tune-up."

He arched a knowing eyebrow at her. "Let's see what an expert has to say."

Two hours later, Erin sat behind the wheel of a pretty blue SUV. She inhaled that wonderful new-car smell and melted into the plush leather seat as she turned off the highway that led to the ranch.

"So you like how it handles?" Austin asked from the passenger seat.

"Of course. It's a great car. You'll enjoy driving it, too." She glanced at the baby in the back. "And it's more practical for Lilly. But there was no reason for you to leave my van at the dealership. I have a mechanic."

"But leaving your car at the dealership isn't going to cost you anything, because I bought this new car."

She was still leery of that deal, but her van did need a tune-up. She started to argue when she spotted a dark car in front of the house.

So had Austin. "Damn, I didn't want to deal with him today."

"Who?"

"Jay. I have a feeling he knew about Lilly and he didn't tell me."

"Then I'll take care of her and let you talk to him in private." She checked her watch. "The furniture should be here in an hour or so." She parked by the porch, and the middle-aged man climbed out of the luxury sedan.

Erin got out, opened the back door and unfastened the safety seat. The baby was awake, and Erin began to talk to her. Lilly's arms were moving up and down. "I bet you're hungry again," she crooned. "Well, let's get you inside and fed." She lifted the child out as Jay walked up to the car.

"Hello, Erin."

"Hello, Mr. Bridges."

He glanced down at the baby. "I see that Dan Lynch has been here."

Erin didn't say another word, but went to the door and unlocked it, and took the baby inside.

Austin made his way out of the car and reached in the back and took out his walker.

Jay raced over. "Here, let me help."

"I've got it." Once he had some support, he looked up at his manager. "Why didn't you tell me?"

Jay didn't even play dumb. "Because you were in the hospital having surgery."

He glared at the man. "How long have you known?"

Jay stood there for a long time, then finally said, "The day you took the ride on Sidewinder."

"Dammit, Jay! I could have seen Megan before she died."

"How? You were laid up in traction."

"I would have figured out a way. She's the mother of my daughter. Did she ask to see me?"

Jay frowned. "Have you had a DNA test done?"

Austin gripped the metal walker to keep from swinging at the man. "Get the hell off my property and don't come back."

Jay was taken aback by his words. "I know you're angry, Austin, but I only have your best interest at heart. That's my job."

"Don't worry about that. You won't have that job any longer. Goodbye, Jay."

Chapter 9

Later that night, Austin watched at the door as Erin laid Lilly down in her new crib, in her new bedroom. Once the baby was tucked neatly under the blanket, the infant let out a sigh, then gave in to slumber. Erin backed away from the bed as Austin turned his walker around and stepped into the hallway. After she shut the door, he wondered if the baby would be too far away.

Erin motioned him into the equipment room, now his bedroom. He walked in and sat down on the bench. They silently went to work with his exercises, until she finally had to stop him.

"Austin, you know if Lilly wakes up we'll hear her through the baby monitor."

He glanced at the white box across the room. "Are you sure it's turned on?" His daughter hadn't been this far away from him since she arrived.

Erin sat down in front of him on the carpeted floor. "After our busy day, Lilly's probably exhausted. We're all exhausted, especially you." Her pretty face showed concern. "Your body is trying to heal, and taking care of an infant is a lot of work."

He sighed. "She's so little."

Erin smiled. "And cute and precious…and if you don't get some sleep, you aren't going to be any good for her."

She got up from the floor with ease and grace, then walked across and pulled out the massage table. "You need to relax." After setting it up, she took towels from the stack on the dresser and spread them out on the surface.

As much as he tried, Austin's body still reacted to the anticipation of her touch. Oh, yeah, having her hands on him was going to help him sleep. He stood and took two hops to the table, then lay facedown. It wasn't long before he felt the warm oil on his back, then her hands.

He bit back a groan of pleasure. This woman had far too many talents. Her fingers began to work into his tense muscles. *Oh, that hurts…so good.*

After about ten minutes, his thoughts turned to their day together. How well she'd fit in with him, with adding a baby to his crazy life. Barely two weeks together, yet he hated to think about her moving on after he was back on his feet.

"Hey, cowboy, stop tensing up," she said.

"Sorry. I guess I can't turn off my mind."

Her hands moved down to his lower back. "You've had an eventful week."

"You could say that. Instant fatherhood."

"That's one of the best things," she said.

"Yeah, I'd say I hit the jackpot in that department." He made a mental note to call his lawyer. He didn't want any problems about custody. He liked Dan Lynch, but he wasn't going to give up his daughter.

She swatted at him. "Relax."

"I'm trying."

Her magic hands moved down his legs. No way could he settle down with her touching him. "That's enough," he said and sat up. "Thanks, but I think I'll be fine now."

"Okay." She retrieved his leg brace and strapped it on. She stood back and studied him a moment. "Look, you had a lot thrown at you, and I'm not talking about your accident. Are you thinking about Jay?"

"Yeah. I believe he tried to pay off Dan. He wasn't even going to tell me about Lilly."

"I'm sorry. I know you trusted him. He never should have kept Lilly from you."

"Yeah, you're right. He's had to do his share of crowd control over the years, but he should have known that Dan Lynch wouldn't lie. I deserved to know about my daughter."

She rested a hand on his shoulder. "You have Lilly now, and a chance to be her father."

He looked into those mesmerizing green eyes. She'd been so giving and caring about everyone but herself. "What about you, Erin? Have you thought more about your dream?"

She backed away. "Sure."

She didn't sound so sure. "What I told you the other day, Erin, I meant. You can start your treatment right away. I'll even advance you the money if that's a problem."

She couldn't hide her surprise. "Oh, Austin, that is

so…nice of you. Thank you. I can't tell you how much I appreciate the offer. But there are so many risks, and while I'm on this job, I'm going to hold off for just a little while. A few weeks isn't that long. Besides, I want you on your feet before I get all hormonal on you."

"It can't be that bad."

Erin shot him an incredulous look. "I take it you haven't read up on the procedure. I'll need to have shots every day, and there's no guarantee on my mood swings."

He opened his mouth to speak, and she stopped him when she came closer. "Do you really think you can handle me high on hormones, cowboy?"

Erin caught that sexy smile of his, and it took her breath away. This man kept surprising her. But getting any more personally involved with Austin Brannigan wasn't wise. Already she'd let herself go from a therapist to a stand-in mom. Sharing her pregnancy just might be too risky to her heart.

"You're not so tough." He reached for her hand, and she felt his warmth. "I just want you to have that baby you want. You'll make a terrific mother."

She couldn't help as tears filled her eyes. "I will." She didn't want to think about if the procedure didn't work out. "There's no guarantee that I'll get pregnant."

He shrugged as he played with her hand. "You never know unless you try."

This situation was suddenly getting too intimate. "Hey, you need some sleep, because I'm going to work you hard tomorrow. So don't think about getting up with Lilly tonight. That's what you pay me for."

He saluted. "Yes, ma'am." Then he stood, grabbed his walker and made a trip to the bathroom. She glanced over at the twin bed, hoping that he would be able to sleep. She hated taking his room, but he'd refused to compromise. She yawned. She needed to get some rest, too, so she could be alert for the baby.

Grabbing the monitor, she headed out the door just as the shower turned on. Visualizing the man standing naked under the spray of water caused her body to warm. Funny, she hadn't had this much desire for sex since before her husband had returned home. Now she could barely be in the same room with Austin without getting stimulated.

She walked across the hall and opened Lilly's bedroom door. A night-light illuminated the space as she made her way across the floor to the crib. She looked down at the precious baby, and her heart constricted in her chest. She was half in love with the child already. Who was she kidding? Both father and daughter had already stolen her heart. How was she supposed to walk away when her time here came to an end?

Friday morning, Erin drove the new SUV east along Interstate 70 to Denver and their eleven o'clock visit with orthopedic surgeon Dr. Michael Kentrell. She glanced in the back at Lilly. There wasn't much to see with the infant's safety seat turned toward the back of the car. Since there wasn't any movement or crying, she figured the baby was still asleep.

"Is she due for a feeding?" Austin asked.

"Not yet, but you never know with infants."

She looked across the car at Austin. He was dressed in a burgundy pullover sweater and a pair of black sweatpants, with one leg cut open to make room for his cast. "I'll handle Lilly and her feedings. You only worry about you today."

He sighed. "I'll try."

"You know Brooke and Trent offered to watch the baby for you."

He shook his head. "No, she's not used to all her aunts and uncles yet. And I didn't want her to think I'd abandoned her."

What had happened to the cocky, arrogant cowboy she met only weeks ago? "You can't be with her all the time, Austin."

"I want her to know that I'm her father, that I'm here for her."

Erin was touched by his concern. "Right now, you need to get back on your feet."

The car's GPS interrupted their conversation to direct them off the interstate to the large medical building just outside Denver. She drove into an available handicapped spot, then hung the blue card on the rearview mirror. Before she could argue with Austin about waiting for her, he had climbed out, hopped to the back of the car and opened the tailgate to retrieve his walker. After she unfastened the carrier, together they went inside and up the elevator to the doctor's office.

They didn't have to wait long before a nurse led him back to take an X-ray, then into an examination room. "It's good to see you doing so well, Mr. Brannigan."

"Thank you. I hope to be doing much better once I talk to the doctor."

The pretty brunette glanced at the baby, then at Erin, then back to Austin. "Your daughter is adorable. You both must be over the moon."

Before Erin could correct her, Austin spoke. "Thank

you. We are. We also might be a little prejudiced about Lilly." He sat up on the exam table, grinning.

The pretty nurse left, and Erin asked, "Why are you letting her think I'm the mother?" A pain circled in her chest because it wasn't true.

"Because I'm not ready for my personal life to hit the tabloids. Sorry, I should have warned you."

His argument did make sense. "What if they ask if I'm Mrs. Brannigan?"

He shook his head. "They won't. Not here, because my medical information is private."

Erin knew the medical profession. Information still got out. "Okay, but if you'd like, I can leave you alone with the doctor."

He frowned. "Damn, woman. You've seen me naked. So there isn't much more to hide."

She'd caught a quick glance a few times, but would deny it. "I haven't seen you naked."

He grinned at her, causing her heart to skip several beats. "If you say so." Austin loved to tease Erin. She usually gave as good as she got.

"In your dreams, cowboy." She brushed her glorious auburn hair back from her face. "I'm not one of your buckle bunnies. Just remember, I've seen my share of naked men. You should be more wary that you're being compared."

He couldn't help but laugh. "So how do I size up?"

She was fighting laughter. "Behave—your child's in the room."

There was a knock on the door, and then the middle-aged doctor walked in. Michael Kentrell was in his late forties, with just a little gray streaked in with his brown hair. He wore wire-rimmed glasses and a warm smile. "Hey, how come I wasn't invited to the party?"

"You give me good news today, and I'll throw an even bigger party," Austin told him, and they shook hands. "Hello, Doc."

"Good to see you, Austin, especially looking so healthy." He turned to Erin. "You must be his therapist, Erin Carlton. It's good to finally meet you."

"Yes, Doctor." She stood up. "I hope you've received my emails with Mr. Brannigan's progress reports."

Erin had been sending the doctor daily reports?

The doctor noticed the baby carrier. "Who do we have here?"

"This is Lilly," Austin said, introducing his daughter. "So you can see I need to be walking."

"I understand," Kentrell said, then went to the wall and began to look over the X-ray on the illuminated screen. He was silent for a few moments, then said, "I have to say, I like what I see." He went over to Austin, rested his leg on the table and removed the cast. "The incision is healing nicely. Your muscle tone is coming back." He smiled at Austin. "This is some of my best work."

Austin had to laugh. "I appreciate that I was the recipient. Just tell me if I've healed enough so I can have a walking cast."

"You're not healed enough to throw that big party, but you are progressing enough to graduate to a walking cast—but I want you to use a cane to help with balance."

Austin didn't want to bother with a cane, but he'd agree to anything right now. "It's a deal."

An hour later, after Austin had been fitted for a removable cast and Lilly fed her bottle, they went outside and were greeted by strong winds mixed with sprinkles of rain.

Once inside the car, he said, "I don't think we should be on the road during the storm. My place is only a few miles away. I need to stop by anyway and pick up some more clothes."

She studied the threatening clouds. "Just tell me which way to go."

He gave her the directions along surface streets, since the rain was starting to come down hard and he didn't want to be on the highway.

"Are you okay to drive?"

She gave him a big frown. "Really? I grew up in the desert, and we had flash floods all the time. Besides, do I look like a wimp to you?"

He thought she was beautiful and strong. "Hardly." A woman who was left alone when her husband had gone overseas. "I bet you've even had to wrestle a few tough patients."

"When I had to," she agreed.

They finally arrived at the security gate to his town house complex, and the guard came out of the small building. He looked in the car and smiled upon seeing Austin. "Hello, Mr. Brannigan. It's good to have you home."

"Hi, Cody. It's good to be back."

"Sorry about your accident, but I'm happy you're on the mend."

"Not as happy as I am. We'll be staying for a while to wait out the storm."

"Well, it's best to take cover because there are severe storm warnings." The guard walked back into the shack and opened the gate for them.

Erin slowly drove through the flooded streets in the neighborhood until they came to his house. He used his phone and opened the garage door. "Just pull inside." Once the door rolled down behind them, the sound of the rain was muffled.

"Wow, it's really coming down," she said.

"It's Colorado. Give it thirty minutes and it will be sunny again. Come on—let's get inside and warm up."

He got out of the car and loved the fact that he could put weight on his leg again. He grabbed the diaper bag while Erin got Lilly.

He opened the door, reached in and turned on the lights, illuminating the large kitchen with granite slab counters and dark wood cabinets. The place was immaculate. Even though he didn't really need it, a cleaning crew came in once every two weeks. He stepped into the living space with the dark hardwood floors, tan area rug and burgundy leather sofas that were angled toward the stone fireplace and large flat-screen television hanging above the mantel.

It had two bedrooms with an office, plenty big enough for him. Maybe he had to rethink the living arrangements with Lilly, mostly about where he was going to live. Would that be here? He went to the fireplace and flipped the switch to start the flame. "It's a little chilly, but it will warm up soon."

"This is very nice," Erin said as she looked around. She set the carrier down on the thick pile carpet. Lilly was awake and making cooing sounds.

Erin stayed busy unfastening the straps and lifting her out. "I think she needs a diaper change and to be out of her seat for a while."

"I can change her," Austin said.

"You can get the next time." She already had his daughter on the blanket-draped sofa and was popping the snaps on her little stretchy suit. She had replaced the wet diaper with a fresh one.

He smiled as Lilly waved her arms, and then she put her fingers in her mouth and began sucking on the digits. He replaced them with a pacifier. "Is she hungry again?"

Erin checked her watch. "Let's hold off. She seems content for the moment. Remember, she's had a pretty eventful day. She's been in the car for hours, and the storm has to be a little unsettling."

As if on cue, lightning flashed in the darkening sky. She looked at him. "Could you find out about the weather?"

"Sure." He reached for the remote on the coffee table and clicked on the television to discover for the next several hours the Denver area was under a severe weather watch, including high winds and the possibility of tornadoes. "Looks like we're stuck here for a while. How much formula do we have?"

"Enough. I brought the powder canister along, so there's plenty."

He wasn't sure about the next question. "How do you feel about spending the night here?"

Chapter 10

Austin held his breath as he waited for Erin to answer him.

She sighed. "Honestly, I don't want to drive back in this weather. Not with the baby, anyway."

He was relieved. "I agree. Even though we have a good car, I don't want to chance it, either. Upstairs, there are two bedrooms, but the refrigerator is bare. I haven't been back home in months. There's probably some soup and maybe something in the freezer..."

Then an idea came to him as he limped over to the counter. "Maybe I can send out for some necessities." He picked up the phone and called down to the gate. "Hey, Cody, it's Austin Brannigan. How do you feel about making a food run before the worst of the storm hits?"

"Of course, Mr. Brannigan. What do you need?"

Austin went to check his coffee supply to see that he

had plenty. "Write this down. I need diapers, size two, and a dozen eggs, bacon, bread and milk. And I'll call in for a pizza from Gino's next to the market. I'll pay you when you get here, and with a nice bonus."

"Not necessary, Mr. Brannigan. I'll be happy to go. The night shift guy will be here in twenty minutes. Is that okay?"

"Perfect. I'll call in the pizza. Would you like anything? My treat."

"Sure. I'll have a medium supreme."

"You got it. See you later." He hung up and looked at Erin. "What kind of pizza do you like?"

She shrugged. "I'm not particular, but I wouldn't mind a few vegetables on top."

Erin tried to ignore her uneasiness as heavy rain poured down outside while she entertained Lilly. The little one wanted some attention, so she rolled the baby over onto her tummy. She was surprised when she raised her head up. "Well, look at the big girl."

Lilly grinned and cooed until she flopped back over onto her back again. Erin helped her onto her tummy again when Austin made his way over to them.

"I ordered the food and groceries."

Erin glanced up at Austin, looking for any sign of discomfort on his face, and didn't see any. "It must be nice to have someone to run your errands."

He nodded. "At times like this, it's nice to have name recognition."

"For your daughter's sake, I'm glad you do, too." Again, she realized the different worlds they'd lived in. She glanced at the plush surroundings. This was a high-end town house. "Money does have its privileges."

"Hey, my life wasn't always this way." He sat down

at the end of the sectional. "I've had to work hard to get where I am. I mucked out stalls and curried a lot of horses to earn my way to pay for some bull riding lessons."

She shook her head. "I'm amazed at what you've accomplished with your career. Just how does one become a bull rider?"

She watched his cleanly shaved jaw tense. "At first it was to irate my dad. After our real mother, Mary, died when Cullen and I were about ten, I couldn't seem to do much to please the man, or maybe I just didn't want to." Austin shrugged. "Then when Dad married Leslie, Trent came to live with us. All he talked about was his dad, Wade Landry, the world championship bronc rider. It was kind of that my-dad-is-better-than-your-dad." He shrugged. "I got interested in rodeos, and I started competing in high school and found I enjoyed the thrill, the competition. I discovered bull riding later on. And I was pretty good. Everyone was surprised because I'm tall, and bull riders need a low center of gravity to help stay on. Luckily, my height comes from my long legs."

Erin enjoyed the easy conversation between them. She glanced at the baby to see she'd fallen asleep. After covering Lilly with a blanket, she looked back at Austin.

"So how do you stay on?"

"With good balance, strength, skill and a helluva lot of luck." He lifted his injured leg onto the ottoman. "There was this one time in Dallas when I drew the worst bull ever, Brutus. He had a reputation, but you were never sure which animal would show up on any given day, the crow hopper or the bucker." He leaned forward. "That day, I had the rope wrapped around my hand and I made the nod to open the gate. That damn bull just stood there. Finally I had to boot him, and he finally got going." He grinned. "It ended up being one of my better rides."

The excitement on his face told her how much he loved the sport. "I wish I could have seen you ride." Had she really said that?

"Well, maybe when our meal gets here I'll show you one or two of my videos."

She rubbed the sleeping baby's back and smiled. "Why am I not surprised you've recorded yourself?"

"Nope. My agent recorded them. It helps me see what I need to improve on so the next time, I'll give a better show."

"I'd say you have determination, too," she added, realizing this was more than just a sport. "You give a hundred percent in your therapy."

His gaze met hers, and she felt a little shiver. "That's because I need to recover."

She tensed as several flashes of lightning lit up the sky. "Are you reconsidering riding again?"

He shook his head. "I'm not thinking anything right now." He rested his head back on the sofa. "I've only been a father for a week." He glanced down at his daughter, and she could see tenderness in his expression. "Wow, it's hard to think about everything right now." His gaze met hers. "Just because I'm financially in pretty good shape doesn't mean I want to sit around all the time."

"Well, your brother and father are right next door,

and your stepbrother is down the road. You might want to invest in something together."

He sat there for a moment as the thunder rumbled outside, and that stirred Lilly awake.

Austin reached for her and cradled the crying baby in his arms. "Sorry, sweetheart. Did the noise scare you?"

The touching scene between father and daughter got to her. "I'll go fix her bottle." She got up, grabbed the diaper bag and went into the spotless kitchen. She mixed the formula and heated the bottle. Everything looked different here in Denver. This was Austin's life. He had all the advantages that money and his name could buy. Now he had a sweet little daughter. And somehow, Erin had to keep from wanting to share in their life. What she needed was to go and make her own life.

When the bottle was heated, she walked back into the living room and handed it to Austin. Immediately the baby quieted as she began to suck on the nipple. Erin swiftly felt the imaginary pull in her own breasts. This was crazy. She needed her own baby.

She looked across the room. She was seriously thinking about taking up his offer to help her have a baby. That was crazy, but he was her best option. No, he wasn't her option—his offer of money was. There wouldn't be a man connected with her child. That thought brought her both relief and sadness.

Austin smiled at her, and her heart did a flip. No, she couldn't get involved with a good-looking cowboy.

There was a loud knock on the door. "That's Cody." Austin managed to reach into his pocket and pull out his wallet. He took out two one-hundred-dollar bills. "Here, give this to him."

Erin took the money and hurried to the door. A wet

raincoat-covered man greeted her. He was holding two grocery bags in one hand and balancing a large pizza box in the other. "Cody, please come in." She stepped aside and motioned him in.

"Hello, ma'am."

She led him into the kitchen and took his bags. "Oh, my. It must be miserable out there."

"Yes, it is. And it's going to get worse."

Austin called out from the living room. "Hey, Cody. Thank you."

"You're welcome, Mr. Brannigan."

"Here, Cody," Erin said, handing him the two bills. "This should cover it."

The younger man's eyes lit up. "Oh, this is too much."

Austin called out, "No, you risked life and limb going out for us. Thank you."

The good-looking twentysomething grinned as he pocketed the money. "Anything else you need, just call down to the gatehouse. Mike's working tonight, and I'm headed home."

He walked to the door. "Good night, ma'am." He left and closed the door behind him.

Erin put away the groceries and took down paper plates she found in the cupboard. She grabbed flatware and napkins and walked into the living room to find Austin burping Lilly. "Good—she about finished. What do you want to drink?"

"I think there are some bottles of iced tea in the refrigerator."

She went back and got two bottles and the pizza box. There was also a container of salad. That was thoughtful of him. She grabbed a couple of bowls and returned to see him lay the tiny girl back in the carrier and adjust the handle so her toys were dangling in front of her.

Austin nodded. "Hopefully that will entertain her for a while."

Erin arranged the food on the glass coffee table. Austin opened the box and the wonderful aroma filled the room. "Oh, I've missed this. Gino's pizza is one of the best."

"We'll see about that." She dished salad in a bowl. "Do you want some?"

He shook his head. "I have everything I need right here." He took a big bite and groaned. "So good."

She picked up a slice. Always watching her weight, she didn't indulge in pizza very often. "I guess I'll have to do an extra workout tomorrow."

That brought a look from Austin. She tensed, hating to have her body scrutinized. Jared had done it all the time. He was a hard-core marine with an unbelievable work ethic routine, top fighting shape.

"I happen to think your curves are perfect."

"I fight a stubborn ten pounds constantly."

He shook his head. "Too skinny." He took a bite, then motioned for her to do the same. "Eat."

"No matter how good this pizza is, you and I can't eat like this all the time and stay in shape."

"I agree, but tonight we can indulge a little."

Austin tried to concentrate on his pizza, but having Erin so close, he couldn't help but react to her. What was wrong with him? She'd been around for the past few weeks, and he'd managed. Lightning flashed across the sky, and he glanced up at the television to see the weatherman standing in front of the board showing the area and the severe weather crossing their path.

"Do you think there's going to be a tornado?"

"Not sure, but we'll need to be alert. We can move downstairs in the rec room."

"You mean sleep down there?"

Just then lightning flashed again and again, causing the lights to flicker. Then a big boom of thunder reverberated throughout the house. Lilly began to cry. Food forgotten. "I think we should go down just to be safe."

Austin got up and took hold of the carrier. "You get the diaper bag," he called as he headed to the stairs. Instead of going up, he took the steps going down to the lower level. He flicked on the light on the stairs and illuminated the path to the bottom. There was a large main room with a sectional centered in front of a fireplace. A long bar stretched against one wall, and another room had been set up as a workout space and for laundry. There was also a bathroom and an exit to a small patio outside.

Erin looked around. "Wow, this is nice."

"Thanks. The house is built into the hillside. It's not a complete basement, but we're safer down here." He went to the fireplace, turned on the gas and lit the wood inside the hearth. "It should warm up soon. I'll be right back." He went upstairs, rounded up several blankets and pillows, and tossed them down to her. Then he went to retrieve their pizza and carried it down.

"I could have helped you with that," Erin said.

"No, stay here with Lilly." Thunder rumbled through the house like a supersonic jet. "I can move around easier now, and I like doing things for a change."

Austin made two more trips upstairs, for some candles and flashlights. After adding two more logs to the fire, he pressed the remote, and the large flat-screen television came on. He changed it to the Weather Channel.

Austin saw Erin's uneasiness, but there wasn't much he could do about it. Lilly had quieted down.

"Man, I'm glad we weren't on the road." The wind blew hard outside as hailstones pelted the glass doors. They tried to finish their meal, but the bad weather was too distracting. Finally Erin gathered the rest of the food, found a small refrigerator behind the bar and put the leftovers there.

Austin went over and closed the lined drapes at the sliding door, to protect them from any flying debris and because he was tired of watching the storm. It was getting dark, or was it just dark clouds?

They sat down on the sofa. Lilly had dozed off, and he turned down the sound on the television. He spread out the blankets and pillows on the floor and sat down in front of the fire. Suddenly the lights flashed overhead, and another crash of thunder rattled the house.

Erin sat down in front of a sleeping Lilly. "Darn, I wish this would just get over with and move on."

The sudden piercing sound of an air-raid siren went off. "There's a tornado sighting." Austin got to his feet and looked around. Where was the safest place to be? "Come on—we need to find more cover. Grab some blankets and pillows." He picked up the carrier and a flashlight. He headed to the small bathroom and motioned Erin into the double shower stall, then placed the carrier in with her.

"Come in here. There's room for you, too," Erin said. She pressed up against the tiled wall, making room for Austin beside her. After he lit a decorative candle by the sink to give them some light if the power went out, he stepped into the confined space. He eased in beside her, the baby at their feet. Blankets were spread out below them and all around the baby's carrier, with the visor pulled down for added protection. Surprisingly there was enough room for all three.

Erin couldn't help but shiver. She'd been in storms before, but nothing like this. And there was tiny Lilly. She had to protect the baby.

The storm seemed to intensify, and she felt Austin reach for her and pull her down to sit next to him. His mouth moved to her ear. "I'm not going to let anything happen to you or Lilly. I promise we'll get out of this, Erin."

He pulled her close against his chest. She could feel the strong beating of his heart, and it gave her solace as the storm raged on. His strong arms held her close, his hands stroking her arms.

"Sorry, I'm not usually such a baby about storms."

"This is more than a storm. Just hang on to me."

The house seemed to rattle with the force of the wind, but he held her tight. Suddenly the lights went out, and except for the candle, darkness blanketed them. They both sat up. Austin turned on the flashlight and shone it away from the still-sleeping baby.

"She seems to be fine," Erin said as she peeked under the visor.

"Good." Austin sighed and pulled Erin back into his arms, and they lay down on the blanket-covered shower floor. He wrapped his arm around her shoulders. "This is pretty cozy. All we need is a little wine and music."

She couldn't help but chuckle. "You're crazy."

He shifted so he could look at her in the dim light. "I'm trying to distract you."

The man did that all right. From the moment they'd met, Austin stirred something inside her. She didn't want to explore it, knowing she could only get hurt if she let herself care about this man. Well, too late for that. She already cared, for the man and his daughter.

"Hey, you okay?" he breathed against her cheek.

"Yeah. I just wish this was over."

"I'm not wild about the storm, either, but I like hanging out with my two favorite girls."

"What a sweet talker you are, cowboy." She had to lighten the mood. Being pressed against this man, it was hard not to react to him.

"It's not a line, Erin. I mean it. You've come to mean a lot to me." His hand cupped her face. "I think you feel it, too."

She couldn't speak, mostly because she was afraid. Afraid to care about someone else who might not return her feelings. "This isn't a good idea, Austin."

He paused. "Aren't you curious about the sparks between us?"

Oh, yes. Her heart ached from wanting this man. "I'm not the right person to ask right now. It's been a very long time since I've let anyone get this close."

His hands moved over her back, then her shoulders. "It's been a while for me, too. But it's a different kind of wanting with you." His head lowered, and his mouth brushed over hers.

She gasped, knowing she should stop him, but she couldn't. Her arms came up his chest, feeling his strength, solid muscle and warm skin through his shirt, and dreams for happily-ever-after rose in her heart. His touch caused her to groan with a hunger she didn't know existed.

Austin Brannigan made her dream again. And right at this moment she was ripe and ready to believe him, at least for one stormy night.

Chapter 11

By the next morning, the violent weather system had moved out of the area and traveled east. But the storm within Austin still raged on. Damn Cullen for interrupting them with his worried phone call.

Austin glanced at Erin in the living room as she fed Lilly her bottle. Being with her during the storm had only pushed the issue about how much he wanted her, and he would have shown her exactly how much.

Even though Austin had kept his brother's call short, the mood between them had been broken. Maybe that was a good thing. The intimacy might scare her off. He didn't want to lose Erin's friendship over a quick hookup during a storm. For him, there wouldn't be anything quick about it. He truly cared about her.

And this morning, without saying a word, she relayed to him she wanted to forget what almost happened between them. Okay, he understood that. His life came with a lot of complications, and even he didn't know what the future held.

His cell phone rang. He looked down at the ID. It was his brother again. "What, Cullen?"

"Just wanted to know you guys survived. It would be nice if you'd called me back."

"Sorry. By the time things calmed down, it was late and we were exhausted." Hell, he hadn't been in much of a mood to talk. "We're all fine."

"Thank God you found cover. The storm caused havoc here, too. We lost a roof off one of the outbuildings, but all the livestock seems to be accounted for."

"Good. That was enough excitement for one night."

A picture of Erin flashed in his head. The taste of her kisses, the feelings she caused in him. He'd never experienced anything like it before. His thoughts turned to Megan, and guilt hit him hard.

"Hey, bro, are you and Erin coming home today?"

Austin shook away the guilt. "Yes. We'll be starting out in about an hour."

"Drive safe, and take it slow."

"Will do. See you soon."

Austin hung up and walked into the living room to see Erin burping Lilly. The two together tugged at his heart.

"Hey, how about I fix you some breakfast?"

Erin looked at him, but her startling green eyes didn't meet his. "No, thank you. I'm fine. I had a granola bar."

Her pretty face was scrubbed clean of any makeup, and her red hair was pulled back into a sloppy ponytail. "Look at me, Erin."

She placed the baby back in the carrier, then turned to him. "What?"

"We need to talk," he went on.

"If it's about last night," she began, "let me first apologize. And I think you should find a new therapist to work with."

He blinked at her words. That wasn't what he'd expected her to say. "Stop right there." He sat down beside her. "I should be the one to apologize to you. I took advantage of the situation. But the last thing I want is for you to leave. Lilly and I both need you." The next words were more difficult. "I promise I won't approach you in any way but professionally. I was out of line, and it won't happen again. Just don't leave us yet. I need you and Lilly needs you. At least stay a few more weeks."

"I don't know, Austin."

He held up a hand. "Okay, you said you wanted to start the IVF. We were going to wait, but why should you? You stay and I'll pay for the treatment. Call it a bonus."

She shook her head. "Oh, no, Austin. You can't—it's too much. What you're paying me is plenty."

"No price is too high for my daughter's well-being. She needs you right now, Erin. We both need you."

As if on cue, Lilly began to gurgle sounds at them. "See, she wants you to stay, too."

Erin's wary gaze locked on him. "We have to keep it business. I don't want a relationship, Austin. And you have your recovery at stake and your daughter to think about."

"I know that." Then why couldn't he think of anything else but how much he wanted to pull her into his arms and kiss her? "I'll keep my distance. Promise."

Lilly let out a loud squeal, and they both laughed at the baby's antics.

"Okay, I'll stay the next two weeks for your therapy and be Lilly's nanny. But I should hold off starting my IVF until after that time."

"I wish you'd reconsider that. There's no reason to wait. You can stay with us as long as you need, through the shots and the transfer."

She put her hands on her hips. "Look who's been reading up on the procedure."

He nodded. "If it's important to you, Erin, it's important to me. If you want, I'll even put it in your contract."

After the long three-hour drive, Erin was so happy to be back at the ranch. She brought Lilly into the house, fed her, then put her down for a nap. Then she let Austin know that they'd do therapy later, but now she went into her room and fell back onto the bed, exhausted.

She'd spent far too much personal time with Austin, and last night had nearly done her in. What had come over her? She'd nearly had sex with the man. She closed her eyes and tried to imagine what kind of lover Austin would be.

She recalled the tenderness in his touch. The kiss that nearly drove her over the edge, that caused her to stop thinking and only feel. She closed her eyes and her heart rate increased as her breasts began to tingle with need.

There was a soft knock on the door. "Erin."

She sat up. "What?"

Austin peeked in the door. "Sorry to disturb you, but Shelby is here and wants to know if we want to come over for supper tonight."

She didn't need to spend any more time with this

man. As much as she wanted to turn down the invitation, she saw the flash of sadness on his face and changed her mind.

"Sure. Ask her what she wants me to bring."

With a nod, Austin backed out of the room and closed the door as he made his way down the hall to the living area to his sister-in-law. "She wants to know what to bring."

Shelby shook her head. "Nothing. You both have been through so much in the last twenty-four hours, I only want you all to relax tonight."

Austin wasn't sure if that was possible. He hated that things had changed between them. All he wanted was the old Erin back.

"Are you okay?" Shelby asked.

He shrugged and laughed. "Sure—why not. I just rode out a category-four tornado with an infant. Why wouldn't I be?"

He'd been lucky that the tornado hadn't been that close to them, but there were a lot of trees down around his town house. He was grateful the storm hadn't been worse.

"Hey, at least you're back on both legs."

He glanced down at his walking cast. "It'll probably be another month before I'm really free, but the doctor is happy with my progress. And I can drive now since it's my left leg."

"Good. Then you can walk down to the corral and watch the kids ride on Tuesday. I know Ryan would love that."

He wanted to get out of the house more, but he wanted Erin to be with him. "I'll try."

Shelby studied him for a moment. "How is Erin doing?"

"She's a little tired from the two-day ordeal."

"And you. How is instant fatherhood?"

"It takes some getting used to, but Lilly is worth it."

"You're a lucky man, Austin."

"I knew that the second Lilly came into my life." He silently added, he was lucky to have Erin, too.

Shelby stood. "Well, I should go. I need to go into the bakery for a few hours today. See you tonight." She walked out the door, leaving Austin standing there by himself.

After checking to see if Lilly was asleep, he went into the workout room and began doing arm curls with some light weights. He needed to focus on something besides the woman he'd nearly made love to last night. Now all he had to do was figure out a way to get things back to where they were before.

The way he felt about Erin Carlton, it might be an impossible feat.

The evening was cooler, and autumn was definitely in the air. Erin hugged her sweater closer to her body as she walked out to the car where Austin was waiting with Lilly fastened into her safety seat.

The drive across the compound only took a few minutes, and it was the first time Austin had driven a vehicle since his accident.

"Wow, I didn't think it would feel this good to be behind the wheel. I won't ever take it for granted again."

"I'm not sure you should be driving at all. I didn't hear the doctor tell you it was okay."

He smiled at her across the car. "I guess you were out of the room."

She liked the fact that they were able to banter back and forth again. She never wanted to lose that with him.

He pulled up in the driveway beside the large Victorian home, which had recently been painted gray with white trim. She could easily live in a home like this. Realistically, never in a million years could she afford it.

Austin parked at the back door and got out. Erin was out, too, and grabbed the diaper bag while he lifted Lilly out of the car.

The back door opened, and Shelby and Cullen greeted them. "Come inside," Cullen said. "It's too cold out there."

The couples embraced, and Austin set the carrier down on the long trestle table. The kitchen was huge, with plenty of wooden cabinets and a large stove and refrigerator. It was so homey, and whatever was cooking smelled heavenly.

Quickly the attention went to the baby. "Move aside," Shelby said. "I didn't get to see her earlier."

Lilly rewarded her aunt with a bright smile and started moving her arms and legs.

"Oh, she's so precious."

Cullen looked at Austin. "I'm a goner now. She's been talking about nothing except babies since Lilly showed up."

Five-year-old Ryan came racing into the room. "Hi, Erin and Uncle Austin." He climbed on the chair and looked at the baby. "Can she talk yet?"

Shelby cradled the tiny girl. "Not yet, but soon." She held the baby close. "She smells so good."

Austin laughed. "Not always."

Cullen spoke up. "Sorry, we're being bad hosts. Can

I get either of you something to drink? There's wine, beer, iced tea, lemonade…"

"I'll have some tea," Erin said. "Maybe some wine with dinner."

"I'll have the same," Austin said.

Cullen went and filled the orders. Then the men walked into the family room.

Erin watched the two handsome brothers leave, trying to ignore the feelings Austin had created in her. She shook away the thought and turned back to Shelby. "What can I help with?"

Shelby shook her head. "Not a thing. This is a really simple pot roast. I can take it out of the oven whenever we're ready to eat." She sat down with Lilly and smiled. "I think I convinced Cullen to speed up our timeline to get pregnant. I don't want to wait any longer."

A painful ache centered in Erin's chest. "I think that's wonderful. You have a full load with Ryan and the shop."

"I have a lot of good help, and if I need to, I'll hire a manager to run the bakery. Some things are just too important to wait for."

That struck Erin. Shelby was right. Maybe she shouldn't wait, either. Wouldn't it be easier for her to deal with the shots' side effects while working for Austin, rather than working at the hospital?

Ten minutes later, Shelby handed the baby back to Erin and began to take the food into the dining room. There was a large green salad, pot roast with potatoes and carrots, and homemade crusty bread.

Austin took a bite and groaned in appreciation.

"Austin Brannigan," Erin began, "if you make one complaint about my cooking, I'll walk off the job."

He gave her an innocent look. "Your cooking is great, Erin. But maybe you can get this recipe from Shelby."

Shelby raised her hands in defense. "Hey, we all have our specialties. Erin is a very qualified nurse and therapist. Brooke raves about your care of her mother."

"I do miss my patients, especially Hattie."

"Who's Hattie?" Ryan asked from across the table.

"She's a sweet woman who lives at the center and I take care of. Sometimes she forgets things, so we have to watch her closely." She glanced at Cullen. "Her husband was a decorated WWII pilot." She looked back at Ryan. "He died and went to heaven a long time ago. Hattie misses him."

Ryan spoke up. "Like when I miss my real mom and dad, but now I have a new mom and dad." The boy smiled at Cullen and Shelby. "Maybe I can go see her and tell her that heaven is a good place to live."

Erin blinked back tears. "That's so sweet. I might take you up on that and have you come visit the center." She realized how lucky she was to have these friends; she had to stop wishing that they were her family. It was time she got her own.

It was about nine o'clock when Austin opened the front door and allowed Erin in ahead of him. She was carrying a crying Lilly.

"Oh, my, someone is hungry." She set the carrier down on the coffee table and unfastened the baby, then lifted her out. "Here, Daddy, you change her while I fix her bottle." She handed Lilly to him and went into the kitchen.

Austin tried to soothe his daughter, but she wasn't

having any of his sweet talk. "Hey, it's okay. Erin is fixing you supper."

He worked as quickly as possible. He unsnapped her stretchy suit, took out her legs and stripped off the wet diaper, then lifted her little bottom and arranged a fresh diaper under her. After the tapes were secured, he snapped her up, then picked her up in his arms. He stood and took her into the kitchen.

Erin was at the stove, taking the bottle out. On the table was a small bowl with powdery flakes inside. "What's this?"

"Lilly is four months old now, so I'm gonna try a little cereal. Her bottle doesn't seem to keep her satisfied." She mixed in some formula. "Sit down and hold her."

Austin was in the chair, ready for the experiment. With a small amount on a baby spoon, Erin guided it to Lilly's mouth. She touched the baby's lower lip and her tongue darted out to taste the new food. Like a champ, Lilly took to the cereal.

He grinned. "I think she likes it."

Erin smiled, too, pulled up a chair and continued to feed her. "I can't give her too much at first. Her system needs to get used to the new food." She fed her another spoonful of cereal.

Austin suddenly realized how close Erin was to him as she leaned toward Lilly. He inhaled her fragrance, and her hair brushed against his face, reminding him of the previous night. His body quickly let him know how much he still wanted this woman.

"You should try to burp her."

Austin lifted his daughter to his shoulder and began patting her back. "Do you think this will help her sleep longer, maybe until the morning?"

"That's what I'm hoping for." Erin put the bowl in the sink and rinsed it.

After Lilly let out a hearty burp, Erin retrieved the bottle and gave it to Austin. He popped it into Lilly's eager mouth. "She does have an appetite."

"That's a good thing. Babies need to gain weight to help brain development and strengthen their bones."

Austin smiled. He was glad they'd been able to talk again. He didn't want Erin to feel awkward around him. "Sounds like you've been reading up on baby development."

She glanced away. "I have. For a long time."

Of course she had.

She put on a smile. "Lilly's good practice for me." She looked at him. "And if your offer is still good, I want to start my IVF procedure right away."

"Seriously?"

She tried not to think about how sexy the man looked, sitting there, holding his daughter. "Yes, seriously. I have one condition. I don't want anyone to know until it actually happens. Too many things can go wrong."

Holding Lilly, he stood and walked toward her. "Agreed. Now, don't take this wrong." He wrapped his arm around her shoulders and pulled her against him. A strange longing came over her.

"It's going to happen, Erin. You're going to have the baby you desire."

Chapter 12

Three days later, Erin walked out of the doctor's office with a smile on her face, but worry in her mind. Ready or not, she'd started the IVF procedure with her first in the series of hormone shots.

She walked down the hall toward the pharmacy to pick up her medication for the next week. Package in hand, she started to leave when she heard her name called.

Erin turned around to see Brooke Landry. "Brooke." She put on a smile. "This is a surprise."

The pretty honey-blonde returned a bright smile. "I had a doctor's appointment. I had to confirm what I already knew. I'm pregnant."

"That's wonderful." Erin's heart tightened in her chest as she managed to hug her friend. Brooke had been through a lot in her life, with a mother who didn't really take care of her and a father who never knew she existed until two years ago. Now she was happily married with a son and another child on the way. "I bet Trent is happy."

"He will be as soon as I tell him." Brooke blushed. "So please don't say anything yet."

"Not a problem. I'll keep your secret until you tell me otherwise."

Brooke's expression changed. "Are you okay?"

"Of course," she answered a little too quickly. "Well, I have been kept busy with Austin and Lilly."

"She's so adorable," Brooke gushed. "Oh, I hope this baby is a girl."

Erin wanted to tell Brooke about her attempt to have a child, but held back. What if this procedure didn't work? She didn't want the pitying looks and sympathy. So she changed the subject. "How is Coralee doing?"

Brooke's smile died away. "As well as can be expected, I guess. She doesn't remember me much. She sometimes knows my name, and other times she just stares into space."

Erin saw the sadness in her friend's eyes and took her hand. "I'm sorry, Brooke. I haven't been there much for Coralee."

"It's not your fault, Erin. She's getting great care, but I hate her not knowing me and my child." Tears filled her eyes. "I even miss when she'd yell at me or call me by my sister's name. I hate that Alzheimer's has robbed her of knowing her family."

"It's heartbreaking, but just know that you're giving your mother the best possible care. Mountain View is a wonderful facility. And when I go back next week, I'll make sure I stop by to see her."

Brooke's eyes brightened. "You've always been so good with Mother, especially taking her into your home. Thank you, Erin, for all those years you took care of her."

Erin blinked back her own tears. "Stop that. You're making me cry. And you don't need to thank me. I was doing my job."

Brooke broke into laughter. "I'm blaming mine on pregnancy hormones."

"I'm just tired, I guess." Was this from her hormones? "And Austin Brannigan is a handful."

Brooke grinned. "I bet he is. And very handsome, with a cute little daughter."

Erin raised her hand. "Oh, no, you don't. I don't need an ex-rodeo bull rider in my life."

Brooke arched an eyebrow. "Not even with the added bonus with Lilly?"

She pulled her friend aside for privacy. "Look, Brooke. I know Austin is handsome, but so was Jared. I don't want to risk my heart again, especially when love doesn't get returned."

Brooke nodded. "Sorry, I was mostly teasing about Austin. I'm so happy with Trent that I want everyone else to be happy, too. You deserve that much, Erin. I hope you find it someday."

If she could have this baby, she would be happy. "I am happy, Brooke."

Her friend eyed her curiously. "It's probably a good thing that you're not interested in Austin. There's no guarantee he'll be staying around here anyway."

"Did he say something?"

Brooke shook her head. "No, but he's been on the

road for years. I'd be surprised if he settles down. Of course, a child can make you change."

Erin didn't want to think about Austin moving on, telling herself that she was only thinking about Lilly. Surely he wouldn't take her along. She looked back at Brooke. "Well, I'd better go. I need to get back."

"Give Austin our best, and I want to have you over for dinner. Hey, I know. We can do a girls' night out and invite Laurel and Shelby along, too."

Erin wasn't so sure she needed to spend an evening with three happily married mothers. "Sure. That sounds great." She hurried out the door, praying she would soon have her own baby. The family she'd always wanted.

That afternoon, Austin looked at the clock again. Erin had been gone a few hours. She needed time off, and he was handling things here.

He listened down the hall, but no sound came out of Lilly's bedroom. She would be up soon from her nap.

"You can do this, buddy." Why did being alone with his daughter still terrify him? Soon, he'd be on his own, so he'd better get used to it.

He sat down on the sofa. What was really on his mind was Erin. She'd gone to her doctor's appointment. Was she going to start her shots today? When he'd asked her earlier, she'd refused to discuss anything with him.

He thought back to the night in his town house and cursed himself for how he'd acted with her in the shower. How each kiss grew more intense, and she hadn't pushed him away. Suddenly his body tensed with need for her. He laid his head against the sofa and closed his eyes. Would they have made love if Cullen hadn't called? He groaned, thinking about her luscious curves pressed against him.

He sat up straight and rubbed his hands over his face. No, getting involved with Erin Carlton right now was a bad idea. For both of them. He had his daughter to think about. He needed to make a permanent home for her. And just where would that be, he wasn't sure.

Since his rodeo days were probably over, maybe the best idea would be to live here. He could sell his town house, then use the money to do some more improvements on this house. He thought about his family. It was nice that his brothers were here. Then Neal Brannigan came to mind. He still had issues with the man. No doubt his father would be willing to offer his opinion on what his son should do with his life.

A soft sound came through the baby monitor. He smiled on hearing the familiar babble. He walked down the hall and opened the door. When he approached the side of the crib, a big smile appeared on Lilly's cherub face.

His heart swelled so full he thought it would burst. "Hey there, little darlin'. Did you have a nice nap?"

She began to pump her arms and legs faster and make a gurgling sound.

"Well, I'm glad to hear it." He lifted her out of the bed and carried her to the changing table. He unsnapped her suit, removed her wet diaper and replaced it with a fresh one. He continued to talk to her about anything and everything, from the color of her bedroom to her cute nose, getting sweet laughter from her.

His chest tightened with such intense feelings, pride and love. He never knew he could feel this way about anyone—then this sweet baby came into his life. Once

Lilly was re-dressed, he picked her up and turned around to see Erin in the doorway. She was smiling at him.

He got another kind of feeling in his chest. "Oh, hi. How long have you been standing there?"

"Not long. I didn't want to interrupt your conversation." She came over and took Lilly's hand. "I know how much she likes to talk."

"I wish I knew what she was saying."

"She's telling you how happy she is. Look at her." Erin stepped closer. "Smiling all the time."

He inhaled Erin's nice fragrance, and his yearning grew stronger. She was driving him crazy. "Why don't you hold her, and I'll go fix her bottle?"

"Sure." She took the baby, and Austin limped out of the room. He couldn't believe how easily he was getting around. This time, he could make a quick escape.

In the kitchen, he concentrated on measuring out the formula and water, and was heating the bottle as Erin walked into the kitchen.

Once she was settled in a chair, he handed Erin the bottle and Lilly quickly grabbed for it. They both laughed. "She's smart, too."

"Yeah, she'll be feeding herself before long," he agreed as he studied Erin. "How did it go this morning?"

Her head shot up. "Fine."

Okay, that was all he got. "So the doctor gave you the okay to start the treatment?"

A smile appeared on her face. "Yes, she did."

"Wow, that's great. I feel like I should open a bottle of champagne to celebrate."

"Whoa, don't do that," she cautioned. "It's just the beginning of the procedure."

"Okay." He was just so happy for her. Then an odd feeling came over him as he thought about other factors. "Have you picked out a father yet?"

The following night, Erin rode into town with Shelby. True to her word, Brooke organized a girls' night out. Erin was more than eager to get out of the house and away from Austin. She didn't want him to ask any more personal questions. Six months earlier, she had no problem on deciding to go with a sperm donor. A stranger who wouldn't want to lay claim to her child. There was no other choice for her. *So don't go getting in my head, Austin Brannigan.*

Shelby parked the car at Joe's Barbecue Smokehouse. Laurel and Brooke were already waiting at the double-door entrance. After exchanging hugs, they walked inside the family restaurant. The owner, Joe, came to greet them.

The good-looking thirtysomething man smiled at the group. "How in the world did those husbands of yours let all you lovely ladies out of the house tonight?"

"Really, Joe?" Laurel said. "Since when do we need to ask permission?" She shook her head. "No wonder you're still single."

"I'm still single because I'm here all the time." He waved them to follow him as he escorted them through the restaurant and into the bar. There was a big circular booth in the corner with a Reserved sign on the table. Joe scooped it up. "I'll send the waitress over. Behave yourselves, ladies. I'd hate to have to call the sheriff."

"Funny," Shelby answered. "I have his direct line if you need it. Cullen is home babysitting."

Laughing, the owner walked away.

Laurel looked at Erin. "Glad you could join us tonight. It's nice once in a while to get away from kids and husbands."

Erin didn't agree, but she didn't have either a husband any longer or a child. "I'm happy you included me."

Brooke jumped in. "I would have done it sooner, but you're always working at the care center."

"I do have odd shifts."

"How was Austin with you going out tonight?"

"Now that he has his walking cast and can get around, he doesn't need me 24/7. And since I start back at the center next week, he needs to get used to being on his own."

"And a girl needs some time off," Shelby added.

The waitress came over with four tall glasses of beer. "Hello, ladies. I'm your waitress, Jenna. The boss sent over these beers and wings, compliments of the house."

"Hi, Jenna," Laurel said. "Erin, Jenna is Joe's sister. She works here but is going to nursing school. Jenna, Erin is also a nurse."

"Nice to meet you, Jenna," Erin said. "When do you graduate?"

"This spring. I hope to go into pediatrics."

"Good choice."

Jenna passed out the drinks. "Anything is better than working for my brother."

Brooke looked at the waitress. "Jenna, could you bring over a soft drink?" Once the girl walked off, Brooke glanced around the table. "I won't be drinking for the next seven and a half months." She beamed. "I'm pregnant."

The table erupted in cheers, then hugs. Erin joined in and threw up a special prayer that she could make the same announcement in a few months. Tonight was for Brooke.

The waitress brought Brooke her nonalcoholic drink, and Erin raised her glass. "To a healthy and happy baby. Maybe a little girl this time."

The other ladies raised their glasses. "To a girl," they all cheered.

Erin took a drink of her beer. It tasted good, and it felt good to relax and enjoy herself for a change. She had been so busy over the past three weeks. Her vacation ended on Monday when she had to go back to her regular routine; tonight was her mini vacation.

"So, how is that good-looking bull rider doing?" Laurel asked.

Erin smiled. "Austin is doing great with his recovery. Thanks to his new walking cast, he's able to get around on his own."

"I haven't been able to come by to meet that sweet little princess yet," Laurel said teasingly. "Jack and Katy have been sick. I didn't want to spread the twins' germs."

"I appreciate that. But now that they're well, bring them by."

Brooke jumped in. "I think we should do a family get-together. I know—we can have it at the lodge."

Erin knew that Laurel and Brooke's father, Rory Quinn, and Brooke's husband were partners in hunting cabins and a lodge that they rented out for weddings and parties.

"We aren't booked this weekend," Brooke added. "So what about Sunday? The weather is still warm, and it's the last week for our Sunday brunch."

Shelby added, "I'll have leftover rolls and desserts from the morning menu. The guys can grill, and the kids can play outside."

Shelby was already on the phone. "And good news—Cullen doesn't have the weekend duty. So it's a go for us."

"Then it's settled. We're doing the family get-together Sunday, one o'clock, at the Q & L Lodge."

"To family." Brooke raised her drink in salute. Erin took another drink of her beer and looked around the table. Her thoughts turned to Austin and Lilly back at the house. She did her own share of fantasizing about going home to her husband and child.

She had to nix that dream in the bud.

When Austin was awakened by a noise, he raised his head off the pillow and checked the clock that was beside his bed. It was after midnight. There was another thump. He got up, quickly strapped on his cast over his pajama bottoms and went to look to see what was going on. He checked on Lilly first. Seeing that his daughter was asleep, he tucked the blanket over her, then closed the door.

He saw a shadowed light under Erin's door. Good—she was home. Then he heard the muffled sound of crying. He knocked on the door softly and opened it a crack.

"Erin… Are you okay?" He peeked inside the dimly lit room and found her sitting on the bed. She was wearing a nightshirt and in her hands was a photo album.

"Erin?"

She looked up at him as she brushed her hair back and wiped her eyes. She quickly closed the book and set it aside. "Austin, is something wrong with Lilly?"

"No. I heard a noise and I was worried about you." He limped inside, sat down and looked into her wide eyes. "What's the matter?"

She shook her head. "Nothing. I guess too much excitement. I couldn't sleep. I probably had too much food and drink tonight."

"So you partied hearty?"

"Yeah, two whole beers. We were celebrating Brooke's pregnancy. She's going to have another baby."

"That's great." He doubted the news made Erin feel good. He reached for the discarded photo album. He opened it to see a man in a Marine Corps uniform and a younger version of Erin in a long white wedding gown. "You made a beautiful bride."

"Thank you." She studied the picture. "I was a foolish, headstrong twenty-two-year-old."

"You look happy."

"I thought I was marrying the man of my dreams and was going to have a lot of babies. But he lied to me. Jared didn't want a family."

She leaned toward Austin, and he got the scent of her hair. "He only wanted to play soldier," she said as her gaze met his. "Do you know he deployed three times?"

"That's a lot."

"Thirty-two and a half months. That's a lot of time I was alone. The last time he came home on R & R, he'd said he wouldn't reenlist. But he did."

Tears formed in those beautiful eyes. "And he left me alone again." Her head dropped to Austin's bare shoulder, and her soft hair draped against his bare skin. "Jared didn't even want to stay around and have a baby with me. He said he would. Then he left again."

She raised her head and looked at Austin. "So don't go asking me why I don't want to marry again. I think I have a good reason." Her gaze studied him. "Guys don't hang around."

His heart was breaking for her. He didn't like seeing her like this. "It's not true, Erin. Jared was only one man. Look at Trent and Cullen. They're happily married family men." He gripped her shoulders and made her look at him. "You're beautiful and funny and, God knows, desirable…"

She smiled, and her arms went around his neck. "That's a nice thing to say, cowboy. So you think I'm desirable?"

He swallowed hard and gave her a nod. He couldn't manage much else. "Jared was a fool. If I had someone like you waiting for me, I'd rush home."

She cocked her head to one side. "And I bet you'd know what to do when you got there, too." She then leaned in and brushed her mouth over his.

His pulse began pounding in his ears. How was he supposed to resist her? "Erin, this isn't a good idea."

"Of course it isn't, but aren't you curious about how it would be between us?"

He cupped the back of her head and held her still. "Hell, yes, I'm curious. I've wanted you since the first day you walked through the door. Every time you put your hands on me, it kills me that I can't pull you into my arms and do this."

His mouth closed over hers. Hearing her gasp, he deepened the kiss, then pulled her against him. Soon, they were stretched out on the bed, trying to get closer. His hands roamed over her body, and she arched against him. Begging him for more.

Even aching with need, Austin's common sense prevailed, and he managed to tear his mouth away. Working to slow his breathing, he pressed his forehead against hers. "We can't do this, Erin. You'd regret it in the morning, and I'd be exactly the man you thought I was."

He sat up and looked at the beautiful woman stretched out on the bed. "You mean too much to me to let that happen." He stood. "When our time comes, there'll be no ghosts between us."

As he headed for the door, he began to ache, and it wasn't his leg this time. It was his heart.

Chapter 13

The next morning was cold and dreary outside, making it difficult for Erin to wake up. Plus she wasn't eager to face Austin.

She groaned. Maybe it was the hormone shots that had caused her to react so strongly to everything, and Brooke's pregnancy, and maybe being with happily married women when her own marriage had failed so miserably. Thank God Austin stopped when he did last night, or they'd both have a lot more regrets this morning.

To her relief, he acted as if nothing had happened between them; their morning routine went on as usual. Once Lilly had been fed, Erin dressed her and played with her for a bit. Still Austin mentioned nothing as they moved on to his therapy session.

Lilly was content in her bouncy seat on the floor in

the corner, busy with her dangling toys, so Erin had Austin begin his routine.

Erin spotted him as he lifted weights for upper body strength. Oh, God, he had massive arms and an unbelievable chest. She had to tear her gaze away and focus on business. Austin had been working hard over the past weeks, and she could see that he wouldn't need her help much longer.

Soon her time here would be ending, at least the nanny job, and then she'd be back on the graveyard shift at the care center. She smiled. She would be happy to see her friends, especially Hattie.

Only three more days here, yet so much had happened between her and Austin during the past few weeks. They'd seen the worst and the best of each other. She closed her eyes momentarily, recalling his kisses, his touch. A warm shiver rushed along her spine as she thought about what could have happened between them.

She looked at Austin to find him watching her. "Sorry—did you say something?"

"Yeah. Are we about done here?"

She glanced at the clock. "Sure."

"Good." He strapped on his leg brace and stood. "How about we go for a ride to get out of the house?"

"Where do you need to go?"

"I don't gotta go anywhere, but it would be nice to get some fresh air." He came to her. "How are you feeling this morning?"

She glanced away. "I'm fine." She opened her mouth to apologize, and he stopped her.

"Don't you dare say you're sorry, Erin. I don't want you to be embarrassed about what happened."

"How can I not be? It was so unprofessional."

"I don't give a crap about what's professional. We're friends first, and if I thought you wouldn't hate me this morning, we'd be lovers." He closed his eyes momentarily. When he opened them, his gaze was darkened with desire. "Believe me, I wanted you so badly, it took everything I had not to stay with you."

Her heart clenched with his confession, fueling her own hunger. She couldn't think of a single reason why she shouldn't fling herself into his arms and beg him to make love to her.

She swallowed hard. "You shouldn't say things like that, but thank you for playing the gentleman."

Mischief gleamed in his eyes and he drew her into his arms. "I seem to be doing a lot of that lately. You're a bad influence on me."

Unable to help herself, she reached out and wrapped her arms around his waist. It felt so good to have his strength, but it was more than that. She truly cared about this man. Maybe too much for her own good. She also knew that this attraction between them couldn't last. She had to leave and make her own life. And he had to make his. "You're a nice man, Austin Brannigan."

He pulled back. "Don't make that mistake, Erin. I want you. And the next time we start something up, I'm not stopping. Understand?"

She swallowed and nodded.

"When it happens between us, I want you to want me as much as I want you. One thing for sure—I won't be a substitute for your husband. For damn sure, you'll know it's me who's making love to you."

She started to deny it, but he stopped her and placed a kiss on her nose. "Why don't you and Lilly go for a ride with me to see my dad? He wants to play grandpa for a while."

She was glad for the distraction. "Are you okay with that?"

He shrugged. "I still have issues with him, but I'd never rob Lilly of her grandpa."

"It's nice to know that all those times being bucked off a bull didn't hamper you from making good decisions."

He arched an eyebrow, and she got a full dose of his sex appeal. "Bucked off, yes, but until my accident with my leg, I've never had any serious injuries."

She stepped back. "If you say so."

"Yes, I say so," he argued. "I've been riding since I was eighteen, and I've worked hard to develop techniques to stay safe. Not every yahoo can climb on a bucking bull. Well, they can, but it's a possible death sentence."

His look told her he wasn't kidding around, and he went on to say, "As careful and vigilant as I was, I couldn't prevent my accident."

She suddenly realized what this sport meant to him. "I'm just glad you're okay."

"So am I." He glanced at his daughter, who'd been amping up her vocal protest for being ignored. Austin lifted her out of her seat and held her in his arms.

Erin's heart squeezed when Lilly laid her head against her daddy's chest and began to coo.

"Come on, darlin'," Austin told her and kissed her head. "Let's get you changed so we can go see Papa Neal."

Ten minutes later they were walking out to the car

and loading Lilly into her seat when a familiar sedan pulled up to the house.

Erin tensed when Jay Bridges climbed out and walked up to Austin. The middle-aged manager pulled off his sunglasses and looked up at Austin. "We need to talk."

"I don't think so, Jay." Austin shut the car door.

Jay didn't budge. "I guarantee you'll want to hear what I have to say. It's about your future."

Austin stood there a minute, then looked at Erin. "Why don't you take Lilly on down to Dad's and I'll be there soon?"

She wanted to argue, but she had no right. She wasn't a part of Austin Brannigan's future.

Thirty minutes later, Erin sat on the small sofa at Neal Brannigan's cottage, which was right behind the main house, where Cullen, Shelby and Ryan lived now. Since Neal had retired from the Denver police department and he'd begun running Georgia's Therapy Riding Center, this had become his new home.

Neal held his granddaughter in his arms while encouraging her to make cooing sounds. Lilly loved the attention from Papa Neal.

Yet Erin couldn't stop wondering what Jay and Austin were talking about. Several scenarios played in her head, none of which did she like. Surely Austin wouldn't be convinced to return to bull riding. Not when he had to care for a baby. She shook her head. No, this wasn't her business.

Neal looked at her. "What's got you so tense?"

She jerked her head toward him. "Nothing. Okay,

maybe I was thinking about going back to my regular job next week."

Lilly grasped her grandfather's finger. "It's funny how life turns out," Neal began. "Six months ago, I showed up here to mend some fences with my son Cullen, and I end up running a horse therapy center. Not what I thought I'd be doing in my retirement, but I wouldn't change it, especially since Austin has come to live here, too." His gaze met hers. "And look at you. You hired on as a therapist, and you suddenly became a nanny to this little sweetheart." He grinned at his granddaughter. "Aren't you the sweetest little girl. Yes, you are."

"Yeah, it's a tough job, but someone has to do it." She tried to joke about the situation, but it only made her sad. "The really tough part will be leaving Lilly."

Neal looked at her. "Only Lilly?"

She could see the strong resemblance between Austin and his father. Even with Neal's gray hair, he still was a handsome man. "I'll miss everyone."

"What about Austin?"

"Of course. Even though he wasn't easy sometimes, he's worked hard...and we've become friends."

Neal arched an eyebrow at her. "Friends is a good start, and you have developed a bond with this little one."

Erin felt her heart breaking, and she couldn't let this go on. "Look, Neal, there isn't anything between your son and me. I was married once, and I don't want another serious relationship. And I don't think Austin does, either. He only wants to make a home for his daughter."

Just then the door opened and Austin walked in. He

had a smile on his face, and suddenly she wondered what he and Jay discussed that had made him happy. No, she didn't think she could stand to know. It wasn't her business anyway. She was leaving in a few days.

"Hey, how's it going?" his dad asked.

"Good. Sorry I'm late. I had to talk with Jay."

"Is everything okay?" she asked.

He shrugged. "Sure. It's nice to know people still want me, but Jay's expectations are pretty high. So I sent him away." He held up a set of keys. "A guy from the dealership just dropped off your van."

Suddenly, she needed to get away. "Thanks." She took them and grabbed her purse. "Would you mind if I tested it out?"

Austin smiled. "Sure—not a problem."

She said her goodbyes and was out the door, feeling a sudden rush of emotions. Darn those hormones. She had to stop worrying about what Austin was doing in his life. She wasn't going to be a part of it. Problem was, no one had told her heart before she'd gone and fallen in love with the man and his little girl.

Austin wanted to go after Erin, but he had a feeling that she was angry about Jay showing up. He was, too, but he couldn't help but think about his business proposition.

He looked at his dad. "Did you say anything to her?"

Neal shrugged. "Only about how much she was going to miss being around Lilly. Of course, if you asked her to stay, I bet she would."

Austin groaned as he dropped into the chair. There were so many things his father didn't know about Erin's situation, and he had no right to tell the story.

"Look, Dad. I know you want me to settle down, but I have to be the one to decide that."

"What about Lilly? You can't go running around the rodeo circuit with a baby."

This was always their fight when he was younger. "I'm over thirty, Dad. I can make my own decisions about myself and my daughter."

Austin braced himself for an argument, but he didn't get one.

"I know, son. And I know you'll make the right one. I just hate to see you let a good woman like Erin go. This little one has lost one mother already."

The last thing Austin wanted was for Erin to leave on Monday. But he didn't have a future to offer her, either. Not yet, anyway.

Sunday afternoon came too fast for Erin. This would be her last day with Lilly. She dressed her in cute pink pants and a frilly print top and a matching headband for the big family get-together.

Austin drove them to the Rocking Q Ranch. There was a picturesque two-story house, several well-kept barns and a large horse arena. Down the road through a wooded area were several log-style cabins, then came another clearing and a larger two-story log lodge with a wraparound porch. Erin had been here once before when Brooke married Trent a few years back.

"It's so lovely here."

"I agree. And according to Trent, they've done well with rentals on the property."

He parked the car beside several others in the gravel lot. She climbed out and glanced down at her own black jeans, tucked into her knee-high ebony boots, and a royal blue oversize sweater under her peacoat. The early November day was cold, warning them that winter was coming.

Austin limped around the car, dressed in jeans and one deck shoe with his cast on the other. He wore a collared Western shirt and a leather jacket.

The man looked so good. No wonder women followed him around.

He came to her holding the carrier. "Is something wrong?"

"No. It's just I feel a little out of place. This is a family get-together."

"We consider friends to be family, too." He moved in closer, too close. She inhaled his wonderful scent. "I want you to have a good time, Erin. And I was hoping that when we get home tonight we'll have a chance to talk."

She nodded, but the last thing she wanted to hear from Austin was that he was going to return to the rodeo. "We've had opportunities to talk the past few days. Why now?"

"Because there have been some offers made to me. I haven't made any decision yet, because I need to talk to some people." His gaze zeroed in on her. "You're one of them."

Before she could respond, Brooke rushed over to them. She hugged them both. "Come on inside. It's cold out here."

Grabbing the diaper bag, Erin followed her friend, and Austin brought Lilly. Once inside, she couldn't help but be struck by the beauty of the large room. The rough-hewn walls, the huge cultured-stone fireplace that took up part of one wall. Two long sofas were arranged to get the full benefit of the fire. Pretty curly-haired six-year-old Addy was sitting quietly reading a book to Ryan and eighteen-month-old Christopher. She turned toward the other wall, where a picture window overlooked the majestic Rocky Mountains.

"This is incredible."

Brooke smiled. "Yeah, I'd say Trent and my dad did a good job designing this place. And especially for times like this when we get to use it for the family."

Erin had to be happy for her friend. Brooke hadn't had an ideal childhood back in Las Vegas, but she survived it, then came here and found love and a family.

She glanced across the room to see Austin with his brother. If only she still believed in dreams. She quickly shook away the fantasy of any future with the man and concentrated on the party.

Several people were mingling around the long buffet counter. Erin knew most of them—Rory and Diane Quinn with Neal; Brooke's twin sister, Laurel, and her husband, Kase, and their twins, Jack and Katy, parked in their strollers. Shelby was setting out the food, and her husband, Cullen, was right there with her. She felt out of place with so many happy couples.

Trent came up behind his wife and wrapped his arms around her middle. "Hi, sweetie." Then the tall rancher came to Erin and gave her a friendly hug. "Hey, Erin. Sorry I haven't been by to see you, but roundup has kept me pretty busy."

"Not too busy," Austin joked. "I hear you're going to be a father again."

Trent nodded. "Yeah. Come spring. I can't wait." He glanced down at Lilly. "I think this time I want one of these. A pretty little girl."

"Of course a girl would be nice, but I just want a healthy baby," Brooke said.

Austin looked down at the baby in his arms. "That's all you can ask for."

Erin couldn't stand the direction of this conversation much longer. "I should see if Shelby needs any help." She took off, and Brooke went with her.

Austin wanted to stop Erin, but knew he had to let her go.

His stepbrother caught his eye. "Is Erin okay?"

Austin nodded, but knew seeing all these babies had to be difficult for her. "She's been dealing with the two of us. We've been a handful. Starting tomorrow, we'll be sharing her time when she goes back to the center and her regular job."

Trent studied him a moment. "How do you feel about that?"

Austin didn't want to share his feelings with his brother. He'd save them for Erin. "Erin has given up a lot to care for Lilly. Now she needs to go back to her real job. Besides, she'll still be coming by for my therapy sessions."

"So you're just going to play dumb and pretend you don't care about her."

Lilly began to fuss, so he rocked her a little. "Of course I care about her, but as you can see, I kind of have my hands full with this little one."

A smile twitched at Trent's mouth. "Yeah, a pretty redhead with big green eyes doesn't draw your attention at all."

"Just shut up," he hissed.

"Such language in front of your daughter." Trent grew serious. "You shouldn't lie, either—that's setting a bad example, too. Another word of advice—if you care about Erin as much as I think you do, find a way to let her know."

"Look, Erin has her future mapped out, and that doesn't include a man in it."

Trent paused, then said, "I'd heard a little about Jared." He raised his hands. "I won't speak ill of a man who served our country, but don't let their rocky marriage stop you. Erin is worth it." He slapped his brother on the back, then walked off.

Great advice. But was he ready to prove to Erin that he was worth the risk?

Two hours later, Erin looked around the table and smiled. Everyone seemed to be enjoying the meal of barbecued ribs, tri-tip roast and hamburgers, along with several side dishes from Shelby's catering service. Once the meal was finished, the men took charge of the children, and the ladies gladly went into the stainless-steel kitchen and began cleaning up.

Erin was happy to spend time with other women, something she hadn't been able to do in a long time. Diane Quinn came up to her. "So you're going back to work tomorrow at the care center. I hope that you won't be a stranger. Come back to see us often."

"I'll still be stopping by to help with Austin's therapy. I'd love to come by, but my schedule doesn't always allow for that."

Diane looked around the busy kitchen. "Then you girls need to have more of those girls' nights out together."

That got her cheers of approval from Shelby, Laurel and Brooke.

The older woman turned back to Erin. "Rory and I want you to know that you're part of our crazy family, and if you ever need us for anything, please just call."

She was so touched by Diane's kindness. "Thank you, Diane. You have no idea what that means to me. And when Brooke comes to see Coralee, I'll make sure that I'm around."

The older woman took her hand. "Good. Remember, call me anytime."

"Thank you, Diane." It had been a long time since she'd felt like she belonged to a family. Even Jared's parents had disappeared from her life.

Suddenly Erin realized the past two weeks she'd led an entirely different kind of life that had been filled with friends and family. Soon she'd be back to her solitary life.

After the kitchen was clean, the ladies found their way into the main room to claim their husbands and children. After a long day, the kids were getting fussy, and that included Lilly.

Austin came up to her as if they were a couple. "You about ready to go home?"

Tightness circled in her chest, gripping her heart. She nodded. She wanted to pretend Austin and Lilly were her family, if only for a few more hours.

After saying their goodbyes, they walked out and strapped the baby in the car and drove home together for the last time.

Chapter 14

After sunset, the temperature had dropped considerably, but the heater kept the car warm for the ride home. Erin laid her head back and enjoyed the lull of the soft music. Of course, her insides were not as calm as she tried to ignore the man seated so close. Why couldn't she resist Austin Brannigan? He wasn't her type, and she definitely wasn't his. The only thing they had in common was Lilly.

She closed her eyes, wishing for a whole different scenario, one with a family, a husband…and children. The familiar pain hit her, but this time it was worse because she'd already gotten too attached to father and daughter.

"We're home," Austin announced.

Erin sat up as he parked at the front of the house. She got out, then went to the back and reached for Lilly.

Austin opened the front door. "I'll feed her," he offered.

Erin paused, then asked, "Since I'm leaving tomorrow, would you mind if I did it?"

He smiled. "Of course not. I'll get her bottle ready."

Erin took Lilly down the hall to her bedroom. She changed the baby out of her cute outfit and into a fresh diaper and pajamas. "There. Doesn't that feel better?"

The little one tried to talk, and gurgled sounds came out.

"Oh, I'm going to miss you," Erin breathed as she picked up the baby and cuddled her close. Those familiar maternal feelings erupted inside her, bringing tears to her eyes. "Just remember I love you, Lillian Katherine." *And I love your father,* she added silently as she rocked the sweet bundle in her arms. She closed her eyes, trying to hold in check all the feelings she had for dad and daughter.

After composing herself, she walked down the hall and into the kitchen. Austin was testing the bottle temperature with droplets on his arm.

He looked up at her and gave her one of his sexy smiles. Her heart raced in her chest. Would she ever stop reacting to this man?

"Timing is perfect." He walked over to her. "Here, you feed her."

Erin took the bottle and their hands brushed, and she worked hard not to show any response to the jolt she got from his touch. "Thank you."

She sat down in the chair and put the bottle in Lilly's mouth. She watched the baby suck contently.

Austin pulled up a chair close to her. "She's going to miss you."

Erin glanced away. "And I'm going to miss her." She couldn't resist anymore and looked at him. His face was so close, she could see the shadow of his beard. "Have you thought about hiring a nanny?"

He shook his head. "No, not right away. I'm home for now, so I should be able to care for her." His gray eyes met hers. "Unless I can convince you to stay on here."

Erin wanted nothing more than to continue this fantasy. "It will only complicate things more. And I have my job at the center."

He nodded as if he understood, and then he placed his hand on hers. "And of course when you have your own baby."

She prayed that would happen for her. "There are no guarantees."

Austin shifted in his chair, stretching his injured leg out. "But you deserve to have your own baby."

She was touched by his kind words. "Thank you."

He snapped his fingers. "That reminds me… I have that check for you."

Erin shook her head. "No, I won't take your money. You've paid me generously for my time here. I'll be fine."

She brought the sleepy baby to her shoulder and began patting her back. "I already have enough, thank you."

"But you could use the extra for a rainy-day fund."

She couldn't let him make this any harder for her. He wasn't paying for her to have a baby when it wasn't going to be his. It was hard enough not to pretend that Lilly was hers.

Austin reached out a hand and covered hers. "I only want to help you, Erin. I care about you."

Oh, God. Why did he have to be so nice? "I know. And I appreciate the gesture, but I can't accept. I have to do this myself."

He finally nodded. "I guess I can understand that."

After a hearty burp from Lilly, she carried the now-sleeping child down the hall to her bedroom, then laid her down in the crib. After placing a kiss on her cheek, she stepped back and right into Austin.

Erin gasped as his arms snaked around her to keep her from falling. With him still holding on tight, they made their way out into the hall. Then he closed the nursery door.

She managed to get out of Austin's grasp. If not, she wasn't going to be able to resist the man.

Unable to look at him, she said, "It's late. We should probably go to bed. I mean, you go to bed and I go to bed." She motioned to her bedroom. "Good night."

He reached out and touched her arm. "Erin, don't go. I don't want you to leave."

She paused, aching to turn around and walk into his arms. "I must, Austin. I have to go back to work."

He stepped toward her, and she took a step back but met the wall. "If you leave this house, I have a feeling I'll never see you again. I can't bear that."

"I'll still come by for your therapy sessions."

"It's not enough time."

She couldn't give him any more than that, or she'd lose herself and end up getting hurt. "It has to be. I can't give you any more."

He leaned in closer. "I don't want to lose you, Erin."

"Oh, Austin…"

That was all she could manage when his mouth closed over hers, and she melted in his arms. The taste of him, the feel of his body pressed against her. She was in heaven.

He finally tore his mouth away. "I need you, Erin." His voice rumbled through his chest. She could feel his heart hammering against her hand. "Let me show you how much."

There was an ache in her throat as she fought to keep from sliding her hands around his neck and seizing his mouth again.

"Tell me, Erin, that you want this, too."

There was no denying it any longer. She wanted to see where their passion took them. Just once.

"I want you, Austin."

He sucked in a breath as he lowered his head and his mouth captured hers. By the time he finished the tender assault, she could barely draw her next breath. He leaned down and swung her up into his arms.

She started to protest about his injured leg, but he kissed her again. Then he carried her into her room and set her down beside the king-size bed.

He raised his arms and cupped her face between his hands. "Just so you're clear about my intentions—"

She placed a finger over his lips. She didn't want to think about common sense or doing the right thing. All she wanted was Austin. "Don't say anything, Austin. Just make love to me."

He quickly went to work. After removing her sweater, he tossed it aside, and then he removed his shirt as well. At the first touch of his hands against her bare skin, her mind began to float, and she gave in to the touch of his fingertips gliding over her body, raising goose bumps. When he finally covered her breasts, she released a shuddering breath.

"Oh, dear God," she whispered into the dark room. "It's been so long…"

"Let me remedy that," he said, and his mouth covered her nipple and sucked gently. She arched her back, desperate for him not to stop. Like a starved man, he continued the wonderful torture. He raised his head and looked at her. She could see the desire in the depths of his eyes.

Austin was shaking like a teenage boy, but he'd never had feelings like this before. His hands trembled as they slid down over Erin's hips, bringing her closer to him. Waves of pleasure rolled through him as she gasped his name. Her hands touched him, causing a jolt of awareness he'd never experienced before. Once again his mouth covered hers, tasting her, unable to get enough. So was she as she reached for the waistband of his jeans and began to pop the snaps.

He pulled back, trying to compose himself. "Ladies first."

He undid her jeans and tugged them down. He stood back in the dim light, admiring her body. "You are so beautiful." He couldn't resist touching her some more. She was toned, yet also soft and feminine, and what curves.

She reached out to him. "Please, Austin."

He quickly shed his leg brace, then chucked his shoes, jeans and underwear and returned to her. "I'm going to show you how much I want you, Erin." Praying silently that he could let her know how much he wanted her to stay, to be a part of his life. His mouth covered hers, and she linked her hands with his. Soon, he was lost in this woman, and together they rode out the storm and made it to paradise.

* * *

Austin glanced at the bedside clock in the dark room. It was one in the morning. Good—he still had some time with Erin. His hand moved over her naked back, and immediately she arched against his touch. She started to shift in her sleep, but was she really asleep?

She placed nibbling kisses along his jaw to his ear and whispered, "Haven't you had enough yet, cowboy?"

He rolled her over on her back and kissed her deeply, leaving them both breathless. "Never. I want you here more than ever."

She giggled. "I should kick you out of bed." She grew serious. "I thought you wanted a quick roll in the hay."

He raised his head. "Are you saying I was too quick?"

She shook her head. "So I need to stroke your ego now."

"I wouldn't mind that at all."

She wrapped her arms around his neck. "Last night was incredible. Thank you, Austin."

"No, thank *you*. And I think we were pretty incredible together."

"I agree. So for tonight, we live out the fantasy and enjoy being together."

He looked down at her. "Erin, why can't you give us a chance?"

"Austin…we've talked about this before. You know that I want a family."

"I have a family—more than I need at times, but it's a family. And a cute baby, too."

He felt her shudder beneath him. "I know. And you know my dream is to have a child of my own."

"You can. There's no reason why you can't go through with your IVF." He fought to keep from asking her about the sperm donor. It might not be his right to question, but he cared about Erin. Maybe even…loved her. He tensed at the realization. But just the thought of another man fathering her child made him crazy. He wanted to be the one to share that experience with her, but that confession might push her over the edge.

He had to go slow. "I know we've only been together a month or so, but we get along. We care about each other." He still needed to decide something about his career. "Why can't we go on like we have been…and see where it leads?"

"You mean no commitment?"

He froze. Okay, how did he handle this not to scare her off? He knew how she felt about marriage. "We can make a commitment to be exclusive to each other. Erin, I care for you."

"I care about you, too," she admitted. "But I can't live here, Austin. As much as I want to stay for Lilly, I need to go back to my job. I promised them. But I'm doing three day shifts, so I'm off four."

"Really." He pressed his body into hers. "Maybe I can convince you to do a few sleepovers."

She wiggled under him. "Maybe. Show me what you got, cowboy."

The following morning was a little more awkward for Erin when she awoke and found Austin next to her. He reached out to her and quickly convinced her since Lilly was still asleep, they should take advantage of their private time. Then once again, he proceeded to make tender love to her.

An hour later, she'd managed to leave the bed and take a quick shower before going to get Lilly. Once the baby was changed into a fresh diaper, she took her into the kitchen for breakfast. Erin couldn't help but blush, thinking about her night and morning with Austin as she prepared Lilly's cereal.

"Your daddy is a persuasive man," she told the baby as she sat down in front of the carrier. She scooped up a tiny spoonful of cereal and guided it into Lilly's mouth. "I'm going to have to be a lot stronger if I want to have my own way."

The little one squealed. She was such a happy baby. "You won't have so much trouble. Just turn the cute smile on him."

Her mood was dampened as she thought about packing up and heading back to her apartment in a few hours. She hadn't worked the graveyard shift in over a week, and she wasn't looking forward to doing it tonight.

She sighed. Mainly because she wouldn't be in Austin's bed. Her body began to heat up just thinking about what the man did to her. She'd never been so in tune with another person. Their connection had been incredible. That was the problem: she was letting him get too close. Too late—Austin Brannigan had broken down that barrier last night.

She felt a hand on her shoulder, and then he brushed her hair aside and placed a kiss against her neck, causing her to shiver.

"Good morning," the familiar voice said against her ear.

She leaned back, giving him better access. "Good morning to you, too."

His lips found their way to her mouth, and soon, she was lost in the man as his tongue pushed past her lips in a deep, hungry kiss. He groaned as his hand reached in front of her and cupped her aching breast.

This time she whimpered.

Suddenly a vocal little girl made her presence known. Austin broke off the kiss, his gray gaze still on her. "Seems I need to give my other girl some attention."

He moved to his daughter, and soon Lilly was grinning again. Erin was amazed to see the transformation of the two of them. He was a good father.

He took the cereal bowl from her and continued to feed his daughter. "Hey, Cullen just called to tell me that there's a horse therapy session this afternoon, and he wanted me to look at a new horse that has been donated to the program. Do you think you can hang around so we can go down there together?"

She didn't want to leave at all, but she had to. "Yes, but I'll need to leave right afterward. I haven't been home to my apartment since last week. Luckily, I pay my bills online, or I wouldn't have any heat or water."

He leaned down and placed a quick kiss on her lips. "Oh, darn. You might have to stay here."

She smiled. "Nice try, cowboy, but it's time we both head back to reality. Besides, I guess I'm a little independent and need my own space."

He took her hand and brought it to his mouth and kissed the back. "I don't want to take your independence, Erin. I just want you to know you have people to depend on. That would be me and my family."

By noon, Erin had packed up her bags, cleaned her bedroom, then carried her things out and put them in her van. She was ready to go, but her heart wasn't in it. Not after last night and being with Austin. She had to stop dreaming the fairy tale, too. She was leaving, and nothing was going to change that.

"Hey, we're ready."

She swung around to see Austin pushing a bundled-up Lilly in her stroller.

"Sure." She had on her jeans and a bulky oatmeal-colored sweater. She grabbed her jacket off the chair. "We're walking?"

"I figured it would be easier this way. It's only about a quarter mile."

"I was thinking about your leg."

He shook his head. "My leg is fine." He drew her into his arms, holding her against him. "I thought I proved that last night…and this morning."

"Yes, you did," she admitted as she buried her head in his chest. Why suddenly was she shy with him? It was because they'd gone from a business relationship to an intimate one. "I'm glad that you've gotten your strength back." She pulled back. "We should get going."

With Lilly covered to protect her from the cooler weather, they pushed the stroller over the gravel road to the arena for Georgia's Therapy Riding Center. Georgia Hughes had gotten a job here on the ranch to flee her abusive boyfriend. She didn't make it, but Shelby and Ryan ended up in Hidden Springs.

Erin realized that she, too, had come to the small Colorado town to escape her memories, hoping to build a new life. Maybe this was to be her happily-ever-after for her and her child.

She heard her name and looked up to see Neal Brannigan waving at them. She acknowledged him, and Austin picked up his pace and she hurried to keep up. His leg must feel fine.

They reached the front entrance, where there was a long ramp to help with the disabled kids and for the kids who needed help getting on the horses.

At the moment there didn't seem to be any children around.

After they greeted Neal, Austin asked, "Are we early?"

His father smiled. "Just a little, but I was wondering if you'd look at a horse that I was thinking about adding to the program. We can't seem to keep up with the volume of kids who want to come and ride. So we need more horses."

Austin turned to her. "Do you mind?"

"No—go ahead. Lilly and I will wait here on the ramp." She looked down at the child, who was content playing with one of her teething toys.

She watched from her elevated post as Austin and his father walked into the corral. Both men were tall, broad-shouldered and slender and had the same rugged look, dressed in jeans and Western shirts and cowboy hats. Not even Austin's leg brace detracted from his appeal.

Soon another man came out of the barn and walked toward them. Cullen joined up with his brother and dad. Although twins, he and Austin weren't identical, but close enough, and both were gorgeous males.

She heard her name and turned to see Shelby come up the ramp. They exchanged a hug, then turned back to the men in the corral.

"It's hard to decide which is the most handsome." Smiling, Shelby released a sigh. "But it sure makes you glad that they belong to us."

Chapter 15

Austin looked across the corral at Erin. She was watching him, and he liked that. Was she thinking about last night, remembering that he was the man who had sent her soaring, leaving her contented and thoroughly satisfied?

"Hey, bro."

Austin jerked around to find his twin brother leading a buckskin gelding. "Hi, Cullen. Who you got there?"

"Dad and I wanted your opinion of our new boarder." His brother rubbed the horse's muzzle. "Sundance here was brought to us from a ranching family. Before that he belonged to a rough stock company." He grinned. "The owner told us Sundance had failed at being a good bucking horse."

Austin ran his hand over the docile animal as he made his way around the horse. "As far as I can see, there don't seem to be any signs of him being jumpy or nervous. Do you think I could give him a test ride?"

Cullen frowned. "Sure, and have your doctor and Erin kill me. Besides, how are you going to mount him with your cast?"

"The ramp." Excited, he took hold of the reins and walked the saddled horse to the outside ramp to where Erin stood with Shelby and Lilly.

"Hi, Shelby."

"Hi, Austin. Are you going to help out with the kids today?"

"Yeah, but first, I'm going to test-ride Sundance here."

Erin was the first to protest. "That's not a good idea. What if you fall off?"

Austin swung around, a little irritated by her lack of confidence in him. "The last time I fell off a horse I was a four-year-old." Then he bent down and brushed a kiss across her surprised mouth. "Nothing is going to go wrong."

"Again, Austin, not a good idea," Erin warned him again.

"It's the best idea I've had in a long time." *Except for being with you last night*, he added silently. His gaze connected with hers again. "Trust me, I need to do this." He might never get on a bull again, but he sure as hell could ride a horse.

Before anyone else could stop him, Austin was at the top of the ramp and easily slid his good leg over the rump of the horse and into the saddle. He used the pommel to get seated right, then took control of the reins. He made a clicking sound to get the horse to move and started around the corral. After he got the feel of the animal under him, he wished he had the open pasture to take a run. He had a feeling this horse could handle a little speed, but he wasn't going to push it when he couldn't fully control the horse.

He walked the buckskin back to the ramp and prayed he could make a clean dismount. When he stood in the stirrup, he was happy that his braced leg held him. He climbed off and walked to Erin.

"Now it's your turn."

She brushed the rich auburn hair from her face. "You're kidding, right?"

"Come on. You aren't a chicken, are you?"

"Yes, I am, and not afraid to admit it." She eyed the animal. "He's so big."

"How about I just walk you around the corral once? By the time we return, I guarantee you'll be smiling." He leaned forward and whispered, "Take a chance with me. I promise not to let you fall."

He pulled back and could see her green eyes widen with wonder.

"What if...?" she began.

He shook his head. "Come on. You've challenged and goaded me into doing things I didn't think possible. You need to take a chance sometime, Erin. I'll be there to catch you."

"Okay, fine."

Shelby walked up to them. "I'll watch Lilly."

Austin took Erin by the arm and took her to the horse. "Sundance, this is Erin. Now, you be a gentleman and I'll give you an extra carrot."

Sundance bobbed his head and blew out a breath.

Austin laughed and glanced at his brother. "You better have some extra carrots."

"We have plenty. The supermarket in town keeps the therapy center well supplied."

He turned back to the horse. "Hear that, Sundance? You lucked out coming here to stay. There's plenty of kids here and all the carrots you can eat."

The horse made a neighing sound.

He took Erin by the arm toward the end of the ramp. "Now, put your foot in the stirrup."

Erin glared at him, then leaned closer and whispered, "Look, cowboy, just because you had your way with me last night doesn't mean you can push me around." Her mouth twitched in amusement.

His body suddenly stirred to life. "Yes, ma'am. Will you *please* put your foot in the stirrup?"

"That's better." She did as he asked and climbed onto the horse. Since she looked a little frightened, he continued to keep her distracted by adjusting the stirrups.

"You ready?"

"I guess," she hedged.

Austin walked down the ramp tugging on the lead rope, then into the arena. "Let go of the saddle horn and hold the reins loosely in your hand. This horse is trained to take both voice and touch commands."

"What does that mean? I say 'turn left' and he does?"

He smiled. "Try saying *W-H-O-A.*"

"Whoa, Sundance," she said.

The horse stopped and waited patiently. Austin looked up at Erin in the saddle and caught her big smile. "Good job." He patted the horse. "You, too, Sundance."

He decided to keep instructing Erin. "Okay, now if you want to turn right or left, you use the reins, and tug a little in which direction you want to go."

She tried it a few times and it worked perfectly. He

then showed her how to back up, and once that was completed, he took another chance and unfastened the lead rope and had her handle the horse on her own.

He followed closely, and with his father and Cullen inside the arena, she walked off on her own. Once at the end, she managed to turn the horse around and came back. With praise from the growing group of bystanders, she dismounted as he lifted her into his arms.

"I did it," she said, amazed.

"And with a smile." He added, "I believe I won the bet."

"I don't think we had a bet."

"Maybe not, but shouldn't I get a reward?" He leaned closer and placed a kiss on her surprised mouth. Suddenly the arena erupted in cheers, but Austin didn't care. He had Erin in his arms.

Early the next morning at the care center, Erin checked her watch, not only because she was anxious to leave work, but also because she wondered how Austin was handling the baby's routine on his own. Had Lilly missed her? She thought back to when she'd rock the baby and listen to her sweet babble. Sadness washed over her. She hated that the little one might feel abandoned by her.

Erin continued down the corridor to the nurses' desk, but she couldn't help but look in on Hattie. When she'd come on shift, the older woman had been asleep. It had only been a little over a week, but with Hattie's declining health, she wasn't sure if she'd remember her.

Erin peered in the door and saw the white-haired woman sitting on her bed, still in her gown and robe, going through her photo album. She looked up and frowned as if she were trying to remember her.

She walked into the room. "Good morning, Hattie. I'm Erin."

A smile appeared on her lined face. "Hi, Erin. I think I know you. You help me sometimes, don't you?"

"Yes, I do. Do you need help this morning?"

Hattie looked thoughtful. "Would you help me find my husband? He was supposed to come and pick me up, but I think he's lost." She shook her head. "And you know men—they never stop and ask for directions."

Erin couldn't help but smile. All the memories that Hattie had retained seemed to be mostly of her husband. How wonderful to have that kind of love. Her thoughts went to Austin, and then as quickly she shook them away.

She turned back to Hattie. "Well, I could have the nurses' station keep an eye out while I help you get dressed all nice and pretty for when he gets here."

Hattie agreed. "I like to look pretty for Johnny." The woman's hand shook as she held out the picture book. "See. He's so handsome."

Erin glanced down at the young couple in the grainy black-and-white photo. She wore a lacy white wedding dress, and the man was in his military uniform. The date was July 5, 1945.

"You make a handsome pair. How many years have you been married?" She hated to think about her own marriage, and how Jared had been away so much.

Hattie sighed. "Sixty-three years. Not all wonderful, but we were blessed with three children and eight grandchildren." Tears came to the older woman's eyes.

"Johnny's been really sick and I'm scared he's not going to get better. I need to go to him."

Erin reached out and gripped the woman's arthritic hands to calm her. "It's okay, Hattie. Johnny isn't sick anymore. He's coming here later to see you, so we should get you dressed and ready for him."

Hattie smiled at Erin. "Oh, you are so kind and pretty. I bet you have a special man in your life, too."

She wanted to deny it, but the truth was, she did care about someone. "Yes, I do. And he's handsome and kind, and I love him very much."

She froze at her own admission. She loved Austin Brannigan. Oh, God. She was in big trouble.

At noon Austin tried to get some things done while Lilly slept. She'd been fussing all morning and had woken up twice during the night. She had a runny nose. He put the baby monitor on the table and sank into a chair. Thank God, Lilly was finally asleep. He was going to ask Erin if he should call the doctor, but there had been no sign of her.

He was doubly worried now. Erin hadn't shown up for his morning therapy session, nor had she answered any of his texts. He tried to rationalize that she'd gone home to her apartment and fallen asleep.

He knew she'd gone two nights with little sleep. One of those times she was with him, and then going back to work last night had to have been exhausting. He only wanted to know she was safe.

He heard a faint knock on the door, and then Erin peered inside. "Hi."

He got up from the table and went to her. He was glad to see she looked rested and absolutely beautiful.

"Hi, yourself. I was worried about you when you didn't show up this morning."

"I apologize. Remember, my shifts are now ten hours. When I went home to change, I lay down for a few minutes and I guess I fell asleep." She met his gaze. "I left my phone in my purse, so I didn't get your messages."

"Why don't you just come here after work to sleep?" He caught her hesitation. "What's wrong, Erin?"

"Maybe it would be better if I didn't come by here in the mornings."

"Why?"

"It's not good for Lilly to get too used to me."

What is she talking about? "She's already used to you being here, Erin. I'd hoped to convince you to spend more time with her." He wrapped his arms around her and brought her close. She resisted at first but finally relented and rested her body against him.

"I want to be with you, too," he confessed. "Erin, the other night meant a lot to me."

She pulled back. "It meant a lot to me, too, Austin. Please understand, I care about you, but I can't handle a relationship with you or anyone. You know what my plans are."

Her rejection broke his heart. What had suddenly changed her mind? "Okay, okay, I won't pressure you into anything you aren't ready for, but I don't see why we can't still be together as friends."

She raised a hand. "Really, you're okay with us being *just* friends?"

He shrugged. "Of course, I want to have more of a relationship with you. Right now, I have to think about my daughter. She lost a lot of people in her life. She needs you, Erin."

He saw her worried look and wished he could soothe her fears. "Do this for Lilly."

"Okay, I'll still come here after my shift is over in the morning, go through the morning routine, sleep a few hours. Then we'll do a second therapy session while she's down for her nap. Then I need my own time."

He hated that she needed to be away from him, but he'd take whatever he could get. He tossed her his best grin. "Maybe we can negotiate that sometimes you might stay for supper. I hate eating alone, and I know you do, too."

She released a sigh. "All right, maybe sometimes we'll share a meal."

"So do we need to write up another contract?"

She finally smiled. "I think I can add it to the original and just have you initial it."

"Okay, that settles it."

Just then the sound of Lilly's crying came over the monitor, followed by coughing, and they both hurried down the hall. Austin picked her up and quickly noticed she was warmer than usual. Lilly began to cough again. "Oh, God, she's hot."

Erin touched the baby's cheek. "How long has she been coughing like this?"

"Only a few times this morning before I put her down, but not like this."

Erin took the baby. "Austin, would you go out and get my bag in the van?"

"Sure." He turned and rushed out of the room.

Erin held Lilly against her chest. "Oh, sweetheart,

I'm sorry I wasn't here for you. We're going to make you feel better real soon."

She walked into the bathroom and turned on the faucet in the shower. By the time Austin returned, the room was starting to steam up.

"Why are you in here?"

"I'm pretty sure Lilly has croup. The steam will help reduce the symptoms. It's a viral infection in her throat and trachea."

Austin frowned. "Should we take her to the doctor?"

"Let me examine her first." She handed the baby to her daddy and had him sit down on the toilet lid. She reached into the medical bag and took out her stethoscope. The fussy baby wasn't in the mood to cooperate.

Erin began to talk to her as she examined her. "You're such a good baby." She listened to Lilly's chest and was relieved it was clear. Next she moved to her ears. No inflammation there, either. By this time, Lilly cried out, letting her know she didn't want any more.

"We'll keep her in here for about ten minutes. I'll go and start up the humidifier in the bedroom."

After filling the machine and turning it on, Erin pulled her phone from her pocket. She found Lilly's pediatrician in her contacts and made the call. She talked to the nurse and related Lilly's symptoms. Then the doctor came on and suggested they bring the baby into the ER as a precaution.

Erin returned to the bathroom and saw Austin cradling his baby daughter. He looked up at her. "She looks pale to me."

Erin glanced at the child and nodded. "Don't panic. I called the doctor, and he suggested we take her into the ER."

"So you're worried, too."

"Of course I am. This precious little girl means a lot to me."

They made it to the hospital in record time. Once in the examination room, Erin stood at the end of the table while Austin held on to Lilly's tiny hand, trying to reassure her. The diaper-clad baby coughed and cried as the young doctor examined her. Finally Dr. North finished, and Austin lifted his daughter into his arms and began soothing her once again.

The physician looked over Lilly's case file, then at Austin. "Your daughter has croup."

Austin looked at Erin. "You were right."

The young doctor continued to explain. "It's a condition that causes constriction in the airway. Her breathing isn't too bad, but with her elevated temperature, I'm concerned about infection."

Austin looked at Erin in panic. She immediately went to him. "Lilly will be okay."

The doctor agreed. "Since she's only four months old, I'd like to keep her here for a few hours to monitor her long enough to give her a moist breathing treatment. It should help improve her condition. Let me go and instruct the nurse." He walked out of the room.

Austin released a long breath. "Oh, God... I had no idea. Lilly was fine last night when I put her to bed. Wait—she did cough a few times, and she didn't want to finish her bottle." He sent a terrified look to Erin. "I shouldn't have taken her out in the cold yesterday."

Erin shook her head as she rubbed Lilly's back. "This isn't your fault, Austin. Kids get sick, and croup is very common."

"But we had to bring her to the hospital."

"Because Lilly could be seen faster here."

Austin paced around the room, gently patting his daughter's back. She had quieted down and her eyes were closed. Erin felt just as helpless. She ached for this child, too. Even though she was a nurse and had seen a lot of medical conditions over the years, she was still fearful seeing Lilly struggle to breathe.

The baby opened her eyes and looked at Erin. She reached out a hand. "Hi, sweetie. You're such a brave little girl."

Lilly let out a soft cry and reached out for Erin. Austin gave her up. "See, she misses you, too," he told her.

Erin wasn't listening. Holding this baby close was so soothing for her, too.

Two hours later, after Lilly's treatment and follow-up exam with the doctor, they left the ER. All that time, Erin never left the baby's side. She even sat with the baby in the backseat on the drive home.

By the time Austin arrived at the house, Lilly was sound asleep. They went into the nursery, where the humidifier had been running most of the afternoon.

"Just set her carrier on the floor," Erin whispered. "Poor thing is exhausted from the ordeal."

"What about her feeding?"

"They gave her fluids in the ER. If she's hungry, she'll tell you."

Austin sank into the rocker and faced his sleeping daughter in the carrier. He closed his eyes, and Erin could see the anguish across his face.

"I don't know if I can survive this." His voice was

low but filled with raw emotion. "She scares me to death."

Erin tried to make light of the situation. "Wait until she starts driving and dating."

He just shook his head as tears formed in his eyes. "I never thought I could love anyone like this. She's my world." He looked at Erin. "How did that happen so fast?"

Erin's chest constricted. She felt the same way. She'd come to care so much for these two. But she had to remember they weren't her family. "It's called being a parent."

He looked at the sleeping child. "I can understand why Megan fought so hard to keep her. I love Lilly so much." Austin reached for Erin and pulled her into his lap. She went willingly. "Thank you for being here for us."

"I'm glad I could help."

His hand cupped the side of her neck. "Your being here helps me, too." He pulled her close. "Please, Erin, don't leave us tonight."

She wanted so desperately to stay, and even knowing the possibility of Austin breaking her heart, she couldn't turn him down. "I'll stay until Lilly is over the worst."

That was her problem. She was borrowing them both to fill in for what she didn't have in her own life. That had to stop. His arms pulled her tighter against him. Soon.

Chapter 16

Four days had passed since Erin moved back into Austin's house. She'd rationalized it by saying she wanted to be there for Lilly, but in fact it had been for her, too. A temporary fix for the problem, but knowing sooner or later she had to let go of both father and daughter.

Besides, she couldn't keep giving her shifts away at the center and expect to keep her job. Her supervisor, Shirley, had been patient so far. And as long as she stayed in Austin's and Lilly's lives, the longer it would take to begin her own. She'd stopped her IVF treatment, deciding to wait until her life was more stable.

All she had accomplished was falling in love with a man who had pretty much kept his distance from her since they returned from the hospital.

"Hey, where did you go?"

She looked up to see the bare-chested Austin dressed

in a pair of gym shorts and seated on the bench, working with weights. Dear Lord help her.

"You say something?"

"I asked if we're done yet."

Seated on the floor, she glanced at the wall clock. "Pretty much." She started to get up when he reached for her.

"Erin…did I do something wrong?"

She couldn't hide her surprise. "No. Why do you ask?"

He didn't look convinced. "You've been frowning all day."

She glanced away. "Sorry. I have a lot on my mind."

He didn't release her. "I'm not buying it. I thought I'd done everything you wanted. I've given you space. Even though it's been killing me, I haven't laid a hand on you. Yet you jump every time you come near me."

Excitement raced through her as she picked at the carpet fibers under her hand. "You thought keeping your distance was what I wanted?"

"Damn straight. I didn't want you to think sex was the underlying reason I wanted you to move back in here."

The heat rose through her body to her face, but she grew brave. "Was it?"

A slow grin appeared on his handsome face. "Hell, yes, it was, but not the only one. Maybe I should just show you how much I want you."

A thrill raced through her.

Austin tugged on her arm and she rose to her knees. He swooped down and captured her mouth, letting her know immediately how he felt about her.

When he finally released her, his eyes searched her

face. "If I had my way, you'd never leave." His hands wrapped around her back, and he made room for her between his legs. "I want you to stay because you want to be with me, to build on what's between us."

Her heart soared at his words, but they terrified her at the same time.

He leaned down and kissed her, then lowered her to the floor. "I want you right now." He cupped her hips, bringing her against his aroused body.

She could barely think. "What about Lilly?"

He glanced at the clock. "I'd say we have about thirty minutes before she wakes up from her nap." He grinned and placed tiny kisses along her jaw. "We should take advantage of the time."

His mouth closed over hers as he lowered her to the carpeted floor. He had her tights stripped off, then her T-shirt before she could argue.

She shivered as she lay there completely naked before him. His heated gaze roamed over her.

"You are so incredibly beautiful."

His words were like a caress. "You're not so bad yourself, cowboy," she breathed, wanting more.

He stood. "You think so, huh?" He came back to her and kissed her hard and deep. His hand moved over her rib cage, causing her to arch her back at the torturous sensation.

"Please."

His gaze met hers. "I love seeing you like this, knowing how much you want me."

"I do want you." She rested her trembling hands against his chest as she caressed his lean and sculptured body. With a quiet growl, Austin took hold of her wrists.

Resting on his elbows, he confessed, "I can't stand any more. I want to feel all of you."

Austin stayed true to his promise and took her to places she'd never dreamed two people could reach together.

Later that day, Erin was preparing supper. Well, she'd heated up the food that Shelby had brought by earlier. They'd nearly gotten caught with their pants down. She thought back to the afterglow of her lying in Austin's arms when a knock sounded on the door. Thankfully Austin had been quick to slip on pants and went to answer it to find his sister-in-law.

Shelby had quickly figured out what she'd interrupted, handed over the casserole to them and said a quick goodbye. Erin wasn't worried that Shelby would say anything. The young chef, wife and mother was a good friend and Erin knew she'd also keep this private.

Five minutes after the departure, Erin's phone chirped, alerting her to a text. Shelby had sent her a message: So happy for you both. Talk later.

Erin smiled, but in truth, for the first time in a very long time, she was eager to be part of this loving family. In reality, her days here were numbered, and soon, she needed to make some decisions about her own life.

Was she willing to try to be part of a couple? The thought scared her to death. It meant she'd have to take a chance. And what about Austin? Would she and Lilly be enough to keep him here?

She shook her head, then released a long breath. "Stop trying to overthink it," she argued. Right now, she only wanted to dream about spending time with Austin…and Lilly.

She glanced out the window. He'd gone to help out his father and brother during the therapy session. She was happy that he was getting out. The past several weeks, he'd been with his daughter full-time. And she also knew he needed to work through some issues with his dad. The only way was to talk and spend time together.

Erin checked on the pot roast in the oven, then on Lilly in her swing. Seeing that the baby was content, she walked down the hall to get her clothes ready for her shift at the center.

There was a knock on the door. Maybe it was Shelby coming to get the scoop. "Coming," she called as she hurried to open the door. Her heart sank upon finding Jay Bridges on the stoop. "Hello, Mr. Bridges."

He nodded. "Mrs. Carlton."

"If you're looking for Austin, he's down at the corral with his brother and father."

The older man nodded and started to turn away, but stopped. "I know you have to be pretty happy to have Austin in your clutches."

She froze. "I beg your pardon?"

"Your playing house isn't going to last very much longer. Austin likes to be in the limelight—he always has. He likes going town to town, each rodeo a challenge."

She worked to keep her calm. "You seem to think I'm trying to stop him."

"You might be one of the reasons, but like I said, nothing is going to stop his plans." A smirk came across his face. "You might be his flavor of the month, but you only serve a purpose because of his daughter. That doesn't mean you'll keep him content in the long run."

She hated that this man could play on her insecurities, as doubts came rushing back. It did the trick. Her thoughts went to her marriage and all the times Jared had left her alone. She shook it off. "I'm Austin's therapist, and I watch his daughter until he's capable of doing it on his own."

He nodded. "And in the end that's all you'll be to him. You seem like a nice person, so that's why I'm giving you this advice." The manager shifted his briefcase to his other hand. "You can't keep Austin from going back to what he loves—the rodeo. And he will go back."

Her chest constricted painfully, making it hard to breathe. "Still not my business, Mr. Bridges."

"You don't believe me?" He arched an eyebrow. "Then why has he asked me to set up a meeting with several rodeo managers?"

Erin gripped the doorknob, trying to handle the pain shooting through her heart. Suddenly the sound of Lilly's cry brought her back to reality. "Like I said, you need to discuss this with Austin. I have to go and take care of Lilly. Goodbye, Mr. Bridges." She shut the door in his face and went to get Lilly out of the swing.

She cuddled the baby close, enjoying the sweet scent of her skin. Closing her eyes, she knew soon her arms would be empty again.

Austin led Sassy Girl back into the large barn, past several stalls until he reached the aging black mare's home. Once he'd removed the tack, he made sure the animal had some feed and fresh water before he stepped out and latched the gate. He'd had a good time working with the kids today. He could now understand why his father loved this job. Yet he had his own ideas on what he wanted to fill his days. Lilly and Erin. He'd been thinking about nothing else.

He heard his name and turned to see Cullen walking down the aisle toward him. "Hey, good job today, bro. Thanks for the help."

"No problem. I really enjoyed it."

Cullen studied him. "Dad enjoyed it, too. I hope you can come by more often. He really wants to spend some time with you."

"Not easy with Lilly, and I can't keep asking Erin to watch her."

"Why don't you bring them both down to the arena? Usually Shelby's around, and she would love to get her hands on the baby." Cullen took off his hat and combed his hair back, then replaced it. "Of course, that would heighten the discussion about us having a baby."

"She putting the pressure on you?"

"And I'm crumbling, too."

Austin laughed. "Four months ago, women couldn't wait to get their hands on me. Now I'm a dad, and I love it."

Cullen looked at him. "I'm pretty proud of you, too, bro, for how you've handled yourself. You're a great dad."

Austin was touched by his twin's words. "Thank you. It's not easy, especially when Lilly got sick last week. I was glad Erin was there."

Cullen nodded. "Erin's a good person. We all like her a lot, and I think you do, too."

Austin sat down on the stall's trunk and stretched out his leg, enjoying the fact that there wasn't much pain. "Yeah, I do. More than I ever thought possible to care about another person." He thought about all the tragedy in Erin's life. "I want to keep her in my and Lilly's life, but I need to offer her a future."

"That's good." Cullen's smile began to fade. "Look, don't make the same mistake I did and let your stubborn pride get the best of you. I shut out Shelby because I didn't have a permanent job." Cullen paused. "You're not thinking about going back on the rodeo circuit, are you?"

Austin shook his head. "Not in the way you think, but it's been a huge part of my life. Bull riding helped make me who I am today. It's hard to shut the door completely." He shrugged. "I need to make some personal appearances to keep sponsors. At least ride out my fame a little while longer."

"You can always raise cattle. There's plenty of room on this ranch."

Before Austin could speak, he heard someone call his name. He looked up to see his business manager.

He walked toward him. "Jay, what are you doing here?"

The older man shrugged. "I needed to talk with you, and I thought I'd come by and tell you the good news. Two of your sponsors still want your endorsement."

The sun had gone down when Austin made his way back to the house almost an hour later than he'd intended. He hated that Jay had kept him so long, but they had a lot to go over. He just didn't expect they'd handle their business in the barn's tack room, but knowing how Erin felt about his manager, it was the best place.

He was happy about retaining two sponsors, but not so happy with the conditions on the contract. Jay had agreed to too many appearances before talking to him. Finally, after arguing back and forth, Jay agreed to go back and make the deal more to his liking.

Austin smiled. He hadn't thought he'd be able to get any sponsor without getting on a bull again, but if his new plan worked out, he'd be set for his and Lilly's future. He wanted to include Erin in that, too. He only needed to convince Erin.

He opened the door and found the living room empty. "Erin," he called.

A few seconds later, she walked out of the back and his heart raced just seeing her. She was dressed in a pair of jeans and a blouse. Her glorious red hair hung free and was longer now, nearly to her shoulders. He loved running his fingers through the silky strands when he kissed her.

She put her finger to her lips to let him know that Lilly was sleeping. He was disappointed he wouldn't see her, but it would be nice to have some alone time with Erin.

"Sorry I'm late," he whispered as he reached for her, drawing her close. He felt her stiffen, and he pulled back. "Look, I know you're angry, but Jay stopped by the barn."

She shook her head. "I know. He came here first. Why don't you go in the kitchen and eat?"

She started to walk away, but he pulled her back. "Not before this." His mouth closed over hers in a tender kiss that quickly grew into more. He loved how she responded to him. How her sweet body was pressed against his, fitting him perfectly.

Suddenly she pulled back. "Look, Austin, I don't have a lot of time. I took a shift for one of the other nurses tonight."

Erin saw his surprised look before she glanced away. "I know it's short notice, but I need to repay a lot of people for taking my shifts." It wasn't exactly true, but she couldn't keep being around Austin like this. "Come and sit down." She rushed to pull his plate out of the oven. "I kept it warm for you."

Austin didn't sit down. "Okay, Erin, but before I eat, tell me what's really going on. Did Jay say something to upset you?"

She shrugged. "Maybe, but he was only telling me the truth."

Austin folded his arms over his chest. He tried to look intimidating, but she knew a softer side of this man. "Then you tell me what that is and let me decide."

She couldn't tell him everything. "He just said what I already knew. That our lives are very different, and we were foolish to get involved in the first place."

"So you think I was a mistake?"

"Letting it get personal between us, yes," she lied. "You knew I didn't want to get involved again. And I knew that you wanted to go back to the rodeo."

He shook his head. "That dream passed me by when Lilly entered the picture. So I changed my dream. I want to tell you about it."

She raised a hand. She didn't want to hear any promises. "It's not your fault, Austin. It's me. I just can't do this again." She couldn't bring up Jared's name. "It's better if we break it off now before anyone gets hurt."

"So you're just walking away, from me, from Lilly."

She blinked back tears. She didn't want to, but eventually, she'd lose Lilly, and it was hard enough now. "You'll see it's for the best." She couldn't be angry with this man just because he wanted something different from life. "It's okay, Austin. The last thing I want is to hold you back." She released a breath. "That's why I feel it's better that

I go back to doing what I love." Besides him and Lilly. "My job. And I also realized I can't do two jobs anymore."

She walked out of the kitchen, hurried down the hall and grabbed her packed bag. She walked by the nursery and paused, but didn't go in. She'd already kissed Lilly goodbye. Now she just had to get out the door before she broke down.

She took out a piece of paper and handed it to Austin, who hadn't moved from the doorway. "I called Jason, the therapist you used before, to take over for me. If you don't like working with him, call your doctor. I'm sure he can recommend someone." She glanced at him. "Goodbye, Austin."

He reached for her arm. "So you're just going to walk out and not let me even tell you my plans?"

She shook her head. "I don't want to argue with you, Austin." She just wished for once in her life that she would come first. "I want you to be happy."

"And you think I'll be happy without you in my life?"

"In the long run you will be."

He glared at her. "You're just afraid that I'll be like Jared. I'm not him, Erin. Dammit, I'm not gonna run out on you."

She couldn't listen to his promises. She was safer not believing. "Goodbye, Austin."

Somehow, Erin managed to walk through the open door and climb into her van. She started the engine and headed down the road. Tears ran down her face as she tried to convince herself she'd done the right thing, the safest thing to protect her heart. If she knew this day was coming, then why did this hurt so badly?

Chapter 17

Later that evening, Austin held Lilly against his chest as he walked the floor trying to get her to sleep. She let out a loud cry, letting him know she was having none of it. The baby knew something wasn't right, that Erin wasn't here to soothe her.

"Sorry, sweetheart. I wish I could make it better."

He wasn't feeling any better, either. How could Erin leave them as if they hadn't meant a thing to her? That was what hurt the most. Why couldn't she stay and give him a chance?

Moving his daughter to his shoulder, he swayed back and forth. "It's going to be okay, sweetheart. Daddy's here. I'm not going anywhere."

The baby released a shuddering breath as Austin continued to rub her back in a soothing motion.

There was a soft knock on the door, and a spark of

hope raced through him. Had Erin come back? Soon disappointment struck him when Trent poked his head inside. Austin put his finger to his lips, as Lilly seemed to have quieted. A few seconds later, he felt the baby's motionless weight against his chest. She was finally asleep.

He carried her down the hall and gently laid her in the crib. He watched her precious face, rosy with sleep, and his heart squeezed with overwhelming emotions. He never knew he could love like this, realizing he'd do anything for his little girl. She was his life. He wanted to share these moments with Erin.

"Looks like it's just you and me, kid," he whispered as he tucked the blanket over her.

He returned to the living room and found his stepbrother seated in the chair, leafing through a magazine.

"Is Lilly asleep?" Trent asked as he put the publication down.

"For now. She had a pretty rough day."

Trent frowned. "What happened? She's not sick again, is she?"

Austin shook his head. Not that kind of sick. "Erin quit earlier. Said she couldn't handle two jobs any longer."

Trent studied him a moment. "Well, you've been a handful, and add in Lilly. Babies take a lot of time and energy."

"I know that, and I offered to pay enough so she didn't have to work at the care center. She turned me down."

Austin sat there a moment. His stepbrother was so different from him and Cullen. Dark coffee eyes that still held that authoritative glare; even his stance was more rigid. A dozen years in the military would give you that edge.

"Yeah, Erin is pretty independent that way," Trent said. "Isn't the job here temporary?"

Austin nodded.

"I can understand why she'd go back to the care center. One day you and Lilly could just move on and she'd be left without a job."

"Whoa. Who said I was moving?"

"I don't know—you tell me. Cullen said your manager came by to give you news about rodeo appearances."

"Nothing is for sure. He's still working on the details."

"Were you going to include Erin in your plans?"

"I thought we were working in that direction."

Trent gave him a half grin. "It's a funny thing about women. They need to be reassured and included in those decisions."

"Erin told me from the beginning that she didn't want anything serious, no commitments." *She only wants a baby*, he added silently. "I know she loves Lilly. That's why I can't believe she left so suddenly."

Trent shook his head. "Then you have to come up with a reason for her to change her mind. And leave the work part out of the equation."

"That's the problem. I'm not sure about my future. It's always been the rodeo." Austin had hoped that he and Lilly were enough to keep Erin with them.

His stepbrother stood. "From what I've learned from Brooke, Erin had a pretty rocky marriage even before her husband came home severely wounded. She worked so hard to help with his rehab, to get him to walk again, to teach him to speak again."

"I had no idea Jared was that bad off physically."

Trent nodded. "Bad enough that Erin turned their home into a care facility and took in more patients to handle her being off work. She wanted to be there full-time for her husband."

And she lost him anyway. "She said he committed suicide."

Trent frowned. "She told you that?"

Austin nodded. "Yeah, she said he just gave up. I think she's still angry about it." He didn't want to say what else Jared took away from his wife. Was that why Erin left him? Was she afraid he would leave her, too?

Trent released a long breath. "I'm sorry, Austin. I kind of thought you two…hit it off."

He'd thought so, too. "It's probably better this way." He glanced down at the cast on his leg. "I still have a lot to deal with, especially now that I have Lilly. Maybe I was wrong to let my daughter get attached to her."

"Babies get attached to people, especially when they help take care of them."

"Yeah, but Lilly already lost her mother only a few months ago. Erin is the second person…" Austin couldn't talk anymore. She chose to leave them, even when he asked her to stay. He did everything but beg.

"Look, Trent, did you come by for something, or just to bug me?"

Trent grinned. "Although the idea is intriguing, there was a reason. Like I said, Cullen told me you've been offered some rodeo appearances. Does that mean you're planning to leave?"

Word traveled fast. "Not permanently, but I need to

keep my name out there, especially since I'm not riding anymore. But if I'm not out in public so people remember me, I could lose my last two sponsors. You
can't believe the money they pay me." He didn't need
the money that bad, but he didn't know what the future
held for him.

"I know, but do you really want to travel? What about
Lilly?"

Hell, he didn't know what to do. "I'll figure it out."

Trent hesitated, then finally said, "You know, if you
really want to keep your name out there, you might
think about teaching."

"Teaching what?"

"Your craft—bull riding."

"You're kidding, right?"

"No, I'm dead serious. You didn't get to be a world-
class bull rider without learning a lot of skills. So teach
others to ride. With your name and ability, I bet you'd
have a lot of students."

His chest tightened with pride at his brother's words.
"Thanks. That means a lot to me."

"You've earned the praise, Austin, so take it. In my
mind, this is the best way to stay in the sport without
getting back on a bull. And the best part, you get to stay
home right here with your daughter and your family."

The idea sparked in his head. "You really think I
could do this?"

"You don't know until you try." Trent shrugged.
"You've got land right here on the ranch. There's about
ten acres right off the highway on the west end of the
property. It's away from the main house and the therapy
riding school. Of course, you'll have to build a corral
and all the other structures. But there is plenty of good

pastureland for the bulls. If you think it's a viable idea, then you should talk to Cullen about laying claim to that section."

Austin was awestruck that his brother had come up with this plan. "So you feel I can make a living at something like this?"

Trent nodded. "Hell, yes, bro. And I wouldn't mind at all putting up your clients in my hunting cabins, or I'm sure Rory and I could work out a deal to build a few cabins on your land." His brother grinned at him. "I can see it now. Brannigan Bull Riding School, all training done by World Champion 'Ace' Brannigan."

Austin was crazy to even think about this big of a project, but he was. Then his thoughts turned to Erin. Maybe this would prove to her that he wasn't going anywhere.

Three days later at the care center, Erin's shift had ended, and she was headed to the nurses' station in the next building as a visitor when she heard her name called. She turned around to see Brooke and little Christopher walking toward her.

She smiled. "Hello, Brooke. Hi, Chris. I was just going to sign in."

The pretty blonde gave her a hug. Her hazel eyes sparkled as she pulled back and said, "I'm so glad you made it today."

"I said I would." Erin leaned down to hug the toddler. "Hey, cutie, I have something for you." She reached into her uniform pocket and pulled out a palm-size fire truck.

"Fire truck," the curly-headed boy said as he took it. "Thank you, Erin."

"You're welcome." Erin stood up and looked at her friend. "I explained I couldn't get away."

Brooke looked doubtful. "If I didn't know better, I'd say you've been avoiding me."

"Why would I do that? You're my best friend."

"Maybe because you don't want me to ask about what happened between you and Austin."

"There's nothing to tell. I couldn't handle the hours. I needed more sleep, so I had to give up my extra job." She couldn't meet Brooke's eyes. Darn, she hated to lie, but she wasn't going to admit how much she missed seeing Lilly every day. How she'd thought about Austin's touch, his sweet loving. How many times had she wanted to drive out to the ranch? Then what? Start dreaming again about what would never happen between her and Austin…

Brooke watched her. "So have you managed to catch up on sleep?"

Erin's gaze went to Christopher, who was playing with his new truck. "Not really," she admitted. "Third shift is exhausting." And she couldn't sleep worrying about Lilly…and Austin. "I can't wait until I switch to the day shift in another month."

"That's great! Then you can live like the rest of us. And I want us to go out again before the baby comes." Her friend rubbed her flat belly. "More girls' nights with Laurel and Shelby, too. I have a feeling Shelby will be the next one to end up pregnant. Little Lilly has given her that nudge."

Erin's heart tightened painfully. Would she ever be able to make that announcement? She didn't know if she could handle seeing someone else have a baby when she hadn't made that dream happen for herself.

"So are you ready to visit Coralee?" Erin asked, wanting to end this conversation.

Brooke released a long breath. "Sure." She turned to her son. "Come on, Chris. Let's go see Grammy Cora."

The toddler ran to her, smiling. "Gammy," he repeated and took her hand.

After signing in, Brooke and Erin walked down to the private room that Coralee Harper had been living in since Brooke had moved her here when she learned about the existence of her father, Rory Quinn. After father and daughter, and her twin sister, Laurel, discovered one another, Brooke moved here from Las Vegas. Of course, falling in love with Trent Landry was the icing on the cake. Erin couldn't be happier for her friend, and she decided to relocate also to leave her bad memories behind and start fresh in Hidden Springs.

Brooke pushed the door open. "Mother," she said softly.

The fifty-five-year-old Alzheimer's patient sat in a chair looking out the window. Brooke called out again. "Coralee."

The once-beautiful Las Vegas singer with the striking blue eyes and smoky voice turned and looked at the intruders without showing any expression. Then Christopher broke free and ran to the woman.

"Gammy Cora," he cried and laid his head in her lap. "I love you."

Erin's eyes filled as the child did more than any therapy could. He got a reaction from the woman.

Coralee's hand stroked the boy's head. "Hello, little boy," she said. Surprisingly, she showed affection toward the child, when years ago she had neglected her own daughter Brooke and given Laurel to her father to raise, all for her career. About three years ago she had been diagnosed with Alzheimer's.

"Mother, remember me? Your daughter Brooke."

Coralee's pretty blue eyes narrowed. "You're not my daughter. Her name is Laurel."

Erin saw the flash of pain in Brooke's eyes as she took the chair across from her mother. "Okay, I'm Laurel." Then she pointed to Erin. "Do you remember Erin?"

"Hi, Coralee."

The older woman stood and went to Erin. "Hello, Erin." The woman touched her face. "You are pretty."

"Thank you. You are pretty, too."

Coralee primped her hair. "Men tell me that all the time."

Brooke stepped forward again. "Mother, I came to tell you something. I'm going to have another baby. Christopher is getting a little brother or sister."

Coralee tilted her head as if trying to understand what her daughter said. "A baby? I have babies. Two beautiful baby girls."

Coralee turned her attention back to Erin, then stepped forward and looked down at her stomach. "Oh, are you going to have a baby, too?"

The next morning Erin sat in her van after her shift ended and made a phone call to Dr. Gail Evans. She needed to make another appointment with the fertility specialist. Needless to say, the doctor wasn't happy that she'd stopped her shots. Before Erin could start the series once again, she needed to go in for an appointment.

She couldn't blame the doctor for her concern. Hormones weren't anything to mess around with. Neither was Erin. She wasn't getting any younger, and her window to have an easy pregnancy was quickly closing. This might be her last chance. A thrill rushed through her at the thought that in a few weeks she could be ready to be impregnated.

Even though her doctor told her she was in good physical shape, she was going to spend a lot of time praying that the insemination would take. She would have a healthy baby.

And nothing was going to stop her this time.

Her thoughts turned to Austin, and she was saddened knowing she couldn't share this with him. She'd known on the first day they'd met, the man wasn't for her. Yet she'd been foolish once again to start to hope that they could build something together. But she was wrong. Again.

In all fairness to Austin, he hadn't made her any promises. She brushed a tear off her cheek. He didn't want to set down roots, and she couldn't give up her dream of a home and family. Truth was, she wasn't enough to keep him here. She had to move past it and make her own life.

She drove down Main Street toward her apartment and decided she should eat something, recalling the three pounds she'd lost. After parking the van, she climbed out and quickly wrapped her coat around her as the cold air chilled her. November was here, and soon there would be snow and frigid temperatures. This was when she missed Las Vegas just a little bit.

Erin walked through the door into Sweet Heaven. Passing the glass case filled with bakery items, she somehow resisted the temptation.

"You need to eat healthy," she murmured and looked

up at the chalkboard menu overhead. One of their sandwiches to go would be nice. She glanced around. And
she wouldn't mind saying hello to Shelby.

The place was busy with the breakfast crowd, and
she questioned her decision. She started to leave when
she heard her name and looked around to see Shelby.

She was wrapped in a hug. "Erin, it's so good to
see you."

"Good to see you, too. Glad your business is doing
so well."

"Yes, I'm happy about that." Shelby looked around
at the filled tables. "Let me find you a place to sit."

"No need. I'll just take one of your turkey cranberry
sandwiches with me if it's not too early for lunch."

"Of course not, but please stay a little while. We
haven't talked in forever."

Reluctantly, she agreed. "Okay, sure. But I'll need
to get home to sleep."

"Sure." Shelby took her by the arm. "Oh, look,
there's someone who's been missing you."

Erin tensed, but followed her friend to the back of
the restaurant. Her heart stopped suddenly, then sped
up when she saw Austin sitting at the small café table.
He was dressed in faded jeans and a henley shirt, holding the baby on his lap. He looked sexy and endearing
at the same time.

Shelby's voice woke her from her musings. "I'm sure
Austin wouldn't mind sharing his table."

Austin looked up at her. He seemed just as surprised
as she was. "Erin…"

"Austin." She didn't take her eyes off the baby. Lilly
had grown so much in only a week.

Hearing a bell sound, Shelby said, "I've got to go back to work. I'll bring your sandwich."

Before Erin could call her back, Shelby was gone. "Really, I shouldn't intrude."

The baby let out a cry, and suddenly Erin's arms ached to hold her.

Then Austin said, "Don't go, Erin. Please, stay, if only for Lilly."

As Erin turned back around, Lilly was reaching for her. The baby grinned and cried out for her.

"Could I hold her?" she asked.

Austin held his daughter out to her. "Of course."

Erin took the sweet bundle dressed in navy tights and a red ruffled long-sleeved shirt and a matching headband that Erin had picked out the day at Baby World. She cradled the baby close. Lilly immediately grabbed a handful of her hair. Erin smiled and sat down in the vacant chair. "How has she been? Any recurrence of croup?"

Austin shook his head. "Just had her to the doctor this morning, and she's in perfect health."

Erin finally looked at him, in those beautiful gray-green eyes, and was nearly lost. He had day-old growth along his jaw. He looked tired. "Is she sleeping all right?"

"She's been waking up a lot."

Erin sat the baby down on her lap. "Maybe you should increase the amount of cereal."

"She's not hungry. She misses you." His gaze locked on hers. "I do, too, Erin."

Oh, God. She missed him more than she thought possible. "I miss you both, too. But I need to move on with my life."

Austin sat back and watched Erin with his daughter,

and his heart ached for her. "Does moving on mean that you're planning to do the IVF?"

She looked surprised at the question, but then she nodded. "I've never changed those plans. They only got delayed a bit. I'm hoping in a few weeks, I'll be ready…"

He tried not to react, but his insides were churning with anger and jealousy. Erin would soon be pregnant with a stranger's baby. "I know you've wanted that for a long time, and I'm sorry if we caused you any holdup."

She shook her head. "No, I'll never regret my time with Lilly."

What about your time with me? "Well, I'm happy for you." That was true, but that didn't stop him from wanting to be the father to her child. By the look on her face, she wasn't ready to hear anything he was about to tell her.

So he changed the subject. "I've made a lot of changes in my life, too. In a few weeks I'm getting this cast off." He might have a limp, but he could deal with that. At least he'd be standing on his own two legs. That gave him a lot of possibilities, and hope.

She rewarded him with a genuine smile that had his pulse racing again. "That's wonderful."

"What would also be wonderful is if you'd be a part of our lives. And I'm not talking about being Lilly's babysitter."

Suddenly her smile faded as she pulled back. "I can't, Austin." She glanced around, avoiding his eyes. "With my schedule right now, I'm pretty busy. And in the long run, it's better this way."

He reached out and covered her hand with his. "Dammit, Erin. It doesn't have to be this way between us. Why can't we be together?"

Seeing the tears form in her eyes, he felt like a heel. But her show of emotion also gave him hope that she still cared.

She hugged Lilly close, then handed her back. "I'm sorry, Austin." She stood. "I can't do this again. Goodbye."

He started to call her back, but Lilly began to fuss. He rested his daughter against his shoulder and rubbed her back as he watched Erin walk out the door. "It's okay, sweetie. I'm not giving up on your mommy." He knew he only had a few weeks to convince her that he was a family man.

Chapter 18

"So, what do you think?"

A week later, Austin stood alongside Dan Lynch, looking over the empty pasture at the ranch. The temperature was downright cold, and he was grateful the baby was strapped inside the warm truck. He held down the engineer's building plans on the hood.

Dan remained silent.

"At least tell me if you're interested."

The older man nodded toward the papers. "Those are some mighty fancy plans you have here."

Good—he was interested. "As you can see, this land is pretty much untouched, so I'm needing to build arenas and outbuildings." He pointed toward the drawings of the four small cabins. "These structures are for the students to stay in during the training. I thought it would be better if the rookie riders had a onetime cost for everything since we're far from town for lodging."

Dan turned to him, showing every one of his sixty-three years in his lined face. "Sounds like a great idea, but I don't have the capital to put into this business. All my money is wrapped up in my livestock."

Austin wondered if a lot of Dan's money had gone to pay for Megan's medical bills. "I don't need capital, but I need bulls to help train the rider. You have bulls. At least I'm hoping you'll want to retire some of your stock here on the Circle R, so I can use them in the school."

Dan shook his head. "I can't believe you're serious."

"Dead serious. I own part of this ranch, so this will be my and Lilly's permanent home. That little girl in the truck means more to me than any championship I ever won. I meant what I said before. I'd like you to be a part of her life." He raised a hand before Dan could speak. "You can continue your rough stock business or just retire and live here. Once I build my new home, you're welcome to move into the foreman's place. All I ask is that you supply my stock."

"Why me?"

"Because you're good at what you do. But most importantly, you're Lilly's grandpa. She needs you in her life."

The old man blinked and glanced away. "I wouldn't mind seeing that little girl on a regular basis." He sniffed and looked back at Austin. "I think Megan saw a lot more in you than any of us did. You've been a good father to Lilly, Austin. She seems so happy."

"She's been the best thing that's ever happened to me. I'm building this school for my daughter's future. I'm finished with the rodeo, but I'm hoping my name and experience will make this business successful."

Dan let out a long breath. "Since Megan died, I

haven't had much desire to travel, either. With her gone, I've been lost these past months." The man looked at him. "You and Lilly just gave me a reason to start a new job. Thank you for this opportunity."

"Hell, Dan, to carry this off, I need you, too. And Lilly just plain needs you around."

Dan nodded. "I need her, too."

Austin paused a moment, and Dan noticed. "Is there something else you want to say?"

Austin needed to put everything out on the table. "Yeah—there's also a woman in my life. Well, she's not in my life at the moment. I'm still trying to convince her that I'm the man she deserves. She adores Lilly and has taken care of her for the last month. We both love Erin, and I want to make it permanent between us." He had to prove to her that he needed to be part of a family as much as she did. He hoped this was the first step.

Two days later, Erin made it to work at the care center. She had taken yesterday off because of the flu. Not wanting to get out of bed, she canceled her doctor's appointment with Dr. Evans, afraid she might make others sick. She was able to get another appointment, but not until Friday. Then she was hoping she'd finally be able to focus on her life, and chance for a baby.

The halls were quiet as she walked around doing her room check. Everyone was in bed for the night, but that didn't mean they wouldn't try to get up. There were sensors and monitors in every room. So far, so good.

She went to the nurses' station and took a drink of her herbal tea. It seemed to help her still-unsettled stomach.

She glanced at the clock to see it was only 2:00 a.m.

She had a long night ahead of her. Her thoughts turned to Austin. Was he asleep, or thinking about her? Was he with Lilly? Her chest tightened with feelings she couldn't shake. She kept telling herself that she'd get over the two of them.

"Hi, Erin."

Erin jerked around to see her supervisor, Shirley. She stood. "Oh, hi. I was checking the room monitors."

Shirley took the seat next to hers. "Sit and take a minute. It's not against the rules to take a few minutes. Besides, I want to find out how you've been."

"I'm fine. Sorry about yesterday. I didn't want anyone else sick."

"You must have been feeling bad, because you never call in." Her supervisor eyed her closely. "I hope you're getting some sleep. You still look a little pale." She paused. "You know if there's something wrong, I'm a pretty good listener."

Although she fought it, tears gathered in her eyes, but Erin couldn't talk about Austin. "I appreciate that, Shirley. This is something I have to work out on my own."

"Sounds like man troubles." She patted her hand. "Since my divorce, I can bash with the best of them."

"No bashing. We just wanted different things." She shrugged. "It's better we learn it now instead of later."

There was a beeping sound on the screen and they both looked. "It's Hattie's room. I'll go see what's wrong."

"Holler if you need help," Shirley said.

With a nod, Erin took off down the hall and went into the patient's dimly lit room.

She found the frail white-haired woman out of bed

and going through her picture book. "Hattie," Erin whispered. "What are you doing? You need your rest."

"I can't sleep. I'm afraid."

She saw tears in the old woman's eyes and took hold of her hand as she knelt down beside the bed. "What are you afraid of, Hattie?"

The woman looked at her. "If I go to sleep I won't remember my Johnny. I can't forget him—I promised. All the time he was gone overseas, I never forgot that he would come home to me." A big smile appeared. "I never forgot him."

"Oh, Hattie, you're not going to forget him." That was a lie. Erin reached out and touched Hattie's forehead. "Johnny might not always be in here..." Then she touched her chest. "But he'll always be in your heart."

Erin took Hattie's favorite picture of her beloved Johnny and helped the woman back into bed. "Here, you hold on to this."

Hattie gripped Erin's hand. "Stay with me."

Erin nodded, then took her phone out of her pocket and texted Shirley at the desk.

Her supervisor texted back. Stay.

Once Hattie was settled in the bed, Erin sat down in the chair beside her and took hold of her hand. For the next hour, Hattie talked about her life with her husband. Erin cried, feeling the love that these two shared.

Finally Hattie whispered, "I miss him so much. No one understands that. I want to go and be with him."

Erin stroked her hand. "Then you go be with your Johnny."

Sometime before dawn, Hattie got her wish, and with her children around her, she went to be with the man she'd loved for decades.

* * *

It was several hours later, and Erin had managed to get away from the care center and drive home. She was exhausted; her emotions were drained. After she parked her car, she walked through the courtyard to her first-floor apartment. She stopped when she saw a beautiful bouquet of flowers on her stoop. Who had sent them? Hope soared in her as she reached for the blooms, but stopped upon hearing her name. Turning around, she found Brooke. What was she doing here?

"Brooke, is something wrong?"

Her friend frowned. "No, I just haven't been able to get ahold of you. You need to check in once in a while, because we worry about you. I understand why you didn't come to Thanksgiving dinner…but I need to see my friend."

Erin was touched. "I appreciate your concern, but I'm fine. Just trying to catch up with work."

Brooke glanced down at the flowers. "And your admirer. Who are they from—Austin?"

"I don't know." Erin managed to unlock the door and carried the vase inside. After setting the flowers on the table, she searched for a card, her friend looking over her shoulder. She opened it to read, *I'm not giving up on us. Please come to the house for dinner tomorrow night at 7:00. Love, Austin.*

"Oh, what does it say?"

Erin handed her the card, and she closed her eyes. What did that mean? And what was she supposed to do about it? She couldn't deny she loved the man.

"Oh, they're from Austin." Her friend grew serious. "Please, don't even try to deny there's something between you two."

"Not anymore. I mean, there was, but Austin had different ideas."

Brooke's pretty hazel eyes locked on hers. "Surely it isn't anything you can't work out."

Erin sucked in a tired breath, inhaling the overly fragrant flowers. Suddenly her stomach rumbled, then flipped over. Not good. She hurried to the bathroom and proceeded to empty her stomach. Once she finished, she sank to the floor in the bathroom.

Soon she felt a cool cloth being placed against her face. It felt good. "Thanks."

Brooke sat down across from her. "You're welcome."

"I thought I got rid of this stomach bug." She took the washcloth from her face and looked at her friend. "I guess not."

Brooke nodded. "I know that so-called stomach bug. I can say that you'll get over it, eventually. It might take a few months, but it's so worth it when you're handed that precious baby."

Erin's heart suddenly stopped, then began to race. "How can I be pregnant?"

Brooke gave her a smile. "Really, you never had your way with a certain handsome cowboy named Austin? If not, you're not as smart as I thought."

"No, not that." She blushed. "It's just that I could never get pregnant and I tried, that's why…" She gasped. "Oh my God, I was taking the hormone shots then." She went on to explain to Brooke about her IVF procedure and her plans for a baby.

Brooke frowned. "Wow! That's a lot to carry on your own."

"I'm sorry I didn't tell you. If I failed at getting pregnant, I didn't want everyone's pity."

Brooke hugged her friend. "Well, I'm here for you now. First, we need to take a pregnancy test just to make sure. Then you're going to go and tell Austin."

She sucked in another needed breath. "Oh, no, Austin. He has a baby."

"Really, you think he's not going to love this baby every bit as much as Lilly?"

"No, not that, but he's going to be shocked because I basically told him I couldn't get pregnant. Maybe he'll think I tricked him so I could have the baby I wanted so desperately."

"Look, Erin. I don't know Austin that well, but from what I've seen, whenever he looks at you, I know he cares. He sent flowers and said he wasn't giving up. And he signed the card 'love, Austin.'"

"Okay, I shouldn't worry. I don't know for sure if I'm even pregnant." The words thrilled her as her hand covered her stomach.

"Only one way to find out. And since you planned to get pregnant, I bet you have a test around." Brooke turned and began opening the doors to the bathroom cabinet. "Found it." She held up the box. "And as soon as we take it you'll know for sure." She grinned. "I wish I could be there when you tell Austin that he's going to be a daddy. Again."

At five minutes before six the next evening, Austin checked the chicken casserole heating in the oven. Shelby had left instructions to keep it from drying out, and he was following them to the letter.

He glanced at the white-cloth-covered table. The plates and napkins were laid out just right. Even a small vase of flowers adorned the center. Lilly was asleep, for now at least, so he could have some private time. All he needed was the guest of honor. Erin.

He released a long breath and wiped his suddenly sweaty palms on his new jeans. He glanced down. Thanks to his surgeon, his cast was a thing of the past. He was wearing a protective support sock over his calf. Not bad, because he could finally wear cowboy boots. And he had on his best pair, coffee-colored full quill ostrich.

Not that they'd impress Erin, but they gave him a little boost. Maybe the extra confidence he needed to convince her that they should be together.

Headlights flashed by the window as the van pulled up. She was here. Suddenly he got nervous again. He pulled open the door just as Erin was about to knock.

She gasped. "Oh, you startled me."

"I'm sorry. I guess I was a little anxious." His gaze traveled over her soft hair, to her pretty face and gorgeous green eyes. Then he took in her rich blue sweater under her peacoat, a pair of jeans and boots. She was a jolt to his system.

He realized he had left her standing there in the cold. "Sorry—please come inside."

She walked across the threshold, and he caught a whiff of her scent and his body stirred instantly. *Whoa, boy. You don't want to scare her off.*

After taking off her coat, she looked around. "Where's Lilly?"

"She's asleep for now. She's been fussy all day, so I have a feeling she'll wake up soon."

"She could be cutting a tooth."

Austin stood there shaking his head. "A tooth?"

Erin smiled at him. "She could be."

"Should I go check on her to see if she's okay?"

"I think your daughter knows how to get your attention."

He nodded, but didn't move. "God, you're beautiful, Erin. I could stand here and look at you all night. I've missed you."

He started to reach for her when Lilly's cry caught their attention. "I can't wait until my daughter is a teenager. I'm going to pay her back in spades."

"Do you want me to go and get her?"

Austin didn't hesitate. He'd use any means to get Erin back in his life. "Go for it. And I'll set dinner out."

She rewarded him with a smile and hurried down the hall. Damn, he'd missed her so much. He went into the kitchen to finish with the food.

Erin's heart pounded with excitement as she went into the nursery and walked to the crib. Lilly was crying, and then suddenly she stopped when she saw Erin. Then came a smile.

That did her heart good. "Hello, baby girl." She scooped the precious child in her arms and held her close, savoring the feel of her. "I've missed you so much."

After pressing several kisses against Lilly's head, she realized she felt a little warm. She took her out to the kitchen to see Austin taking out their meal.

Erin handed the baby to him, went to the sink and washed her hands. Then after she dried them, she ran a finger along the bottom gum line and felt a bump. "I think she's cutting a tooth."

Austin paused, looking concerned. "Poor kid."

Erin went to the cabinet, took out some infant pain

reliever and something for the inflammation. Once she spread gel along her gums, Lilly stopped fussing.

"Okay, let's eat," Austin announced. "I slaved over this meal."

He moved the baby swing closer to the dining table and put Lilly in it. Once she was entertained, they could eat. He helped Erin take her seat.

In the chair across from him, she wasn't sure if she could eat, or maybe just tell him why she came tonight.

Austin reached for her hand and squeezed it. She was quickly reminded of his strength, and also of the gentleness of his touch and how those fingers traveled over her body, bringing her pleasure.

She jerked at the sound of her name. "Sorry. What did you say?"

He smiled. "I'm glad you're here, Erin." Giving her hand one last squeeze, he released it. "Now, please, enjoy the dinner."

The meal was pleasant, but it was still strained between them. How would Austin react to her news?

Austin started up the conversation. "Brooke told me about you losing Hattie. I'm sorry, Erin. I know she meant a lot to you."

Her throat tightened up and she could only nod.

"You have to think she's in a better place, and I bet you were with her so she wouldn't be alone."

She blinked at the emotions. "I have to think she's much happier now. She's with her husband."

The silence was broken as his cell phone on the counter began to ring. He glanced at the ID and Erin could see the name Jay appear on the screen. He sent it to voice mail.

"You should talk to him. It might be important."

He shook his head. "Not as important as being with you."

Her doubt overrode his sweet words. "Isn't he setting up your rodeo appearances?"

"He can wait."

She couldn't stand it. "Please, I don't mind if you answer."

He scooted his chair back. "All right. Excuse me." He grabbed the phone and walked into the other room, but the small house didn't give much privacy. "What do you want, Jay?"

As Austin talked, Erin glanced down at his injured leg and discovered he wasn't wearing his cast any longer. Although she saw the slight limp as he paced back and forth. Would he be going on the circuit soon?

All her past fears started to return as she remembered how Jared would pack up and leave her. Again and again. Tears filled her eyes. Even telling herself that her husband's deployments weren't the same, the deep ache in her chest didn't know the difference.

Lilly began to fuss, and Erin got up and went to her. "Oh, sweetheart." She lifted the baby from the swing, went to the refrigerator and took out a bottle. "Are you hungry?"

Erin heated the formula, then sat down to feed Lilly when Austin returned. "I'm sorry. This isn't how I wanted things to go tonight."

"It's okay." It wasn't how she wanted things to go, either, but this was who Austin Brannigan was, a rodeo star. Suddenly she wasn't in the mood to talk. She glanced at the clock. "Look, Austin, I have an early shift." That was a lie. She had the night off. "I'll finish feeding Lilly, and I should take off."

He stood there staring at her. Then he finally said, "So this is how it goes. When you get scared you're just going to run off again?"

"I'm not scared," she argued. "You and I just have different ideas about the future."

"That's not true, but you don't have the guts to stay and find out what my plans are." He took Lilly from her. "Fine. Go ahead and leave."

He walked out of the room, leaving her more alone than she'd ever felt in her life.

Chapter 19

Austin sat in the rocking chair in the nursery, feeding Lilly the rest of her bottle, waiting to hear the front door close. If he wasn't holding his daughter, he'd probably be running after Erin, trying to get her to stay. But he had his child to think about.

He watched Lilly's eyes drift shut and he removed the empty bottle, then lifted her to his shoulder and began to pat her back. Once she burped, he put her down in her crib and covered her.

He rested his arms on the rails. "I tried, Lilly. I wanted so badly for you to have Erin for your mommy. Someone to love you as I know Erin does. Problem is she doesn't want to take a chance on a beat-up rodeo cowboy." He kissed her forehead. "Night, sweetheart. Daddy loves you."

Lilly released a shuddering breath, and then she

made a sucking noise before she settled down. How could his heart be so full, yet so empty?

He turned and stopped when he saw Erin in the doorway. He was thrilled she hadn't left, but he was also angry as he motioned her out into the hall.

"Why are you still here?" His words came out too harsh, but he couldn't take them back.

Her back straightened. "I need to tell you something before I go."

Great—he didn't need for her to explain fifty different ways why they couldn't work. He walked her across the hall to the workout room that he'd turned into his office. There was a long table with the building plans spread out on top. He was going to show her their future together, but now…

He faced her and folded his arms across his chest. "Okay, say what you need to say."

She started to speak, but got distracted and went to the table. "Looks like you're doing some construction."

"Yes, I am. And we want to get our permits so we can break ground before the first snow." He didn't want to talk about a life she didn't want to be a part of. "Erin, what do you need to tell me?"

She jumped and refocused her attention back on him. "Oh, right. I thought you should know…" She hesitated again.

"Dammit, Erin. Whatever it is, just tell me and get it over with."

"Stop trying to intimidate me."

"Then quit stalling."

"All right. I'm pregnant," she blurted out.

Suddenly, he felt as if he'd gotten thrown off a bull and had the wind knocked out of him. "You went ahead with the IVF?" He didn't wait for her answer and crossed the room. She was going to have a baby. Not his, but the baby she'd always wanted. He pushed aside his own feelings and tried to be happy for her, and concerned. He went to her. "Are you okay? Should you sit down?"

"I'm fine, really. Just some morning sickness. And I'm still in shock."

He led her to a desk chair, sat her down, then knelt in front of her. "I know how much you wanted this baby." He was dying inside. She didn't need him. "I guess your wish came true."

"Part of it," she admitted.

He couldn't let her go without giving it one last shot. "This doesn't change my feelings for you. I want you to be a part of my and Lilly's life. I'll love your baby just as much as if it were my child."

She blinked. "What about the rodeo?"

He stood and pulled her up, too. "That's what I was going to tell you tonight. I'm not going back on the road. Well, I am for a few months, but only to advertise my school for bull riders."

Those gorgeous emerald eyes widened in surprise. "What? Where?"

He turned her to the building plans. "Right here on the Circle R." He pointed at the architect's plans. "There are ten acres of sweet grazing land along the west end of the property. Both Cullen and Trent gave me their blessing to lay claim to it. I need to build a couple of corrals and outbuildings." He went on to tell her about the cabins, and Dan Lynch coming in as his stock manager.

"Wow! When did you decide to do all this?"

"The moment you left me, I knew I had to plan a future, and I want it with you."

Trembling fingers went to her mouth, and she was holding back tears. "Oh, Austin."

"I love you, Erin. I don't want to go back on the road. I want to stay right here. I discovered I want a home, too. And I'm going to build us a bigger one for our family." He touched her stomach. "And our babies."

"I love you, too, Austin."

That was all he needed to hear. He pulled her close and his mouth covered hers. Heat suddenly exploded in him as her body instinctively leaned into him, and her arms circled his neck and deepened the kiss.

He tore his mouth away. "I want you so much, Erin."

She moved enticingly against him.

"I want you, too."

He groaned, trying to resist. "Hold that thought, woman." He kissed the end of her nose. Then he went to a desk drawer, took out the small box and returned to her. He drew a deep breath, then went down on one knee.

She gasped.

"Erin Carlton, you are the most precious woman in the world to me. I think I fell in love with you that first day you marched into my room. I need you in Lilly's life and mine. Will you spend the rest of your life with me, raise our children together and build a permanent home here on the ranch? I'll even put it in writing, draw up a new contract. Just know this one will be ironclad, and forever." He opened the box to reveal a square-cut diamond surrounded by tiny emeralds. "The emeralds reminded me of your eyes. Please say yes."

"Yes! Yes! I'll marry you."

Erin held out a shaky hand, and he slipped the ring on her finger, then leaned down and kissed her.

Suddenly she tore her mouth from his and backed away. "Austin, I need to explain about something." She took hold of his hand and pressed it against her stomach. "This child I'm carrying is yours."

He was touched by her words. "That means a lot to me, Erin, and I'll love this baby as if it were mine."

"No, listen to me, Austin. You and I made this baby."

He stared at her, not understanding.

"Come on, cowboy. You can figure it out. I didn't go through with the IVF. You and I made this baby the old-fashioned way. Out of love."

A thrill shot through him. "*I* got you pregnant?"

She grinned. "Darn right you did."

He let out a whoop. "We're going to have a baby." He stood and swung Erin up in his arms, then put her down and kissed her. It was not enough. "I think this calls for a celebration." He lifted her into his arms and started off to his bedroom. He wanted to show her how much he loved and cherished her. "Tonight is just the beginning, our beginning to our family. Welcome home."

Epilogue

The end of February, Erin drove up to the construction site, parked and climbed out of the SUV. The build was progressing quickly. The corral and bucking chutes were nearly finished and ready for the first bull riding class in early summer. When Austin was determined to get something done, he didn't mess around.

She rubbed her slightly rounded belly under her coat, then reached in the back and released Lilly from the safety seat.

"Dada," she said, pointing toward the man talking to the contractor.

"Yes, that's Daddy. Come on, sweetie. We need to tell him our big surprise." Erin was thrilled at the news she'd gotten at her doctor's visit. She only hoped Austin would feel the same.

She carried the eight-month-old through the busy

construction site. Thanks to a mild winter, the new
buildings were nearly completed, along with a small
barn with six stalls. Austin had insisted they have horses
on their property, too, so the family could ride together.
He'd finally purchased two horses he wanted, the stallion named Wildfire and the small filly for her, Peanut. She didn't mind at all as long as she was with her
cowboy.

Erin had officially become Mrs. Austin Brannigan
on the Saturday before Christmas with all the family
around them at the Q & L Lodge. Brooke was her ma-
tron of honor, and Cullen was Austin's best man. They
stood in front of the minister, Austin holding Lilly in
his arms as they became a family.

Shelby had prepared a delicious wedding supper and
a beautifully decorated wedding cake. It was a perfect
day. The best Christmas she ever had was her upcoming adoption of Lilly. The holidays with the Brannigans
were the best ever.

Erin heard her name called and looked to see Austin hurrying toward them. Lilly spotted her daddy and
squealed in delight. When the little girl reached out,
Austin scooped her up in his arms. He held her high in
the air and she giggled, and then her father pulled her
close and kissed her chubby cheeks.

Warmth spread through Erin's chest and circled
her heart as she watched father and daughter. Their
bond was so precious it brought tears to her eyes. Darn
emotions. She hoped her news was going to make him
happy, too.

Austin turned his attention to her, giving her that
sexy grin she loved. Then he leaned down and kissed
her. "Hey, what brings my two favorite girls out here?"

She blew out a breath. "Well, I didn't want to wait until you got home tonight to tell you my news."

He looked concerned. "Is it the baby?"

She raised a hand. "Not in a bad way, but Dr. Evans wants us to come in later today."

She watched the color drain from his face.

"Stop, Austin. It's okay. I'm healthy, but the doctor found one kind of irregularity. She wants to do an ultrasound to be sure, and I didn't want to do it without you there."

He paused, then asked, "That's when we get to see the baby and tell the sex?"

"Babies!" she corrected him. "That's my news—there are at least two babies."

Those gorgeous gray eyes rounded in shock and he grinned. "Oh, God. You're not kidding, are you?"

She shook her head. "I'm sorry. I guess I neglected to mention that fertility drugs might cause multiple births."

A slow smile crossed his face. "Wow, it's a good thing you only took the shots for a few days."

"You're not upset about this?"

He pulled her close against his side and kissed her. "Are you kidding? I'd say if we have more than one at a time is good—then you don't have to go through this again and again."

She was truly blessed to have Austin in her life. "Here I thought I couldn't even have one child…" Joy spread through her. "Oh, we still have to find out from the doctor if there are twins, or more."

"My only concern is you, and for these babies to be healthy. But I suddenly want a large family."

She laughed. "I love you, Austin Brannigan."

"I love you, too, Erin Brannigan."

Lilly got into the act. "Dada. Kiss. Mama."

"You got it, kid." He gave his daughter a big smacking kiss. Then he turned back to his wife and kissed her, too. "Now let's see that doctor so I can find out how many bedrooms we need in our new house."

Five months later and summer had arrived in Colorado, and Austin's first bull riding class had finished up the previous day. He'd sent twenty aspiring world champions off, satisfied he'd given them skills they needed to improve their rides.

And not once during the four-day school had he been tempted to climb into the chute and show those young riders how he'd done it. He knew he wouldn't risk his life again. Not with what he had waiting at home, a wife and three kids, daughters Lilly Katherine and Nora Christine and son Logan Austin.

He'd been relieved when they'd learned the news that there were only two babies. First and foremost was for Erin to have a safe pregnancy and give birth to healthy babies. And she had, with only the last month on bed rest.

That was when he knew he had to get the house finished for his growing family. He stood in the new kitchen Erin had designed for their two-story home. The large room was adorned with white cabinets, dark granite counters and stainless appliances. The massive island made it easy to feed kids, and also would entertain the entire Brannigan clan. And soon his family would all be descending on them to meet the new Brannigans.

Just then the back door opened and Shelby arrived with her arms filled with platters of food, followed by

Cullen and Ryan. Soon their family would be growing, too. Shelby was expecting a baby in about four months.

"Bro, have I thanked you for marrying a chef?"

"No need." Cullen winked at his wife. "It was my pleasure."

"Uncle Austin, did you know we're going to have a baby girl? And we're going to name her Georgia, after my mom in heaven?" Ryan announced.

Austin looked at his brother and sister-in-law. "That's wonderful. And I bet you'll be a great big brother."

The boy beamed just as Lilly came running into the kitchen. "Ryan…play."

Ryan took the toddler's hand. "Sure." They went off into the other room.

"Be forewarned—never tell a kid your news unless you want him to announce it."

"Well, congrats on the baby girl."

Shelby nodded. "Hey, where's the new mama?" Shelby asked as she began to arrange the food on the counter.

"She's upstairs feeding babies. I better go check on her. Can you handle things here?"

She gave him an annoyed look. "I can't believe you're asking me that. Go. Hurry and bring the babies down." She waved him off.

Austin walked out of the kitchen and into a hall that had an office on one side where he ran the business and a formal dining room on the other. He continued into the great room with the stone fireplace and the huge sectional sofa and big coffee table. The dark hardwood floors gleamed, just like the smile that Erin showed him when everything had been completed.

He went to the open staircase as more family came in the front door. He tossed a wave toward Rory and Diane, along with Laurel and Kase, and their eighteen-month-old twins, Kate and Jack, and their older sister, Addy. Then Brooke and Trent appeared with Chris and baby daughter Leslie. She was named after Trent's mother. "Make yourself at home. Be right down."

Down the hall he passed Lilly's pink bedroom with the crib and toys scattered on the floor. Then he came to the nursery with two cribs for the newest family members. Brother and sister would be sharing a room for a few years yet. There were two empty bedrooms farther down, but he headed for the master suite, where he'd find his wife.

Austin opened the door and paused, seeing her seated in the familiar rocking chair. Behind her were large windowed doors that led to a balcony and a view of the Rocky Mountains. The afternoon sun was like a halo around Erin as she held their son to her breast. The picture was so beautiful that he wished he were an artist so he could paint them. Love surged through him. How could one man get so lucky?

Erin sensed someone and she raised her head to see Austin. He walked across the room toward her, dressed in a burgundy Western shirt, snug black jeans and those fancy ostrich boots.

Her heart skipped a beat. "Hey, cowboy. Who's holding down the fort downstairs?"

"Who else? Shelby. I thought I'd come up to see if you need any help." He nodded to her breast. "I can see you're doing a perfect job without me."

"You can burp your son." She handed him a protective cloth, then the baby.

She refastened her nursing bra, noticing her husband was watching her. Another thrill shot through her. "I know it's been a long time." She stood and placed a sweet kiss on his mouth. "But hang in there an extra week. And I'll make it worth your while."

The babies had been a little premature and had to stay in the hospital a few weeks to put on weight. Now they were finally home.

He grinned. "You already made it worth my while with these two healthy babies." He continued to pat Logan's back. "I love you so much."

Her heart was full. She couldn't believe this wonderful man she was married to. How caring and loving he'd been to her over these past months of her high-risk pregnancy. "I love you, too. Thank you for giving me these wonderful babies."

He placed Logan in the bassinet, then turned back to her. He took her in his arms. "You're the one who saved this crazy bull rider from a life of endless wandering. You showed me what a home really is supposed to be." He lowered his head to hers and captured her mouth in a loving kiss.

"Oh, no, none of that."

Hearing Trent's voice, Erin broke off to see several family members filing into the bedroom.

"Since you wouldn't come downstairs, we decided to come up and meet the newest Brannigans," Trent said.

"We were headed down."

Erin smiled fondly at Shelby, Cullen, Trent and Brooke. Rory and Diane went to stand next to Nora's bed.

"Oh, she's so precious," Diane said. "Leslie would love knowing that her grandchildren were living on her family's ranch. And all together."

Erin knew she couldn't have a home more deeply rooted in heritage.

Brooke's twin sister, Laurel, and her husband, Kase, came in with Addy along with their two toddlers in hand. They walked over to see the babies.

"Family is important," Erin began. "We want our children to know about theirs."

Austin and Cullen's dad, Neal, arrived with Dan and Lilly, and they went to see the babies.

Austin took Erin's hand. "I kept my promise. Is this enough family for you?"

"Yes, you have, cowboy. More than enough." Erin stepped into her husband's embrace. "You gave me more than I could have ever dreamed of."

She was finally home with her man.

* * * * *

*Harrison McCord was sure he was the rightful owner
of the Dawson Family Ranch. And delivering Daisy
Dawson's baby on the side of the road was a mere
diversion. Still, when Daisy found out his intentions,
instead of pushing him away, she invited him in, figuring
he'd start to see her in a whole new light. But what if
she started seeing him that way, as well?*

*Read on for a sneak preview of the next
book in Melissa Senate's
Dawson Family Ranch miniseries,*
Wyoming Special Delivery.

Daisy went over to the bassinet and lifted out Tony,
cradling him against her. "Of course. There's lots
more video, but another time. The footage of what the
ranch looked like before Noah started rebuilding to the
day I helped put up the grand reopening banner—it's
amazing."

Harrison wasn't sure he wanted to see any of that. No,
he knew he didn't. This was all too much. "Well, I'll be
in touch about that tour."

*That's it. Keep it nice and impersonal. "Be in touch"
was a sure distance maker.*

She eyed him and lifted her chin. "Oh—I almost
forgot! I have a favor to ask, Harrison."

Gulp. How was he supposed to emotionally distance
himself by doing her a favor?

She smiled that dazzling smile. The one that drew him like nothing else could. "If you're not busy around five o'clock or so, I'd love your help in putting together the rocking cradle my brother Rex ordered for Tony. It arrived yesterday, and I tried to put it together, but it has directions a mile long that I can't make heads or tails of. Don't tell my brother Axel I said this—he's a wizard at GPS, maps and terrain—but give him instructions and he holds the paper upside down."

Ah. This was almost a relief. He'd put together the cradle alone. No chitchat. No old family movies. Just him, a set of instructions and five thousand various pieces of cradle. "I'm actually pretty handy. Sure, I can help you."

"Perfect," she said. "See you at fiveish."

A few minutes later, as he stood on the porch watching her walk back up the path, he had a feeling he was at a serious disadvantage in this deal.

Because the farther away she got, the more he wanted to chase after her and just keep talking. Which sent off serious warning bells. That Harrison might actually more than just like Daisy Dawson already—and it was only day one of the deal.

Willow Emery approached her brother and sister-in-law's two-story home in Brooklyn, New York, with a deep sense of foreboding. The white paint on the front door of the yellow-brick building was cracked and peeling, the windows covered with grime. She swallowed hard, hating that her three-year-old niece, Lucy, lived in such deplorable conditions.

Steeling her resolve, she straightened her shoulders. This time, she wouldn't be dissuaded so easily. Her older brother, Alex, and his wife, Debra, had to agree that Lucy deserved better.

Squeak. Squeak. The rusty gate moving in the breeze caused a chill to ripple through her. Why was it open? She hurried forward and her stomach knotted when she found the front door hanging ajar. The tiny hairs on the back of her neck lifted in alarm and a shiver ran down her spine.

Something was wrong. Very wrong.

Thunk. The loud sound startled her. Was that a door closing? Or something worse? Her heart pounded in her chest and her mouth went dry. Following her gut instincts, Willow quickly pushed the front door open and crossed the threshold. Bile rose in her throat as she strained to listen. "Alex? Lucy?"

There was no answer, only the echo of soft hiccuping sobs.

"Lucy!" Reaching the living room, she stumbled to an abrupt halt, her feet seemingly glued to the floor. Lucy was kneeling near her mother, crying. Alex and Debra were lying facedown, unmoving and not breathing, blood seeping out from beneath them.

Were those bullet holes between their shoulder blades? *No! Alex!* A wave of nausea had her placing a hand over her stomach.

Remembering the thud gave her pause. She glanced furtively over her shoulder toward the single bedroom on the main floor. The door was closed. What if the gunman was still here? Waiting? Hiding?

Don't miss
Copycat Killer *by Laura Scott,*
available April 2020 wherever
Love Inspired Suspense books and ebooks are sold.

LoveInspired.com

HARLEQUIN

Heartfelt or suspenseful, inspiring or passionate, Harlequin has your happily-ever-after.

With new books published every month, you are sure to find the satisfying escape you know you deserve.

Love Harlequin romance?

DISCOVER.

Be the first to find out about promotions, news and exclusive content!

Facebook.com/HarlequinBooks

Twitter.com/HarlequinBooks

Instagram.com/HarlequinBooks

Pinterest.com/HarlequinBooks

ReaderService.com

EXPLORE.

Sign up for the Harlequin e-newsletter and download a free book from any series at **TryHarlequin.com**

CONNECT.

Join our Harlequin community to share your thoughts and connect with other romance readers! **Facebook.com/groups/HarlequinConnection**

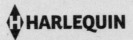